praise for *mathematicians in love*

"Full of quirky, charming life-forms h[...]
by a god who's the female jellyfish-cre[...]
characters, off-the-wall situations, and [...]
writing SF spoofs, like Bela's rock music avocation, 'beats the hell out [...]
publishing a math paper.'" —*Publishers Weekly*

"May well be Rudy Rucker's best novel—funny, wise, fast, and inventive."
—Gregory Benford, author of *Timescape* and The Galactic Center Saga

"In *Mathematicians in Love*, Rucker has created a love story wrapped up in a cross-cultural mystery tour that could only have happened inside the mind of a crazy mathematician. Buy a ticket. It's well worth the price." —*SFRevu*

"[Rucker] is palpably and quiveringly tuned in to the zeitgeist and can offer cultural and scientific commentary and satire better than almost any other SF author practicing today." —*SciFi.com*

"Percolates with off-the-wall characters and trippy extra-dimensional shenanigans. Nobody writes math-based science fiction like Rudy Rucker does. Rucker keeps the tone light and the action playful, even as his characters grapple with the meaning of tragedy and the ultimate mechanics of the universe. A definite high point in his singular writing career." —*San Francisco Chronicle*

"All the pleasures of a Rucker novel come forth abundantly: playfully weird higher physics and math; bizarre conceptual psychedelia; distinctively Californian counter-cultural comedy; zany romance; doppelgangers; generally happy endings ... *Mathematicians in Love* is an engaging and entertaining book, light yet thought-provoking, funny yet of some gravity." —*Locus*

praise for rudy rucker

"Rudy Rucker should be declared a National Treasure of American Science Fiction. Someone simultaneously channeling Kurt Gödel and Lenny Bruce might start to approximate full-on Ruckerian warp-space, but without the sweet, human, splendidly goofy Rudyness at the core of the singularity." —William Gibson

"One of science fiction's wittiest writers. A genius . . . a cult hero among discriminating cyberpunkers." —*San Diego Union-Tribune*

"Rucker's writing is great like the Ramones are great: a genre stripped to its essence, attitude up the wazoo, and cartoon sentiments that reek of identifiable lives and issues. Wild math you can get elsewhere, but no one does the cyber version of beatnik glory quite like Rucker." —*New York Review of Science Fiction*

"What a Dickensian genius Rucker has for Californian characters, as if, say, Dickens had fused with Phil Dick and taken up surfing and jamming and topologising. He has a hotline to cosmic revelations yet he's always here and now in the groove, tossing off lines of beauty and comic wisdom. 'My heart is a dog running after every cat.' We really feel with his characters in their bizarre tragicomic quests." —Ian Watson, author of *The Embedding*

"The current crop of sf humorists are mildly risible, I suppose, but they don't seem to pack the same intellectual punch of their forebears. With one exception, that is: the astonishing Rudy Rucker. For some two decades now, since the publication of his first novel, *White Light*, Rucker has combined an easygoing, trippy

by rudy rucker

FICTION

White Light	THE WARE TETRALOGY
Spacetime Donuts	Software
The Sex Sphere	Wetware
Master of Space and Time	Freeware
The Secret of Life	Realware
The Hacker and the Ants	
Saucer Wisdom	Postsingular
Spaceland	Hylozoic
As Above, So Below: Peter Bruegel	
Frek and the Elixir	The Hollow Earth
Mathematicians in Love	Return to the Hollow Earth
Jim and the Flims	
Turing & Burroughs	STORY COLLECTIONS
The Big Aha	The 57th Franz Kafka
Million Mile Road Trip	Mad Professor
	Complete Stories

NON-FICTION

Infinity and the Mind
The Fourth Dimension
The Lifebox, the Seashell, and the Soul
Nested Scrolls: A Writer's Life

style influenced by the Beats with a deep engagement with knotty (or 'gnarly,' to employ one of his favorite terms) intellectual conceits, based mainly in mathematics. In the typical Rucker novel, likably eccentric characters—who run the gamut from brilliant to near-certifiable—encounter aspects of the universe that confirm that life is weirder than we can imagine." —*The Washington Post*

"Rucker stands alone in the science fiction pantheon as some kind of trickster god of the computer science lab; where others construct minutely plausible fictional realities, he simply grabs the corners of the one we already know and twists it in directions we don't have pronounceable names for." —*SF Site*

"Reading a Rudy Rucker book is like finding Poe, Kerouac, Lewis Carroll, and Philip K. Dick parked on your driveway in a topless '57 Caddy . . . and telling you they're taking you for a RIDE. The funniest science fiction author around." —*Sci-Fi Universe*

"This is SF rigorously following crazy rules. My mind of science fiction. At the heart of it is a rage to extrapolate. Rucker is what happens when you cross a mathematician with the extrapolating jazz spirit." —Robert Sheckley

"Rucker [gives you] more ideas per chapter than most authors use in an entire novel." —*San Francisco Chronicle*

"Rudy Rucker writes like the love child of Philip K. Dick and George Carlin. Brilliant, frantic, conceptual, cosmological . . . like lucid dreaming, only funny." —*New York Times* bestselling author Walter Jon Williams

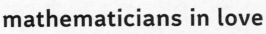

mathematicians in love

a novel by

RUDY RUCKER

night shade books
new york

10 9 8 7 6 5 4 3 2 1

Library of Congress Cataloging-in-Publication Data

Names: Rucker, Rudy v. B. (Rudy von Bitter), 1946- author.
Title: Mathematicians in love : a novel / by Rudy Rucker.
Description: New York : Night Shade Books, 2019.
Identifiers: LCCN 2018041193 | ISBN 9781597809634 (pbk. : alk. paper)
Subjects: | GSAFD: Humorous fiction. | Science fiction.
Classification: LCC PS3568.U298 M38 2019 | DDC 813/.54--dc23
LC record available at https://lccn.loc.gov/2018041193

Cover artwork by Bill Carman
Cover design by Claudia Noble

Printed in the United States of America

For Sylvia, my true love.

contents

"RR": An Introduction by Gregory Benford xi

1. Bela, Paul, and Alma 1
2. Cone Shell Aliens... 49
3. Rocking with Washer Drop............................ 99
4. Hypertunnel at the Tang Fat Hotel 154
5. Mathematicians from Galaxy Z............................ 218
6. The Gobubbles... 286
7. The Best of all Possible Worlds 361

Afterword.. 408

"rr"

an introduction by gregory benford

Rudy Rucker (RR) twice won the Philip K. Dick Award for best SF novel.

Here's why, exemplified in this novel, *Mathematicians in Love*, a romantic comedy where a PhD is not required but is useful, with a whole corkscrew of SF twists.

Playwright Tom Stoppard painted the grand achievement of our emotional lives as "knowledge of each other, not of the flesh but through the flesh, knowledge of self, the real him, the real her, *in extremis*, the mask slipped from the face." So how to do this, as a math major? How do we learn to discern between a love that is imperfect, as all meaningful real relationships are, and one that is insufficient, the price of which is repeated disappointment and inevitable heartbreak? Making this distinction is one of the greatest and most difficult arts of the human experience—and, it turns out, it can be greatly enhanced with a little bit of science.

RR does this craftily, humorously. Not that RR can give you the odds of finding your soul mate, or how game theory reveals the best strategy for picking up a stranger in a bar, or the equation that explains the conversation patterns of lasting relationships. He's not *that* into just numbers. He's not like longtime singleton Peter Backus, who calculated that there are more intelligent extraterrestrial civilizations than eligible women for him on earth. RR's more a romantic optimist, and his life proves it.

Mathematics is ultimately the study of patterns—predicting phenomena from the weather to the growth of cities, revealing everything from the laws of the universe to the behavior of subatomic particles. Love, like most of life, is full of patterns: from the number of sexual partners we have in our lifetime to how we choose who to message on an internet dating website. These patterns twist and turn and warp and evolve just as love does, and are all patterns which mathematics is uniquely placed to describe.

RR knows and shows this: Mathematics is the language of nature. It is the foundation stone upon which every major scientific and technological achievement of the modern era has been built. It is alive, and it is thriving.

Peter Backus's calculation, for example, yielded 26 eligible women for him on all of Earth. Being able to estimate quantities that you have no hope of verifying is an important skill for any scientist—a technique known as a Fermi estimation, which is used in everything from job interviews to quantum mechanics. Backus was an anti-RR: unreasonably stringent. Backus assumed that he'd find only 10% of the women he meets agreeable and only 5% attractive. He made similar estimates about women, without of course having met many. As any mathematically minded person will tell you, it's a fine balance between having the patience to wait for the right person and the foresight to cash in before all the good ones are taken.

RR did this, maybe intuitively. He married his college girlfriend Sylvia a week after graduation, in 1967, and they're still together. Perhaps his life informs *Mathematicians in Love*.

In 1983, RR published "A Transrealist Manifesto," readily available online, and he later included the essay in his non-fiction collection *Seek!* In it he states, "Transrealism writes about immediate perceptions in a fantastic way . . . Transrealism tries to treat not only immediate reality, but also the higher reality in which life is embedded." This manifesto has been widely influential, and *Mathematicians in Love* mirrors it.

Rudy's book on Bruegel, *As Above, So Below*, is also written in a Transrealist way.

RR knows a remark by Robert Sheckley: "A writer's first problem is how to write. The second problem is how to write a story. And the third is how to write about himself or herself."

When RR read Philp K. Dick's *A Scanner Darkly*, it spoke to him as no other book spoke to him before. PKD writing directly about his real life was a technique that appealed to him. PKD led him to call himself a Transrealist, and write that manifesto about it. PKD represents SF that stops being about the future in favor of being about the present—and better still, the writer's life, though maybe unconsciously. What's essential is that the quotidian story has a 'wonky,' crazy element to it.

Rudy loves Asimov, but Asimov never really wrote about his own life. A good idea, overall. Transrealism is an attempt to write science fiction that's also realistic. PKD is at one extreme on this scale and Asimov at the other.

Usually in Rudy's books, characters leave reality in some way—they take a trip to another dimension or the center of the earth—and that really stands for his being a writer, who gets to go to another, more fun world himself. And the "trans" move lets RR put in things that are less socially acceptable. The warts and stuff. The folks on the bus.

Manifestos are usually written because the writer feels disempowered and is having problems getting published. Rudy was a transrealist before he was a cyberpunk. The cyberpunk stuff was less like him, I think. Rudy's stuff uses real characters, always breaking out of the quotidian. They're grounded in mundane, then the fantastic breaks in on the character. Rudy likes characters breaking out.

When I first met Rudy, he told me he felt that a transrealist novel is not plotted beforehand. He used to never plot, anxious that he wouldn't be able to finish because the more he thought about it, the less likely it would be he would stay the course. Now he's more confident, I think, and *Mathematicians in Love* shows him at his peak, wings spread wide.

This romantic comedy is about two mathematicians in love: the roommates Bela and Paul who are working towards their PhDs under the direction of a mad math genius named Roland Haut. They invent a para-computer called "GoBubble" that predicts the future. Bela leads a rock band on the side; he says it "beats the hell out of publishing a math paper."

Some of RR's mathematical flights may stun hapless mathophobes, but his wild characters, off-the-wall situations and political riffs inform this SF spoof, packed with hypertunnels, alien shellfish from a parallel universe, and an improbable resolution to a threesome's romantic dilemma. RR pulls out all the stops for one of his most entertaining yarns.

RR encapsulates his tone best in a poetic invocation of the muse:

Time, saucers, sex, and goo
Elves, mutants, robots too
Muse of strangeness old and new
My blank pages call to you.

mathematicians in love

ONE

bela, paul, and alma

My tale begins on an alternate Earth in the university town that we called Humelocke, a close match for your Berkeley. And the book will end with me here in your San Jose, California, writing up my adventures—and preparing to move on.

To make my story easier to read, I won't use each and every alternate place name we had on my original world. But I'll keep "Humelocke," in fond memory of that specific place and time where I first came to know wonder, madness, and love.

It was an April morning in Humelocke, and I was working on my Ph.D. thesis; that is, I was staring out my apartment window and imagining Minkowski hyperplanes buttressed by homotopy sheaves, with the whole twinkling cloud castle tethered to a trio of animated figurines shaped like, oh, a rake, a fish, and a teapot. Three morphons.

Say what? I'm a mathematician.

My thesis adviser, Roland Haut, had set me in pursuit of a fabulous mathematical unicorn called the Morphic Classification Theorem. I was up to my ears in student loan debt, and I wanted to finish very soon. Another doctoral candidate was on the hunt as well, Paul Bridge, who happened to be my roommate. Paul was making better progress.

As I thought of Paul, my view of mathematical paradise dissolved and I was staring at a puny tree in our apartment complex's dingy courtyard. Mathematics lent even this humble object some borrowed glory. The leaf-bud-studded branches were rocking in the fitful spring breeze and, the branches being compound pendulums, their motions were deliciously chaotic. I savored the subtle whispering of the wind. Combining the sights and sounds, I could visualize the turbulent air currents in the wind-shadow of the tree: corkscrews and vortex tubes, realtime physical graffiti far gnarlier than the sheaves and hyperplanes I kept trying to dream. Why was I trying to outthink Nature? Why not embrace the world and go surfing?

I glanced down at my binder full of penciled thesis notes, with little turds of eraser rubber stuck to the pages. I had a nice big sketch of my latest image: the hyperplanes like disconnected floors of a building, the sheaves like bulbous elevator shafts, and the morphon figurines off to one side like control knobs. I dug it, but Roland Haut wouldn't like it. My monthly meeting with him was in an hour. I seemed unable to produce the kind of thesis he expected. I'd lost my way in the enchanted forest, and a magic pig was eating my lunch.

Literally. I could hear him behind me, rooting through the fridge, popping off a container's plastic lid. It made a faint B-flat note.

"Leave the mashed peas alone, Paul. They're mine."

"I'll only take half." He was dipping the peas out with two fingers that he kept pressed together and slightly curved, as if to mimic a legitimate spoon. "How much did they cost?" asked Paul. "You can add half that amount to my share of the rent."

"Plus a thirty-four-dollars-an-hour personal-shopper fee prorated for my twenty-seven minutes at the market *plus* eight-and-a-half percent sales tax, an eleven-percent convenience charge, and a per-transaction accounting charge of a dollar seventy-seven," said I.

"How many items did you buy on that particular shopping trip?" challenged Paul. "If you're charging for shopping time, you need to divide by the number of items you bought." He mimed a brisk division-slash in the air, keeping his spoon fingers stiff and bent, the fingers clotted with green paste, wet with spit.

Paul's wallet was on the counter, the wallet's edges precisely aligned with the counter's. I plucked it up and extracted a five-dollar bill. Even though Paul argued about money, he usually had some. His arguing was more for sport. My arguing, on the other hand, was more for money. I'm—call it frugal. I get that from my mother, Xiao-Xiao; she's half-Chinese, a widow, runs a tiny eatery in the South Bay. My father, Tibor, had been a Hungarian computer-chip engineer and a willful tyrant. Right before his heart attack, he'd blown all of the family's savings in Reno. Jerk. My big sister Margit and I had needed to take out big student loans to go to college.

"Peas all yours now," I said, pocketing Paul's five.

A good deal. Although the mashed peas had been the tasty kind with the picture of sweet-pea flowers, they'd cost only $3.89, and were a week old, on the point of tasting metallic. I walked over to my desk by the window and put my worn spiral notebook into my knapsack.

"I get lichees," said Paul, still at the fridge. He tipped some of my jellied lichees from their tub into his mashed-pea container, using his relatively clean thumb to coax them along. Although Paul was orderly with his possessions, he was like a wild animal when it came to food.

"Help yourself," I said, pulling back from being stingy. "What's mine is yours."

Paul drifted back to the kitchen table, his attention once again on the screen of his laptop. His hair was lank and medium length, of no particular color. He wore flesh-colored plastic glasses; he had the notion that a pinkish frame color made glasses less visible. When he was uneasy, he always adjusted his glasses, pushing the bridge higher on his nose. He had a firm, handsome mouth, although there was a slight gap between his front teeth. His short-sleeved white shirt was translucent, with his loop undershirt showing through. His neck usually had red razor rash. He was from Saint Matthews, Kentucky, and talked with a hint of a country accent. I'd heard another student say that Paul looked like a Bible salesman who rents a room in a house trailer from a retired school teacher, and she catches him screwing her poodle dog. But that was going too far. Paul was a good guy. He wasn't obese; he didn't smell bad; he had a sense of humor.

Paul was my friend, and hip or not, he was a great person to hang out with, perhaps the most interesting person I'd met in my life. He was smart, well organized, and intellectually generous. Paul liked to hold forth to me on this work, showing me his latest pages and going over the details, but after a bit, his spaceship of thought would always lift off and leave me stranded on my own dark and lonely planet.

We each had our own take on how the big Morphic Classification Theorem should go: Paul's thesis was symbolic and analytic; mine was to be visual and geometric. We had radically different styles of doing math. I'd try to explain my drawings, he'd try to explain his tidy rows of symbols, but for all the communication we achieved it was like we were showing each other scratches and dings and barnacle clusters on rocks and seashells.

Paul had recently given a well-received math colloquium at Stanford on his preliminary results—even though I'd tried to talk him out of it, fearful as I was of being scooped. There was a big universal dynamicist at Stanford named Cal Kweskin; he and his student Maria Reyes were closing in on the Morphic Classification Theorem, too. I was kind of disorganized about attending conferences and seminars, so I hadn't actually met those two even though I'd read, or had tried to read, their papers. Paul was a lot better at networking than I was.

It would have been hard for me to put together a good talk on my work thus far, although I did have some nice drawings scattered through my hundred or so penciled pages. Neither Paul nor Haut fully appreciated my pictures; Haut's style of math was more like Paul's than like mine. Haut kept asking me to prove a theorem. After six month's work, I still didn't have that one solid result to hang my Ph.D. thesis upon. Although I'd found some interesting conjectures, they remained stubbornly undecidable, in limbo, neither provable nor refutable.

Paul and I lived in the crummy old wood-shingled Ratvale student co-op with its gray carpeting on undulating floors and permanent smells of puke, pot, and cat piss.

How we two met is that we happened to sit next to each other at the math grad students' orientation session. Paul endeared himself to me by spilling a full cup of coffee into the open knapsack sitting between his feet.

"You do that often?" I asked him.

He paused, analyzing the query. "Less often than once a month, more often than once a year," he said finally. "Are you looking for a roommate?"

"Probably." I liked the implicit *fuck you* in Paul's narrowly logical answer. And I liked that, despite this bit of bravado, he looked even more anxious than me. Although I'd survived the math undergrad program at UC Santa Cruz, math at Humelocke was intimidating. The big leagues.

Paul and I chatted a little about our backgrounds. He'd started out as a chemistry major at the geek heaven of BIT, the Boston Institute of Technology, and had gotten bored with having to learn chemical recipes and compounds by heart. For him, math was easier—once he understood something, he could reproduce the proof, and there was nothing left to memorize. He'd switched over to mathematics his junior year in college.

"What kind of math are you interested in?" I asked him.

"Universal dynamics," he said, and that sealed our partnership. Both of us had come to Humelocke in hopes of writing a thesis in this hot new field with the great Roland Haut.

Our shared dream had come true, but only Paul was making the most of it.

Walking down Telegraph Avenue towards campus, I bought a fat slice of squid pizza and an XL coffee. I was worried about my meeting with Haut. By now he was more than disappointed in me; he was contemptuous. And, for my part, I resented his attitude. I've never been one to take criticism calmly.

The only redemption would be to show Haut something amazing—which I seemed quite unable to do. I was still hoping to become a genius mathematician, but it was a lot harder than I'd imagined. What if Ma were right? She kept saying I should stop borrowing money for grad school and get a job at a high-tech company, like my thuggish cousin Gyula Wong, who was on the security staff at Membrain Products down in Watsonville; they made various kinds of sophisticated membranes for, like, drums, pumps, filters, electrical transformers, and medical apps.

As usual, Ginsberg Gate at the edge of campus was lined with people at card tables: army/gay/fraternity/anarchist/Islamic/corporate recruiters and the like. I like the sounds of crowds, of the voices layering upon each other.

Today there was extra activity at the gate, stirred up by a hotly contested special election. The Humelocke district's congresswoman had died in plastic surgery, and the vote for her replacement was today. A computer genius and self-made billionaire by the name of Van Veeter was running as a Heritagist, trying to win the spot from the painfully inept Common Ground Party candidate, Karen Barbara—for whom I was planning to vote.

There'd been so many gaffes and scandals involving Barbara that, inconceivable as it sounds, this time around a Heritagist had a chance at representing Humelocke. Our benighted country was three and a half years into the reign of the Heritagist Joe Doakes, the least intelligent and most repressive president ever. But even now, every election seemed to sweep more Heritagists into office—with no great hope for a Common Ground victory in the upcoming November national election. We'd suffered a series of terrorist attacks which had our citizens in a state of fear. Most recently a terrorist named Tariq Qaadri had blown up the Roebuck skyscraper in Chicago—and was still at large. Even though our troops had cornered Qaadri in Lilliputistan, he'd somehow escaped to a safe haven in Blefescustan, only to mastermind more bombings from there.

Instead of blaming President Doakes for Qaadri's continued terror, the voters clung to Doakes the more. And it was looking like the Common Ground presidential candidate was going to be a patrician stuffed shirt named Winston Merritt, a painfully awkward man too polite to ask the hard questions about why Doakes didn't catch Qaadri. Doakes's only real liability was Vice President Frank Ramirez, an unpleasant character dogged by rumors of graft and of personal violence.

Although he was a Heritagist, our local congressional candidate, Van Veeter, was no extremist; he was a logical computer guy, seemingly quite honest. His reasons for wanting to be a congressman had to do with some quirk of corporate tax law that had particularly outraged him. He'd begun his career by patenting some clever new chip designs, and had built up a successful company called Rumpelstiltskin, making specialized chips for cell phones and other wireless devices. Recently Rumpelstiltskin had been using its sky-high stock to acquire several other companies. According to Veeter, there was one particularly obstreperous tax law relating to his maneuvers that had made him decide to go to Washington and debug the system. A lot of people seemed to like the idea of a geek debugging DC. There was even talk of having Veeter replace Ramirez on the national ticket for November. But first, of course, he'd have to win the Humelocke election today.

As I imagined yet another Heritagist victory, I seemed to hear a downward beep like a character dying in an arcade game, and a stomach cramp hit me. Coffee, pizza, stress. I darted into the student center for a pit stop. While I was washing up, I looked in the mirror, working on my self-esteem.

I liked what I saw. Bela Kis. Being three-quarters Hungarian and one-quarter Chinese, I have this nice warm skin color. I've been bleaching my thick, blunt-cut hair since high school. I have virile dark stubble on my jaw. I'm fit-looking, thanks in part to having taken up surfing in Santa Cruz. I play electric guitar well enough to have been in a little college band called E To The I Pi. And this particular day, I was wearing an orange plaid golf shirt and purple bell-bottoms which looked good on me.

In short, you'd never have guessed I was a math student. Maybe if I'd been all robotic and Martian and autistic like the others, then it would have been easier for me to prove the Morphic Classification Theorem. On the other hand, perhaps a truly radical proof could only come from a suave surf dog like me.

I headed up a grassy green slope towards the math building, Pearce Hall, a handsome relic of the NeoDeco 1970s, fully twelve stories tall, with chrome falcons decorating its cornices. I was avoiding thinking about Haut and the election by staring down past Humelocke towards the bay and San Francisco. It was a blue-sky day with puffy white clouds, the living air like cool clear water. A nice offshore breeze. Good day for Ocean Beach, over on the other side of San Francisco. I hadn't been in the water all winter.

"Hi, Bela," said a woman right outside Pearce Hall, smiling at me. About my age, deep brown eyes. A wide mouth and fragile jaw. A dimple beside the corner of her lips. Wavy brown hair teased and sprayed into a fashionable shag with three streaks of blonde. A Peter Pan collar white shirt with an anarchist bomb drawn on the back in black marker-pen, a plaid red miniskirt worn backwards, gold golf shoes. Cute, hip, happening. A nice up-and-down rhythm in her voice. She seemed familiar, but—

"Pleasure Point?" she said, making a wavy gesture with one hand. "Pink and green wetsuit?"

"Alma the local!" Of course. I'd occasionally seen her surfing at Santa Cruz, and one time we'd actually met at a beach party. Not that the locals down there mingled all that much with the college kids. They called us hairfarmers, even though most of us were dreggers, the same as them. "You're a student at Humelocke?" I asked Alma.

"My senior year. I'm—" she paused to giggle prettily. "A Rhetoric major. We studied this rant by one of the former math professors."

She meant *The Unabomber Manifesto* by Ted Kaczynski, the most famous crazy mathematician of them all, one-time professor of our own University of California at Humelocke.

"My roommate says anyone who mails bombs to computer scientists can't be all bad," I said, thinking of Paul. "But, hey, that was last century. We're too big for envy anymore. Thanks to universal dynamics, math is going to rule the world."

"That's what I was hoping to see you about! I'm reporting a feature on universal dynamics for this webzine called *Buzz*. It's my final project for Sci Lies—what we call Rhetoric of Scientific Discourse."

I noticed now that Alma was wearing a digital video camera tucked behind her ear. A little red diode glowed on its side. I'd looked at *Buzz* a couple of times. Cartoons, interviews, radical politics, minifictions. "You're, like, stalking me?"

"I saw you listed as a student of Roland Haut's," said Alma, circling me, sizing me up. "And I found out you had an appointment with him today. I can't believe we never ran into each other before."

"This place is too big," I agreed. "I'm glad to see you." I'd always been interested in Alma Ziff, but too shy to talk to her. She was intimidating in the lineup, with a loud mouth and usually some hard-looking older surf-rats at her side. Guys who wore shades in the water and preferred to speak Spanish. Indeed, I'd left that one beach party soon after I heard Alma's brother Pete and one of his brahs say they wanted to "kick the *pinche* hairfarmer's *culo*." Pete was a foul-mouthed long-haired beanpole, notorious on the scene, a stoner/surfer/biker/dreg with a beat-up motorcycle sporting a surfboard rack. His comrade that night had been an ugly gnome with a pompadour and giant grommets set into his earlobes.

In any case, Alma was alone with me now, and all smiles. "What have you heard about universal dynamics?" I asked her.

"I saw that article in the *San Francisco Chronicle* last month, and I looked at the introduction on Roland Haut's website. But *Buzz* needs it in your own words." She tapped the camera at her temple. "Tell us, Bela. I'm vlogging you."

"All right," I said, standing up straight for the camera, delivering the party line. "Plants and animals, the weather, political movements, your personal shifts of mood—all of these are what we might call chaotic dynamical systems. The key new insight is that any given dynamical system can be precisely modeled by a wide range of other dynamical systems, often of a quite different kind. Recently my thesis adviser Roland Haut proved that real-world orchid blossoms have the same shapes as computer-simulated water splashes. That was the first big success for universal dynamics. We're expecting many more to come. We'll read the weather in a teacup; watch a flapping flag for a medical diagnosis; model the legislature as a pile of rotting fruit. Am I talking too fast?"

"Thank you, Bela Kis," intoned Alma.

"You said it wrong," I put in.

"What?"

"My last name. You said 'kiss,' but it's 'keesh.' Means 'small' in Hungarian. Kiss the Kis and see him grow."

"*Be*-la." Her voice was sweet music. "Can I follow you inside? I want to see some demos of, like, universal dynamics predicting something."

"If Roland says it's okay, I can show you the splashes that look like orchids."

"Good. And maybe something newer?" Alma stepped close and ran her hand across my biceps. "Are you still surfing?"

"Lately I'm always worrying about my thesis. And Ocean Beach is so gnarly in the winter."

"I was there last month with my big brother Pete and his friend Wrong Wave Jose. They came up from Cruz. They're both working on a fishing boat now. At least I hope it's a fishing boat."

"I think I've met them."

"Yeah, they were always out at the Point with me. And that time you were talking to me at the beach party? Pete looks like a crusty long-haired dreg but he has a motorcycle, and Jose is—"

"The aggro guy with the giant holes in his earlobes?"

"Oh, did he scare you, Count Dracula? Pete and Wrong Wave Jose aren't vicious, they're just shy. Poor self-esteem. Pete's had a lot of problems." Women always cover for their loser friends and relatives. You gotta love them for that.

"Jose has this not-so-secret crush on me," continued Alma.

"Even though he's utterly, totally out of the question. Sorry, Jose! I'm looking for a handsome boy with a good future. I learned all about it in this course I took last fall. Rhetorics of Sexual Exchange."

"It's okay that I'm part Chinese?"

We were in Pearce Hall now, riding the elevator to the tenth floor. Alma gave me this goofy smile. "It's a plus." She rose up on her toes and kissed my cheek. "And you *are* cute."

"Thank you." My heart was beating fast. I hadn't had a date in months. And here I was alone with a woman in a metal box. Wonderful. I smelled the faint scent of Alma in the air: her breath, perfume, and hair spray.

I went ahead and brought Alma into Haut's office with me. He was a stocky man with dark hair worn in an old-fashioned pageboy. Every now and then he'd go off the deep end and spend a few weeks in the psych ward. Right before his last breakdown, he'd shed his glasses for corneal surgery, as if to look less like a mathematician.

"This is my friend Alma from Santa Cruz," I told Haut. "Alma, this is Roland." I noticed that the light on the side of the camera behind Alma's ear was still glowing. She'd been vlogging me in the elevator. So what.

Haut was forty, but he liked for students to call him by his first name—not that we wanted to. He had a basic coldness about him, and he could be quite cutting if riled. But people forgave him everything. He was a genius, a fount of fascinating new ideas.

"Why?" said Haut testily, meaning why had I brought Alma to meet him. He was sitting with his back to the window at a long desk scattered with pieces of paper and natural curiosities. Seashells, bits of driftwood, oddly striated rocks, dried seaweed, seedpods, animal teeth, crystals. On his left was a sunlit wall covered with orchids growing in little tubes.

Pinned up next to each plant was a graphical image of a computer simulation of a water splash shaped exactly like the plant's blossom. Like I'd told Alma, this was the big success of universal dynamics so far. Two years ago, Roland had used the equations of fluid flow to predict the patterns of orchid growth. And for this work he'd won the Fields Medal—which is a very big deal in mathematical circles. Haut hadn't yet published another result that dramatic, but he was hinting that something new was in the works. Something about crystals and discrete decision systems. But the details were for him to know and the rest of us to find out. He was secretive about his research, even among his students.

As usual, Haut was wearing high-quality yuppie clothes: a pink silk shirt with a green bow tie, black velvet plus fours, argyle cashmere knee-socks, and red leather running shoes. (Note that the tastes and fashions of my birth-world differed a bit from those of the world in which I describe my adventures for you, dear reader.)

Haut was fastidious about his appearance, in fact he had a full-length mirror beside his door. Mathematics had been good to him. But it hadn't done much for his personality.

"Why, Bela?" repeated Haut, stubbornly hassling me

for bringing Alma along. As if it was this huge deal. His eyes hadn't focused in on us, he was doing his zillion-mile stare, possibly watching himself in the mirror, which was positioned in such a way that he could see himself and the window behind him.

"I told her what a freak you are, and she didn't believe me," I rapped out, expecting it to come across as a joke. My idea was to break the negative loop of contempt and resentment that Haut and I had gotten into. I was fantasizing that we were both so socially inept that normal standards of politeness didn't need to apply.

"Believe it," said Roland, smiling with his teeth. "Can you get Bela to start his thesis, Alma? We're not the only ones working in this area. The Stanford team might beat us out. Time is of the essence."

"I'm powerless over the boy," said Alma. "It's an honor to meet you, Professor Haut. The thing is, I'm reporting a little segment on universal dynamics for this Humelocke-based webzine called *Buzz?*" She touched the camera poking out beside her eye. "Do you mind that I'm vlogging you?"

"Call me Roland."

"I was wondering if I could show her the universal dynamics lab," I suggested.

"No," he said coldly. "Some of the work's confidential. You know that, Bela."

"But not the orchid simulation. That was on TV."

"I don't have time to supervise what you show her. Now, Alma, if you could wait outside for a minute, Bela and I have to talk. You've seen enough, yes?"

"Thank you, Professor Haut," said Alma brightly.

"Roland," he corrected. "You're beautiful. *Au revoir.*"
He gestured at me to close the door with Alma on the other side of it.

As soon as we were alone his face turned dark. "Where do you get off calling me a freak? And in front of a camera. *Vlogging?* This isn't an art school." The barking words echoed in the little room.

"I thought—"

"You don't think, Kis, you feel. You're conscious only of your needs. You have no awareness of other minds. When cornered, you mimic intelligent behavior. But I've seen no evidence that you *think*. Or am I wrong? Do you finally have something substantial to show me?"

The savage outburst wounded me. I fumbled my notebook open to my most recent drawing and tried to say something, but there was a lump in my throat. "I've been thinking about sheaves of fiber bundles connecting hyperplanes to these little Dr. Seuss seeds that—" I managed, and then my voice broke. I admired this man's work so much, and he hated me. My own stupid fault.

"You're emoting," said Haut coldly. "In hopes of provoking pity. No use. I won't carry you any longer, Bela. Please look for a new adviser. And if you can't find one, settle for the master's degree you've already got. That's enough for teaching high school or community college."

Wordlessly I stumbled from his office. On the way out I glimpsed myself in Haut's wall mirror. I looked pathetic. Alma was right there in the hall. Her face softened when she saw me.

"He harshed on you? Poor Bela. Here." She fished a fashionably lacy hankie from her purse.

"Don't need it," I said, rubbing my eyes in the crook of my arm. Following an obvious chain of association, I was remembering all the times my father had yelled at me and called me an idiot. I was starting to get mad. "That prick Haut. He fired me." I glanced around; nobody else was in the hall. "I don't need this. I'm a musician as well as a mathematician, you know. Come on, I'll let you tape as much of his fucking lab as you like. It's in the basement."

"*Right* on." Alma's camera was still running.

At some level, I must have been riding the Tao, for we were alone in the elevator again. Once more Alma kissed me, and I kissed her back. Lips and tongue. In a way, I had a lot going for me. I'd done something outrageous and had been punished—so she was both impressed and sympathetic. Also I was about to escort her into a place she wanted to see.

"I like elevators," I said when we paused for breath. "They're a temporary autonomous zone outside of ordinary spacetime."

"And you know it's going to be of a limited duration," added Alma. "So things can't get too seriously out of hand." She started laughing, fending me off from kissing her again. "I still can't believe you said that to your thesis adviser. 'I told her what a freak you are, and she didn't believe me.' Did you *want* him to drop you?"

I had to think about that for a second. "Sounds that way," I said finally. "You are what you do. But now I wish I hadn't done it. I've got this feeling I can still turn my thesis around. But Haut might make it hard for me to get my work approved."

"Especially after you let me webcast his private goodies," said Alma. We were stepping out in the Pearce basement. We passed a couple of lit-up open computer labs; at the end of the hall was the universal dynamics lab, sealed off with a metal door. "I don't want to get you in more trouble," continued Alma, holding my arm with both hands. "This story isn't that important to me. I'm only doing it as a favor for my roommate Leni Pex. She hosts *Buzz* on a server in our apartment. Mostly just students read it. If you're scared, let's not bother."

Even as Alma was saying all this, she was marching me towards that metal door. Body rhetoric. And I was fully going for it, eager to show her my spunk. Of course I realized that once her camera images were posted on *Buzz*, Haut would hear about them—there are no secrets on the web. But I had this reckless urge to piss the man off. Yeah, Haut would be mad, but he'd probably get over it. It wasn't like I was planning to show Alma anything that hadn't aired a dozen times before.

"Nudge some of your hair forward so your camera doesn't stand out so much," I told Alma. "We're goin' in."

I punched my keycode into the door's pad and greeted the woman proctoring the lab, a fellow first-year grad student sitting at a desk studying.

"Hi, Lakshmi," I said. "I want to show Alma around. She's working on some applications. I checked with Roland." Sort of true. "Fine," said Lakshmi, hardly looking up from her topology textbook. "Just sign in."

So we signed in, using our real names. I led Alma over to Haut's multiprocessor supercomputer, funded by a fat grant from the NSF. As it happened, my own login ID wasn't working—already disabled by Haut? So I used his login and password, which I happened to have learned by watching him log in from his office. It was easy: user ID rolandhaut; password Iamagenius.

I stepped Alma through the standard demo that Haut always showed his interviewers, split-screen pairs of water splashes and orchid blossoms, with each half of the screen containing an image and some equations. The paired images were similar in shape, although not in texture and color—you could tell that the ones on the left were simulated water and the ones on the right were actual plants. And of course the paired equations were totally different. I explained to Alma that Roland Haut had gotten the Fields Medal for proving that the equations really *were* at some deep level the same, which in turn implied that the forms shown in the images could indeed be made identical, were it possible to precisely match the equations' parameters.

"Do you have any other pictures?" asked Alma, not interested in the mathematics.

I moused around and found a file labeled aprilvote.nb in Haut's documents folder, time-stamped with today's date. I hadn't seen this one before, or even heard about it. I was intensely curious to see it—keep in mind that, despite our personal differences, I was a passionate admirer of Roland Haut's work. So I went ahead and launched aprilvote. nb, with Alma and her camera peering over my shoulder. I figured that later, if necessary, I'd have time to tell her not to post these images. But right now, I just had to look.

The left side of the screen showed a beautiful simulation of frost forming on a windowpane. The right side of the screen showed a table of precinct-by-precinct vote tallies for Van Veeter and Karen Barbara. A simulation of today's election. At the bottom of each image were, once again, sets of equations.

As the fingers of frost grew and exfoliated, the table entries changed, the numbers spinning like digits on a hit counter. The way my brain is wired, I often imagine sounds when I look at pictures. And the sounds of the pictures were matching pings and crackles. After a minute or two of frenetic activity, the two on-screen windows settled down. The frost pattern looked like a duck or maybe a rabbit. And Karen Barbara was the election winner by a razor-thin margin of seventy-nine votes.

"Is that for real?" whispered Alma. "You absolutely can't put this on *Buzz*," I said. "It's Haut's next research paper."

Physicists conjecture that when a test individual B falls past the event horizon of a black hole, he himself doesn't immediately notice this. He's doomed, but at first only his stationary observer A knows.

"I'm vlogging in real time," said Alma in a small voice. "My camera has a wireless link; it posts an upload every ten seconds. I thought you understood that."

Lakshmi the lab proctor's phone was ringing. Could it already be Haut? We didn't stick around to find out.

Outside Pearce Hall, I got Alma to turn off her camera and put it away, and then I had her phone her friend Leni Pex and ask her to remove the hoarfrost-and-voting movie from the *Buzz* server. Listening to Alma's end, I gathered that Leni was sitting at her keyboard, doing the delete right away, and, then, just for the hell of it, checking how many downloads the aprilvote segment had gotten in the minute or so it had been up and—*ow*—it was 476.

"That many?" I said to Alma as she put away her cell phone. "Four freaking hundred and seventy screw-me six?

"The *Buzz* server runs this news-feed software? A client can, like, register their preferences so that their browser gets an alert whenever news about a favorite topic appears on any news server. And then their browser can do an automatic download. And there's a lot of interest in the election today. So . . ."

I glanced up at Pearce Hall, wondering if Haut might just possibly be aiming a military-grade sniper rifle at me from his office window. An unexpected shoal of clouds had filled the sky with marbled gray. In my possibly-soon-to-be-exploded head I could hear guitar metal chords and a chorus chanting, "Paranoia, *the* destroyer," at a rate of many, many repetitions per second—followed by the sudden crack of gunfire.

"Come on," I said, cutting around to the other side of the tall cylindrical bell tower that stood next to Pearce Hall. Getting out of Haut's line of fire. "Better here." I took a big shaky breath.

"Lighten up, Bela," said Alma. "Tell you what, I'll take you surfing at Ocean Beach."

"For sure," I said guffawing sarcastically. "I don't need to do no fuckin' homework. I'm gettin' expelled."

"You don't know that," she said soothingly.

In the back of my mind I'd been going over the frost and voting equations I'd just seen, and now I was beginning to see the outlines of a miraculously simple geometric proof of why the two would be equivalent. What a radical concept. Haut was a genius. "I'm going to have to tell him that I'm really, really sorry," I said.

"Not today," said Alma. "Lie low. You think Barbara will really win by seventy-nine votes? Maybe Haut will thank you for getting his prediction out there. This could be good publicity for him. Maybe he was feeling shy."

"*Shy?* Roland Haut?"

"Let it go, Bela. Be in the now. We're going surfing. I hope you have a car?"

"A big old station-wagon muscle car," I said proudly. "With squinty little windows on the sides in back. It's a Bel Paese Squire, no less."

"Don't tell me you polish it all the time and take it to classic car shows where they play, like, The Crooners," said Alma with a giggle.

"Well, no, my car's a beater. Mostly white, but one fender has red primer, and the hood is yellow. It's a pie-bald battle-scarred squinty-whale surf machine. Let's go vote. My polling place is at the YWCA on Bancroft Way. We can walk by there on the way to get my board."

"You live in Ratvale too?" She was smiling broadly. I noticed something a little needy about her smile; it made me want to care for her.

"Lend me some sugar, baby, I *am* your neighbor!"

We drove across San Francisco to the end of Golden Gate Park where it meets the ocean. The sky was getting cloudier all the time, a spring shower coming on. We suited up and walked onto the damp, gritty beach, boards under our arms.

To the right were the wild, rocky Marin headlands. Out in front of us lay the vast Pacific, the horizon line scalloped by far outsider waves.

There were golden holes in the cloud cover, with shafts of sunlight like slanting pillars. The waves near the shore were sliding gray hills, breaking in sharp lips with crowns of spray blowing back off them towards the sea.

As always, the sound was wonderful: the crunch of the big waves, the hiss of the foam bubbles popping, the low tones of the wind—oceans make the best sonic chaos of all.

"Snowy plovers," said Alma, pointing to some little white birds running past, their legs spinning like wheels and their bodies not even bobbing. She was wearing her pink and green wetsuit, the wind bouncing her blonde-streaked brown hair. "I've always wanted to hold one of them in my hand and feel his—his quickness. His racing heart, his little twitches."

"Yes. And I like those birds over there with the long slightly up-curved bills, the way they're rummaging in the deep sand. Like people eating noodles with chopsticks."

"Marbled godwits," said Alma, giving me a look that held a hint of a challenge.

"I'm impressed you know the birds," I replied. "And what do I know? Hmm. The water surface between those two waves is a hyperbolic parabaloid. And the steep, rippled front of the one about to break? That's the Cartesian product of an exponential curve and a sine function."

"From China," said Alma, pointing at a boxy container ship on its way to the straits under the Golden Gate Bridge. "Ha Jin line."

I elaborated on this, keeping up my end of the courtship display. "Carrying cast iron tractor parts, flash memory chips, plastic action figures, jasmine tea, and dried sea cucumbers."

"Look out for the rhetorician and the mathematician!" cried Alma, running into the surf.

We paddled past the breakers and started catching waves. At first I was lagging, but then the water got good to me. It was so nice to be surfing again. Alma was lovely on her board, like a flickering flame. Our final ride was a king kong magic slide right into the heart of a double-wide tube, the two of us together inside the curled wall of water for a shared heartbeat of forever.

Boom.

We came out wet and laughing. In the spitting rain of the parking lot we changed out of our rubber suits and into our clothes; me getting a few glimpses of Alma's shapely nude body—she wasn't prudish. We scampered across the tropical plants in the street divider and hit a coffee shop at the corner of Judah and La Playa. It was cozy inside: checkered floor, black leather couches, a craggy old man wearing a red carnation, SF State students doing homework on laptops, the smell of coffee. We found a spot on a couch by the window.

"How did you end up majoring in math?" asked Alma. "I remember people would talk about it in the lineup. Like, *that stud's a mathematician*." Once again I noticed the tiny dimple below the corner of her mouth.

"They did not," I said.

"Oh, yeah," said Alma, nodding. "And I was curious about you."

"I *was* going to major in physics, but I took the wrong courses. I guess math is what I really wanted. I have this way of backing into my decisions. Math has always been easy for me. There's nothing to memorize. It all follows from a few basic ideas. Like the trig formulas come from a single image of a circle. What about you and rhetoric?"

"I'm a woman of modest means," said Alma. "My father's a termite exterminator, and my mother's a part-time realtor who sells about one house a year. Gary and Sarah. They smoke *mucho* pot. They're comfortable bumping along the bottom. Sarah has a bunch of salt-water aquariums, and Gary's biggest interest is his pumpkin patch in our backyard. We live in a little house in those flat blocks off Seabright Avenue near the harbor; every October, we sell pumpkins in our driveway, it's the high point of the year. We make about twenty dollars and buy a couple of new fish. I've always wanted to have more stuff than my parents when I grow up, but I don't want to give up being mellow. I studied pretty hard at Santa Cruz High, and I was on the debating team, but I'd cut school to surf. *Hell* yeah. I picked rhetoric as my major because I like to talk. I'm like you—I'm doing what's easy for me. And I figure rhetoric could lead to a career in business, law, or politics."

"A dreg yuppie larva," I said, and put on the plummy tone of a nature show voice-over. "This voracious pink and green caterpillar is destined to pupate into an aristocratic highflier!" In the background I heard the whoosh of the espresso machine, the crackle of the milk steamer.

Alma cocked her head and appraised me. Her eyes were a nice shade of gray. "Are you upwardly mobile, Bela?"

"What is this, a job interview? My father's dead and my mother runs a little Chinese restaurant in a strip mall in San Jose. It's called East-Vest. My big sister is an accountant. No bucks. But I could have a huge future in universal dynamics. Even if I do get expelled. Not that money is very important to me. Day to day, it's being interesting and funny that counts. And, maybe, in the long run, getting some fame." I glanced around the crowded room, at the black and white tile floor, the chatting students, the man with the red carnation. How would it be if all these people knew who I was?

"I think about money so much," said Alma. We'd turned to face each other on the couch. The rain outside was running down the windowpane. As she talked, Alma idly ran her finger along the path of a rain rivulet, following the motion of the water. "You've got no idea. Wanting the good clothes and the nice car. I'd like to get past it. One way or another. Talk about something interesting or funny, Bela."

"Those trickles of rain. They're just the kind of thing I dig thinking about. I like that you notice them too. Let's understand them."

"How do you mean?" She had a wonderfully intent gaze.

"What are their forms, what are their laws of behavior. Science project! The drops stuck to the glass, for instance, they're not round or oval like people draw them in cartoons. Their edges are jagged. So their surfaces are concave as well as convex."

"There's drops of all sizes," chimed in Alma. "Most of them aren't moving. But then one of them gets fat enough to start rolling."

"And this drop bumps into others and that helps her keep going for awhile," I said. "But—whoops—sometimes she comes to a stop. Trickles of all sizes. According to universal dynamics, we can emulate these gnarly processes by snapping together a few standardized morphons in Minkowski sheaf hyperspace and—"

"Techie jargon is bad," said Alma. "Alienating."

"Follow the happy throng to Mathland!"

"Interesting?" said Alma, leaning back and shaking her head. "No. Funny? No." But her mouth was spread in a long smile.

The rain rivulets had merged in my head with that tube we'd surfed. And yes, oh, yes, I was beginning to see a proof for the Morphic Classification Theorem. Five of the animated shapes, or morphons, that I'd been drawing—the fish, the dish, the teapot, the birthday cake, the rake—surely I could connect them to make a universal emulator. And this would be the key to the big proof. A lovely series of diagrams was taking form in my mind with a sound track to match. Proofs without words. I wanted to start sketching on the folded-in-four sheet of paper that I always kept in my back pocket. But more than that I wanted to advance my relationship with Alma. The lively curves of her mouth were as interesting as any math I'd ever seen.

"Let's drive back," I suggested. "I could pick up some food and make us rabbit paprika for supper." At some deep level I felt myself wondering how it might be to live and eat with this woman for the rest of my life.

"Can I invite my roommate Leni?" asked Alma.

"I guess so. I've got a roommate too, did I mention that? Another math grad student. Paul Bridge. If we're lucky, he might not be there."

"Don't you like him?"

"I do like him, in fact I'm eager to talk to him about that new demo I saw today. And about the raindrops, and my ideas on how to prove the big theorem. Lots to talk about. I meant 'lucky if he's not there' in the sense of enhancing the probability of you and me fully hooking up tonight."

"I loathe that expression," said Alma. "It sounds like two dragonflies fucking in midair. They do that, you know. They're always going at it above our pumpkin patch. The sprinklers attract them. One year my father grew a pumpkin that was six hundred pounds. Even though it was stiff, its shape was soft and slumped. It was a grotesque, bloated parody of a healthful natural phenomenon, in some sense comparable to humans mating as fecklessly as insects." Although she was looking down at her coffee, she shot me this stealthy half-smile from under her brow.

"Nice rhetoric," I allowed. "Rabbit paprika, yes?"

"Yummo. I haven't had slow food in weeks."

Back in Humelocke, traffic was a mess, with a bunch of fire trucks on Bancroft Way. We didn't mind, we were cozy in my motley high-horsepower wagon, holding hands in the dusk, with some of my E To The I Pi songs softly playing. Alma's profile was as crisp as a face on a new-minted coin. And all the while, part of my attention was on the mathematical symphony taking shape in my head.

I dropped Alma off before going to the garage, she was planning to come over for dinner a bit later. With Leni, she said. They were going to bring something to drink. She gave me a nice, long wet good-bye kiss. Oh, Alma. It struck me that the onset of love was an aspect of universal dynamics as well.

After I got the squinty whale stashed, I took a gander at the fire trucks—they were parked by the YWCA building where I'd voted. Crap. Most of the windows were broken out, the walls were black with smoke, there was water everywhere. Somebody on the sidewalk said the fire had started at five o'clock, sparked by a short circuit in the electrical boxes. All the votes were lost. Haut had predicted a Barbara win by seventy-nine votes. If the election were really going to be that close, the unexpected fire might have tipped the balance the other way. Maybe the Heritagists had set the fire.

Sadly I traced the karmic chain in my mind: my insulting Haut, him firing me as student, me breaking into his account and viewing his files, Alma uploading his images to the web, the multiple downloads of same, the very real possibility that a Heritagist Van Veeter operative had drawn the conclusion that trashing a well-chosen polling-place would swing the election. I wondered if Haut had already set in motion the steps to get me expelled.

But that was all mundane bullshit. My big new ideas about universal dynamics were still in place. Mentally I pushed on them; they stood firm. I stopped under a streetlight to scratch a few marks on the piece of paper from my hip pocket, humming the sounds of the pattern as I drew. I'd meant to detour to a fancy organic market, but I wanted to get to my notebook before I lost any of this. I felt like the Cat in the Hat juggling a teapot, a rake, a birthday cake, a dish, a fish, and a seven-dimensional hyperplane.

I grabbed some brown'n'serve rice balls and a tired-looking pack of rabbit quarters at a smelly little grocery on Telegraph and rushed back to the apartment. I'd have about an hour before Alma showed up. Paul was there, bent over his laptop at the kitchen table, tuned out of the workaday world, his laptop and his papers all neatly aligned parallel to the table's edges.

"I'm worried about that fire," I remarked.

"What fire?" said Paul, not looking up. I had a paranoid flash that there was something sly and calculated about his response. But, no, he was just deep into Mathland. "I saw the frost and vote demo," he said, still staring at his screen. "Good work liberating that, Bela. Haut was holding out on us. Cal Kweskin and Maria Reyes at Stanford saw the demo too. I got an email from Maria."

"How . . ."

"My browser watches for posts about universal dynamics. I downloaded the movie thirty seconds before it went away. It's terrific. All these doors are opening." He made a *deedle-deedle* guitar sound, finally looking up at me, the gap between his teeth showing as he smiled. "The stairway to heaven."

"I have an idea for a new diagram," I said. "I want to show you. I feel close to some very big results."

"Yes," said Paul, right on my wavelength. "And it'll take big results to make Haut forgive you. I say let's team up. He already phoned here looking for you. Aging popinjay. He was steamed when I told him I'd seen the movie too.

We'll pull ahead of him, we'll take him down, and we'll beat Stanford, too. I was looking at your notebook again this afternoon. After the frost-vote demo, your drawings are making sense to me."

"Yes," I said. We were feeding each other's excitement. "I've been thinking about your equations. I'm finally seeing what they mean. I want to crank some math."

"I'm ready."

I noticed I was holding a sack of groceries. "Two girls are coming over in an hour," I told him.

"No," said Paul, pushing his glasses up on his nose.

"I said I'd make supper."

"No."

"I went surfing with one of them this afternoon. The girl who reported that *Buzz* story. Alma."

"I saw the movie of her kissing you in the elevator," said Paul with a slight snicker.

"She's bringing her roommate Leni," I told Paul. "That's who you talk to. Don't be flirting with Alma."

"I don't want to flirt," said Paul righteously. "I want to do math."

"Women, Paul," I said, pouring some oil into a frying pan and adding the rabbit. "The fair sex. The civilizing influence. All relevant influences must be factored in. Observe. I dredge the meat." The pan clanked happily, I sprinkled on flour and paprika. "I show you my partial sketch of the universal emulator, a morphon construct capable of simulating any process at all." I skimmed my pocket-scrap of paper over to him. "I complete the meal preparations." I poured a can of bouillon into the pan and put on a clattering lid. "And we have a brief and cogent predinner discussion about our revolutionary plans for universal dynamics." Everything was math: the sounds of our voices, the flow of expressions on Paul's friendly face. "We share a healthful repast with our lovely guests, and come the morrow, you and I will make mathematical history." I made mystic passes in the air.

"Come sit down and tell me about this new picture," said Paul coaxingly.

I pulled a chair over beside him and smoothed out my scrap of paper. "I think that all we need is those five basic morphons. Fish, dish, rake, birthday cake, teapot. They're like the cross-cap and the torus in algebraic topology, Paul. All-purpose building blocks. Each of them is a sound, too." I sang the sounds to him.

The fact that I was using Cat-in-the-Hat-style names for the morphons made perfect sense to Paul. As I talked and sang, he began turning my images into rows of symbols on a lined pad of paper. Our conversation was like telepathy, with one plus one becoming more than two.

Seeing Haut's second demo had hipped us to a fundamentally new technique for finding patterns. Haut had matched plant growth to water splashes and election results to frost crystals, well and good, but now we were pairing ocean waves with trickling raindrops, mood swings with candle flames, food fads with fluttering leaves, city neighborhood distributions with the acoustics of church organ music, and the spread of rumors with milk swirls in coffee cups.

Each of these resonances could be explained by modeling the processes as combinations of my five morphons.

Each morphon had a characteristic activity—the fish swam; the dish shattered; the teapot poured; the rake dragged; the cake blazed with candles. And implicit in these behaviors were five fundamental processes: rhythm, fracture, flow, aggregation, transformation. I hadn't been quite sure that these basic modes were sufficient to model everything, but now, in just a few lines of symbols, Paul confirmed my intuition.

"Draw your picture again," said Paul. "It wasn't correct before, but, you know, I think if we use the rake handle, we really *can* get a universal emulator."

"Yes," I said, my pen springing to the page. "The dish morphon goes under the birthday cake, with the teapot sitting on the cake inside the circle of candles. The fish is in the teapot peeking out. All just like in my first version. But this time the rake has its teeth embedded in the side of the cake and the handle is all rubbery. The rubbery handle swoops under the plate and coils to make a helical spring holding up the plate, and then the tip-ass end of the handle grows out to the side and up over the top and—and then what, Paul?"

"The handle gets thin and it threads in through the teapot's spout!" exclaimed Paul. "It dips into the tea, squeezes past the fish, pokes out the top of the teapot and wraps around the—"

"Around the handle!" I cried. "Yes! The rake is holding the dish and lifting the teapot! And it goes like this." I sang the picture as if it were a musical score.

"Math loves us," said Paul. "We've sketched a proof for the Morphic Classification Theorem!"

"Using a five-morphon universal emulator," I gloated. "Hmm. Do you think we can prove that we have to use all *five?* Or can we get it down to *four?*" Math is never over.

Paul said, "Five," and then he showed me why, and then a knock on the door brought us back. Nearly two hours had passed.

It was Alma and her roommate. "Sorry we're late, we got into watching the election returns. This is Leni Pex. Leni, this is Bela Kis and—you must be Paul?"

"Hi," said Paul, beaming at her and actually turning off his laptop.

"Is something burning?" asked Alma, an asterisk between her eyes.

"The rabbit!" It had boiled dry. I poured in some water. Great hiss and steam billow. In my present state of mind, I saw it as compound morphon, a cartoon explosion made up of rakes and teapots. I turned on the oven and put in the foil pan of rice balls. A compound of the dish and cake morphons.

"Your interview was good," said Leni, screwing the top off the half-gallon of red wine she'd brought. She was a slight, clean-cut woman, with her blonde hair in a tight bun. She was pleasant, but by no means flirtatious. Tidy, healthy, confident. "We got so many hits today," she continued. "I hope you're not in trouble about that secret demo."

"How's the election going anyway?" I asked as I rinsed out some dirty glasses from the sink. Paul was setting the table, aligning each dish and fork just so.

"It's close," said Leni. "I guess you heard that the votes

from the YWCA polling place are all lost. That's bad for Barbara." She seemed content with this.

"You're Heritagist?" I blurted out unbelievingly.

"Hello? I'm gay. But party lines aren't everything. Van Veeter's a smart guy. He could get a lot of good things done. I don't mind admitting that I support him."

We were interrupted by a snort of not-quite-laughter from Alma. Paul had just told her one of his Kentucky jokes, this one involving a country boy who has sex with animals.

"Swell icebreaker," I said. The tasteless joke was like a rake morphon, poking and dragging. Who even *told* jokes anymore? "Don't mind him, Alma, he gets weird around women."

"Bela was so eager to get back here and talk to you," Alma told Paul. "I expected you to be this, like, genius?" She threw up her hands and shook her head. "Did you two discover anything while you were burning the dinner?"

"Something big," said Paul. "Times like this it's better not to check the details for a few hours. Then you can still be happy."

"And you're from Kentucky?" said Alma. "That's why you told the—joke."

"I grew up near Louisville," said Paul. "In a place called Saint Matthews. My father's a Pentecostal Charismatic minister."

"Pentecostal?" said Alma.

"It means he rants in gibberish," I put in. "Real hard-core Kentucky."

"It's not necessarily gibberish," said Paul. "They call it the unknown tongue. To me it always sounds somewhat the same no matter who speaks it. Like a real language, almost." He made some sounds to demonstrate. "*Ungh waah oonk y ay aya du bogbog ah smeepy flan*. When Pop got going in the pulpit, we'd feel like he was telling us important stuff. His church is still quite successful, you know, even though he had an affair with one of the parishioners and my mother left him. She's a potter in downtown Louisville now. That's where I finished high school. They've never spoken to each other since she left. It's sad."

"Can we eat soon?" said Leni, not sure what to make of Paul. "I need some protein before the wine clobbers me."

"Sure," I said. "I'll set it out."

"Raaa-bits?" bleated Paul as I put the food on the table, echoing the punch-line of his lame joke. I guess the wine was hitting him too. Nobody laughed.

"You seem like a colorful character," Leni said to Paul as they helped themselves. "What color do people mean when they say that? Cerise with flashes of lemon? Maybe I should get you to vlog for *Buzz*."

"I still haven't looked at that news report Alma did today," I remarked, wanting to steer the conversation my way. "That was great surfing, wasn't it, Alma?" I was sitting next to her. I passed her the food and took some for myself.

"It was a blast," said Alma. "Better than with Pete and Jose."

"Your big brother and his friend?" said Leni. "Anything's better than those two. They know about eight words between the two of them. And six of the words are *fuck*."

"Oh yeah?" said Alma. "How about your mom dragging you along for shopping at Brashears-Normandy when she came to visit last month, Leni? And giving you all that lipstick and foundation makeup that she got for free."

"You don't want to start on parents with me, Alma," said Leni. "I've met yours."

"I used to see Alma in Santa Cruz," I put in hastily. "We surfed some of the same places."

"I saw you playing in a brewpub once, too," Alma recalled, smiling at me. "That surf-music trio you were in—you were playing some of the songs in the car today? I keep forgetting the name?"

"E To The I Pi," I said.

"Which equals minus one," said Paul, his mouth full. "What a great name. You didn't tell me about this, Bela. Were the other guys math majors too?"

"Physics on drums, computer science on bass, math on guitar. That's me. Our drummer was a woman, by the way. She and the bass player got married."

"He really *is* cute," said Leni. "I wish you'd vlogged yourself surfing with him today, Alma. That camera's shockproof and waterproof, you know. I want to get some people to start vlogging everything they do. *Real* reality TV. I'm getting these special wearable cameras called vlog rings."

"Vlogging?" said Paul. "That means video blogging?" He shook his head. "That reminds me of this boy Jim Ardmore I knew at church camp in Kentucky, a really witty guy, very dry, almost like an English person. I was in a cabin with him and this kid named Randy Karl Tucker from a blue-collar neighborhood called Shively. We could hear Randy Karl beating off every night. And Ardmore

would call out, 'Flog it, Tuck.' He had kind of a lisp, Ardmore did, so it came out more like, 'Fwog it, Tuck.'" Paul
smiled, savoring the richness of Ardmore's wit. "That's
what the word 'vlog' makes me think about," he added.

"I'd let you vlog yourself masturbating if that's what
you really want to do," said Leni, maneuvering some rabbit onto her rice ball. "Is that what you're getting at?"

"No!" said Paul, looking surprised. "Not at all." He
tended to have very little grasp of how oddly his utter-
ances came across.

"Tell me more about the vlog ring," I said, to get my
friend off the spot.

"Just like it sounds," said Leni. "You wear it on your
finger, and it has a bulgy little fish-eye lens that pulls in a
hemispherical field of view. Looks kind of like those tacky
rings they try and make you buy when you're a senior in
high school? My first girlfriend actually wanted to give
me one. Ugh."

"Doesn't a fish-eye image look warped on the screen?"
I asked. "Like those freak-out TV commercials of your
parents pushing their faces up against you? Have you
done your homework, honey? Did you take your meds?"

"The users download some software that flattens out
the image," said Leni. "And since there's so much visual
information coming from the vlog rings, the users can
vary their point of view. Like you're following a person
around and deciding what to look at. It's the latest tech.
What if I gave vlog rings to thousands of people? Today I
found a way to get vlog rings very cheap. For free, really."

"Clever you," said Alma in an oddly hostile tone.

"You could get a bunch of contestants wearing vlog rings, and have the viewers vote on who's more interesting to walk around with," volunteered Paul, wiping up sauce with a rice ball. "Half of the contestants get eliminated every week. And eventually there's only one left."

"Start with a thousand and twenty-four people, and after ten rounds, you're down to one," I put in. "Call the show *One in a Thousand*."

"Or do twenty rounds," said Paul. "And make it *One in a Million*."

"I can't believe I'm having dinner with mathematicians," said Alma with a pleased expression. She poured herself more wine and, beneath the table, she ran her bare foot along the top of mine.

"They seem colorful," said Leni. "Gray and beige *are* colors, right?"

"You're a rhetoric major like Alma?" I asked her. I had my shoe off too now. Alma and I were tapping toes.

"No, I'm in business," said Leni. "With a minor in communication. I'm gonna start a media empire. I like *One in a Million*. Normally I hate reality shows. They always tilt towards the most average kinds of people. But this could be the opposite. The whole point of the web is that we can track the outriders and ignore the flyover zone. No more goobers and jennas."

"Who?" asked Paul, looking around the table for more food.

"That's surfer slang for uncool people," explained Alma. She giggled then, feeling the wine. "Like groovy mathemagicians." She pulled her foot back under her chair.

"I may not be cool," blustered Paul. "But I'm going to be rich and famous. Right before you two tough cookies turned up, Bela and I figured out how to prove a big theorem. It'll change the world."

"Does it have something to do with Professor Haut's secret demo?" asked Leni. "The frost crystals predicting the election? That was awesome. Too bad he was probably wrong."

"If he's wrong maybe it's *your* fault, Leni," said Alma, giving her a sharp look. "Heritagist robot."

"Shut *up*. It's your fault for smooching Bela and vlogging that demo in the first place. Slut. How are you going to change the world, Paul?"

Paul hesitated, as if waiting to see if Alma or Leni were about to throw something at each other. But they weren't all that worked up. It was just wine and rhetoric.

"We've found a new family of—of cosmic harmonies," said Paul finally. "A way to see all sorts of processes matching up. The key is that you can emulate anything by hooking together these five morphons that—"

"Mighty Morphin Power Rangers," interrupted Alma giddily.

"LeapFrog LeapPad. Newborn Baby Tender Love. Did you ever notice that toy names are strings of trochees? *DAH-da DAH-da DAH-da*. Designed to be whined." She made her voice super-nerdy and keened, "Teenage Mutant Ninja Turtles."

"I had a bunch Power Rangers when I was a kid," said Paul, accepting the interruption. "I liked them."

"Growing up in Orange County, I was into G.I. Joe," said Leni. "I put all my Barbie dresses on him. Joe's always been my role model. See?" She flexed her biceps. Paul looked, but he didn't touch.

"Here's a picture of our morphons," I told Alma, fetching my drawing of the fish in the teapot on the birthday cake on the dish with the rake wrapped all around.

"Boing boing," she said, touching the part at the bottom where the rake handle coiled around to hold up the dish. "And this is a model of—what?"

"A universal emulator," I said. "You can adjust the number of candles, the turns of the rake, the angle of the teapot spout, like that. And you get a thunderstorm or a baby or a crooked election or a barking dog."

"That's so poetic, Bela." She gave me a soft pat on my head, and let her hand stay on my shoulder, gently caressing my neck.

"Minkowski sheaf space is *very* groovy," put in Paul, reaching over to align my papers to match the table's edges. "Meaning that it has lots of attractors. Ruts. Things *want* to match."

"I don't understand what you're saying at all," said Leni. "But the language is—"

"Colorful!" said Alma, and she and Leni clinked wine glasses.

"The key practical application is that Paul and I can finish our theses," I said. "And maybe get good jobs."

"Can I turn on the TV now?" asked Leni. "I want to check the election news."

"Don't be a jenna," said Alma. "Let's listen to the radio. To KALX."

"Music," agreed Paul. "Pure undulating form."

So we flaked out on our long couch, smoking some joints

Leni had brought, and listening to the good, thick, electric sounds—a typical college-station playlist of groups you'd never heard before and would never hear again, many of them sounding, in the evening's context, insanely great. Alma sat between Paul and me, with Leni on the other side of Paul. Paul had to be careful not to sit on the crack between two couch cushions, he couldn't stand that. He was trying to talk math to Leni again, and I grabbed the chance to have a personal conversation with Alma.

"You seem a little tense," I said.

"I—this afternoon was so much fun. I'm worried the magic will go away." She was leaning her cheek against the couch cushion, looking at me. Her chin seemed especially fragile. She was so precious, so finely made, and at the same time so cuddly-looking.

"I know what you mean exactly. I want it to keep it going. A lot of things came together today. Patterns meshing."

"The mighty morphons."

"I'm noticing them everywhere. Like—hear that guitar feedback? I love playing that stuff. It's computationally rich. Those bent notes—they're a model of what's in my heart. The first flowering of love. Reaching out, drawing back, turning in on itself, stretching out again—you know?"

"Oh, Bela. Would you like to show me your room?"

Paul was uncouth enough to ask us where we were going.

"Hooking up," said Alma, keeping a straight face until I'd closed my door behind us. I actually got out my shiny metallic guitar and played a little for Alma, but then she started kissing me and we lay down together on my bed. We made love twice, the first time fast and fierce, the second time slow and thoughtful. And then lay staring into each other's eyes, the room lit by a candle in a bottle on the floor beside my mattress, the flame reflecting *in* the chrome of my guitar.

"Tender Bela," she said, her voice a perfect flower.

"Sweet Alma."

"Are you going to keep seeing me? Now that you've gotten what you wanted?"

"You wanted it too."

"Answer the question."

"Yes, I'd like to keep seeing you."

"Would you like to see me *every night?*" asked Alma, running her hand across my cheek.

"I don't know. Probably. Where are you going with this?"

"I don't have any money left, and Leni says if I can't pay rent, I have to move out so she can make my room into a server room. She's getting free vlog rings and servers and bandwidth from—never mind. She's creeping me out. Could I stay here with you till graduation? It's just six weeks."

"Maybe. If I'm not expelled, I'll be working on my thesis a lot."

"I won't bother you, Bela. Say yes."

"Yes, Alma." It felt good to think of myself as her protector. It made me feel like a grown man. And she was adorable.

"Do you mean it?" Her voice was so lovely. I kissed her.

"I mean it." And then we had sex again.

I woke early. Alma was already gone. She'd left a note with hearts and Xs on the bottom. The note said she had an early class, that she'd be bringing some of her stuff over later today, and that she could hardly wait to sleep with me again. I kissed the note.

On my way to the bathroom, I spotted Paul with his laptop at the kitchen table, the dirty dishes piled and neatly aligned on the counter. His face was quietly exultant.

"Up all night?" I asked. "Sorry I, uh—"

"Easy life for you," he said. "The first draft of our paper's almost done. I scanned in your drawings for the illos. *Morphic Classification*, by Paul Bridge, Bela Kis, and Roland Haut. Don't protest. You deserve the credit. We wouldn't have the result without you. You're smarter than you seem. For instance, you're the one who spent the night with Alma."

"Sure I deserve the credit. But Haut? You really want to give that windbag a cut of our action?"

"We tell him he only gets to be co-author if he lets you finish your thesis with him," said Paul. "We coopt him before he starts trying to get you expelled. We throw him a bone. He's going to want this one."

"What a concept!" Paul's generosity was overwhelming. I'd been scared to even think about what was going to happen to my academic career. And now everything was okay? I leaned over the sink, splashing water on my face while the good news sank in. "You'll really do this for me?" I said, drying myself.

"I print it out and we go see Roland. The sooner the better. Front and center, Kis."

"I have to tell you something about Alma."

"She's beautiful. I wish she was my girlfriend."

"Don't say that, Paul. She wants to move in with me. Probably just till her graduation next month."

"*Sproinng.*"

"Don't be hitting on her, horn-dog."

"I won't need to. One of these days she'll drop into my hand like a ripe fruit. I just hope that you and I will still be friends."

He grinned up from his laptop and adjusted his glasses, snugging them against the bridge of his nose. He was wearing the same see-through white shirt and tank-top undershirt from yesterday, complete with a greasy rabbit-paprika stain on the slightly bulged-out belly of his shirt. I really had nothing to worry about. Let him fantasize.

"We'll stay partners no matter what," I agreed. "Math first, love second."

On the way to Pearce Hall, I bought a newspaper, looking it over as we walked along. Thanks to the electronic voting machines, the tallies were already final. Van Veeter had beat Karen Barbara by ninety-seven votes. A mocking mirror image of Haut's prediction. For sure the YWCA fire had made the difference. The fire was being reported as accidental, caused by defective wiring in the fuse-boxes. I figured that was bullshit.

Paul was uninterested in these issues. He was busy leafing through his print-out, making precise corrections with his fine-point pen as we walked.

I threw the newspaper away. It was nicer to think about Alma, to relish the delightful memories of last night. And she was coming back to me this afternoon! With a song in my heart, I followed Paul into Pearce Hall.

"You have the nerve to show up here?" shouted Haut as soon as he saw my face. He was almost at the breaking point. I was tempted to nudge him over the edge.

"Take it easy, Roland," said Paul, stepping in between us. "We've got really good news."

"Good news? The fascist earth rapers have stolen another election!" Haut pushed past Paul and shoved his face in mine. "Kis here told Van Veeter just how many votes he needed to swing the deal. My prediction might have been correct if it hadn't been for that fire. I'd registered that prediction, Kis, it was time-stamped. Designing and running it cost eighteen thousand dollars worth of billable research time. So first of all I'm losing credibility, secondly you've wasted my grant money, and thirdly, I'm losing my representative in Congress. You're out of here, boy, your career is over."

"We proved the Morphic Classification Theorem!" said Paul, brandishing his printout.

Haut wasn't hearing him. He dragged us over to look at a university regulation that he'd accessed and highlighted on his screen. He read it out loud in a strident tone.

"Any student making unauthorized access to university computer accounts is subject to suspension or other sanctions. In cases of legally actionable offenses, the sanctions may include expulsion." Haut paused to glare at me, then poked me in the chest. "And yes, Kis, your stealing my paper is *legally actionable*. I'll be talking to the UC legal staff today. How does a midterm transfer to San Quentin sound?"

"Please, please look at this," said Paul, holding our paper right in front of Haut's face, its bottom edge precisely parallel to the floor.

"*Morphic Classification*, by Paul Bridge, Bela Kis, and Roland Haut? If you think I'm sharing a credit with a jackass like—"

"Just look it over, Roland," said Paul. "Skim it. We'll wait in the hall."

When Haut emerged, his face had relaxed. "The Bridge-Haut-Kis Morphic Classification Theorem. Good work, boys." He was chuckling with pleasure. "A landmark in the history of mathematics. The BHK theorem. I can see it in the textbooks." I noticed that he'd moved his name one notch closer to the front.

"Bela gets his thesis?" said Paul.

"Oh, all right. That frost-vote work of mine—maybe I can still use it after all. And, listen, I've got some ideas for making our joint paper better. I'll earn my credit fair and square. Come into my office and let's get down to it. With a little focus, you two can graduate next month. There's definitely enough here for two separate dissertations. I'm going to announce the result by email today before Cal Kweskin and Maria Reyes over at Stanford beat us to it."

Haut was smiling, albeit not at *me*.

TWO

cone shell aliens

Paul and I spent the next five weeks preparing our theses and the joint research paper, Alma living in my room all the while. Everything was more complicated than I'd expected. For one thing, I was noticing some sexual tension between Paul and Alma. Paul was not above accidentally opening the bathroom door when Alma was showering so as to get a look at her. Often Alma just laughed. For her part, she'd become increasingly concerned with improving Paul's personal habits, as if prepping him for some future role. She found him both too tidy and too messy.

Alma's increasing interest in Paul might have related to the fact that he was doing so well in his job search. We'd both been sending out letters and emails, and mine were disappearing into the special limbo reserved for Nobody from Nowhere. Paul, on the other hand, was getting interviews: UCLA, UC Santa Cruz, Washington State, and even, god help me, Stanford.

Meanwhile of course our glorious rake-cake-fish-dish-teapot proof had any number of holes. One by one we patched them, but some of the patches introduced sec-ond-order holes of their own, and a few third-order holes cropped up in the margins of the patch-patches.

I was good at finding the holes; if I read through the proofs quickly, I could hear their music, and the holes would sound like pops and clinkers.

When the holes were all patched and we'd fully solidi-fied the statement and proof of the Morphic Classification Theorem, Haut weighed in with five freaking anomalies that we characterized as the fish with legs, the teapot with an infinite spout, the rake with no tines, the cake with a hole in the middle, and the dish with only one side. Each of these led to additional special cases in the proof, which meant more holes, more patches, and so on.

In the past I'd sometimes visualized the corpus of mathematical knowledge as an ample goddess, a Mamma Mathematica who nourished her adepts with perfect hemispherical teats. But now I saw the goddess in another aspect: wrinkled, querulous, vindictive. Mamma Mathe-matica had become a warty cackling witch, her cold bony finger poking the soft spots beneath my ribs, testing if I might be ready for the oven.

There weren't enough hours in the days; I longed for some way to veer off into perpendicular time and live a year in the space of an afternoon. Lacking that ability, I drank very much coffee. And Paul began using methe-drine.

"They wouldn't like that in Saint Matthews," tut-tutted Alma, seeing Paul taking tight little snorts from the tiny yellow glass vial he'd begun carrying. "Filthy street drugs.

I thought you were a finer person than that, Paul. You should at least be using Ritalin." It was a Thursday afternoon, a little over a week before commencement. Paul and I were very nearly done. Haut was scheduled to sign off on our theses on Tuesday, and we were supposed to get our diplomas next Friday.

"Many Kentuckians are amphetamine enthusiasts," answered Paul, laying a finger along the side of his nose. He was wearing bottle-blue clip-on shades over his glasses. Although the clip-ons were just a cheezoid item he'd found in the tourist-trap head shop where he'd bought his little meth holder, they had the effect of making Paul look quite demented, especially as combined with his unvarying short-sleeved white shirt and loop undershirt.

"Think of carnies and truckers," he continued. "Jockeys and fiddlers. Crystal keeps Kentuckians lean and mean. And, yes, I know the dangers full well. Don't worry, Alma. I'm only using speed for three more days, and then I stop. A localized degeneracy, you might say. Home stretch. We're almost done. You should snort some too, Bela. And then we could arrange all our books in order of size."

"It's not funny, Paul!" cried Alma. "I grew up with an addict in the family. My big brother Pete. He'd get violent when he was coming down; he'd start breaking up the house, punching holes in the walls. My Mom would have to call the sheriff. I'd hear the police loudspeakers crackling and whining outside, and the cherry ball on their car would be flashing red and blue light across our curtains, and they'd come in and take Pete away. And

Mom would be like, okay let's have supper. She and my father wouldn't ever talk about it because they're addicts too. You're playing with destruction." The main message I took from this rant was that Alma cared about what Paul did. And that was bad news for me.

Paul grinned, basking in Alma's attention. He was a little proud to show he could be a bad boy, too. He held the little yellow bottle out towards me, shaking it invitingly. "Crank 'er up, Bela."

"Nah," I said loftily. This was all about posturing for Alma. "Everything seems too important when I'm stoned. And all we're really doing is writing a math paper."

"*We?*" shot back Paul. "It's me who's actually writing it." He bent over his laptop, peering though his blue shades at the symbols on the screen. "Crankity-crankity-crankity-crankity-crank," he said, with a sly glance at Alma.

"I saw Haut today to set up our thesis defenses for Tuesday," I said, changing the subject. "And that's all fine. But he's stonewalling my requests for letters of recommendation. I finally got a nibble from Chulo State and when I asked Haut to write them a letter he said—stop looking at your screen and listen to me, Paul!—He said he got up last night and saw a pair of cockroaches reflected in his bathroom mirror, running around on the floor, and that the patterns told him that he shouldn't help me get a job at all. I tried to act like it was a joke, but he said, no, it was an instance of the Morphic Classification Theorem at work, and that the cockroaches were emulating him and me. And I said that was complete bullshit, and he said, yes it was, but that now he'd tell me the real story, which was that the cockroaches in the mirror had been human-sized, and they'd been telepathically communicating with him by beaming rays at him, telling him that Bela Kis should work for a certain high-tech company instead of becoming a professor. And then he holds up his fingers like little antennae and he wiggles them at me and sticks out his tongue. And tells me to get out of his office. He's losing it, Paul. He's an evil madman."

"Cockroaches?" said Paul, cocking his head. "We have cockroaches too."

"Haut was *teasing* Bela," said Alma. "Don't you two have any common sense at all? What *is* it with you and Haut, Bela? Did you do something new to piss him off?"

"I bet he did," said Paul. "You talked against his consulting gigs, didn't you, Bela?"

"So?" I admitted. "I'm right! Listen to me, Alma. Haut wants to start marketing a prediction service based on our new theorem. I say it's way too early. Mother Nature doesn't want power-tripping greedheads looking up her skirts."

"Can't you stop fighting him?" said Alma gently. "You're just transferring your old issues with your biological father. It's self-destructive, Bela."

"Alma's right," said Paul. He'd turned his attention back to his screen now. He was in the math zone.

I was indeed pained by my memories of how my father had treated my family. If only I could forgive my old man and let go. Maybe then I wouldn't always be starting fights with father figures. I needed to be working on my thesis instead of stewing and arguing. I was bad and wrong.

So of course I lashed out at Paul the more. "You're so wired that you haven't bathed for a week and you're giving me advice? Not everyone has it easy like you, fair-haired boy. Teacher's pet. Ass kisser."

"Call me Professor Bridge," said Paul, closing his laptop and picking up his neatly aligned papers.

"Paul got the letter from Stanford today," said Alma. "His job offer. Cal Kweskin wants to have Paul there working with him. We didn't want to tell you. To spare your feelings. But you're acting like such a—"

"Loser," said Paul, getting to his feet.

"You're a sellout," I snapped. "A bullshitter."

Paul shook his head and went into his bedroom to work in peace. It was always tidy in there: all the clothes folded and stacked, the bed made, no litter to be seen.

"Stanford?" I said forlornly to Alma.

"An assistant professorship," she said. "He can start on salary right after graduation. He gets summer research money. And they have a slot in faculty housing ready for him. They even gave him a big advance to help him move. He's going to use it to buy a camper van."

"Only one school has even written me back, Alma. And you heard what I said about the letters of reference. Haut's blackballing me. It's not all my fault."

"Poor Bela. I never knew math was so political." She stepped over and gave me a hug.

I looked down at her shag hair-do with its three stripes of blonde. We'd been living together for about five weeks, and she'd become very familiar to me. It was like she was with me even when she wasn't with me. I had an emulation of her inside my mind. But, wonderfully enough, she actually existed outside of me, and I could look at her and soak up her endless happy surprises for free. I ran my hand down the side of her face, ending at her precious dimple. But she broke away before I could kiss her.

"Don't give up," said Alma, shaking her finger at me. "Finish the thesis, no matter what. Who knows, you just might be in my long-term future. But now I'm off to the library."

Although Alma had already passed her final exams, she still had to finish her Rhetoric of Science report on universal dynamics. She was arguing that universal dynamics was a male strategy for decontexualizing reality, a kind of scientific pornography designed to isolate natural phenomena from their social and emotional matrices—her paper was a "biology good, mathematics bad" rap. Although I felt that Alma was neglecting the really interesting aspects of universal dynamics, her argument was cleverly constructed and beautifully written. It made things more interesting to have this woman disagree with me. I just hoped I could keep her in my life. Whenever I focused on my affection for Alma, it helped me calm down.

After Alma went out, I walked over to Paul's closed bedroom door. "I'm sorry I yelled at you," I called. Somewhere off in Mathland, Paul made a friendly pig noise. No need to bother him any further. I made another cup of coffee and got back to mathing. What else was there to do?

Sometime late Saturday night Paul and I finished. We posted our theses to the math department website. And without even bothering to check again with Haut, Paul went ahead and submitted an electronic copy of our joint paper to the prestigious *Annals of Mathematics*. We were all set to become published Ph.D.s—Paul a Stanford professor, and me unemployed. It was time to cut back on coffee and drop the meth.

We went to bed and slept right through till Sunday evening. When we awoke we were still pretty sketchy. And very hungry. Alma was done with her report and she was hungry too. We headed up to Telegraph Avenue.

Some local Buddhists had opened an Italian gelato-style ice cream parlor. It had a glowing electric sign in the window with a divine eye and an "Om Mane Padme Yum" mantra in pastel neon script. The three of us went in and had an eating contest. The idea was to keep doing rounds, and see who lasted the longest. We took turns picking the flavor.

Banana, anise, pistachio, espresso—and Alma was out. She probably could have eaten more, but she wasn't into pointless contests. Paul and I went head-to-head with ginger, violet, cinnamon, pear, chardonnay, and green-tea gelato, which was the one that shut me down. Paul ordered a victory scoop of vanilla and somehow forced most of it out through his nostrils, making two gnarly, dripping tusks.

"I am cleansed," said Paul, wiping his face with a towel that the disgusted counterman threw to him. "Om *shanti.*"

Vibrating with the sugar rush, we walked the warm spring Humelocke night, seeing morphic parallels all around. The leaf-shadows and our thoughts, the car headlights and our emotions, the sounds of the night and our beating hearts. Alma walked in the middle, holding hands with both of us. And that night she slept on the couch. I was losing her.

Monday around noon we went over to Pearce Hall to check with Haut and make sure he was all set for the thesis defense tomorrow. Some maintenance trucks and campus cops were busy outside the building; a tense buzz filled the hallways. Haut's tenth-floor office door was sealed shut with yellow tape. We hurried to the departmental office.

"You didn't hear yet?" asked Lupe the attack secretary. "I was about to phone you. Professor Haut went on sick leave. 5150."

"He's in the hospital?" I asked.

Lupe sighed and rolled her eyes. "They're evaluating him." She was a basically pleasant woman who'd been toughened by her years of dealing with demanding, out-of-it mathematicians. But if you came out of the fog enough to achieve some minimal level of socialization, Lupe could be quite humane.

"He has to sign off on our dissertations tomorrow!" said Paul.

"Yeah, Professor Kitchner and I were talking about that," said Lupe. She gestured towards the chairman's dark, empty office behind her. "He's out for lunch interviewing a temporary for summer school. He thinks maybe you two can visit Professor Haut with the signature sheets today and it'll be okay. We still have your defense scheduled for tomorrow. But it's better if you can get those signatures. The grad school doesn't like to make exceptions." Her face darkened, recalling past battles with the grad school administrators.

"Where *is* Professor Haut?" asked Paul.

"Thataway," said Lupe, pointing a finger. "Summit Psychiatric Center. It's up the hill past the botanical garden. I already phoned, and you can see him this afternoon between one and two. They can only hold him for seventy-two hours, but we're kind of hoping he'll stay longer. The K bus goes straight up there. I've got your signature pages ready for you."

"He knows we're coming?" I asked.

"I think so," said Lupe. "When the ambulance came for him Friday afternoon, the last thing he said was to make sure that Paul came to see him. And you too of course, Bela."

"What did he *do?*" asked Paul.

Lupe lowered her voice. "He broke the glass out of his window with his desk chair. It's a good thing the chair and broken glass didn't hurt anyone."

"Jeez," I said. "The tenth floor. Was he going to jump?"

"Just go see him," said Lupe, cutting off the gossip and handing us the signature pages. "And don't fold or wrinkle these or the grad school won't accept them."

We found Roland Haut in a room on the first floor of the psychiatric hospital, overlooking a red dirt hillside overgrown with shiny green poison oak.

"I went ahead and sent our paper to the *Annals*," said Paul.

"I could have improved it," said Haut. He wasn't in bed or anything, he was just sitting there in his usual yuppie-type clothes: white linen knickers, a yellow silk shirt, a purple bow tie, yellow-and-purple leather running shoes. "I proved something new on Friday," added Haut in a monotone. Presumably they'd sedated him.

"Save it for the next paper," said Paul.

"I hope you'll be feeling better soon, Roland," I added.

"I don't like it here," said Haut. "I want you boys to get me out right away. I'm not signing off on those dissertations unless we're outside." With the preternatural alertness of the unhinged, he'd spotted the pages in my hand.

"I'm not sure we can do that," I said cautiously. Indeed, the nurse at the desk had told us that although a code 5150 involuntary commitment for inpatient psychiatric evaluation was only for seventy-two hours, Saturdays and Sundays didn't have to count, as those weren't regular work days for the doctors, at least not at Summit Psychiatric. So Haut was legally obliged to stay until Wednesday. The doctors hadn't yet gotten around to evaluating him. For sure nobody was in a rush to put Haut back on the street.

"Why did you throw the chair through your office window?" asked Paul, sitting down on Haut's bed. He was careful to sit precisely perpendicular to the mattress. "Were you going to jump out?"

"Who told you that?" said Haut.

"It's not exactly a secret," I said. "I mean—the window's gone. Maintenance is patching it up."

"Didn't anyone notice that all the glass ended up on the *inside?*" said Haut, lowering his voice. "*I* didn't break the window. Something broke the window to get at *me*. I threw the chair at it." He paused, chewing on the tip of his thumb. "Close the door," he told me. "If the white-coats hear this, they'll want to keep me here for weeks."

When I turned back from the door, I saw Haut making rapid, silent gestures to Paul, like he was trying to get Paul to club me over the head or choke me. Paul shook his head and shrugged.

"You have to sign these papers now," I said, laying them down on the room's rolling table. "Here, I've got a pen. Just sign them for us, Roland. Paul and I kept up our end of the deal. We finished our dissertations and we wrote a joint paper with you. Don't be so—"

"Oh, suddenly this is *my* fault?" said Haut. "I said you have to get me out of here."

"That's not going to happen," I said. "You have to stay here till Wednesday. It's the law. You're 5150, dog."

"It's good for you to be here for a few days, Roland," said Paul. "It's safe."

"What day is it now?"

"It's Monday," said Paul patiently. "Our defense is tomorrow. Graduation is Friday. Sign the papers."

"Don't you want to hear about the thing that broke the window?" said Haut, finally taking the pen from me.

"First sign the papers," said Paul, aligning them. "Don't talk about the window if it upsets you."

"It resembled a flying cone shell snail," said Haut, signing the pages with two quick scribbles. "Like that little shell on my desk that Stephen Wolfram gave me? With the pattern of white and orange triangles wrapping around it like a rolled-up cellular automaton? The pattern is orderly but not predictable, a classic example of computational complexity. But the creature floating outside my window was ten feet long. It wasn't an Earthly cone shell snail, you understand. It was an alien. I saw it while I was working with our theorem Friday, looking for applications. I'd just discovered a remarkable, although stunningly obvious, method for turning a vibrating membrane into a universal paracomputer. A thinking drumhead."

Haut paused and gave me a sharp look, his eyes bright and mad. And then he jabbered on. "The boy is baffled. Yes, Kis, I say 'paracomputer' not 'computer' to point out the fact that this is a *natural object* which behaves like computer. Not a high-tech totem that we monkeys made. Any complex natural process is already a universal para-computer, as our theorem helps to show. But any practical use of a paracomputer requires a coder-decoder method to handle the formats you choose. I was in my office, and about 4:30 p.m. I solved the coder-decoder problem for a paracomputer based upon a vibrating membrane. Find-ing the solution felt like having a light come on in a dark room. I looked up from my work into the mirror on my wall, wanting to admire the face of genius—and I saw a cone shell the size of a canoe hanging in the air outside the window behind me. Not an empty shell. It was alive, with a mollusk inside. I could see its snout, its eyes."

Haut handed Paul my pen, but his hand was still press-ing down on the signature sheets. He continued talking. "The horrible thing was that a tentacle was already extending from the creature's mouth snout to me. Red-dish, quite thin, passing through the window glass and attached to the back of my head. Apparently the cone shell had been communicating thoughts. Tutoring me. Its mouth was like a funnel with transparent edges, the red tendril leading from it like a tongue. Plugged into my brain stem. I saw all this synoptically in my mirror. In a fraction of second."

"You must have been very surprised," said Paul gently. He and I exchanged a glance, edging closer, waiting for our chance to snatch our precious pages back from Haut.

"To the contrary," said Haut. "I'd already had a sense of otherness while formulating my solution to the codec problem. A sense of imminent arrival. But, yes, when I actually saw the cone shell in the mirror I became agitated. I turned and picked up my chair. Although the shell was now invisible, I knew it was still there." His trembling fingers drew together, dragging the papers along, beginning to wrinkle them. "Perhaps it meant me no harm, but I was frightened. The cone shells of the South Pacific harpoon small reef fish and other mollusks, did you know that? The killer snail fires out a detachable tooth that's filled with hallucinogenic conotoxins; it drags the disoriented victim into its floppy maw; and the next day, all that remains of the lovely tropical fish is a pack of bones wrapped in—"

"Look out! Cone shell!" I shouted, pointing towards the window. Haut threw up his hands and shrieked. There was a whinny mixed into his cries; I was loving it. In a heartbeat, Paul had snatched the papers, squared their edges, and shoved them inside his shirt.

"Oops," I said. "Maybe not. Sorry, Roland." Quick footsteps padded down the hall. A nurse and an orderly appeared. "This door has to stay open during visiting hours," said the nurse.

"Would you like a nap, Mr. Haut?" said the orderly.

"I have another little pill for you," said the nurse.

Haut whipped his head around, not quite able to figure out what had just happened. "It was good to see you," I said. "I hope you're better soon."

"Little bastard. I hate you." I pointed quietly at the window one more time, and cupped my hand like a shell. And then we left.

Friday morning the math department had a small ceremony and reception at Pearce Hall. It was cool and cloudy with misty sprinkles of rain. I still felt weird and shaky from working so hard on the thesis. We all wore the traditional red robes and flat triangular caps. The applause was like soft confetti.

Eventually Chairman Kitchner read out Paul's name and my name and said we were Doctors of Philosophy. It was very satisfying. My mother, my big sister Margit, and Margit's husband Bert were there, smiling and clapping and taking pictures. Margit was an accountant for an insurance company in San Francisco; she actually worked in the pointy Transfinita Building. Bert was a very junior stockbroker at Schwein and Son, one step up from a telemarketer—although he talked as if he were a major financier.

I would have liked for Alma to be there, but she had her own graduation to deal with that afternoon. She was spending the morning organizing her stuff and getting gussied up. The plan was that I'd meet her and her parents after the undergrad commencement at the campus's Egyptian Theater, which was this awesome stone Art Nouveau amphitheater dating back to the early 1900s.

Paul's parents weren't at the Pearce Hall ceremony either; what with being divorced, neither of them felt like making the long trip from Kentucky alone. And although Roland Haut was out of Summit Psychiatric now, he was absent as well. I felt just a bit guilty about teasing him the other day. Like I'd been kicking him when he was down. But then I heard something that got me mad at him all over again.

"The University of California is filing a patent on the theorem you two proved with Roland Haut," Chairman Kitchner told Paul and me as we got our cookies and plastic cups of wine from the reception table. Kitchner was a tall, bald man with lugubrious wrinkles running down the sides of his face. "I thought you should know. Roland just told me this morning."

"I already heard," said Paul a little sheepishly. "I was waiting for a chance to tell you, Bela."

"You can patent a theorem?" I said, taking a long pull of wine.

"Sure," said Paul. "Like Lempel, Ziv, Welch and the LZW compression algorithm. Or Rivest, Shamir, Adleman and the RSA encryption method. The Bridge-Haut-Kis theorem could lead to some valuable commercial processes."

"So why does the *university* end up owning it?" I asked.

"It's in the terms of Roland's research grant," said Kitchner. "Standard practice. If you have any lingering questions, he can go over it in person with you when he's feeling less agitated. But I wouldn't bother him for a few weeks, Bela. He seems to have an—attitude towards you. It's unfortunate. The problem when mathematicians go off the deep end is that they still think they're being logical."

"Why does anyone listen to him?" I asked Kitchner. "He told Paul and me that he saw a giant cone shell snail in the air outside his window!"

"I know," said the chairman. "He's still talking about that. Alien cone shells and cockroaches the size of people. He sees them, but only in mirrors." He gave a dour smile and shook his head. "I'm not sure how the window incident is going to play out. The administration is quite concerned over the legal exposure this kind of thing opens up. But Roland's tenured and he does a lot of good work. The patent comes at a fortunate time for him."

"The glass from the window," put in Paul. "Roland said it was all inside his office because the cone shell—"

"He told me that too," said Kitchner, rolling his eyes. "There was glass all over the place—inside, outside, on the sidewalk, everywhere. If it had cut someone—forget it!"

"There's no way to undo his patent?" I said. "I still don't have a job, and I'd been hoping to maybe make some money off our theorem myself. Paul and I did most of the work. It doesn't seem right."

"That's academia," said Kitchner with a shrug. "And there's no reason you can't make money off the theorem. The patent provides a framework. It's really quite an honor to have coauthored a patentable result. The way it works is that you consult for commercial ventures who license your theorem from the UC. In all likelihood you'll find improvements that your new employers can patent on their own. And, Bela, I'll be glad to help you with the job search. The department's very proud of you. Stop by the office next week, and I'll see what we can do." And with that he moved to the next knot of students.

"Smile, Bela," said my sister, and took my picture. She was tall, like me, with her hair bleached, and starting to get a double chin. A comfortable person. "Stand next to him, Ma."

"You get in there, too, Margit," said her husband Bert, taking her camera.

"Doctor Kis," said Ma, adjusting my triangular red mortarboard and patting my cheek. "Wonderful! A Ph.D. in the family!" She was short, with high cheekbones, lots of wrinkles, and eyes that curved like commas. She was always in a good mood, unlike my father, whose moods had fluctuated between anger and despair.

Bert snapped our picture. "Now I'll take a picture of Bela and Paul together," said Ma, hefting her own camera.

Ma had taken a liking to Paul when she, Margit, and Bert had come by our Ratvale apartment this morning. Paul had impressed Ma with his efficiency and liveliness, although I half-suspected that Paul's pep resulted from his having dipped into his leftover methedrine. He'd been up all night packing everything he owned into his new camper van, getting set for his move to Stanford. Everything tidy, everything at right angles. Alma had kept him company, putting her stuff in cardboard boxes in my room, including those of her possessions that had still been at Leni's.

Despite a lot of probing by Alma, I hadn't come up with any good suggestions for where she might live next—other than with her parents. My Ratvale lease was due to run out in a week and a half. Alma was unhappy about this. It was like she expected to me to provide her with a place to live even after graduation. I resented this, although at the same time I felt apologetic about my inability to deliver.

I myself was paralyzed at the prospect of leaving Humelocke. In denial. My stuff was strewn all over the echoing apartment. If I could come up with some money, maybe I'd extend the lease for a month, although this prospect was so unlikely that I hadn't mentioned it to Alma.

Certainly I was in no rush to move back with Ma. She was all set to begin nagging me to getting a job. After I'd told her in the coffee shop this morning that the Chulo State job had fallen through, she'd picked up a newspaper from the next table and begun mock-innocently checking to see, just as a matter of interest, if the category "mathematician" appeared in the classified ads. After being loudly surprised when no such listing could be found, she'd moved on to wondering what kinds of job slots a mathematician could fill. Bookkeeper? Loan officer? Payroll clerk? Teacher? Sign installer?

"You know what Ph.D. really stands for, Mrs. Kis?" said Paul, standing next to me. We had our arms across each other's shoulders.

"Tell me, Paul," said Ma, pointing her camera at us.

"B.S. is bullshit, M.S. is more shit, and Ph.D. is—"

"Piled *high* and deep!" I chimed in as the camera beeped. The sun came out; a breeze caressed us; the sky was a beautiful pale shade of blue.

"Oh, you boys," laughed Ma. "That's all you learned in grad school? Get your frail old mother some refreshments, Bela." Ma was about as frail as beef jerky or a coiled steel spring. But I was happy to tend to her. I was very fond of my mother, and proud to have her here today.

About twenty plastic cups of rice wine waited on the refreshment table. The sunlight danced enticingly among them, making arrows and cusps of light on the white paper tablecloth, bright condensations of energy. At the morphon level, we guests at the reception were akin to the caustic curves of refracted light; we were concentrated fields, like the candles of the birthday cake morphon. I felt a twinge of prospective melancholy, an intimation of my future nostalgia for this particular moment. Graduation was the end of something. Who knew if I'd ever again see so deeply into math as I did at this moment?

"What was that about a patent?" asked brother-in-law Bert when I rejoined Paul and my family. Bert was tan and fit, Filipino with a fair amount of Chinese blood. He'd shaved his head bald last year at the first sign of hair loss. "You dogs ready to run with the venture capitalists?"

"Our results are mostly theoretical," I said. "We can figure out how different kinds of systems *should* match up so that the one system emulates the other. And we have a few pet examples that happen to work. But in general—"

"Can you use it for technical market analysis?" said Bert. "That's the question. Like the Prediction Company, it was

started by those guys from the Santa Fe Institute, Doyne
Farmer and Norman Packard? That big Swiss bank UBS
was funding them to play the currency exchange market."

"There's a stumbling block," put in Paul. "Codec." Paul
and I had been hung up on this concept ever since hearing Roland Haut raving about it. On the street, a codec
was a software or hardware package used to code audio
or video into small files and to decode such files back into
audio or video. But to us, codec meant so much more.

"What's codec?" asked Bert.

"Coder/decoder," said Paul. "Our Morphic Classification Theorem shows that all kinds of natural processes
can act as good simulations for each other. But if you want
to learn something specific from a simulation, you have to
code your data into the simulation's world and decode it
back out. Like suppose you're going to make predictions
about the weather by reading tea leaves. To get concrete
answers, you code *today's* weather into a cup of tea made
with loose leaves. You swirl the cup around, drink the tea,
look at the leaves, and decode the leaf pattern into *tomorrow's* weather. Codec."

"Huh?"

"It's like if you ask a Hungarian mathematician a question," I said. "You have to code your plain English question into Hungarian mathematics, and then you have
decode the mathematician's batshit answer into plain
English. Codec."

"Ah, those genius Hungarians," said Margit, fluffing her
blonde shag with the back of her hand.

"Almost as smart as Chinese people," said Ma.

"What is it with the Chinese-Hungarian connection, Mrs. Kis?" interjected Paul. "Bela's never quite explained it me."

"During the Cold War years, Hungary was one of the only European countries where the Red Chinese could go," said Ma. "Budapest developed a lively Chinatown, where I was born. My father was Chinese and my mother was Hungarian. They had two children: Xiao-Xiao Wong, which is me, and my younger brother Zoltan Wong. My mother died too young, poor thing, run over by a streetcar. And then my father didn't know how to raise us. So he sent Zoltan and me to grow up with his cousin Shirley Woo in San Jose. We adapted, we became Silicon Valley kids. In high school I fell in love with a Hungarian-American boy named Tibor Kis. We married young and were blessed with Margit and Bela. And then my brother Zoltan married Tibor's sister Zsuzsa! Always Hungarian and Chinese in our family. Tibor's been dead for five years. He would have loved seeing this graduation, Bela. He would have been proud. He loved you even if he didn't say so. How come you didn't tell Paul about your family?"

"It's complicated," I mumbled. The truth was, I didn't like thinking about my far-flung, vociferous family.

For one thing, I wasn't crazy about my San Jose relatives—I found them old-fashioned, always talking about money and family, and I felt guilty for thinking that, although, yeah, my bad-ass double cousin Gyula Wong was pretty hip. He'd been almost like an older brother to me when we'd been kids.

Another issue was that thoughts of my immediate family were tainted by my feelings about my father. His gambling bankruptcy had infuriated me. And the very last time I'd talked to him, he'd started ragging on me about "wasting my time" playing in a band. We'd gotten into a terrible argument and I'd told him I wished he was dead. A week later he'd keeled over from a heart attack. Lacking a way to love his memory, I preferred not to think about him at all.

"Math is more important than your family?" probed Ma.

"Don't start on Bela, Xiao-Xiao," interrupted Bert. "He was about to tell me how to use his theorem to get rich. You guys said you could predict the market if it weren't for—what?"

"Codec," said Paul. "We're kind of on our own with the problem right now. Last week our adviser, Roland Haut, claimed he had a big insight about solving the codec problem; he was going to turn, like, a rubber sheet into a programmable paracomputer. But then he went mental and threw his chair through his window, and now he either doesn't remember his codec idea or he doesn't want to talk about it. I visited him yesterday. He's better. He's decided the cone shells and cockroaches were just hallucinations."

"You saw him?" I said feeling a twinge of jealousy. "You should have beaten the freaking codec outta him." I picked up an empty cup and began pouring my rice wine back and forth from cup to cup. It made a gentle gurgling sound. The wine surfaces dimpled with turbulence; small bubbles swirled around. "Here's a simulation of a mutual fund's price, Bert."

"Right," said Paul. "A small-cap mutual fund is a perfect morphonic match to a poured cup of liquid. At the morphon level, you're looking at a pair of rakes with their tines hooked together in overhand knots, and a fish and a teapot perched on the handles, with the fish drinking tea from the spout and wearing a little dish on its head like a straw boater." As he talked, I kept pouring the wine back and forth. "But, you see, Bert," added Paul, "Our problem is how do we feed the market trends into the wine? And how do we get the prediction numbers out?"

"Codec it like this," I said, draining my glass. I was feeling reckless.

"Piled high and deep," said Bert approvingly. "I'll tell you guys a trade secret. If you have enough smoke and mirrors, you can pull in the fees whether or not your predictions work. Business guys are bored. They want to be amazed. You could get steady work dazzling them with those Humelocke math degrees."

I still couldn't believe Chulo State hadn't hired me. I abhorred the notion of getting a normal nine-to-five job. Maybe I should get back into music. Start a band.

I handed in my cap and gown, then took a walk around the campus with my family, showing them some of my favorite spots. For lunch we got yogurt and giant bowls of roast root vegetables at Mondokko, a student-type place near Ratvale. Ma enjoyed the chance to eat in somebody else's restaurant. Just for today she'd left East-Vest in the hands of her brother and his wife, Zoltan and Zsuzsa Wong, who'd sent along their best wishes and a card containing a hundred dollar bill. Good old

Uncle Zoltan. Ma said their son Gyula had to work at Membrain Products today. If he'd had been present, he probably would have tried to scam or strong-arm me out of my hundred bucks. That's the kind of guy Gyula was: guiltlessly predatory.

After lunch, Bert and Margit took off in their car, while Ma and I walked down Telegraph and Shattuck towards the DART station. Ma was interested in all these shops that I'd passed a hundred times without noticing, places filled with imported fabrics and carved figurines. We went into about four of them, and finally she found just the pink-flowered silk pillow that she wanted, a plump round disk to put on her chair by the cash register at East-Vest.

"Hurry home soon," Ma told me at the station. "You're all done in Humelocke now. You did a good job, and you can party, but don't do anything reckless. Mongol rabbit when you get home." Her little restaurant's specialty and my favorite. Ma used organically raised rabbits from Marin County, and had added Hungarian variations to a traditional Chinese recipe.

By the time I got up to the Egyptian Theater, the undergrad commencement ceremony was over. Worming through the hubbub, I caught up with Alma and the Ziffs by the main entrance as planned. It was just her parents with her. Seemingly her aging surf-dregger brother Pete hadn't made it, which was fine with me.

"This is my friend Bela," said Alma. "And these are my parents Gary and Sarah. Bela and Paul have been letting me live in their apartment. I told you about Paul."

"Yo," said Gary Ziff. He had long curly hair hanging down like a welcome mat, with a bald spot on top. He sported a walrus mustache and a Hawaiian shirt. I made him for a parrot head. Sure enough he lit up a joint, right there on the street.

"*Gary*," said Alma. She looked very cute in her yellow graduation robe and three-cornered mortar-board, which set off her dark eyes and intense features.

"Hey, we're in Humelocke," said Gary. "This is a party town. I used to come up here in high-school and freakin' run wild. Want a hit, Bela?"

I waved him off. I was feeling buzzed enough from the wine, the emotions, and the weeks of overmathing.

"I'll shotgun you," said Gary, rounding his lips and blowing a stream of smoke my way. "It's my special Ziff-zone mix. I put termite powder in it." I accidentally caught a pungent whiff and felt instantly dizzy. "I'm an exterminator," added Gary.

"Make him stop, Sarah," said Alma. Sarah Ziff was a stocky woman with a marcelled perm, her hair black with gray at the roots. She had a sweet doughy face behind her pointy cat's-eye shades, and earrings shaped like fish. Hearing Alma's distress, her mouth formed a fierce expression.

"Don't. Ruin. The day," she said to Gary, drawing back her lips to reveal stained teeth. She clamped her hand onto his shoulder and gave him a shake with each word.

"Whoah," said Gary. He took a few steps back, did one more toke, then pinched out his joint and dropped the roach in his pocket. "Bring the band down behind me, boys," he said, flicking an imaginary microphone cord. What a guy.

"I think it's time to feed him," said Sarah, folding her expression into sweetness again. "Is the Triple Rock Brewery still on Shattuck?" asked Gary. "They've got killer nachos."

"That's a wonderful idea," said Alma. "You guys go there and fill up. Order without me. I'll be there in, like, forty minutes. I have to change, and finalize my packing—and it'll be easier without you hovering."

"We *are* taking your stuff back to Cruz, right?" said Gary. "I spent the last three days emptying out the van. You won't believe some of the things I found. Dick Chandler's reflecting telescope that he's been asking me about. I'd totally spaced on that. I borrowed it for our trip to Death Valley." He held his finger out like a gun and mimed shooting himself in the head.

"When he was looking for UFOs," added Sarah. "Never a dull moment around the Ziff household, Bela. I heard you got your doctorate today? Congratulations."

"My van's right outside Ratvale if you want to start carrying some boxes down for her," Gary told me. "We were late, but I got a great space."

"Come to think of it," said Alma, "why don't you guys just come back to Bela's apartment and meet me there after you eat? I'm really not that hungry."

The Ziffs angled off towards the brewery, sharing Gary's roach as they walked. Alma and I headed for Ratvale. Everywhere students were floating along in their red and yellow robes. Like butterflies on a field of flowers.

"I can't believe you're expecting me to go back and live with them," said Alma, apropos of her parents. "Gary, Sarah, and Pete? I'd rather die."

"Maybe we can both move into the city," I said. "Depending what kinds of jobs we get. I didn't tell you there's a slight chance I could renew my Ratvale lease for a month. If I get some money."

"You should have told me that earlier, Bela," said Alma, her voice rising to a shrill note on my name. "Instead of saying you're going to live with your mother? In San *Jose?* Living with your parents is like a comic where time starts running backwards because Bizarro Superman flies around the equator a bunch of times the wrong way. And *now* you tell me maybe you'll stay in Humelocke after all? Like I wanted to all along?"

I was getting a little tired of Alma's dramatics. I loved her, yes, but come on. I needed to kick back for awhile. No way was I up for offering her guaranteed support.

"I don't know what's gonna happen," I said. "Just accept that. Why not hang here with me and find out? I know that graduations are hard. Your relatives think it's a big happy day, but it isn't happy at all. It's like dying. And now we're going into another world."

"Thanks so much for that cheery thought, Bela." She was in quite a state. "You're so right. I *am* going into another world."

"Even if I can't renew here, you can come sleep over at my house in San Jose," I said. "Ma likes you. Or maybe we'll go camping."

"As if." When we were half a block from Ratvale, Alma

stopped by a battered old white Rotgenick panel truck with a ticket on the windshield. "Look what my brain-dead father did." The truck was parked next to a fire hydrant with a paper sack over the hydrant.

"The Ziff family vehicle?" I said, unable to suppress a grin. Somewhere along the line, Gary had glued fake plastic grass to the truck's roof—Bogoturf.

"As if the cops weren't going to notice that the curb's painted red," continued Alma. "As if they don't see the hydrant there every single day. Gary's going to be talking about this ticket for weeks." She was laughing and, I suddenly realized, crying at the same time.

"There's Paul's van," I said, to change the subject. Paul's brand new camper van was parked a few spaces ahead, a high-tech, curvy, low-emission machine, gleaming in the sun. It even had a mattress in back. "Gotta hand it to the boy. He's got it together."

"Yes," said Alma. "He does. Not like the rest of you."

I was sensing something in the air. And when we went up to the apartment I finally got the picture. Paul was sitting there with a bunch of yellow roses.

"Congratulations, Alma," he said hugging her.

"Oh, Paul," she said, kissing him on the mouth.

Paul broke the clinch, embarrassed. "She's coming with me, Bela. We've been talking about it."

"I'm sorry," Alma told me. "I do still care for you. More than you know. But—"

"I already put your boxes in my truck," Paul said to Alma. "I figure the sooner we leave, the better."

"Wait," I said.

"Let's just do it," said Paul. "I feel sick about this too. You're still my best friend. Come see us after things settle down."

"I'll miss you, Bela," said Alma.

I felt a cramp in my stomach, a gag in my throat. I'd had too much wine and food, and that whiff of Ziff-zone hadn't helped either. I ran into the bathroom and threw up. And when I got done, Paul and Alma were gone.

I went down to the corner store and bought some non-filter cigarettes. Self-destruction mode. I sat in my room by my sunny window, smoking and retching a little from the smoke.

I was thinking about Paul's messiness, his self-absorption, his awkward walk, his discordant voice, the ugly rash on his neck. Alma wanted that? I could almost hate Paul—but not Alma. It was, after all, thanks in part to my own ineptness that she had to choose between living with Paul or with her groover parents—at least until she found her own job. Poor Alma. She'd said it was hard to leave me. I'd work to get her back.

A torrent of Alma images was rushing through my mind. The way she craned her neck to look at something. The smell of her cheek. Her dimple. The way she pushed back her hair. Alma naked. Alma laughing. On and on.

Paul had stolen my one true love, and he had the nerve to say I was still his best friend? How pathetically naive he was, how spoiled by good fortune.

I continued brooding, watching the smoke, with the sun and leaf-shadows playing across my face. The chaotic

flickers were hitting me with an almost psychedelic inten-
sity. I was in a very weird state of mind. The wine and
the Ziff-zone had worn off, but I was feeling stranger and
stranger. I had this odd sense of an impending visitation,
of beings on their way to give me a message. Angels in
America? I wondered if I was fully losing it.

I took my electric guitar out of its case, plugged it into
my speaker-amp and started playing riffs. It was a flashy
chromed model, acquired secondhand along with some
amps and mikes during my E To The I Pi days. My hands
were shaking. Alma, Alma, Alma. Life was unbearable.
Think about math, Bela. Music and math can calm you
down.

As I tuned my guitar, it struck me that my instrument's
sounds could perhaps take on the same morphonic structure as my love triangle with Alma and Paul. To begin
with, I imagined three mirror-bright mind dishes reflecting the elusive fish of love like a kaleidoscopic hall of
mirrors.

I began making it real, using my silver guitar to code my
thoughts and feelings into electrical signals that went to
the speaker-amp. The circuitry munged the wave forms,
decomposing, fuzzing, shifting, and remixing them—a
computation whose result was sounds. And the room's
acoustics added a second stage to the computation. The
guitar tones reverberated and beat against each other in
the chunks and crannies of negative space surrounding
my room's furniture and me.

By way of expressing myself the more, I moved around
as I played, letting the speaker's vibrations affect the strings

of my guitar, feeding the signals through multiple cycles of acoustic computation. And all the while my ears were decoding my gnarly guitar noise into thoughts and feelings.

Codec. Brain states, finger twitches, electric signals, air pressures, eardrums, brain states.

Codec. Thoughts _ sounds _ thoughts.

I collapsed the concepts more and more, stripping away the externals, glimpsing the mathy core. It was like staring into the sun. The more I understood, the more certain I became that strange visitors were on their way. It was as if their arrival were sending a ripple back through time, a reversal of cause and effect. I was approaching a solution to the codec problem *because* they were about to arrive. Did that mean I'd forget the answer after they left? And who were they, really? I wiggled my guitar neck, riding the feedback like a witch on her broom.

I thought of the aura that epileptics experience before a fit. Perhaps I was on the brink of seizure? But I kept on playing my guitar, kept on thinking.

Thinking about Alma. Working intuitively, not quite knowing how I did it, I really did find a way to codec the love triangle into sound. The noisy room computed; I listened to what emerged. The grungy metal buzz was telling me what to do. Tweak this, tweak that, and *deedle-yawng-skreek* I suddenly knew how to win her back. I had to become famous by starting a rock band. And somehow Paul should sleep with another woman and have Alma find out. Aha.

I looked in the mirror on the wall above my dresser—grinning with an open mouth, hungry for the next rush.

In the mirror's recesses, I saw the image of my open window and the reflected tiny view of Haste Street with the eternal Humelocke freaks truckin' on down the line. I noticed a couple of characters with heads vaguely like the buds on a fractal Mandelbrot set. They'd come to a stop across the street; they were staring at Ratvale. I had a premonition that they were here for me. Not wanting to face them yet, I peered deeper into the mirror's dark glass. The two figures across the street had waving antennae and feelers; they were humanoid cockroaches standing on two legs, one male and one female.

I turned towards the window now, oddly calm, rocking my guitar, fire-hosing feedback from my amp. I couldn't see the cockroach people through the window, although, glancing down, I could see them as reflections in my guitar, warped and breaking up across the shiny curved surfaces.

I went back to my wall mirror to see them better. The alien cockroaches scurried across the mirror-street, climbed the mirror-wall of mirror-Ratvale, wriggled in through my mirror-window and stood in my mir-ror-room. Their mouths were moving, but I heard no sound other than the wailing and buzzing of my guitar.

Staring through the mirror at them I formed the impression that the aliens were weird but cozy, like awk-ward chatty mathematicians in thick sunglasses—but those weren't glasses, those were bulging, dark-green fac-eted eyes. Bug eyes. The aliens' mouths were humanoid, with thin green lips and yellow teeth like corn kernels. Each of them had two legs and four arms, the limbs purple and muscular with one joint too many. Comfortingly, they had feet and hands.

Their bellies were banded with horizontal stripes of tough-looking elastic yellow tissue, and their gently domed backs were an iridescent shade of mauve. On their heads they wore those whiplike antennae I'd noticed, and writhing purple-green feelers in place of hair.

Was I safe? A quick glance over my shoulder confirmed that, at least so far as I could see, the aliens weren't physically in the real room with the real me. This despite the fact that, within the looking-glass world, they were right behind mirror-me, close enough to touch my mirror-shoulder. A cockroach man and a cockroach lady.

And now, just like a mathematician would, the guy cockroach held up a scrap of—paper? It had symbols and diagrams on it, and it was better than paper, it was animated. The lines and shadings were moving through a cycle of a five steps, repeating them over and over so that I could better understand.

And that was not all. The woman cockroach was beaming green rays out of her eyes, rays that drilled through the mirror-glass and played across my forehead, no doubt penetrating into the tissues of my brain. But, perhaps due to the 'rays' influence, I wasn't scared. And soon I knew the solution to the generalized codec problem for a drum-head-type paracomputer, perhaps the same solution that Haut had claimed he'd learned from the cone shells. Aha.

The solution involved, among other things, sheaves, teapots, and Mobius strips—arranged just so.

All this time I was still playing my guitar, my hands and ears off in a world of their own, and the music getting ever lovelier. On the fly, I was translating my thoughts into smeared and tangled hypersheets of sound.

Grinning and sweating, I labored to imprint the cockroaches' subtle codec solution upon my memory. It was, um, Klein bottles, Minkowski space, cellular automata, and—

"Dude! Where's my sister?"

The mirror-roaches chirped, rotated at some impossible angle and disappeared. I was back to so-called reality, seeing a tall, skinny guy with shades peering in my bedroom door. His face was gaunt, he had long dark hair slicked straight back, he wore a rumpled blue jumpsuit.

"Bag the noise!" he yelled. "I'm lookin' for Alma." It was Pete Ziff. We recognized each other from the surf scene back at Cruz.

I stopped playing—and snapped out of my trance. What had I been doing just now? Had that been real? My solution to the codec problem, if it really was a solution, was shifting like a sand-castle lapped by a rising tide. For the moment I didn't care. I was glad to be alive, glad to be normal again.

"It's good you came," I told Pete. "I was seeing, like, mathematician cockroach aliens in my mirror. Teaching me things."

"Stoned geek," said Pete. "Where the fuck's Alma and her shit?"

"She left," I said. "With Paul Bridge. My roommate." I wanted to tell Pete as much as possible about Paul's whereabouts. That lucky pig was getting off way too easy. "They're moving into the faculty housing at Stanford."

"Where's that at?"

"Duh? Palo Alto? I'd be glad to write down his cell phone and address for you." I tore a scrap off the folded-in-four sheet of paper from my hip pocket and uncapped my pen. I didn't like the way Pete was looking at me. I'd never liked Pete. "You can read, can't you?"

"Fuckhead hairfarmer. Alma's really gone?"

"Here." I jotted down the info and handed it to him. "FYI, Alma said she'd rather die than live with her family," I added.

Pete spat on the floor and stalked out. As long as I had my pen and paper handy, I made a drawing of what I remembered about the generalized solution to the codec problem. A little comic strip of four panels. There had been a fifth frame, but that was one of the parts I already couldn't remember.

As I sketched, I heard Pete and Gary Ziff yelling at each other in the street, with Sarah remonstrating in the background. And then I heard the pop and roar of Pete's motorcycle, the one with the funky bracket for his surfboard welded to one side. Although it wasn't even suppertime, I could also hear the sounds of several post-commencement parties cranking. Humelocke was full of music.

Without looking in the mirror again, I shoved the paper in my pocket and got the hell out of my room. I wanted to be around people. Enough with the math.

It had clouded over again, and was spitting bits of rain. I decided to walk a few blocks and visit my friend Danny Nguyen, a fellow math grad student. He had a couple more years of study ahead of him, and I knew he was sticking around for the summer. Although his field was differential geometry, studying the possible shapes of higher-dimensional surfaces, he was also interested in what everyone else was doing—he'd even come to my thesis defense. Danny was intelligent, preppy, and polite; I could see him as a department chair some day.

To cut down on his living expenses, Danny had signed on as a proctor in Bulkington, which was probably the wildest of the student co-ops. The Bulkington graduation party was well underway when I got there.

The neighbor next door to Bulkington had a problem. He was a fat-necked guy with longish black hair, standing next to his unbelievably large SUV, hollering at three grungy little skate-dreggers: a couple of Asian-Indian boys and an Anglo girl—all of them pierced, short-haired, feral. Apparently the skaters had been grinding the man's front steps as well as those of the Bulkington co-op. One of the boys was wearing a construction-orange vest that he'd wired as a beat box. As the man yelled, the boy's hands played over his vest, making a mocking soundtrack of off-kilter rhythms.

Danny Nguyen appeared at the dorm entrance, alert to the crisis, his eyes intent behind his heavy black-framed glasses. He wore a lot of mousse in his short hair, sculpting it into hedgehog-like pattern of peaks.

"Hey Danny!" I called.

"Hi, Bela. You can help me out." He turned to the skaters. "I know that you guys don't live here, so don't be giving us a bad name. The party's an open house; come on in and have a good time. But don't bother our neighbor Mr. Vitelloni. Or maybe Bela here kicks your butt. Just kidding. It's party time. No fights, no cops, free beer inside. But remember—Doctor Bela is gonna be watching you."

"Nice beat," I said to the skater with the vest, a dark-skinned guy with a beaky nose and a prominent Adam's apple. "I like how off-balance it is. I'd maybe push it a little further, a little closer to random noise."

"Monster music," said the kid, tapping his vest in several places. The sounds thickened and folded, with unexpected wrinkles. "Feedback modulation," he said. "Electronic tabla. You're Doctor Bela? My name's Naz."

"Make it very strange now, Naz," said the other boy skater, holding out his well-muscled, golden-skinned arms and writhing them like snakes. "I'm Thuggee and this is K-Jen." His voice had that subcontinental singsong lilt.

K-Jen was a stocky blonde girl with a strong chin and high cheekbones. Her lips were irregular at the edges, giving her mouth a smeared look. Her eyes had something twitchy and anxious about them. She also had pimples, a nose ring, and a shag that had mutated into matted tufts.

"He said free beer?" said K-Jen in a husky voice. "Eek." She gave Mr. Vitelloni the finger, and led the other skaters into Bulkington.

"Little snots," yelled Vitelloni, thrusting out his jaw and waving a fist. His wife watched from the porch, stick-thin and sour.

"Excuse me? Excuse me?" she called to get Danny's attention. "Mr. Nguyen? I'm expecting your crew to repaint our steps come clean-up day."

"No problem, Ms. Vitelloni," said Danny. "Just remind me if I forget."

College kids were milling around the halls of Bulkington, smoking pot and hitting the kegs in the communal dining area on the first floor. I saw a naked curly-haired guy carrying a dark green plastic trash bag, seemingly with nothing in it. He'd drawn a giant raven beak on his chest, with his nipples painted black for eyes.

"Caw caw," he yelled in a deep voice. "Wak wak. Wak caw bong ork whooo!"

"We call him the Birdman," Danny told me. "He keeps that garbage bag full of nitrous oxide. He got a tank from an auto shop." Danny shook his head. "I might not proctor here next year."

We made our way into the common room and joined the knot of people around the silver kegs. A couple of other math grad students were there, too, Dirk Wronski and Eugenia Fraze. It was interesting to join Danny for the Bulkington parties.

"Congratulations on your degree, Bela," said Dirk, toasting me. He was tall and raw boned, wearing a shiny gray suit over a starched white shirt as if to emulate the 1950s immigrant mathematician look. Very dregger. "Any job nibbles yet?"

"The chairman said next week he'll try and help me," I said, glad to be talking. "Paul's already off for Stanford. And, listen to this, he took Alma with him."

"No!" said Eugenia, whose round, steel-framed glasses were a stern contrast to her sweet, pixyish face. "Poor Bela."

"I want to hear about this too," came a voice from behind me. It was Leni Pex, intimidatingly fit, and all

dolled up in pancake makeup, trailing two equally the-
atrical women in her wake. Leni was wearing a ring with
a lens on it. One of those vlog rings she'd been talking
about. The ring itself looked to be made of plastic, red-
dish with shades of blue.

"You're webcasting live?" I said, not all that glad to see
her. Encountering Leni gave me a pang for Alma; it hit
me like a knife in my heart—to use a favorite Hungarian
expression. We get the most out of our emotions.

"I always vlog live at parties these days," said Leni. "It's,
like, my web show. *Out with Leni.* Glad to see you've got
a beer." She let out an insinuating chuckle. "Graduation
party, hmm? I hope you get drunk and spill your guts for
my viewers. Do you know my friends? Dorothy Hook
and Lulu Cliff, this is Bela Kis, who just got a Ph.D. in
math, am I right?"

"Yeah, I made it," I said. "No thanks to *Buzz* for airing that demo. The thesis kept getting harder at the end.
Like climbing an Alp. You might say I've got altitude sick-
ness now. These are my fellow mathematicians Danny
Nguyen, Dirk Wronski, and Eugenia Fraze. Look out,
guys, Leni is webcasting us live. Dozens, perhaps *scores* of
no-life losers are watching us as we speak."

"You'd be surprised at our hit counts," said Leni equa-
bly. "We've started selling ads. Dorothy and Lulu are my
partners. We all graduated today. Dorothy in communication, me in business, and Lulu in computer science.
We've got big plans. We want to take *Buzz* public in two
years."

"I remember you," I told Dorothy. She had vivid red

lipstick and bobbed black hair. Kind of a 1920s look. "You were in a calculus section I taught a couple of years ago. But you dropped almost right away."

"I found a way to substitute an online philosophy course for it," said Dorothy. "Self-paced."

"You didn't like my teaching?"

"Didn't like anything about you," said Dorothy, laughing. "Shoes, voice, smell, and those questionable stains around your zipper—ugh! Just kidding. You were fine. It was the stuff you wrote on the board. I was all, do I need to know this to communicate? Noooo. I can't imagine how anyone could take math course after math course to get a Ph.D. It must be like memorizing the *Star Wars* movies. All those hunchbacked little deltas and epsilons and their stupid battles. I don't have math anxiety, Bela, I have math *contempt*." Stagily she clapped her hand over her mouth. "And to think I said that live on the *Out with Leni* show!"

"Wasn't Alma living with you?" Lulu asked me. She looked like a depraved schoolgirl, with thick makeup, black bangs, a frilly white blouse, a blue miniskirt and horizontally striped black and red stockings. "I remember she moved out of Leni's when I helped put the extra servers in. She was steamed about losing her room."

"Steamed latte," purred Dorothy. "I love Alma's skin."

"Not that you ever got your hooks into her," put in Lulu, kissing Dorothy's cheek and leaving a lipstick mark. Lulu winked for the camera and Dorothy stuck her tongue in Lulu's ear. They were really camping it up.

"Did I hear you say that *Alma Ziff* left with your roommate *Paul Bridge?*" said Leni, holding up her vlog ring to catch my reaction.

I didn't answer that one. I noticed the three skaters from outside were getting themselves each another pitcher of beer. Naz's beat-vest was booming even funkier sounds than before; synthetic sitars on top of the tabla beat, everything hooked into feedback loops, slowing down and speeding up unexpectedly. I hadn't realized a digital system could sound that wonderfully weird. We hadn't used any electronica in E To The I Pi.

"That kid Naz has a knack for steering his sound algorithms between, *harrumph*, the Scylla and Charybdis of noise and repetition," I said to Leni by way of a distraction. "Threading between the random reefs and the sullen maelstrom." The beer was going to my head. "I need to sit down."

"Let's all go hang in my suite," said Danny. He was eyeing Lulu with the hopeful expression of a dog waiting for a scrap to fall off the table. "It's right behind the community room."

So we retreated into Danny's apartment, really quite sizable considering he didn't pay any rent at all. It was furnished with a decade's worth of Bulkington leftovers, things that students hadn't bothered to take along when they moved on. Just for the hell of it, Danny had bedecked his walls with scavenged psychedelic posters illuminated by black lights—the kinds of things that freshman and sophomore students would acquire and then outgrow. Some of the posters showed figures of real mathematical interest: Escher's Mobius strip with ants walking on it, zooms of the Mandelbrot set, a snowstorm of stellated polyhedra, tumbling hypercubes, like that.

"Cooool," said Lulu, taking it in. "The lair of the mathemagicians."

She was mocking us. But enjoying us too. She was, after all, a computer scientist. Maybe Danny had a chance with her. I flopped into a velvet-cushioned Danish Modern chair.

"You still didn't tell me about Alma and Paul," persisted Leni, pulling over a wing-backed armchair and dangling her hand like a queen offering her ring for a kiss. "Feed the *Buzz*. Tell all." Dorothy and Lulu leaned on the chair behind her: smirking, sinister courtiers.

"Bela's the man," said Danny, pleased to see a fellow mathematician's moment of fame.

"Don't say anything you don't want to," cautioned Eugenia.

But with Leni and her partners laughing and commenting and egging me on, I went ahead and told the world not only about Alma leaving with Paul, but about Haut's breakdown, my fruitless job search, and the weirdness of the Ziffs.

While I was talking, Eugenia checked Danny's computer to see if I was really there on the *Buzz* channel, and indeed I was, but with my voice delayed just enough so that hearing it tripped me up. Eugenia turned the sound back off, but left the picture on. I wondered if Alma was watching me.

Meanwhile Dirk kept bustling out to the common room like some demonic Wroclaw drink-hall denizen, elbows out, forehead glistening, bringing back four pitchers of beer at a time. Normally I'm not much of a drinker, and soon my jaw was so well-oiled that I sang a few of the riffs I'd been playing that afternoon, spilled my whole vision of the cockroach people, and began explaining my new ideas about solving the codec problem. I even got out my little scrap of paper with the four drawings and speculated about the forgotten fifth frame.

A few other people from the party drifted in to watch me showing off—Sue Boo, Kenny Yoder, Amparo Alvarez. Friends of Leni's, business majors into gung-ho hearty games of volleyball. But even they were digging my rant. Something about my worldview struck the non-mathematicians as comical—even the parts that I thought were serious.

When I was about done, Leni got a call on her handheld, a chunky little cell phone with a miniature keyboard and a separate earpiece. "I'll ask him now," she said into its mike.

"You said you need a job, Bela," said Leni, turning her piercing blue eyes to me. "Well, guess what, my main backer wants to make you an offer. You can be the first 24/7 full-time vlogger for *Buzz*."

Although I was sober enough to realize that the gig would be something like working as a sideshow freak, I was drunk enough to consider doing it. "How much would you pay me?" I asked.

"Hold on," said Leni, listening to her earpiece. And then she named a figure that surprised me. The other kids at the party cheered. "That's for a week," added Leni. "*And* you also get a percentage of our ad revenues. The

more people you draw in, the more you make. We might
have you back for more weeks if there's an audience."

"You'll really give me that much money?" I asked.

"Hell yeah," put in Lulu. "*Buzz* is for real. We're paying over a thousand bucks a month for the bandwidth to
download all those megs of video to our clients."

"I'll take the job," I said, impressed.

"Here's the contract," said Leni, passing me her handheld. Dense text appeared on the little screen. "To accept
the terms, say 'Yes,' and press Enter."

"What's in the contract?" asked Eugenia, peering over
my shoulder. "Be careful, Bela."

"Limited time offer!" said Leni in a teasing yet peremptory tone.

I scrolled through the tiny lines of legalese. Essentially
I'd be signing away my right to privacy for a week, with
the contract mutually renegotiable at the end of the week.
I'd be wearing a vlog ring and apparently I wouldn't be
allowed to remove it till the end of the contracted week—
unless I wanted to forfeit my pay and pay a hefty penalty
charge.

"All right," I said, giddily pressing Enter. "Yes."

Leni slipped a dark blue vlog ring on to my left hand's
ring finger like she was knighting me. It was a perfect fit.
The ring wriggled, tightening itself.

"You can tell how you're doing by the color of your ring
band," said Leni. "The more people viewing your current
webcast, the redder the ring gets. If you keep it red a lot,
that means more income for *Buzz*—and a better chance
of us asking you back to do another week."

"Play the guitar for us!" suggested Dorothy. "Like what you played when you saw the giant cockroaches in the mirror this afternoon!"

"All right," I said. There was in fact a band playing in the Bulkington common room now, and I knew the bassist, a skinny guy called Rico. We'd jammed together a few times. The band had an extra guitar, and they let me join in for a golden oldie, Samadhi's "Flop Sweat," my choice, as I'd often practiced their now-dead lead player's wonderfully sinuous guitar line, a buzzing wail like the trail of a homemade dregger airplane looping and rolling and going down in joyous fuck-you flames.

I was playing great, in my humble opinion, and my ring band was nice and red, but after that one number, the regular guitarist asked me to step down. Maybe he was jealous. Or maybe I didn't sound as good as I imagined. I was pretty drunk.

I needed air and decided to head for the roof. On the way up the back stairs, I overtook Naz, Thuggee, and K-Jen. They were lugging a washing machine from the basement. K-Jen seemed less haunted than before; the beer had mellowed her out. She was singing something slow and rhythmic to help them push, her voice older and more worldly than I would have expected.

"Yo," said Naz, noticing me behind them. "Doctor Bela. Heard you playing just now. Old school grime. Lend a hand, bud."

I helped them inch the machine up the steps, not bothering to ask why. "Move the box, men," chanted K-Jen, "Let your muscles bend." Her voice was dark and rough at the edges. I had a fleeting vision of her voice as a pattern of rakes and teapots.

The roof of Bulkington was flat and open, with a parapet around the edges. The Birdman was up there cawing at the misty rain. I tried some of his nitrous oxide. The sky tolled like a bell. K-Jen was ranting at the world below. And then the Birdman helped Naz and Thuggee push the washing machine off the parapet to land on Mr. Vitelloni's SUV in the driveway.

I woke up. Sunlight shone yellow through the worn spots of a window shade, illuminating a poster of a fractal on the wall. I was lying on Danny Nguyen's couch, clothed but barefoot. I was sincerely glad that yesterday was over.

The fractal's buds reminded me of the cockroach-people; hallucinations? Alma was gone; a knife in my heart. My finger ached.

I looked at my hand. Oh god, the vlog ring. I tried to slip it off—no way. It felt like it had glued itself to my skin. Well, I could stand it for a week. Good money.

Somewhere nearby I could hear moans and a bed going *bump bump bump.* I needed to hit the bathroom, but it seemed better not to make noise and interrupt Danny's big score. I lay there waiting, making faces at the vlog ring. Looking at the ring, I noticed that the hue of the shiny ring band was always changing. Like if I mugged at the ring or put it near one of Danny's posters, the band got a little redder from viewer interest, but if I put the ring down in the dark under my cover it soon turned blue with boredom.

Finally the sex noises crescendoed and came to a halt. I went and relieved myself, keeping my vlog hand behind my back.

"Yo, Bela?" Danny's voice from his bedroom. "You okay?"

"I feel like a carnival geek," I said. "No more drinking."

I heard a little buzz of conversation in Danny's bedroom, and then he called to me again. "Put something over that camera, would you? Before we come out." I found my shoes and socks next to the couch. I shoved my left hand into a sock, wearing it like a mitten. "All clear," I called.

The mystery girl was, as I'd already suspected, Leni's friend Lulu Cliff the computer science major. She'd washed off most of her makeup, and she looked kind of plain today. Thin lips, bright eyes, an angular chin.

"How much do you remember?" she asked me in a quiet tone.

Images and sounds blossomed from that question. K-Jen chanting and shrieking. A tumbling washing machine, growing smaller as it fell, then thudding onto Vitelloni's SUV, impacting the front left corner of the roof. The sharp *bang* decaying into a slower *crunch*, followed by the sparkly *tinkle* of the shattered windshield. The startled car's alarm hooting like its outraged owner. Thuggee standing on the parapet, guffawing, rolling back his foreskin, pissing down at Vitelloni. The incredibly prompt arrival of the squad cars with their red-yellow-blue flashers. My stumbling, careening evasion down the back stairs. My hand grabbing a last pitcher of beer. Danny hustling me into his room. Oblivion.

"The cops were here for two hours," said Danny. His hair was all flattened out this morning, combed down over his forehead dreg-style. "You were lucky to miss it. They busted the Birdman and those three skaters. The Birdman flipped; they put him in a straitjacket."

"5150," I said. "Did I vlog the washer drop?"

"Oh yeah," said Danny. "Lulu and I looked at the footage after the cops left. It's awesome. I don't think the cops know about it yet."

"It's such a great launch for your show," said Lulu softly. "Leni and Dorothy and I want to see you do really well this week."

"So why are you making me cover up my vlog ring right now? Like, people are gonna watch the inside of a sock?"

"Look, I'd rather not have everyone totally know that I spent the night with Danny," whispered Lulu. "I mean we two were visible together last night, *possibly* an item, but to vlog me in the apartment in the morning—it's so, you know, hitting every note. Belaboring the obvious."

"I wonder if you're ashamed of me," said Danny in a matter-of-fact tone.

Lulu grunted and made a fishlike face. "Look, if you must know, I don't want Dorothy and Leni to know that I slept with a *boy*. They'd tease me and call me a lug. Lesbian until graduation." She walked over to Danny's fridge and found herself a soda. "Other than having a penis, you're fine, Danny. And frankly I wouldn't mind doing you again. But right now, I've got to run."

"I'll call you," said Danny. "I will." He turned to put on the coffee.

I followed Lulu out towards the common room. Some bleary Bulkington students were eating oatmeal amidst the trash and the puddles of vomit and beer.

"A private question," I whispered to Lulu, shoving my sock-covered hand deep into my pants pocket for still more shielding. "Who's Leni's big backer? Who's giving her the money for the servers and the bandwidth? Who phoned her last night?"

"You could figure it out yourself," breathed Lulu. "If you spent a little time online."

"Just tell me." She made her voice still softer and leaned up to my ear. "Van Veeter."

THREE

rocking with washer drop

As I rejoined Danny, I noticed that my vlog ring was beeping. It didn't like being covered up. When I took the sock off my hand, the plastic of the band was of course dark blue. Virtually nobody was tuned in.

Suddenly the ring spoke to me in Leni's voice. "What do you think you're doing, Bela?" She sounded miffed.

"Danny and I wanted a little privacy here," I said.

"Yeah," put in Danny. "This happens to be *my* room."

"I'm under blood oath to conceal the carnal rites of the mathenauts," I added.

"Covering the ring violates our contract," said Leni, not amused. "Don't do it again."

"Ah, yes, the contract," I said. "Can you email me a copy? I didn't get a super good look at it last night. What with being drunk and seeing it on a display the size of my thumbnail." The ring's band was warming up towards purple now.

"The contract is right here on the *Buzz* website," said Leni from the ring, her voice warming. "People can read it and wonder if they'd like to be vloggers too. We're accepting applications. And, Bela, I have some wonderful news."

"What?"

"Your vlog of the washer drop has been downloaded twenty thousand times since last night! People are loving it. What a great kickoff for *The Crazy Mathematician*!"

"That's what you're calling my show?" I asked, not too pleased.

"I was about to tell you," said Danny, turning on his computer. "We were looking at it last night after you passed out."

"If the shoe fits," said Leni. "Oh, and one more thing. You should go straight back to your apartment. I told some people to meet you there. Bye."

"Look at this," said Danny, pointing to his computer screen, which was displaying a video window surrounded by virtual buttons and controls. The video showed me looking at the screen, slightly lagged. As Danny moved his mouse around, the viewpoint changed; he could effectively look in any direction from the viewpoint of my vlog ring. But by default the image was centered on whatever I happened to be looking at.

The screen bore the caption "*The Crazy Mathematician*" in its title bar. On the left side was a clickable timeline for jumping to arbitrary points of my accumulated vlog stream, also a topic search bar, also some simple buttons linking to the most popular bits that I'd vlogged so far. Lulu had helped write *Buzz* an automated system that took care of all this. Database cinema. The top link was labeled "Washer Drop."

I replayed the washer drop. I'd captured it all. K-Jen's voice was some kind of amazing. And Thuggee's wild grin as he besprinkled the furious SUV owner—an instant icon of rebellion.

After I reset the display to real time, I started fooling

around, adjusting my ring's position and the point of view to get an endless regress going in the onscreen window— like what you see if you point a video camera at its TV monitor. I twisted the camera angle to produce chaotic feedback. "Check it out, Danny," I said.

"Gnarly computation in daily life," he replied. The ring got slightly redder.

"I wonder who makes the vlog rings?" I asked in a just-wondering tone. Given what Lulu had told me, I had a very good idea what the answer would be.

"Does it have a logo?" asked Danny. I peered at the band and made something up. "I see this little embossed image of a sneaky gnome wearing a stolen crown."

"I'll search for *vlog ring*," said Danny, typing the phrase into his computer's main toolbar. A moment later he'd found it. "Vlog rings are made by Rumpelstiltskin, Inc., the company founded by Humelocke's newly elected congressman—"

"Van Veeter," I exclaimed. I'd been dying to say the name out loud ever since Lulu had whispered it to me a few minutes ago. "I wonder if Rumpelstiltskin's backing *Buzz*," I continued ingenuously. "I think I heard that *Buzz* got their vlog rings for free."

"Would make sense," said Danny, not all that interested.

I wasn't going to say anything else just yet, but I was convinced that Van Veeter had another reason for funding Leni Pex—I believed she'd started the fire at the YWCA polling place that had won the election for him.

But for now I let my suspicions rest. Leni hadn't actually given me any money yet. It was too early to bite the hand that fed me.

I said goodbye to Danny and headed toward Ratvale. On the way, I began savoring being a realtime vlogger with my own show. I had nothing better to do, that's for sure—what with my thesis and research paper done, my girlfriend and roommate gone, and still no job offers. Summer vacation. I stopped and looked at shop windows, now and then talking to my vlog ring, making comments on this and that for my audience's benefit, feeling high-tech and important. I consumed a brownie and a big glass of orange-and-carrot juice, savoring them, feeling like a character in a movie.

Eventually I got back to my apartment, and sure enough, some people were waiting for me. Actually just one person: a Humelocke cop about my age. He was friendly enough, but said he had to book me as an accessory and as a material witness to the Bulkington washer drop. People always have bad news for you when they call you "sir."

Leni had sicced the law on me to liven up my vlog. As the police processed me into the jail, my ring was an attentive shade of red. The cops wanted to remove it for safekeeping, but they couldn't get it to budge.

As chance would have it—not that there really *is* any chance in the divine jellyfish's cosmic computations—I ended up in a tiny barred cell right across from Thuggee and Naz, who were in individual cells of their own. Each cell had a bunk sticking out from one wall, plus a utilitarian steel toilet and a tiny sink.

"Doctor Bela," said Naz, a grin splitting his bored face. "How'd they find you?"

"This ring," I said, holding out my hand. "It's a camera that's broadcasting all the time. Whatever I see goes straight to the web."

"This is very bad for our case," said Thuggee. He had an even stronger Indian accent than I'd initially realized. "Video evidence can be highly effective."

A moment of silence passed as we all remembered Thuggee gleefully pissing off the parapet. "Where's K-Jen and the Birdman?" I asked, to change the subject.

"Birdman's in the psych ward, I guess," said Naz. "And women go in a separate cellblock. We'll be here till the court meets on Monday. None of us three is gonna call our parents for bail. K-Jen's Dad beats her whenever she's home. Russian meathead."

"My parents will weep and wail," said Thuggee despondently. "And give long lectures. I was hoping this regrettable incident might go unnoticed. But now you're telling me that you've been posting everything to the web. My sister and her friends are looking at the web all of the time." He went to his bunk and lay down facing the wall.

"Enough about John Law," said Naz, rubbing his big nose. "Let's talk about music. I liked what you were getting at yesterday, about how my best beats steer between repeating and turning into noise. I'm always looking for the secret formula. Do you know some mad scientist tricks about that?"

"Universal dynamics," I said. "The science of gnarl. I just got a Ph.D. in it."

We spent the afternoon and evening talking. It was a good session. First I laid out the theory behind Wolfram's classification of computations into the too cool, the too hot, and the gnarly. And then I got into the practicalities of chaotic nonlinear feedback. Naz was bright and eager for the information, and I was getting the teacherly reward of learning while I talked.

Naz had a regular drum kit at home, he'd played in a high school garage band. As I described some of the rhythms that mathematics could produce, he tapped them out on his bunk and his cell bars. But we couldn't try out any of the more intense and computationally unpredictable algorithms, as the cops had Naz's beat vest in safekeeping.

It struck me that maybe Naz and I could make some music together. I'd thoroughly won his confidence; he was calling me Bela Frankenstein. Yeah, we'd start a band, and I could use my *Buzz* exposure to launch the group. And once I got a little bit of fame, I'd be on my way to getting Alma back.

That was the plan I'd figured out while playing my guitar in my room the other day. Start a rock band. Alma was impressionable; deep down she wanted to love me. If I gave even *one* successful concert, it could be enough. And then, according to my plan, it was just a matter of encouraging some woman to seduce Paul in such a way that Alma found out. That would definitely close the deal.

But I didn't tell Naz any of my schemes yet. I had a feeling that I wasn't thinking all that clearly.

It was a long Saturday night in the clink, with screaming drunks and tweakers coming in at every hour, many of them pausing to glare at me—as if I were one of *them*. Everything was hard, dull, dead. The only visible sign of nature's cosmic computation was the pool of water in my toilet, with barely visible chaotic ripples driven by the breeze from the air vent.

How far I was from where I wanted to be. What a fool I'd been. I kept thinking of Alma, cozy in a ranch-style Stanford faculty home with Paul. Alma sleeping in clean white sheets with her new man. Domesticity was looking pretty damn good. Would I ever get there?

In the midmorning one of the cops came to let me out. "You made bail," he told me. I bid Naz and Thuggee farewell, telling Naz that we should jam when he got out.

"Sweet," said Naz. "We'll build a monster band, Bela." There was a call for me at the front desk of the police station. Leni. "I hope you're not mad about this," she said. "At least we bailed you out. The washer drop's gotten half a million hits!"

"I want my week's pay right now," I told her. "In cash, so you don't bounce the check or something. Otherwise I'm smashing this ring with a rock and you can shove Veeter's contract up your ass."

"No *problem*, Bela. Feeling a little crabby, hmm? Better have some breakfast."

It was a beautiful day outside, warm and sunny. I was happy to be out of jail. But again I had a vision of Alma with Paul. Alma wearing an apron, making scrambled eggs.

Walking past a *Chronicle* vending machine, I noticed my picture on the front page of the Sunday paper with the headline, "Humelocke Washer Drop Vlogger." Of course I bought a copy. The facts in the story were roughly correct. It even showed a few blurry frames from my vlog.

"Look, I didn't actually push the washer over the edge myself," I said to my vlog ring, working on my public image. "And I didn't realize what those kids were planning when I helped them hump the washer up the stairs."

Once again I wondered if Alma might be watching me. It would be good for me to be seen doing something uplifting today, something different from getting drunk or spending a night in the tank.

I didn't bother to eat anything on the way to Leni's; I didn't want to dilute my rage. I figured her angle was this: the more she screwed up my life this week, the better her ratings were.

I found Leni sitting at her kitchen table with Dorothy, the two of them sharing a bowl of fruit salad and yogurt, with three Sunday papers spread out on the table, each with a story on *Buzz*.

"Here," said Leni, handing me an envelope. I peeked inside, the cash was there.

"Thanks," I said. "That's good." But I had my momentum built up, and I went ahead and laid my heavy accusation on her, glad to have it going out live on *The Crazy Mathematician* show.

"I think Van Veeter paid you, Leni Pex, to help him throw the election," I said, pointing at her. "I believe that you, Leni Pex, are the one who set the YWCA polling place on fire."

Give Leni credit, she did a good job of looking surprised. "That's absurd. I was at yoga class that afternoon. You were there with me, weren't you, Dorothy?"

"It was Tuesday, right?" said Dorothy. "We go every week. Four to six."

"Oh sure, get your lover to lie for you," I said.

"It's not a lie, Bela," said Leni tartly. "I'm sorry for you, losing it like this. It's not my fault that Van Veeter likes *Buzz*." She cocked her head, studying me like some struggling beetle in a collecting net. "Are you trying to shock me into canceling your show? Is that it? We're going the full week, and that's final. The crazier you get, the more people watch. But that doesn't mean I have to associate with you. So beat it, loser. Go huff gas with your little skater buddies." She favored me with a smug glare.

Maybe I was actually wrong? I took a deep breath, then another, and then I left. Leni almost looked disappointed. She'd expected me to go ahead and make an even bigger ass of myself. The only way through the rest of this week was to play it cool.

I stopped by Ratvale to shower and change clothes. It was terribly empty in my apartment; I hated the way the sounds echoed and bounced around. I went out and spent the day hiking the trails of Tillman Park, poking around a creek, watching the shadows of the water's eddies on the sandy bottom, thinking about math, forgetting the vlog ring. It was good to get back to the stuff that mattered. I still had that scrap of paper with my codec comic strip solution on it, and I lay in a meadow studying it for awhile, trying to reconstruct the mental states the alien mirror cockroaches had prodded me into. I could almost see the argument, but not quite. The tide had collapsed the sand castle. I'd lost that final fifth frame: the punchline.

Again and again I thought of Alma. It would have been nice to share this beautiful day in the woods with her, to be monitoring her expressions instead of the color-shades of a vlog ring. Was Leni right? Was I a loser? One good thought came to mind. I could use some of the money Leni had given me to renew the lease on my Ratvale room for another month. That could help my chances of getting Alma back.

Thinking about the paracomputational codec problem reminded me of a certain journal article on six-dimensional sheaves, so when I got back onto campus, I went into the library and did research for a few hours. My ring band turned about as blue as it could get, indicating utter boredom and disinterest on the part of the viewing audience. So what.

Night fell as I returned to my apartment. It felt a little creepy in there. Just to prove my courage to myself, I got out my silver guitar and started playing again. The upside of wearing the vlog ring was that if I *did* see the cockroaches, I could check and see if they showed up in the vlog, too. Then I'd know whether or not they were a hallucination.

But I didn't see any aliens this time. I played for about forty minutes, thinking some more about starting a band. I could tell people were digging my music. My vlog ring was bright red.

The bass player and the drummer of my Santa Cruz group, E To The I Pi, had long since gotten married to each other and moved to Seattle. But I liked the idea of Naz being my drummer, assuming he could rock on a real drum kit. It could be very commercial to have a young skater in the band. For bass, maybe I could ask Rico, the guy I'd seen the other night. He'd been pretty friendly.

As for a vocalist—right about then I heard a knock. I set down my axe and hurried to the door. I was imagining that Alma had come back to me.

But no, it was Leroy, a street person who hung around our block. He always carried a silvered plastic ball that he liked staring into, a discarded Christmas ornament. Often he'd sleep in the Ratvale courtyard, filling it with the smell of goat. Paul talked to Leroy sometimes.

"Bela," said Leroy, wearing a sly grin inside his dirty beard. "I followed your sound."

"Um, you like it?" I said, wondering what he wanted. I myself had never spoken to him before. "*Funky*," said Leroy, nodding his head. "Outstanding. I been watching you."

"How do you mean?" Surely he didn't have a—

"Wireless dingbot," said Leroy, fishing a little device from a cranny in his layers of clothes. "My fourth eye." He tapped the tiny computer against his shiny, careworn forehead. "Social services give 'em to us. Final solution to the cyberhomeless problem, know what I mean?"

Yes, I recalled hearing something about this. Low income people in the Bay Area were being issued palmtop computers with paid-up wireless connectivity, thanks to grants from a couple of the big companies. Some kind of tax write-off to clear out their inventories.

"You saw my show, huh?" I said without enthusiasm. Today was Sunday evening. That meant five more days I was going to be wearing the vlog ring. Five days was a long time to have even the bums in the street watching my every move, including my showers and my trips to the toilet.

"You got a lot of space in here," said Leroy, peering into my apartment as if he were in search of something in particular. "I just wanna check if—" He squeezed past me and sidled into my bedroom. "*There* they are." He'd found the half-full pack of cigarettes I'd bought the other day. Apparently he'd noticed them on the web. "Lend me one?"

"Take them all. I don't normally smoke. But, um, we're not really supposed to light up inside."

"*You* did. I saw." I noticed something odd about Leroy's feet. Although at first glance it looked as if were wearing dark slippers, he was in fact barefoot. A crust of filth running across the tops of his feet covered the gaps between his toes.

"Come on, Leroy, let's take this party outside. And I'll give you a half-bottle of wine from the fridge, too."

"Righteous," said Leroy. "I got something to communicate, know what I mean?"

"Fine," I said. Except for the goat smell, I was glad for the company.

So we settled onto a bench in front of Ratvale, Leroy contentedly smoking and drinking the wine, admiring himself both in his little silver Christmas ball and in the screen of his palmtop, which was of course tuned to *The Crazy Mathematician*.

"What it is," said Leroy presently. "I seen how the fire started at the YWCA on election day."

"No way."

"These few blocks are my kingdom, man. Leroyland. Nothing escapes the ruler's eye. I was layin' back of the Y gettin' baked, watching the clouds in my magic ball. And I seen this thing like a big seashell. Yeah. A shell with triangles all over it, orange and white, flying around the yard. At first I thought it was a giant bumblebee. But, naw, it's ten feet long. With a slimy sucker-thing hangin' outta the shell. And I see this shell as a reflection in the mirror ball, but not in the actual air, know what I mean? I'm thinkin' I'm smokin' some *good* shit."

"A cone shell?" I said. "Are you making this up?"

"I might still have some of that same dope," said Leroy, beginning to feel around in his pockets. "I don't want any," I said. "Finish telling me about the fire."

"Yeah. So this, um, alien snail the size of a motorcycle, it's flyin' around in the mirror world, sniffin' something out, know what I mean, and I'm sittin' real still, and then I see it go up near the shed with the fuse box."

"You saw it by the fuse box on the back of the YWCA?" I said.

"Saw it reflected in my Christmas ball, know what I mean, it's like hidden in the workadaddy world."

"And this is behind the building where the voting is?" I pressed.

"Yep. Citizens in and outta there all day, but they're not botherin' me in the backyard, I might as well be a pile of garbage." Leroy barked a bitter, coughing laugh. "Camouflaged. They don't know that Leroy means The King." He finished the wine, and put the empty bottle under the bench, then sighed and rubbed his finger on the palmtop screen. "Look at me in there. King Leroy, yeah. Coulda been a star."

"And the fire?"

"The snail shot a tendril at me. I was the only one seen it, but it was real. I could feel, like, a little dart hitting my skull. I'm Moby Dick, I'm beating my flukes, but the cone shell reels me over to the fuse box and then *zzzzzt*. Danger zone. Move the wires and the short circuit lights off the Y. But don't say it was me that did it."

"Thanks, Leroy," I said, getting to my feet. "That's an interesting story." I glanced down at my vlog ring and adopted a newscaster's barking tone. "Late-breaking news on the YWCA polling-place fire that swept Van Veeter into office! Suspicions that Heritagist operatives set the fire have been contradicted by the testimony of Humelocke's King Leroy! Leroy reports the fire was masterminded by an invisible flying cone shell!"

"What it is," concluded Leroy.

I didn't know what to think anymore. Had Leroy started the fire? Had a cone shell told him to? Or had he invented all this simply because he overheard me talking about aliens on my vlog? I went and got some Om Mane Padme Yum ice cream alone, and then I went to bed.

Late the next morning, Monday, I got a call from Professor Kitchner. He wanted me to come to his office. So, okay, it was back to dear old Pearce Hall.

It was funny, walking in there, to think that now I was a Ph.D. All done. I didn't have to scuttle around anymore. My papers were all in order. What had I been so tense about?

"Good morning, Bela," said Kitchner, a quizzical expression on his heavy lips. "I've been reading about you. That thing on your finger, that's the notorious—what are you calling it?"

"Vlog ring," I said. "Yeah, it's webcasting this conversation. I want you to be clear on that."

"Crystal clear," said Kitchner, running his hand across his bald head. "I'll make this quite brief." He fell silent for so long that finally I spoke up. "This is about the—trouble at Bulkington?"

"*Ooooh* yeah," he said. "You were very much the topic at my meeting with the chancellor and the provost this morning. Our crazy mathematician."

"I didn't pick that name."

"The name picked you," said Kitchner steepling his fingers. "A bit of good news. The university has made the aggrieved neighbor a generous settlement offer. And in return he's not pressing charges and he's signing a release. You're off the hook, as they say."

"Oh, thank you. That's great. And another thing. We were going to talk about me finding a—"

"No we're not," said Kitchner, shaking his head. "That's your bad news." And then he saw me out of his office.

Outside it was another beautiful Humelocke day, with the light dancing off the San Francisco Bay. I was relieved to know my legal worries were over. But it sounded like Kitchner wasn't going to help me find a job at all. I sighed, beginning to absorb the fact that, more than likely, I'd never ever get a job as a math professor. I almost felt tears forming in my eyes. So long a road I'd traveled, and for so little reward.

This *Buzz* gig had loaded me with more baggage than I'd anticipated. But maybe that was the wrong way to think about it. I didn't have to be passive. I needed to be working this gig for my own purposes. I had some cash now. And I could use my web exposure to help get me a career outside of teaching. To hell with academic politics.

To start with, I went by University Housing and renewed my lease. That way I'd have a love-nest for my little sparrow—as well as a rehearsal space for my new band. Yes, I was going to start a band.

I'd begin by recruiting Naz. If Mr. Vitelloni was dropping charges, then Naz and his crew would be getting sprung. I hurried down to the jail and, as fate would have it, Naz, Thuggee, and K-Jen were just walking out the door, squinting at the sunlight, throwing down their skateboards.

"Doctor Frankenstein!" said Naz. "Still wanna jam?"

"You guys can come up to my apartment. I've got it for five more weeks."

"I'm down with that," said Naz. "You got a car? We can pick up my drum kit. Right now is a good time, my folks are working. Maybe they won't notice."

"I can't be doing this," said Thuggee rolling his muscular shoulders like he had a sore neck. "I must face the parents."

"I'll come with you, Bela," said K-Jen, flashing a rare smile. "I have a lot to sing after—that." She jerked her head towards the concrete building behind us. "Jail raga."

Pimply and disheveled as K-Jen was, she had a star quality about her, so much so that I found her a little intimidating. She seemed outside the circle of ordinary society. But Naz wasn't shy with her at all.

Naz and K-Jen skated along with me towards my car, crouching, zigzagging, doing jumps. And then I drove them down University Avenue to the flat part of Humelocke.

As it turned out, Naz's family lived upstairs from a little Indian grocery that they ran. And as soon as Naz started carrying out his drums, his mother did notice us, and she came out into the street. She wore a wrapped sheath of blue silk, and she had a red dot on her forehead. Sari and bindi.

"Behold the jailbird," said Naz's mother in a sarcastic tone. She frowned and adjusted her thick black ponytail. "Everyone was looking at that horrible video of you and the filthy Thuggee." She noticed me now. "The crazy mathematician!"

"I'm not crazy," I said. "I have a Ph.D. I was hoping Naz could help me start a raga-rock band."

"Naz has to go to school immediately. And his hooligan hussy friend should be attending her classes as well. This is the last week before graduation, Naz!"

"You're in high school?" I asked K-Jen, a little taken aback. "How old are you two?"

"We're seniors," said K-Jen. "Eighteen. The last week of class doesn't matter for shit. They *want* Naz and me to graduate, you bet." She walked around and stood on the other side of my Bel Paese squinty whale, not wanting to get embroiled with Naz's mother.

"What if I call your father out here to beat you?" said Naz's mother to him. I noticed a slender bespectacled man watching us from the store's dark door.

"Just chill, Mom," said Naz. "Today it's too late to go to school. I promise I'll make the other classes this week. Now let me go and practice with Bela. It's my big chance to be in a successful band."

"You should wash yourself. You will have gotten lice in jail."

"I have lice from K-Jen already," said Naz, just to torment his mother. "And crabs." He ran up the back stairs to the family's apartment. He was back a minute later with his cymbals and drum-sticks. "That's everything. Gotta go."

When we got to my apartment Naz and K-Jen took a long, noisy shower together, complete with thumps and moans. My vlog ring was loving it. Everyone but me was getting laid.

Eventually K-Jen and Naz were ready to jam.

"If this works, then all we'll need is a bass player," I said.

It didn't take too long to find a groove. Thinking about raga, I put my guitar on open tuning, and began sliding some long electric notes up and down. Naz was indeed a good drummer, and we worked out a kinky way to interface his drum vest with contact mikes on the sides of his drums. The vest's electronics were a Taj Mahal of sonic mirrors, mixing in that boingy tabla sound.

K-Jen used a microphone I'd found in my supplies. Steadily she revealed more surprises: she could declaim spontaneous poetry in a tasty, precise style that had me hanging on every word, warp it into a chant, stutter that into a gravelly dreg roar, thin the blur into a songbird harmony, and return to poetry, the topics running from stories about her daily life to the injustices of society to the eternal mysteries of existence. K-Jen may not have been much of a talker, but boy could she sing.

"We sound good," I said, pausing for breath after maybe an hour. "We're really starting a band."

"And I'm the singer?" said K-Jen, not quite believing this. "I can write and sing about, like, politics and UFOs?"

"You rule," I said. "We'll do this on fast forward. With me on *Buzz*, we can get famous in a week. And then I can get my girlfriend back."

"You're not after me?" said K-Jen, just a little suspicious. "This isn't some ill scam?"

"I'm not attracted to you that way. Pimples and nose rings—never mind."

K-Jen smiled an inward smile, looking around my living room with an almost proprietary expression. "Naz and I can hang here."

"What's the K stand for?"

"Eleven." Jen made a complex gesture with her hands. "There are ten other Jens at my high school—that I *know* of—so I thought it made sense. K-Jen being superior to A-Jen through J-Jen, you understand."

"Sounds like math. My bag. I just got my Ph.D. Do you like math?"

"No," said K-Jen, unengaged by the topic. "What's the band called?" I'd been thinking about this and I had my answer ready. "Washer Drop!"

"Sweet," said Naz.

"If that's our name, we should do a song about it," said K-Jen and chanted a trial verse.

Wash out the dirt, machine bomb a jerk.
Rooftop skater bop, oil pig washer drop.

"Not bad," I said, repeating the words to myself and picking out a rhythm on my guitar. "Try it again."

"Get us some beer first," said K-Jen. "I sing better when I'm drunk."

"I'm not buying beer for you," I said. "Not on camera. You're underage."

"Naz and me can scam some," said K-Jen. "We'll be back after we tank up."

"Up to you."

While they were gone, I phoned Rico from the band last night to ask him if he would play bass in my new group. But he didn't want to. He was doing fine as things stood. So then I called my old bass player Tad at Microsoft in Seattle. But I just got some bullshit smart answering-machine program.

I hit a little lull then, a pocket of doubt. Shouldn't I be doing math? If not for a professorship, then for publication and for consulting gigs? Paul and I had proved the big Morphic Classification Theorem, yes, and we'd found a number of interestingly equivalent systems, but without a codec for any of the natural systems, carrying out detailed simulations was impossible. Although the four drawings I'd made were suggestive of the codec for a vibrating membrane, without the concluding image, they were inconclusive. All the more reason to get back to work!

But I was utterly burnt-out on math for now and, come to think of it, pushing so hard on the math was what had led me to start thinking I was seeing aliens. Not a place I wanted to be. Music was the cure. But I needed a bass player.

There was a knock on the door. Alma? No. Naz and K-Jen? Not yet.

"Hi Bela," said the dark-haired woman standing there. I'd never seen her before. "I'm Cammy Vendt." She was carrying a bass guitar in its case in one hand. "I'm here to try out for Washer Drop." She looked calm, an impression enhanced by the fact that her eyebrows were so long and level. Her teeth stuck forward a bit, pushing her lips out, giving her a piratical air. In old-school rocker style, she was wearing a sleeveless black T-shirt, black jeans, and low-cut black boots.

"The vlog?" I asked unnecessarily.

"I need some gigs," said Cammy tossing her head. She had Bettie Page hair, dark and cropped into a thick bob, with short bangs and purple streaks. "My group broke up. We were called Nutricious? We even cut a CD, but we never really got paid, and we started fighting. And then the frontwoman got her own deal, the drummer got into smack, the guitarist started doing studio work, and I'm destitute. I'm sharing an apartment with five other people in Hunter's Point. There's a resident geek in our apartment, and he saw you talking about needing a bassist, and we recognized Ratvale so, what the hey, I jammed over here." Cammy made a graceful swooping gesture with one hand. She seemed very comfortable in her own skin.

"Excellent," I said. "Let's hear you. I've got a spare speaker-amp you can use." Packrat that I am, I had quite a bit of equipment left over from the E To The I Pi days.

I started a bluesy raga line to match the oil pig lyric K-Jen had suggested. After a few bars, Cammy came into the envelope of the beat, dancing around the time signature in the lively unpredictable style of the true musician, ahead of the count here, behind it there, throwing in grace notes to keep things interesting.

We kept on jamming. I enjoyed watching Cammy's moves. She was taking little dance steps in her black engineer's boots, and swaying her guitar neck in synch with mine. She had stage presence, and without being exactly beautiful, she was sexy. Approachable.

And now Naz and K-Jen came tumbling back in the room, loose and laughing, ready to rock, Naz whacking and boinging his drums and drum vest, K-Jen by turns tuneful and raging. It was wonderful. In the space of an hour we'd nailed Washer Drop's very first song, "Oil Pig."

So now Cammy, who knew the San Francisco music scene better than any of us, got on the phone and tried to get us a gig. She smoked as she talked, her eyes focused in the distance, visualizing the person on the other end of the line. I felt a silly, possessive twinge, wanting Cammy to be visualizing me. My heart is a dog running after every cat.

In the event, all the bars Cammy tried were booked for this Friday, which was when I was hoping to play. And then I had the idea of playing in San Jose at my mother's restaurant, East-Vest. The plan seemed synchronistically apt.

Although East-Vest was too small to hold more than twenty people, there was a big, bleak strip-mall parking lot right outside Ma's front door, deserted on weekend nights. We could set up a stage there, pile up pallets or something. And we'd give a free concert. I phoned Ma and got her okay, even though she didn't quite understand what I had in mind.

So that was Monday. We rehearsed for next three days, writing songs, learning covers, and getting comfortable with long jams. We had at least an hour and a half's worth of music, maybe more if we stretched the jams and faked some extra covers.

Leni really got into the concert idea. She told me we had to get an event permit from the City of San Jose, a necessary step that hadn't crossed my mind. That would have been a deal breaker for me, but Leni sliced right through the red tape, with Van Veeter making a few calls to smooth the way. As well as the event permit, San Ho was charging us for police protection—what an absurd concept, paying the cops to hassle you. But Leni and Veeter sprang for the cop fee, not to mention the rental charges for lights, an outdoor sound system, and a temporary stage. *Buzz* stood to rack up some fat ad revenues from our live event, and Veeter would get nice publicity for the Rumpelstiltskin vlog ring.

Cammy and I drove down together Friday afternoon; K-Jen and Naz were coming in Thuggee's family car. Thuggee's parents were letting him be our roadie, at least for today.

"I've never been to San Jose," Cammy told me on the way down. It was a sunny day, the rolling hills along Route 280 already turning summer-yellow.

"You didn't grow up around here?" I asked. Whenever we'd been together this week, we'd been rehearsing; we hadn't yet done any small talk.

"I'm from Ohio. I've only been in the city for two years."

"What was your day job?"

"Night job. Sometimes I work as a stripper."

"I'm impressed," I said glancing over at her.

"It's performance," said Cammy. "The other women are nice. I was with a, like, classical burlesque group. Kind of liberated. The Fluff Circus? We had jugglers and contortionists."

"I've heard of them," I said, glancing at Cammy once again, reconsidering her figure. "Like my tits?" She batted her eyes and palmed her thick bob of hair. "You have this great vibe, Cammy. You're so sure of yourself. It's attractive."

"Strutting around naked on a stage will do that for you. You should try it sometime. Fluff Circus has male strippers, too."

"This week I'm a stripper every time I'm in the bathroom," I said, wiggling the finger with the vlog ring. "I don't get to hear people cheering—but the ring does get redder when I'm nude. I guess yeah, it's made me more confident."

"We're pros, you and me," said Cammy. "I'm up for our concert. How big a crowd you think we'll draw?"

"Leni figures it'll be several hundred. I hope all the equipment works."

"I'll show you how to do a good sound check," said Cammy. "And we need to have monitor speakers pointing back at us. I did a gig without monitors once, and I couldn't hear myself play. I wish we were charging admission. Am I going to get paid?"

"Ma's gonna give the band half of what she makes selling food and drinks," I said. "She's getting a bunch of kegs. She got a permit to set up tables in front of the restaurant."

"'Your mother's Chinese-Hungarian? Nothing personal, but she's gonna short us. How about your cut of the *Buzz* advertising, are you gonna split that with the group?"

I was feeling a little put-upon. "How much would it take to make you feel satisfied about playing tonight, Cammy?" She named a fairly reasonable figure, a couple of hundred bucks.

"I'll make sure you get at least that," I said. "You're an experienced musician. You deserve to get more than Naz or K-Jen—at least for our first gig."

"Thanks, Bela," said Cammy. "You're a good frontman."

"Look," I added, happy to have this intriguing woman smile at me. "I'll do something else for you. My vlogging contract with *Buzz* runs out tonight. I'll push Leni to let you be her next vlogger."

"You don't want to do it anymore?"

"No, it's—it's getting to be too much." Half the people I saw on Telegraph Avenue knew every intimate detail about me. As if I were Leroy, sleeping on the sidewalk with my face to the sky and my pecker hanging out. I felt like the watching eyes were wearing my personality bubble away; I was starting to feel porous.

"*The Struggling Musician*," said Cammy, happily making plans. "That's what I'll call my vlog show. I'll cut a swath. I'll do my act at Fluff Circus while I'm live. Break a thousand hearts."

"You're not at all embarrassed about the stripper thing?"

"Sex isn't that big a deal to me," said Cammy. "It's like brushing your teeth. I don't see why everyone gets so bent out of shape. Are you still mooning over that girl I heard you talking about? You know, what's-her-name. Uma?"

"Alma," I said. "Yeah, I'm still thinking about her. I had this idea that if I got famous I might be able to get her back. Especially if her new boyfriend Paul Bridge cheats on her. Alma and I are both the type to—like you said—get bent out of shape. Old school."

"Is he cute?" said Cammy thoughtfully.

"Paul Bridge? He's smart, and I used to like him a lot, and we wrote a great math paper together. But I'm not sure I'd call him cute."

When we got to Ma's restaurant it was almost supper time. Naz, K-Jen, and Thuggee were already there, helping set up our rental equipment. Ma and her cooks had been working all day making rabbit-meat skewers and little cartons of East-Vest paprika-fried rice that she could vend to the expected crowd, the food all set behind a long outdoor table. She offered us some. Cammy ate a box of the rice right there, eager to get to work on the sound check. But I went into the empty restaurant to sit down and chat with Ma. She reheated some of the rice for me in the wok, adding a portion of salami the way I liked.

"I hope you stop this vlogging nonsense soon," said Ma, swirling the food. "I'm embarrassed around my relatives.

Shirley Woo said her granddaughter Ling-Ling watched you taking a shower, and now she keeps talking about it. Disgusting brat. I haven't watched it myself. I don't want to be spying on you. I thought I'd raised you to have a little modesty, Bela." She scooped the glistening, fragrant rice onto a plate and set it before me. "Eat."

"Thanks." I loved Ma's cooking.

She sat down across from me, keeping up the stream of motherly advice. "And now you're starting a band with Cammy? She looks like a nice level-headed girl. Competent. But what are you doing with those grubby high school kids? And how's this supposed to help you get a good job as a professor?"

"I'm not so sure that's going to happen. My adviser Roland Haut doesn't like me, and the department chairman's mad at me too."

"How could they not like you? Are they crazy?"

"Haut is, yes. But the music thing could really take off, Ma. And there's always consulting. You never know."

"I say forget about both the music *and* the teaching and get a job in high-tech like your cousin Gyula. That's where the real jobs are. The family's trying to find a way to get you in where Gyula works."

"Aw, Ma. Gyula doesn't know jack. He's not really high-tech. He's a guard, a company goon."

"He's vice administrator of security for some new company that bought Membrain Products, Bela. He sees the new big boss all the time because he's been driving his limo for him. Gyula mentioned you to the boss—without actually saying he's related to you—and guess what, that man knows about your big math paper! Gyula said his boss is very eager to meet you, and that he might even offer you a job!"

"Oh, right. Who's Gyula's new boss?"

"That guy who just got elected. What's his name. Van Veeter."

"Huh?"

As if on cue, a white Hornswoggle stretch limo with dark glass pulled up at the restaurant's front door. Gyula hopped out the driver's seat. He was a swarthy guy with heavy stubble and a low forehead. A tough cookie. We'd always been somewhat competitive with each other—if he actually helped me get a job, he'd love lording it over me in the future.

Gyula offered me a sarcastic salute which included giving me the finger, then opened the car's rear door for, yes, Van Veeter. As if that weren't enough, who else should appear from the dark leather recesses of the limo but—a twitchy Paul Bridge and a smiling Alma Ziff. My life was beginning to feel like a movie script.

"Hi guys," said Gyula, leading the way into the restaurant. "Meet the Honorable Van Veeter. Mr. Veeter, this is Xiao-Xiao Kis and her son Bela."

"Bela," said Veeter. He was a soft-faced sandy-haired man wearing high-end business clothes: matching gray silk jacket and knickers with a pale lilac shirt and a yellow silk Pompano bow-tie, the brand name subtly worked into the fabric. His teeth were preternaturally white, his skin well-tanned. "I'm a big fan of your work." said Veeter. "And that web show of yours has been a total time sink for me this week. Fascinating way to decompress. It's good to finally meet you." He was considerably shorter than he looked on TV. Barely taller than my shoulder.

I shook Veeter's hand, wondering if he'd absorbed the accusations that I'd made about him. Hard to tell. His grip was firm and intense, the Platonic ideal of a hand-shake. It took awhile to get my hand back.

"That was nice of you to help organize the concert," I muttered. I was distracted by the sight of Alma staring at me.

"I'm not nice," said Veeter. "I need something from you. And please don't take offense if I leave early. I'm in crunch mode, even though I've been pissing away time watching your vlog. I have to get back to my ranch early tonight." In person he seemed less like a hard-charging can-do politician, and more like an engineer with no patience for social niceties. One of my people.

"Still friends?" said Alma suddenly planting a kiss on my cheek.

The scent of her intoxicated me. "I miss you," I blurted out.

"I think I made a mistakc leaving you," she stage-whis-pered so that everyone could hear.

"Van just bought the patent for the BKH theorem from the university," announced Paul, drowning her out. "He has some special hardware, it's a membrane of optically sensitive plastic. Limpware, really. He calls it a Gobrane. I've been up to my eyebrows in chemical engineering all week. We've made a programmable paracomputer. Van's awesome, Bela. He knows how to model the morphons. Day before yesterday, we had this big breakthrough over your little comic strip about the membrane codec technique. Believe it or not, you drew a picture of the temporal evolution of long-chain polymer entanglement." He was talking very fast.

I recognized the signs. Paul was high on speed. No wonder Alma was unhappy with him. "And the Gobrane is *made* of entangled polymers," continued Paul. "And your missing fifth frame? We realized that it's—"

"Stop right there," said Veeter, holding his hand up as if to cover Paul's mouth. "I don't want to go into patentable details while we're on the air, for crying in the sink." For a little guy, he had a lot of presence. He smiled at me. "But I will say this much. The Morphic Classification Theorem is manna from heaven. A new model for computation: turn your problems into physics and forget about writing machine code! We're starting a new golden age, the age of paracomputation. I'm here tonight, Bela, because I want to ask your advice about this one particular process I want to model. Paul's not quite sure how to do it."

"It's a cake with a rake handle and a teapot spout jammed into it," said Paul. "And it's supposed to match the—"

"Hold your horses, Paul," said Veeter, giving Paul's arm a gentle shake. He seemed to have a fondness for corny idioms, which was probably a plus for reaching the electorate.

"Why did you decide to have me do a vlog show anyway?" I asked Veeter.

"For me, the Morphic Classification Theorem was Christmas morning," he said. "And you're Santa. When I heard you ranting on Leni's webcast from that Bulkington party—it seemed like a slam dunk to have you vlog fulltime for a week. That way I could pick your brain. I didn't realize you'd be starting a rock band! But why not. Now that your vlog week's over, I'd like to offer you a Membrain consulting contract for this one particular mystery app. Paul's on the project too. Membrain Products has made him a principal investigator for a research grant through Stanford. And President Doakes wants to see that Cal Kweskin and Maria Reyes get a separate morphonics grant from the National Security Agency. There's money all around, Bela; you're in high clover."

I felt a little confused. "But your company is Rumpelstiltskin, right?"

"We acquired a controlling interest in Membrain last quarter," said Veeter. "I'm pulling ashore as many boats as I can before I put my business interests into trusteeship. I take my oath of office next week, you know. This one remaining app is my last hurrah. At least for now. And then I'm off to debug DC."

"You're quite the octopus, Congressman Veeter." I said this with a bit of a sneer.

"Call me Van," he said, with a flicker of aggression in his gray eyes. "You've publicly accused me of arson and election fraud. I'd say that puts us on a first-name basis."

"Sorry about that, Van," I heard myself say, at the same time feeling my mouth form itself into a shit-eating grin. Part of me wanted that consulting contract very much. "Maybe I was wrong about the arson. I have a thing about Heritagists."

"I don't blame you," said Veeter with a shrug. "I'm a citizen first, a geek second, a Heritagist third. One of my goals is to move my party back towards its mainstream roots. But let's not talk politics. Let's talk morphic classi- fication for Membrain Products. We'll set up a meeting tomorrow."

All the while there'd been noise out front from Naz's drums, K-Jen's mike, and Cammy's bass. And now Cammy herself popped into the restaurant.

"Come *on*, Bela!" She looked elated, frisky, full of life. She'd put on heavy lipstick for the show. "Oh, you must be Andrea," she said to Alma, in a casual tone. "I'm sur- prised you showed up."

"Alma. And you're the stripper musician?"

"*Meoowr*," said Cammy, making a clawing gesture. And then she took my hand and pulled me outside. I was glad. If Alma was miffed and jealous, that was good for my cause. I needed to seem hard to get.

A few early arrivals were milling around the parking-lot, and among them was my third-cousin Ling-Ling Woo, the one who'd been talking about the vlog of me taking a shower. She had her strawy black hair up in an excited ponytail. Three of her girlfriends were at her side, all of them waving at me and doing that Asian thing of covering their laughing mouths. Just for the hell of it, I stepped up to the mike and began improvising a song as part of my sound check. I started slow.

> I'm an open-book flatland screen man, you watch me now and then.
> Click on my ads to pay me, I've got pixels in my skin.
> You know me real well, and I don't know you,
> But some of your thoughts, they're comin' through,

I'm glad, little girl, to hear you say,
The crazy mathematician's gettin' real today.

And then I switched to a sing-song chorus.

Bela's weenie,
First I ever seenie,
I'm a happy teenie,
Sock the raga rock.

Ling-Ling and her friends were screaming and jumping up and down, not hiding their mouths anymore. Hello Kitty learns to talk. Cammy was laughing hard. I made a space for her in the sound.

She came in with a funky bouncy bass line, Naz attacked his drums, and K-Jen echoed my verse and chorus, adding iller elaborations of her own. It made for a funny, funky, whacked-out song.

We went on from there, the sound check segueing right into the show, "Bela's Weenie" leading into "Universal Automaton" which set us up for "Oil Pig." Thuggee was up on the stage dancing side by side with K-Jen, switching from cute little Motown-type steps to whirling dervish routines. To thicken the sonic mulligatawny, Naz had wired Thuggee with mikes so that his body was itself a feedback device, altering our music as he moved around. Dog, we were *on*.

People were showing up in packs, alerted by my ongoing vlog. We ended up playing three hour-long sets, playing more or less the same songs each time. As the crowd got more excited, some people reached up towards us; Thuggee did a good job of keeping them off the stage.

To close out the final set, we did a twenty minute jam version of "Sex Files," during which K-Jen and Thuggee took off their shirts and did street theater—K-Jen playing an alien queen abducting Thuggee. Thuggee knelt and begged, K-Jen leered and brandished a green dick-like scepter, Thuggee crawled after her, K-Jen crotch-bumped his face, Thuggee jumped up and humped at her butt—with K-Jen raving in alien tongues all the while.

I was looking down at my chromed guitar, and I noticed some alien reflections. Things like cone shell snails floating above the happy audience, the stage lights picking out the white and orange triangle patterns wrapped around the cone shells, the triangles linked in skeins. When I looked out across the crowd with my naked eyes, the creatures weren't there, but I kept on seeing them in the mirror of my guitar. Two flying cone shells as big as ponies.

Nevertheless I stayed with the music. I was almost afraid that if I stopped playing, the cone shells might burst out of the mirror world and storm the stage.

As it turned out, it was a bestially drunk San Jose guy who stormed the stage. He wanted to get at Cammy in particular. Thuggee bodily lifted up the drunk and threw him back into the crowd, after which the cops none-too-gently dragged him to one side.

After the concert the band retreated into Ma's restaurant, and she locked the door and closed the blinds, lest we be mobbed. Our rented police officers came in handy here, keeping the crowd from busting the glass door. It was that intense.

Although there was no sign of Veeter, Alma, or Paul, Leni Pex had made her way into our sanctum. "Great, great performance," she said, focusing on Cammy. "You were spectacular."

"The most fun I've had in a long time," said Cammy, smiling over at me, eyes dancing beneath her long, level brows. "Good work, frontman. And, yo, Naz, where'd you get those beats, my man?"

"The programs came to life," said Naz. "Thuggee was jammin' it too."

"What about *me?*" said K-Jen, who was pulling her sleeveless T-shirt back over her lacy red bra.

I knelt down and salaamed. "You're a rock goddess."

And the others salaamed her as well, even Cammy. "All hail K-Jen!"

"You children were very professional," said Ma, for want of a better word. "I couldn't believe how you whipped up that crowd. We sold every bit of our food and beer. You should make a CD."

"I'd like to spin off a DVD version of the concert," said Leni. "And market that for people who can't watch it on the web."

"Hello?" said Cammy. "Royalties? Publishing rights? You may have signed Bela, but you didn't sign me."

"Or me," put in K-Jen.

"Don't look so *bad*, girls," said Leni. "I'll have to talk to Van. Maybe we can make a side deal with the band for the DVD. It would be great for your career."

"Let Cammy take over the vlog show, and that'll help," I said. "My time's up, right? Cammy should be the next one."

"I'm more interesting than her," said K-Jen. "Sorry, Cammy."

"I'll keep you in mind," said Leni to K-Jen with a quick smile. "Who knows, maybe we'll do the whole band. But, yes, I like the idea of Cammy going next."

"I thought we'd call my show *The Struggling Musician*," said Cammy, shaking out her bobbed hair, preening.

"You'll be good," said Leni. "You have a certain look. But we'll call it *The Stripper Musician*. More commercial."

"It's not like I'm always stripping."

"Bela's not always crazy, either," said Leni. "You know how it is. People's expectations. Here, check out the contract." Once again she called up some fine-printed text on her handheld device.

"Did Veeter leave any kind of message for me?" I asked Leni while Cammy studied the screen, K-Jen enviously reading over her shoulder. In the back of my mind I'd been thinking about that consulting gig.

"Oh yes, I almost forgot. He said to meet you at Paul's house at Stanford, noon tomorrow. He took off near the end of your first set. His ranch is off Skyline Boulevard above Palo Alto. He gave Paul and Alma a ride home. I think they were fighting."

"Good. So now can I take off this soul-devouring ring?"

"In a second," said Leni.

"So you really only own the rights for rebroadcasting my performances during the vlog week," said Cammy, still studying the fine print on Leni's phone.

"That's right. You still own your songs, of course. All we own is the raw bytes that get blogged—not the intellectual property. Just the sounds and images of this one week of your life. Say you agree, press Enter, and we've got a deal."

"I'm down with it," said Cammy. "Yes." She pressed the button and handed back the phone.

"I'm gonna talk to an agent," grumbled K-Jen.

"Great," said Leni and busied herself with her handheld, which functioned as her all-purpose control center. A moment later my vlog ring loosened up. I handed it to Cammy.

"Put it on now, Cammy," said Leni. "With this ring I thee vlog."

"Right now?" said Cammy, giving me a look. She shoved the ring into her pants pocket. "I have something private I still need to take care of tonight. But I'll put the ring on first thing tomorrow morning."

"I don't like that," said Leni. "It means *Buzz* has dead air."

"Cut her some slack," I said. I had an inkling of where Cammy was going with this. "For tonight you can just rebroadcast our concert—and all the other wonderful highlights of *The Crazy Mathematician*."

"People can click the highlight links already."

"So just for one night they won't have to click," said Cammy. "But that's how it's gotta be. I'll start vlogging by nine tomorrow morning."

"Oh, all right," said Leni. "And as soon as you actually start, I'll pay you."

We spent the next couple of hours helping to tear down the stage and stash the equipment in Thuggee's van, discussing the concert all the while.

"I saw flying alien cone shells reflected in my guitar," I finally mentioned. "Did you guys see anything like that?"

"Sure I saw aliens," said K-Jen, not really understanding what I meant. "All over the place. It was wild. I love that people are dressing up for our shows."

"I'm talking about *real* aliens," I said. "Extraterrestrials."

"What you smokin', bud?" said Naz. "Throw some down for your bros."

"I heard that people used to wear Martian costumes to the Joeys concerts," said K-Jen. "Back in the day."

"It adds wild merriment if the Washer Drop fans are being eccentric," said Thuggee. "Up to a point."

"And beyond that point we've got you to protect us," I told Thuggee. "Thanks for throwing that drunk off the stage. And your dancing was great. I hope you can keep being our roadie."

"My parents are only partially understanding that Washer Drop is a golden opportunity," said Thuggee. "And this is reminding me that we need to be on our way."

We all congratulated each other some more and then Thuggee, K-Jen, and Naz headed north to Humelocke.

"Let's go home too," said Ma, who'd been cleaning up the restaurant. "Come on, Bela, spend the night at our house. Cammy can stay too, we've got room." Ma didn't often encourage my female acquaintances to sleep over.

"Sounds good to me," said Cammy. "I'm definitely ready for bed." Another look from beneath her level eyebrows. Was she thinking what I was thinking? Why else would she have left the ring off?

Ma's house was a little flat ranch house on a tiny lot in a low-cost neighborhood near the train station and under the airport's jet path. Her bedroom was at one end of the house, with two smaller bedrooms at the other end—the lairs where big sister Margit and I had weathered high school. Nominally Cammy was going to sleep in Margit's room. But as soon as Ma had settled into her room, Cammy was standing in my doorway, wearing only her T-shirt and panties.

I was sitting on the edge of the bed, wearing some old pajamas I'd found in my dresser, going over the concert in my mind. It felt like I could remember every note of every song. What a triumph. I was feeling less and less interested in writing math papers that only a few dozen people would ever read.

"Let's visit a little more," said Cammy. "I'm too wired to sleep."

"Come on," I said, patting the bed beside me. Cammy sat down beside me and we talked for maybe two hours. We went over the concert one more time—and the conversation spiraled out from there. She told me about being in a garage band back in Ohio, about hitching to California and working as temp, about the stripping scene, about her cat. I talked about E To The I Pi, about being a math student, about the big theorem I'd proved with Paul, and about the aliens I thought I'd been seeing. We talked about nursery school memories and favorite foods, high-school proms, good and bad drug experiences, rock concerts we'd seen, which states in the US we'd visited, and the best places to find new music. We discussed our past lovers and our hopes for the future.

Cammy looked into my eyes, a gentle smile on her slightly crooked lips. We were going to kiss. We were going to fuck. We were falling in love.

"I wanted this to be private," she said softly. "That's why I'm not wearing the ring."

But just then everything changed. The phone rang a few times in the other end of the house, no great distance away, and Ma fluted my name, clearly relishing the action. "Bela! It's for you!"

"Damn," I said. "I'll be right back, Cammy." I'd had my cell phone turned off all week, lest *Crazy Mathematician* viewers start calling me up at odd times. So who would know to call me on Ma's landline?

I padded into the kitchen and picked up the crufty old extension phone.

"You rule my world, Bela." Alma's voice, warm and husky. "Paul got jealous and made us leave early. I'm so sick of him. He always wants me to fuck him, and I never feel like it anymore. I swear, Bela, I haven't let him touch me all week."

"You, um, liked the concert?"

"Un-freaking-believable. I've been replaying it on the computer. I can't stop watching you. I just had to call. When your cell phone didn't work, I thought of finding your mother's number under Xiao-Xiao Wong. I had a feeling you'd go to earth in old San Ho."

"Clever girl. So now you miss me, eh?"

"Are you coming by our house tomorrow? I think Van set up a meeting? Let's be sure and get some time alone. My beautiful Bela. My big star. I owe you an apology."

"Will you come back to Humelocke with me? I renewed the lease." I was a sucker for this girl. My pulse was racing, and all thoughts of Cammy had vanished from my head.

"Maybe," said Alma. I heard background noises from her end. "Oops, I gotta go." She signed off with a special kissing noise that we'd come to enjoy making at each other. "*Mmwah*."

I responded with a "*Mmwah*," hung up, and there was Cammy across the kitchen staring at me, shaking her head. "How cheesy."

"Lost my temper. Alma and I have something special together. Maybe you wouldn't understand."

"Maybe I wouldn't," snapped Cammy, turning on her heel. "Asshole." She walked down the hall and closed her bedroom door with a slam. A familiar sound from the old days of family drama. I knew that what I'd said was cold and stupid. I could have, should have, gone to her and apologized, but I was tired.

As I fell asleep, my heart was singing Alma's name.

Next morning on the drive up, Cammy and I were all business, discussing our playlist, possible gigs, equipment changes, and ways to make good use of the vlog. She was wearing the ring now, broadcasting *The Stripper Musician* in real time.

We didn't seem to be talking about last night at my house—probably to our fans' bitter disappointment. I had a feeling that maybe I'd let a precious opportunity slip away. But I was too obsessed with Alma to apologize. I sensed that Cammy might be planning some kind of revenge on me for rebuffing her, but I couldn't quite visualize what form this would take.

"You mind if we stop at Paul and Alma's?" I asked as we neared the Page Mill Road exit. "I'm supposed to meet with Van Veeter to talk about this research contract."

"And sniff around that phony little priss-pot. Palo Alto's where she belongs all right. She's a born yuppie, Bela."

"Alma's parents are Santa Cruz stoners," I said defensively. "Her Dad's a termite exterminator, for god's sake. And her brother Pete is—" I remembered the vlog ring. "Oh, never mind. It's not Alma's fault if she wants a nice life."

"Maybe I'll just wait in the car. Or you could drop me off at the train station."

"Oh, come on, Cammy. It might be interesting. My old roommate Paul Bridge, he's quite a character." An unworthy thought passed through my head. My master plan for winning back Alma. If Alma had been freezing out Paul, it would be easy to turn his head. "You might like him."

"I might like him more than you," said Cammy. "That's the pattern, right? All right, then, bring him on." Right away I had second thoughts. "Look, I'm not saying that you're actually supposed to—"

"Make things easier for you? But that's my job, isn't it? Backing up the mighty frontman."

"Look, if you're gonna trip out, I should just drop you at the Cal Train station."

"No, I'm up for this now. I'm going to teach little Alma a lesson. We'll see who's the real whore of Babylon in this lamer crowd. Two math dweebs and a—was it a *rhetoric* major?"

My stomach felt like I'd swallowed razor blades, but then, blessedly, Cammy winked at me. To some extent she was hamming it up for the sake of her vlog. Doing street theater. But I sensed an undercurrent of sadness as well. If only Alma had phoned an hour later last night. If only there were more than one world.

Gyula was parked in Veeter's Hornswoggle limo on the street a few doors down from Paul's house, as if not wanting to make it too obvious where the boss was. Noticing us going by, Gyula pointed at me and grinned, showing his sharp incisor teeth. I parked in the driveway beside Paul's new van.

Alma met us at the door. She looked dreg-style suburban, in a dark paisley jogging suit with her striped shag hairdo teased into a pouf. Cammy pushed right past her to check out Paul in the kitchen.

He was in there with Veeter; they had some equipment spread out on the dining table: a laptop, a little video camera on a tripod, a barcode scanner wand, a shiny low-slung brass teapot. Veeter was wearing the same gray knickerbocker suit as last night, with a white shirt and a red bow tie, although he'd taken the coat off, rolled up his shirtsleeves and untied the tie. He greeted me with a friendly smile.

Before I could talk to the boys, Alma tugged me off alone into the living-room and planted a big kiss on me.

"I'm thinking about what you said," she whispered into my ear. "About coming back. Maybe, Bela, maybe."

In other words Alma was keeping her options open. From the kitchen I heard Cammy laughing charmingly at something Paul had said, and through the door I could see her leaning forward so that her purple-streaked black hair hung across her cheek. My bassist. Maybe she really would close the deal for me. What a girl. Why was I so eager to get Alma back again? And then Alma kissed me again, her tongue hot and avid. Oh Alma.

"Check out our rig, Bela," called Veeter a minute later. So Alma and I trooped into the kitchen and watched. Paul was holding a—magic lamp?

"Van thought it would be funny to mount his Gobrane in this brass teapot he found," said Paul. "In honor of our Seussian nomenclature." The brass teapot was a warm shade of orange-gold, with an elongated profile; it resembled an Aladdin's lamp. Paul set the pot on the table and lifted off the little lid. "Look inside."

An elliptical membrane of shiny multicolored material was snugged into the pot, fitting as tightly as if the pot were half full of tea. The little plastic drumhead was undulating, with slight ripples moving back and forth. The criss-crossing ripples were interacting to form delicate filigrees and fleeting moires—like a tiny wind-ruffled pond. In addition, the membrane was spotted and striped with colors: blues, greens, aquas, yellows, and mauves—like watered silk, like an old book's marbled endpapers, like the mantle of a giant South Pacific clam.

"Oh, Paul!" said Cammy. "It's beautiful!"

"We want to use it to predict the—" began Paul, but Veeter interrupted him.

"Ah-ah!" cried the tycoon, loud enough to drown out whatever Paul might have been about to say. "I'll tell Bela myself in just a minute. And meanwhile, Paul, I wonder if you could take Cammy outside to look at your new van or something?"

"Huh?" said Paul. "Paul, you're so obliv!" said Alma impatiently. "Cammy's wearing a vlog ring. Get her out of here."

"What kind of van do you have, Paul?" said Cammy in a sweet, cajoling tone. "Is it cozy inside?"

I don't think Paul had really noticed Cammy's presence until now. He'd been too busy slobbering over the paracomputer. But now, finally, her voice reached him. "I can show you," he said, turning towards her with a wondering smile that made me think of a blind man enjoying the warmth of the sun. The two of them went outside.

"All right then," said Veeter, pulling some papers from his pocket. "This is your consulting contract. Two copies: one for me, one for you. Sign them both. You'll be under a nondisclosure agreement of course. Your friend Alma here already signed a nondisclosure as well, by the way."

The first thing I noticed that, as with my vlogging contract, the money was considerably better than I might have expected. "It doesn't say how many months it's for?" I asked presently.

"We'll see how it goes," said Veeter. "Could be just the one month, remember I'm off to the Capitol pretty soon. But if our little session today goes well, I could extend it.

You could work with one of the senior Membrain engineers instead of with me; I'm thinking of a bright young fellow named Henry Nunez at our Watsonville plant."

"Well, just a month might be fine with me, too," I said, airily signing the paper. "I could be getting really busy with Washer Drop." I was still floating on the success of our concert.

"You were awesome last night," put in Alma. "I think maybe you're almost too good for the rest of the band."

"You're trying to break us up already?" I said. "The band is incredible. I'm lucky to have them play with me."

"Can you two have this conversation some other time?" interrupted Veeter, puttering around with the little brass teapot, peering at the undulating sheet of colors.

"Yes," I said, glad to duck Alma's comeback.

Fat chance. "I'm not trying to break up your band," said Alma. "It's very good if you take the consulting contract. I'd like to see you being able to get a steady job, if we're going to talk about us having a future together. Van, you really should give him more than a month."

"First let's see what the man can do," said Veeter testily. "Now listen up, Bela. The Gobrane is a membrane of electrically active long-chain polymers. Membrain figured out how to build it, but not how to program it, which is why Rumpelstiltskin was able to buy them out so easily. I was about to close down the project, but then I heard about the Morphic Classification Theorem. And I figured out how to directly map your rakes, cakes, fish, dishes, and teapots into processes on the Gobrane."

"What!"

"I was an engineer before I fed my brain to the computers and sold my soul to Mammon," said Veeter. "And I move fast when I'm hungry. Do you know computer science?"

"I know it's for lamers who can't handle real math."

"Hey, if you've got an attitude, Doctor Bela, let's skip the details. Suffice it to say that I've found an inverse hash-table genetic algorithm approach that produces usable solutions to the membrane codec problem in a reasonable amount of time—assuming you run the search on a network of conventional computers. I call it *devolution*. You guys thought the paracomputational codec problem was unsolvable because you're ivory-tower mathematicians. Yes, a *perfect* solution to a search problem usually requires exponential time to find. So what? If you knew the first thing about applied CS, you'd have realized that in the real world, finding an *acceptably good* solution for most problems takes only polynomial time, hell, linear time. It's no big deal to find an acceptably good codec for a system as simple as a vibrating drumhead. Put away your impossibility proofs, sharpen up your coding sticks—and let the machines do your thinking."

"That's crude bullshit," I snapped. Where did this guy get off? A physics major turned computer jock turned businessman turned politician—and he's telling me I don't know how to apply my own work? "I truly doubt if—"

"The proof's in the pudding," said Veeter intensely. "Whenever I have a clear morphic diagram of a process I can now get the Gobrane to emulate it, thanks to an algorithm inspired by the high-falutin' theorem you boys proved. As for the codec problem, well, Paul and I were able to figure out the missing fifth panel of your little comic strip. Devolution explores the fitness landscape and finds an acceptable Gobrane codec in a tractable amount of time. The codec for the demo I'm about to show you—it took two days to devolve it on Rumpelstiltskin's eighty-machine network. A nontrivial crunch, yes, but totally feasible."

By now I was speechless. This straight-looking little dude was a maniac. It was like seeing John Q. Milquetoast pick up a ukulele and play extreme buzz-saw blitzdreg rock.

"Cat got your tongue?" gloated Veeter, as if reading my expression. "Demo time." He pulled a dice cube out of his pocket, an ordinary red plastic die with white spots. "Rolling a die onto a hard surface is equivalent to a fish swimming inside a teapot, with a rake handle sticking in through the spout, and the six tines of the rake resting on a dish. Morphically speaking, that is. It's a simple enough system that you don't need a cake."

The image clicked for me immediately. The teapot represented the table, the rake the rolling of the die, the fish the chaotic dynamics, and the dish the observation of the result. Why hadn't *I* thought of this? I looked at Veeter with new respect. "So what's the codec?" I said presently. "How do you feed your Gobrane the details of any one particular roll of the die?"

"It's like I said, finding an acceptable codec is easy if you let devolution do the work. The codec can have any form you specify." Veeter gave me one of his aggressive stares. "A mathematician tells you why you can't do what you want. An engineer finds a *crude bullshit* way to do it."

My mind was reeling. The guy had me on the ropes. "The output—can it be something as simple as a picture of the die in its final position?"

"Good, Bela, you're quick. And the input is two successive images of the cube falling towards the table. I video-capture two frames and laser-paint them right onto the Gobrane's surface. I'm using the laser in this barcode scanner." Veeter was growing more and more animated, his small hands repeatedly touching his bits of equipment. He handed me the die. "Throw it past the lens. And watch the Gobrane for the answer." He readjusted the camera one more time and rested the scanner on the open top of the pot. "Roll that sucker, Bela!"

I shook the die and tossed it past the camera, closely watching the teapot. The scanning laser painted two quick images of the die upon the membrane of the Gobrane, painting them so fast that, to my eyes it looked like one image. A cube above the wood-grain-patterned plane of a table, the image in shades of laser red. Immediately the Gobrane began munging the image. In a split second the pattern divided up into a grid of copies of the image—four, sixteen, hundreds, thousands, millions, with the little images rotating and flipping and trading places, and then the undulating red-tinted design congealed back into an image of the die at rest with the six facing up. In the real world, the plastic cube clattered and jittered across the table-top for another moment before settling down to show, yes, a six.

I felt a chill.

"The Gobrane is a paracomputer," said Veeter. "A gnarly natural system can perform computations much more rapidly than any existing network of digital machines. It's a simple matter of resources: a natural system is inherently parallel, with all its parts being updated at once. And ten grams of plastic is made up of something on the order of sextillion molecules. My paracomputer can easily outrun the relevant physics of something as simple as a rolling die. Try it again! I want you to fully believe that it works, believe it right down in your bones. Otherwise you're not going to think hard enough about how to use it."

I rolled the die six more times, and every time the prediction was correct. The patterns upon the Gobrane were mesmerizing; it was as if I were seeing overlays of alternate realities, patterns reinforcing or canceling each other.

"You should take this to Vegas," put in Alma.

"Mickey Mouse," said Veeter dismissively. "The security goons beat the crap out of geeks trying stunts like that. Real gamblers play the futures markets. And politics."

"Futures in what?" I asked, not ready to think about what a faster-than-real-time paracomputer might do to politics. "This brings us to the point of today's exercise," said Veeter. "In order to put Rumpelstiltskin on an even keel, I'd like to place a very large order for a common type of memory chip before taking office. Obviously I want to lock in the best possible price. So I need to predict the futures market for that particular chip, which is traded on the Shanghai commodities exchange. And this, Bela, is the question I'm paying you to answer: How would you hook together your morphons to represent a high-tech futures market?"

I sat in silence for a minute, revolving the problem in my mind. "The model needs a cake for sure," I said presently. "The cake is the chip industry."

"Yes," said Veeter. "And I was thinking of having a rake and a teapot sticking into the cake. Like Paul was starting to blurt out last night. The handle of the rake and the spout of the teapot jammed right into the dough. The rake represents materials, you see, and the teapot stands for manufacturing costs. But then—we're not sure how to include the free market."

"Flying fish," I said as readily as if a voice in my head were dictating to me, which was how some of my best ideas tended to come. "The fish are the competing buyers. They're hovering around the cake's candles like moths. You put a plate up above them, and the fish cast shadows on the plate. The total shadowed area on the plate corresponds to the chip price."

"Tremendous!" exclaimed Veeter after a moment's thought. "A fine mind redeemed from rock and roll. Paul's been trying to help me, but he couldn't make the jump. Of course. The fish are like moths and the shadows are the prices. Aha! I'm going to implement it right away."

"Oh, hold on," I said. "We're talking stochastic measure theory. The chip price will be the *square root* of the shadowed area."

"Now that's why I need a guy like you," said Veeter admiringly. "The square root, of course."

"Way to go, Bela," said Alma.

"So how do you codec this one?" I asked Veeter.

"I've got a terabyte database on my chip market in here,"

he said patting his computer. "That's the data. I updated it just before you got here. I can put your new model into the Gobrane as a pattern of eddy currents, and the data enters as electric potentials along the chip's edge. This is harder than the dice problem. Devolving the codec for this type of data cost me a hundred and twenty hours of network time."

Veeter worked faster than anyone I'd ever seen. He picked up a connector cable from his computer and plugged the computer into the teapot. The brass Aladdin's lamp had a data port set into its side, not to mention a power supply and some subsidiary components in its base. In the space of a few minutes, he'd programmed our model onto the Gobrane as a pattern of whirlpools and eddy currents; the membrane took on a spotty appearance that resembled leopard skin or perhaps a peacock tail. According to Veeter, the chip now embodied the cake, rake, teapot, fish, dish model I'd described.

"You're an animal," I said admiringly.

"Now for the data," said Veeter, and clicked an icon on his screen. His database surged through the connector cable and the chip took on the look of a blue and green doily, with a lace filigree around its edge. The colors seeped inward, growing tendrils that spiraled around each other, forming a tiny red flower at each intersection. The flowers expanded, wobbled, and overlaid each other, canceling out the colors till only a dust of animated black pollen remained. And now the pollen-dots congealed into—the number 72, as if printed onto the chip's surface in a bold sans serif font. Talk about an easy-to-use codec!

"Seventy-two," mused Veeter. "Lower than I would have dared try. Terrific. I'm going to trust this result. No time to waste; the data's constantly changing out from under us, and the paracomputer isn't all that accurate for longer periods of time. Tada, I place my hedge." He typed 72 into a brokerage window on his computer screen, clicked the Purchase button, and looked up with a quizzical smile. "Ever spent point-seven billion dollars with one mouse click? We're all done for now. And Bela, give me your copy of the contract for a sec. Unless I've just roasted my weenie, it looks like you saved me a hundred mill."

Mutely I handed him my contract. He laid out the two copies, scratched some things out, wrote in and initialed some changes, and slid the altered contracts over for me to initial as well. He'd just changed the contracts to run for thirty-six months, with an even better monthly salary. "Henry Nunez will be in touch with you if we need any more help. You'll like him, he's a good guy. But you don't have to work any harder than you want to. Enjoy yourself, you deserve it. And now I've really got to run. Feel free to tell Paul what we did. He's been hung up on this chrome-dome mathematical physics thing your old adviser was talking about. Something about the Margolus-Levitin theorem? Anyway, I'll leave the laptop and the paracomputer for you boys to play with. I've got a couple more rigs just like this back at the ranch. I'll be fascinated to see what you two maniacs get into."

He hurried out of the house, phoning Gyula as he went. We drifted along in his wake, drawn by his energy. Gyula materialized at the end of the driveway, and then Veeter was gone.

"I'm so proud of you, Bela," said Alma, giving me a big kiss. I hugged her, feeling like things were back to normal.

When we broke the clinch I was struck by how quiet it was here amidst the domestic little ranch homes of the Stanford drones.

"Where'd Paul and Cammy go?" I wondered.

"Oh *no*," said Alma, pointing. Paul's van was gently rocking up and down. And to dispel any possible doubt, we glimpsed a flash of Cammy's slender, bare shoulders through the tinted rear window. She was riding Paul.

That crazy Cammy. Vlogging Paul's seduction live on the web! Although I ached with jealousy, I forced a laugh.

I heard Cammy's answering laughter from within the van, rich and confident. She turned just a bit, revealing the womanly curve of her left breast. She could have been mine. I held my fake smile, feeling the tension in my cheeks.

Alma pounded her little fist on my chest. "It's not funny, Bela. That whore. Take me home to Humelocke." She kissed me one more time for emphasis. "Yes, I'm coming back to you. I'll get my stuff."

At one level this felt wrong. I should be the one with Cammy, not Paul. That bastard. Always a jump ahead of me. What was so great about Alma, anyway?

But now here she came, in tears, bumping and lugging her suitcase out of the house, with wads of extra items under her arms. I took the heavy bag and put it in the back of my whale wagon. Comforted her. And then we were on our way.

On the highway I glanced over at Alma, admiring her crisp, perfect profile, really much finer than Cammy's. I took her little hand in mine. How sweet it felt. I wanted to take care of her.

"I could love you, Bela," she said.

"I love you right now," I replied.

Yes, I had my doubts, but mainly I was glad. I had Alma, I had a steady income for the next three years, there were all kinds of incredible applications for my mathematics on the horizon; and I had the burgeoning success of Washer Drop to enjoy as well.

As for Cammy, well, she'd pretty much told me she was going to seduce Paul and I'd pretty much told her to go ahead. In a way, she'd done it as a favor to me. No need to get all bent out of shape—as she would put it. What a woman. I'd still be making music with her in any case. And, who could tell, maybe we'd be lovers yet.

Really, everything was perfect.

FOUR

hypertunnel at the tang fat hotel

I tend to tell my life story as if everything were funny, even though it's not.

Given: the world is absurd. Do we laugh or do we cry? My bent is to laugh; it feels better. But sometimes laughter loses and brutality wins. Sometimes there's nothing left but tears.

Cammy Vendt was murdered while Alma and I drove to Humelocke. The killer was a gardener's assistant named Roberto Sandoval. He stabbed her sixteen times.

Sandoval was riding around town in a friend's mini-pickup on Friday night, smoking pot laced with PCP. They noticed the wild-ass crowd at the outdoor Washer Drop concert, and what the hey, they stopped.

Sandoval and his buddy joined the throng, ready to smoke more shit, drink beer, maybe pick up a girl or get in a fight. Cammy caught Sandoval's attention, the way she was strutting on the stage so fine and proud. After drinking for awhile, he tried to climb up to dance with her. Thuggee slammed him, and the cops sent him on his way without bothering to arrest him. When Sandoval tried to push to the stage again, the people in the audience recognized him from before and called him an asshole, driving him back to the fringes of the crowd. He smoked and drank till he blacked out; his friend gave him a ride home to his sister's apartment on 11th Street in downtown San Ho. His sister waited the counter at a taqueria.

That would have been the end of it, but Sandoval's sister happened to have a computer. After sleeping through the start of work Saturday morning, Sandoval did a web search for that jerk-off washer-something band he'd seen last night, a search for those snots who'd thrown him off the stage, a search for those dreggers with the *puto* bass player—and somehow he ended up at *Buzz* watching *The Stripper Musician*.

Sandoval's senses were raw and preternaturally alert from his hangover. Although relatively uneducated, he was cunning. According to what he told the police, he figured out the route to Paul's place from the visual information in Cammy's vlog, took a commuter train to Palo Alto, and walked to Paul's from the station. This part of the story was a bit uncertain, as no witnesses could recall having seen Sandoval on the train.

In any case, by the time Sandoval arrived, Cammy was dressed and leaving Paul's house, on her way to the train station herself, having turned down a ride from Paul, wanting, she'd told Paul, a little walk to clear her head. Paul said she'd looked tired and sad. Sandoval attacked her in the street with a hunting knife.

He stabbed her sixteen times, nearly severing her head. Cammy's vlog continued for a half hour after she died, the camera on her finger broadcasting the unbearable images. Her paper-white face, her neck wreathed in gore. Her sunglasses lying on the pavement beside her, one lens shattered. All the blood in her vital, wonderful body spilled out onto the gray pavement, making a shape like, oh, like a grove of beautiful trees, like a mass of swaying trunks leading to a pathetic noble crown.

Poor dear Cammy. If only—if only.

When my father died, it took a month until the tears came. But this time the storm came in fast and heavy. I felt terribly guilty. If only I could go back in time and protect Cammy from Sandoval. If only I could kill him. Thanks to the vlog I knew his bestial face like a brother's.

I happened upon the murder videos right after I got back to Ratvale with Alma on Saturday. Alma was already getting on my nerves a little, so I surfed to Cammy's vlog. It took half a minute of mounting horror to understand what I saw: the heaven tree of her blood upon the dry, uncaring asphalt.

I got on the phone to call the cops, who already knew, and then I called Leni and screamed at her to take the images down, but she left them up for twenty-four more hours. She later claimed she had some kind of technical problem in removing public access to the files while at the same time preserving them as evidence for the police. But I'm quite sure her goal was to rake in big hitcounts. Business was what Leni was all about.

The murder vlog files spread across the web, with no-lifer dipshits casting the footage into their own weird obsessive categories: art noir, splatter thrills, puke porno, sick humor, conspiracy theory. And never mind that the images were of a suffering fellow sojourner in this vale of tears.

A short-lived scandal erupted over the fact that Van Veeter had been at the crime scene. This was fueled by a clip from Cammy's vlog that showed him walking past the camper van with an impish, knowing smile on his face. Probably he'd been embarrassedly trying to act cool, but in the hands of a mudslinging pol, that odd smile could have been used to cast Veeter as a callous lecher, criminally negligent and utterly unfit to take office.

But remember, Veeter's political opposition was, sigh, the Common Ground Party. When the press asked Karen Barbara about Veeter's recent actions, she eschewed the red meat, and instead questioned the propriety of the man's huge chip option purchase. Huh? As if anyone cared about commodity futures when there was a televised sex murder in the news.

Early Monday morning, Alma and I were watching network TV over breakfast. Thanks to Alma's civilizing influence, we were eating granola and drinking a pot of tea.

On TV, Veeter was in Washington, DC, emerging from a high-level security briefing with his new buddy, President Joe Doakes, who was of course thrilled to have a Heritagist congressman from California, and never mind any odors in the man's wake. Facing the press, Joe and Van issued a joint statement stating that increased surveillance of vlogs and vloggers was vital. The TV anchorman liked this.

"You see how they're reporting this?" I said to Alma. "The murder's the fault of vloggers? Veeter's home free."

"We must fiercely oppose the lickspittle running-dog imperialist-lackey mainstream media," said Alma with a gentle smile. "To use the traditional Humelocke rhetoric. I'd rather be here than Palo Alto, Bela. I don't think I'd make a good Snodfart wife."

And then the TV showed a clip of Veeter remarking that the still-dynamic research programs of Silicon Valley were on the point of bringing to fruition some truly twenty-first century technologies of terrorism prevention so as to combat the attacks of Tariq Qaadri.

"He's talking about the Gobrane paracomputer!" I cried. "He's gonna hand it over to that crook Joe Doakes! Doakes will classify it as top secret and use it against his political enemies!"

"Would that affect your consulting gig with Rumpelstiltskin?" wondered Alma.

"First thing they'll do is fire me!"

"Why, Bela? They need your ideas."

"I'm a known troublemaker," I sighed. "And Veeter's gonna want to distance himself from the Cammy connection."

"I thought he promised to pay you for thirty-six months. Let me look at your contract. I'm good at deciphering legal rhetoric."

Of course I had no idea where I'd put the contract, in fact I couldn't recall having seen it again after Veeter handed it to me. I'm forgetful about business-type things; they don't engage my imagination. For all I knew, I'd let the contract flutter out the rear window of my car, or maybe I'd recycled it with the accumulated paper trash of my apartment.

Galled by the evidence of my impracticality, I subconsciously chose to flip my mood from depression to anger. This kind of transition is what catastrophe theorists call a chaotic bifurcation, although a universal dynamicist would prefer to regard this type of abrupt mood swing as a bend in a geodesic worldline along the tines of a knotted rake. To put it less technically, instead of giving Alma a straight answer, I threw a hissy fit.

"It's high time someone shot that moron Joe Doakes," I rapped out. "They say that if you don't care about your own life you can always kill someone. I'll take out Doakes and, *hell* yeah, I'll die in a hail of the Pig's bullets. I don't care. I deserve to die."

"*Why* do you deserve to die, Bela?" asked Alma, an edge in her voice. All weekend she'd been nice, tidying up the apartment, comforting me, making meals, like that. But now I was pushing her too far. Well and good. I craved a scene. I wanted the outer emotional weather to match my insides.

"I'm telling you, it's my fault that Cammy died," I said. "I gave her the vlog ring. And—I might as well tell you now—I egged her into seducing Paul. That was my master plan to get you back, see. First I'd get famous, and then I'd get Paul to cheat on you. It worked. But I shouldn't have left poor Cammy on her own at Paul's. She died to make me happy. I should shoot Joe Doakes."

"Back up," said Alma sharply. "You *planned* that with Cammy? You told her to fuck Paul in the driveway? You two big bad-ass rockers were, like, laughing about needy little Alma?" Her lips were drawn very thin. "I'm just a shuttlecock in some weird power-badminton game between you and Paul? Maybe you should be fucking him instead of me!" She was standing over me, her face distorted, once again in tears.

"It's you that matters, Alma," I said quickly. It was very easy to visualize her leaving me again—and I didn't want that. "Cammy was jealous of you," I continued. "I almost slept with her Friday night after the concert. But you phoned me. And I was glad. It's you that I want. I love you. I told Cammy. She got mad. And, yes, maybe at some level she went after Paul to help me. But she also did it to spite me. And to get back at you. And to spice up her vlog. Cammy was a complex person, Alma."

"Don't romanticize her, Bela," said Alma, looking a little mollified. "She wasn't all that stable."

"She was a great bass player."

"I think maybe she had a death wish. Vlogging yourself having sex is like: calling all stalkers."

"You're blaming her for getting murdered?" My voice shook with a fresh gust of passion. Although my mood swings were the logical and deterministic results of my inputs, they were dismayingly hard for me to foresee, let alone control. "You never worried about stalkers when you were doing your news reports for *Buzz*," I said heatedly. "Nobody said I should worry about stalkers when I was vlogging *The Crazy Mathematician*. Why should Cammy be different? Just because she's a woman who does what she likes?"

"Oh—all right," said Alma, relenting. "And of course that vile creep should have left her alone. It's typical, though. This is such a sick country. If I stay with you—*if*—then maybe we should move. Like Canada. Or Hungary?"

"Where I want to go is backwards in time to stop Sandoval," I said. "I have this feeling there might be a way to change the past by using the new tech that Paul and I are inventing. Assuming Joe Doakes doesn't send some agents to seize our magic teapot."

"There's only one way that people change the past, Bela. They stop thinking about it. They move on." Alma's face was kind, intelligent, deeply concerned. She really cared about me.

"I should forget about Cammy, huh?" I could have left it at that. But, God help me, a part of me wanted to fight some more. "That's fine for you. You won."

Alma sighed, but didn't answer. Instead she began walking around the kitchen collecting her stuff. I watched in silence, already starting to regret my behavior.

"I don't need this bullshit, Bela," she announced when she'd filled her purse. She was standing by the door to my bedroom. "I'm sorry for you, but I'm almost thinking it's a mistake to renew our relationship. You and Paul aren't normal. You're pods. Crazy mathematicians."

"I hear that all the time," I said wearily. "Crazy means illogical. Paul and I are logical. Therefore we're not crazy. Note that a system can be at the same time logical and unpredictable. But, yes, I'm acting like a jerk. I'm sorry. I'm stressed out. Too many things at once. Don't give up on me, Alma."

"I'm going to clear out of here for a few days," she said. "And then we'll see. I might as well visit Pete and my parents down in Cruz. I just have to pack a few things."

"Okay," I said, following her into my bedroom. "Remember, I'm going to Palo Alto today. I have to give a statement about the murder. That'll be horrible. And once I get past that, I want to try and organize a Washer Drop concert for Wednesday. A benefit for Cammy? K-Jen and Naz want to do it, and Thuggee says that Rubber Rick will let us use his space. The Globo Club. He says the place is usually blank on Wednesdays. Would you want to come back up for that?"

"I don't think so," said Alma with a little shake of her head, folding a skirt into her suitcase. "Let Cammy have her own night."

"What if I pick you up in Cruz the next day? Early Thursday. I'll bring my board and we'll go surfing in Big Sur. Splash off the blues."

"Now *that* I'd like." She smiled up at me. "I'll have enough of Pete and Gary and Sarah by then."

"Pete's living with your parents?"

"Sad but true." She snapped her suitcase closed. "You can kiss me good-bye, dear pod." I did that. Our bodies always liked each other, no matter what dumb things our heads said.

"You need a ride to Cruz?" I asked after the kiss. "I could go by there on the way to Palo Alto. It'd just be an hour-and-a-half out of my way. I'd still get to the court-house in time."

"I'll get a ride with Leni and Lulu. They're going down to Watsonville today to see the guy they picked for the next *Buzz* vlogger. Henry Nunez, the chief engineer at Membrain. I'm gonna go meet him too. Actually he might not vlog for long. Leni's thinking about doing that *One in a Million* show that you and Paul talked about the first night you met her. It looks like Veeter can steer her to this really huge sponsor. He'd sell a lot of vlog rings that way, and I think the Heritagists would use the data."

"That's cool." I didn't ask for details, didn't repeat my recent rants against Leni and the government, didn't go there. I'd had enough fighting for now.

So I drove to Palo Alto and did my thing at the courthouse, and when I walked out, I encountered a pale middle-American couple, dressed in black, squinting against the California sun.

"Hello, Bela," said the man. "I'm Klaus Vendt and this is my wife Dagmar. Cammy's parents." He looked gently baffled, like nothing made sense to him anymore.

I took his hand. "Cammy was wonderful," I said. "I can't believe she's gone. It's breaking my heart. It must be terrible for you."

"She phoned us and told about the band," said Dagmar, managing a bright, off-kilter smile. Her cheeks were blotchy. "She liked working with you, Bela. And Cammy's cousin showed us the Washer Drop concert on his computer. Cammy looked so strong, so bouncy. She was having fun." And then Dagmar's voice changed, the ragged bird of anger taking wing. "Why did you give her that horrible ring, Bela? You made it so easy for that monster to find her! And then you left her alone to find her way home on her own."

"I'd do anything to change what happened," I said. "I'm sorry all the way through. I even—I even wish I was dead."

"That wouldn't help anything," said Dagmar, giving me a fierce look. "If we crumble, the killer wins even more."

"We think Cammy would have wanted you to come to the funeral," put in Klaus. "We're having the ceremony in San Francisco tomorrow. We think she'd rather end up here than back in Ohio."

"I'll be there," I said. "And the next day, Wednesday, our band—Washer Drop—we'd like to give a memorial concert for her. Would that feel right? I thought we'd donate the money to a charity in Cammy's name. Or give it to you for funeral expenses."

"A charity," said Cammy's mother. "I like that idea."

"There's a musicians' networking group called Fugue," said Klaus. "In San Francisco? We were already talking to them about starting a fund in Cammy's name. One month, when she didn't have a place to stay, they let her live in their office."

"And she used their computer," said Dagmar. "Two or three emails a day, while it lasted. It was nice to know what she was doing for once. Well, of course right at the end, with that horrible vlog, we knew more than we needed to know. I just wonder why—"

"I've heard of Fugue, yeah," I interrupted. "That would be perfect."

"Would we be welcome at the concert?" asked Klaus awkwardly. "Not too old?"

"Of course you should come," I said. "It'll be at the Globo Club, it's a place in the outer Mission district. We'll be onstage starting about ten or ten-thirty Wednesday night."

"Yes," said Dagmar, pushing her hair out of her face. "We'll be there."

I'd promised a lot, considering that I hadn't personally talked to Rubber Rick yet. Nor had I figured out who to get for a new bass player.

I split from the Vendts and phoned Rubber Rick from my parked squinty whale and yeah, man, Rubber was already a Washer Drop fan, he'd talked to Thuggee, and for sure we could use his club, and I shouldn't feel alone, man, because everyone on the scene was way bummed about Cammy, and Rubber had already been talking up our show, man, he had a concert sound system and lights lined up for us, and for sure he'd dig to pass our cut of the door receipts to Fugue for a Cammy Fund, what a beautiful idea, and get this, of all the incredibleness, Jutta Schreck the bassist for AntiCrystal wanted to sit in with us, yeah man, Rubber had talked to her after her show at the Warfield last night, Sunday, it was synchronicity, man, what with AntiCrystal being in the city from Warsaw to play three sold-out gigs, and Jutta totally knew about Washer Drop, she'd seen our webcast when she was loaded in her room at the Grand on Saturday night, and our sound got so good to her that she and AntiCrystal covered "Oil Pig" as an encore for the Sunday night concert, for true, Rubber had been there and seen it, Jutta doing this amazing Cammy-riff solo, and making a speech about the murder, a little hard to understand since Jutta's English isn't so good, but the feeling came through, and Rubber had actually talked to her about Washer Drop at the after-show party at the Cave, Jutta had been there and the lead singer Wacław Smorynski, too, what a party, man, Rubber had seen the synchronicity coming together and he'd all but asked Jutta to sit in for the Globo gig, man, there wasn't gonna be no problem, and Rubber had the cell-phone number of one of Jutta's roadies, although maybe it was a little early in the day just now to try and raise her, what with Jutta being, you know, a junkie vampire, she only comes out at night, but Jutta's guest spot was gonna happen, man, visualize-realize-actualize, and in that same karmic vein, Rubber Rick was picking up some totally off-the-hook art for the concert from the cartoonist Howler Monkey this afternoon, and the Rick's club dogs were goin' out to paper the city tonight, stickin' up little miniposters everywhere, like Washer Drop with Special Guest Jutta Schreck at the Globo Club in a Memorial Concert for Cammy Vendt to Benefit the Fugue Musicians Rescue Fund, it's gonna happen, Bela, you got Rubber Rick pimpin' for you, know what I mean?

"Yeah," I said, kind of stunned by the torrent of plans. That was Rubber Rick all over. "Absolutely."

It was awesome that our single San Jose concert had earned Washer Drop acceptance as a real band. Cammy would have loved it. If only. A lump constricted my throat. I free-associated to an *I Ching* throw I'd gotten the day that I learned both that Roland Haut was willing to be my thesis adviser, and that Haut had no idea about how to prove the Dynamical Classification Theorem: "One pushes upward into an empty city." The only thing that had ever been blocking my way to success had been my own limited expectations. I'd cast my doubts aside and become a mathematician and a rocker. Loud in the empty city. I took a deep breath.

"About Jutta," I told Rubber Rick, "tell her just come by my apartment when she wakes up. We'll start rehearsing maybe five or six. Gotta wait till Naz, K-Jen, and Thuggee get out of school. It's their last day of class."

"After school special, man. Jutta Schreck meets the crazy mathematician and his savage skate-dreggers. Can you even believe it?"

"What I can't believe is that Cammy's dead."

"I hear you, man. How dark. This is gonna be such the epic show. How about webcasting it? I got a video rig right here in the club and a radiant geek living on our best couch. Andrew Silverfish. He can stream your show through my club's website."

"Okay. And run it with a text crawl at the bottom of the screen asking for donations to the Fugue Cammy Fund. Say 'Cammy Fund' on the posters, not 'Musicians Rescue Fund.' It's gotta be all about Cammy."

"I hear you."

I drove over to Paul's. He hadn't been at the courthouse today as he'd already spent most of Saturday and Sunday with the cops. I'd gotten email from him last night, urging me to come by. He wanted to talk about the Gobrane, about Alma—and about Cammy.

Two TV trucks were encamped outside Paul's house, and when I got out of my squinty-whale station wagon, the reporters were on me like flies on shit, asking questions about Cammy and Van Veeter.

I looked past them, trying to see the spot where Cammy had died. But by now of course the cops had hosed it off.

I pushed past the cameras and made it onto Paul's little lawn. The reporters had to stay in the street unless you were talking to them. Those were the rules of the game. I knocked on Paul's door until eventually he peeked out and let me in.

A reporter with slick black hair began hollering our names. "Mr. Kis, Mr. Bridge, Mr. Kis, Mr. Bridge!" He had a peremptory tone that was hard to ignore.

"I need to get out of here," said Paul, closing the door and leading me into his kitchen. He looked wretched. All the blinds were drawn. He was wearing slippers and pajamas. "The cops still have my car. They impounded it for evidence."

"Poor Cammy," I said.

"She was so hot," said Paul. "What a waste. I hope I don't have to meet her parents. I keep thinking I should have driven her to the train. I hope you're not mad at me, Bela." He flopped down and filled a bowl with Raisin Bran. He had the cereal box and a plastic gallon of milk sitting right next to the dish. The magic teapot was off to one side of the messy table. "You hungry?" asked Paul, his mouth full.

"No thanks."

"My fifth bowl today," he said indistinctly. "Helps my stomach. I'm kicking Ritalin. I got some at the Health Center; I told them I had an attention deficit disorder. Boy, have I been attentive this week. I'm telling you, Ritalin's worse than meth. How's Alma?"

"She's fine. Settling into Humelocke with me." No point mentioning she'd temporarily bailed for Cruz.

"I want her back," said Paul.

"Alma's insidious, isn't she?"

"Like Scarlett O'Hara," said Paul. "The belle of the ball, the steel magnolia. She's powerful and manipulative, but she gives off this vibe of needing a man, and you want to be, like, her knight."

"Mr. Kis, Mr. Bridge, Mr. Kis, Mr. Bridge!" The voice bayed like a hound on a scent.

"I love Alma," I told Paul. "She's got me hypnotized too. But I'd give her up if that would bring back Cammy. And if I'm not mad at you it's because I feel like it was *my* fault." I picked up the magic teapot, peering down at the lively skin of the Gobrane. It was still connected to Veeter's laptop; he'd left that for us too. "Do you think there's any way to change the past?"

"Funny you should mention that," said Paul. "Roland Haut says that a Gobrane paracomputer might be able to tear a hole in spacetime. And then who knows? I talked to Roland for three hours Saturday night when I was on my Ritalin run. I hadn't meant to call him at all because I figured he'd try to muscle in on my grant from Veeter. But, you know, I got on this telephone kick. Tweak out and jabber someone. And it turns out Roland has this cool idea for a self-referential prediction paradox that would create a singularity. A tunnel. He thinks it could lead to those aliens you guys talk about."

"You've seen the aliens, too?"

"No. But if my crazy mathematician collaborators are encountering giant roaches and flying cone shells, it's my job to explain why. Me, I've been having bizarre, loath-some dreams—but that's from the murder and the Ritalin rebound. I'm lucky the cops didn't give me a blood test. This has been a wake-up call. I'm off speed for good."

"I hope so," I said. "Did you see Veeter on TV with Joe Doakes? I think Doakes is gonna make our paracomputer top secret. We might not have our magic teapot for much longer."

"President Doakes? Wow. Have you ever noticed that he always sounds angry—like just on the point of lashing out? He's the strict father that serious losers wish they'd had. I haven't been watching television at all. I've been eating cereal and doing math."

"Mr. Kis, Mr. Bridge, Mr. Kis, Mr. Bridge!" The voice had taken on a tone of angry reproof. Like how dare we ignore someone so important.

"I wish I had a rifle," said Paul, rising to peek out through the curtains. "Explode his head like a rotten pumpkin. That'd be good to see on the news."

"They're about to give up," I said. "The networks are dropping the story. Veeter will get a free pass. What kind of math have you been doing?"

"Axiomatizing the Gobrane. And working on a morphic model for individual human decision making. A prize problem, don't you think? I already told Van; he definitely wants it solved."

"Show me."

Paul handed me a pad of paper covered with lines of symbols, many of the lines overwritten and crossed out. An old-school mathematician's way of doing things. Nail the theory before starting any experiments.

"I know it's messy, I'm about to rewrite all this," said

Paul. "The first part is about the Gobrane axioms. And
the rest is my model for predicting people's actions. I start
with the assumption that your mind is a bunch of obsessive thought loops, with your external inputs sparking
trains of thought that plow through your thought loops .
And I turn that model into morphons."

I looked over his symbols, asked questions, read some
of the formulae again.

"The thought loops are cakes on dishes and the thought
trains are fish dragging rakes, and they fit inside the teapot of the skull," I said after a bit. "Very elegant. But I
still don't understand why these simulations work on the
Gobrane. Do *you* understand the Gobrane?"

"It's a mat of some sextillion long-chain polymers," said
Paul. "An activator-inhibitor reaction-diffusion system
with ten-to-the-twenty-first-power computational nodes.
What makes it programmable is that there's different species of molecules in there, and as long as they get a little
solar energy now and then to power up the reactions,
the molecules keep converting back and forth from one
species to another, with some species catalyzing certain
reaction paths."

"Sounds like chemistry," I said uneasily. I didn't like
getting too far from the diamond clarity of math.

"Never mind," said Paul. "I found a way to abstract away
from the details. I've discovered a set of universal paracomputation axioms to specify how the Gobrane behaves.
And I think lots of other systems can obey the very same
axioms. You'll help me clean up the axioms, and we'll
publish them. All sorts of naturally occurring systems can

become paracomputers, just like we expected: dripping faucets, wind-blown ribbons, candle flames. Van's opened a lot of avenues."

"But now he's gonna be closing them down," I said. "Van and his new pal Joe Doakes won't want anyone to have paracomputers except for their secret police and the Heritagist party central office. And maybe their business buddies." Out in the street, the two trucks started their engines with a roar—and drove away. "The word's already come down from the top," I said. "They're leaving so nobody sees the goons come to kick our butts and take away our Gobrane."

"You're so paranoid," said Paul. "We signed contracts. Here's yours by the way." It was lying face down where I'd left it two days ago, duh, in a puddle of milk under the cereal box.

"Thanks," I said, examining the stained paper. Sure enough, a bail-out provision lurked in clause twenty-three: Premature termination of the agreement would be allowed at the discretion of Rumpelstiltskin with a settlement of ten percent of remaining monies to be paid to the contractor after all Rumpelstiltskin equipment had been returned as specified in clause seventeen. I read this part to Paul.

"But we're not done," he protested, in a calm, reasonable tone. "We're just getting started. Van knows that. He's excited about my mind model. He'll want us to finish our work. This is Nobel Prize territory. Hell, if Haut's right, it could be even bigger than that. Newton, Einstein, Gödel!" He pushed back on the bridge of his glasses, worry setting in. "I wish I hadn't called Haut. He really is crazy, you know. And of course now he wants to see the Gobrane. I'm a little scared of what he might do. He'll flip if he hears about Veeter sharing our work with Joe Doakes. Maybe if I can keep Haut out of it, Veeter will still be okay with us."

"To the media we're filthy tar babies, Paul," I said, folding my contract into my pocket lest I misplace it again. "Listen to me. We're beyond redemption. The networks have been showing that vlog clip of Van with Cammy's face and your face in the foreground, and you're all flushed and sweaty. The other clip they show is from the concert when that prick Sandoval is trying to grab Cammy, and Thuggee throws him off the stage, and I'm in the foreground yelling and holding my crotch. In the public mind it's almost like we killed Cammy. Van's gonna cut us loose, dog. Let's hide the magic teapot before it's too late."

"Van wouldn't double-cross us," said Paul stubbornly. "He's an engineer. One of us. A scientist."

"Scientists are nice guys? Did someone mention Roland Haut?"

"Look," said Paul, growing agitated. "I told the secretary I'd be in my office at Stanford this afternoon. I have an appointment with Cal Kweskin and his student Maria Reyes. They're doing some morphonics research for the National Security Agency. You've got a new career as a rock musician, so whatever you do is fine. But I can't afford more craziness. I'm a rookie professor."

"We need to hide you *and* the Gobrane. It's not like you're teaching classes. And even if you were, summer school isn't even in session yet. The campus is dead, Paul."

"Stop it. You're freaking me out. Everything's set. I want to start my job." Paul hated unexpected change.

"Why don't we ask the paracomputer if Van's going to invoke clause twenty-three?" I suggested. "Good way to test if your mind model works. If the Gobrane's so fast, maybe it can predict Van's moves before they happen."

"Well, I don't have a very good codec yet," said Paul, getting his excuses ready. "That ham-handed computer-science hack Van came up with—devolution—it works, but it's computation-intense. To get your codec, you use a genetic algorithm that runs evolution backwards to arrive at a linked list of inverse hash tables, and the tables grow so big that you have to use a network of computers to hold them. But I still don't have that kind of account on the Stanford system, and Van says he can't give me time on the Rumpelstiltskin network either."

"See? He's getting ready to dump you."

"Shit." Paul turned on Veeter's laptop. "Well, anyway, I do have a crude, toy version of a codec for the mind model. Instead of devolving it, I figured it out from first principles."

"Mathematics is the way. Does your codec work?"

"Kind of," said Paul. "A little. Some of the time. What data would we use to simulate Veeter?"

"We web search for Veeter's biography," I said. "His speeches and interviews. Feed in the news stories from the last few days. And especially use his news conference with Joe Doakes." I cast out a hook for Paul's vanity. "But I don't guess you could program our little question as fast as Veeter programmed his chip-futures inquiry the other day."

"Oh, yes I can," said Paul, his fingers busy on the laptop.

"I looked at Veeter's chip futures market hack, by the way. It was good. Were you the one who thought of measuring the shadows of the fish?"

"The square roots of the areas," I said.

"Yeah," said Paul. "Alright, here we go, we'll see if we can simulate Veeter making his plans." In a remarkably short time, Paul was ready. "You talk to the paracomputer and it talks back," he said, rubbing our teapot like a magic lamp. "That's the best part of my homemade codec. It talks. I ripped the guts out of some public domain speech-recognition software. The Gobrane membrane vibrates with the sound of your voice, munges that into a morphonic computation, and then it vibrates the answer back like a little speaker." He leaned closer to the pot's colored, shivering surface. "What's your name?"

"Van Veeter," said the brass teapot. The synthesized voice sounded ever so slightly like Van's.

"What's your latest invention?" continued Paul.

"A Gobrane paracomputer," said the teapot. "Publicly it's for antiterrorism, and privately I'll be using it for market speculation and political strategy."

"Let's get to the point," I said to the pot. "Are you going to break your contracts with Paul Bridge and Bela Kis? Are you going to confiscate their Gobrane?"

"I'm sorry, I don't understand," said the teapot. "Please restate your input."

"Will you send someone to take the Gobrane away from Paul Bridge?"

"Yes," said the teapot. "This is likely."

"How soon?" asked Paul, getting to his feet.

"They could arrive anytime within the next sixty-five thousand five-hundred and thirty-six years."

"That's not an actual number; that's an overflow error," said Paul. He leaned over the laptop. "Is it possible that Veeter's agents could arrive within five minutes?" I asked the teapot.

"This is tautological," replied the paracomputer. "Five minutes is less than sixty-five thousand five-hundred and thirty-six-six-six—*urk*."

Paul was furiously typing and mousing on the laptop.

"Oh, let's turn this bullshit off," I said, closing the teapot's little lid. "Use common sense, dog. They could be here any minute."

Paul sighed and looked up. "I need more time with this apparatus. If Haut's Paradox were to come into play—well, things could get very interesting. I have to tell you more about that." He rose to his feet. "All right, Bela. I'll get dressed." He hurried into his bedroom.

"Bring your toothbrush and pajamas!" I called, closing the teapot's lid and powering down the laptop. "We might be gone for a couple of days."

"What about my office hours?" hollered Paul, still anxious about this point.

"Tell them you're overcome by grief. Tell them you're doing special research on how to change the past and save Cammy's life!" Until I said this, I hadn't quite realized that was my real hope. The paracomputer felt like magic, and once you had magic, there was no telling where it might end. I put the teapot and the laptop into a plastic shopping bag.

"I'm ready," said Paul charging out of his bedroom with a red nylon Stanford duffel bag of neatly folded clothes. "Let's go!"

Sure enough, we passed Gyula on the way out, tooling down Page Mill Road in the long white Rumpelstiltskin Hornswoggle. A thick-necked Asian guy sat in the front seat next to him, and in the back were two figures shadowy behind the dark glass. Gyula saw me, but he didn't veer or slow down. All he did was lick his index finger and mark an imaginary tally in the air. Like, "You owe me."

"They're not busting us?" said Paul, noticing. "The driver's my cousin," I said. "Gyula Wong. Almost like a brother."

"Then why would Veeter send him to get you? He's not that dumb."

"Van doesn't know Gyula and I are related. We Chinese don't leave much of a paper trail."

"I thought you were Hungarian," said Paul.

"Whatever works. Have you ever seen that guy riding with Gyula before?"

"Oh yeah. He's bad news. I'm glad we didn't have to face him. They call him Owen but his name's really Yuan. He was with Van the other day, and Van was bragging that he smuggled Owen from Shanghai in a shipping container and that Owen will do anything Van says. He barely speaks English."

I drove a few miles on the main highway up the peninsula and then, just to be evasive, I cut over the Santa Cruz Mountains to the less traveled coast highway, Route One. Meanwhile Paul used his cell phone to call the Stanford math department and cancel his meetings through Wednesday, his voice serious and sad.

It was foggy on the coast. I headed north. As we drew ever further from Paul's new life, he looked less and less enthused.

"So where are we going?" he asked. Out to the left the surf was breaking in long tubes below the low cliffs, everything soft and pale in the mist.

"I myself am going back to Humelocke," I said. "But I figured I'd park you and the magic teapot in, like, a random motel that Veeter won't be able to predict even if he's using your new mind model."

"Incommunicado in a motel. Great. Maybe I'll hang myself."

"I've been feeling suicidal myself," I admitted. "Because I keep flashing on those images of Cammy dead in the road and hating myself for not being there for her."

"Exactly," said Paul. "But at least you have Alma. If you were a real friend, you'd tell Alma to come back to me."

I didn't touch that one. After a bit, I tried a change of subject. "That was kind of weird what we just did—to ask the teapot to make a prediction about itself," I said. "Asking it if Veeter would confiscate it. Is that the kind of self-reference Haut was talking about? Did he explain the details of his paradox?"

"I don't feel like talking about it now," said Paul, disconsolately staring out the window. The fog was getting thicker. You could hardly see the ocean.

"How about this for the paradox," I said coaxingly. "We program the Gobrane to predict its own predictions, and to then say the opposite of what it predicts it'll predict. So that it says yes if and only if it predicts that it'll say no. Boom, contradiction, and that tears a hole in spacetime?"

"You're on the right track," said Paul, grudgingly. "But it's not quite that simple." He opened my glove compartment and began refolding and arranging my maps. "I'm too upset about changing my schedule to talk math."

We drove in silence for a while. Paul stacked all the maps in order of size and closed the glove compartment. "I really really shouldn't be leaving my new job," he repeated. "Everything was all set. I had office hours today." We were passing through the ever-gray beach town of Corona. "Look, Bela, let's get this over with. Drop me in one of these motels here. I won't hang myself. I'll just get back to my research."

"About the motels," I said. "I'm thinking that if Veeter is really serious about finding us, he might ask Joe Doakes to sic the Secret Service on us. The SS handles federal threats to computer security, you know. They could pick up on your credit card when you register."

"I'll give a fake name, and pay cash. Pull over at the Joe Crouch Motel next to the Monogrub burger place."

"They'll ask for your license," I said, not slowing down. "And, dog, I love you too much to strand you in Corona. Especially if you're feeling down. As many times as I've been through Corona, I've never seen it sunny. And I just remembered that I've got a second cousin who does the books for a cheap place in Chinatown. I can get you in with no questions asked."

"Chinatown!" said Paul. "Fine. But I've totally, absolutely, unequivocally got to be back at Stanford by Thursday afternoon. I'm having dinner with the chairman and Cal Kweskin at the Faculty Club. If you make me miss another appointment, I'll turn into a hysterical vegetable."

"I'll check back with you late Wednesday night after the Washer Drop concert," I said soothingly. "And then I'll drive you straight home. We're doing a benefit for Cammy Wednesday night. Would you want to come?"

"No! I want to duck Cammy's funeral, her memorial, her whatever. No more reporters, no more confusion, no more pictures of me. I'm ashamed to show my face after Cammy's vlog. I hate to think what they're saying about me in Kentucky." He sighed and straightened the folds of his pants and shirt. "What's the name of this Chinatown place you want to stash me in?"

"Tang Fat Hotel. It's really a rooming house, not a hotel. Old people live there. And immigrants might stay there after they come off the container ships. Maybe some Chinese hookers work it, too. For sure nobody's gonna ID you."

"Sounds louche," said Paul, cheering up. He had a country boy's fascination with the seamy side of San Francisco. "Coolies, opium smugglers, marrying maidens with tangy fat. I'll be off the grid. Peace and quiet to write up my new results. Let the Cammy thing blow over. I'll try a few more experiments with the Gobrane. Maybe I'll even get Haut to come by. What the hell. I know he'll want to dip into the futures markets, even if we don't get around to tearing a hole in spacetime. And, come on, Bela, *why* can't you send Alma to keep me company?"

"She's back with me for good, Paul. You were a temporary aberration."

"If I'd given up speed earlier and if I hadn't slept with Cammy, I'd still have Alma," said Paul. "I'm a better prospect. You keep talking about changing the past. If we can bring back Cammy, maybe we can save my relationship with Alma, too."

"I don't think so."

"I do."

"Forget it."

"Fuck you."

"Kiss my ass."

Although this exchange was only half-serious, we didn't talk much more for the rest of the drive. I sank into my own thoughts—about Cammy, about Alma, and Paul's axioms for the Gobrane. Those notes he'd shown me were amazing. The math thoughts always came better when I was around him. It was like intelligence-enhancing Buddha rays were continually beaming out from the guy.

It was foggy in the city. I pulled into Stockton Street and stopped by the Tang Fat Hotel, a weathered three-story wood rooming house with a faded sign. Each room had Victorian bay windows. Most of the windows were filled with clothes on hangers, maybe drying or airing out. The whole first floor was occupied by the Wang Kee Bargain Market, with a low awning above its bins of gnarly roots and stalks. Next door was the *Mee Mee Bakery*. The sidewalk was crowded with lean-faced men and stumpy dark-clothed women carrying bags.

Paul and I got out of the car. The Tang Fat Hotel's front stoop was tiled in red and white; behind its plate-glass door was a plain stairway leading to the upper floors. A horse-faced guy was sitting by the stoop on a plastic chair, chain-smoking generic nonfilter cigarettes. I asked him in Chinese about getting a room. He pretended he didn't hear me.

I told him about my cousin Jackie Wang, who did the accounting for the Tang Fat Hotel, Jackie the son of Mabel and Wing Wang, Mabel being the sister of my mother's father's first cousin Shirley Wong. Upon hearing of my relationship to Jackie, the horse-faced man acknowledged me. His name was Wu. He offered me a cigarette, but I was off cigs again. I told Wu that my friend Paul wanted to stay there for three nights. Wu said he had a single bed on the third floor.

"Three night two hundred dollar," he told Paul in English. Paul handed him a couple of hundred-dollar bills, and Wu unlocked the front door, passing Paul the key.

"See you Wednesday around midnight," I told Paul and got the two bags from the car: Paul's duffel and the Gobrane.

"Here," said Paul, taking his lined pad out of his duffel and tearing off the written pages. "You study what I wrote about the Gobrane and the mind model. I know it by heart. I'm gonna write it out in a nicer form as soon as I get to my room."

"Thanks, dog."

Wu coughed and hawked a lunger onto the sidewalk. A cop car turned the corner, alert to the traffic jam behind my squinty whale. I hopped into the whale and drove off.

I got back to Humelocke about five o'clock. Gyula and his companions were parked in their white limo by the same fire hydrant where Gary Ziff had been. And they already had a ticket on their windshield. But they didn't care.

Gyula beckoned me over, a condescending smile on his lips. He'd given me one break, but now it was time to reel me in. I noticed a paracomputer rig just like ours on the seat next to him. A shimmering teapot and a laptop. I wondered if they'd been using Paul's mind model to predict my actions. Veeter would have had the resources to devolve a proper codec, which meant the system would be working better. But it didn't seem as if they'd picked up on my Tang Fat Hotel detour. They'd come straight to Ratvale.

Owen the Shanghai muscleman was scrunched down so he could glare out the window at me. He was a really big guy. His neck was as wide as his head; his eyes were gun-turret slits. Now he extricated himself from the car and stood beside it, twitching the kinks out of his shoulders, never taking his eyes off me. The bridge of his nose was very flat. He wore a skin-tight sleeveless red tank-top with a Chinese character for good fortune on it. Around his neck was a heavy gold chain with tight, flat interlocking links like an attack dog's collar. Dangling from the necklace was a gold medallion bearing an X-eyed smiley face.

The passengers from the back seat got out as well. Two lawyers: A thin, snooty one and a short fat one with a full black beard. "I'm August Cochon," said the taller one. "And you would be Bela Kis?"

"Yeah," I said, reluctantly shaking his hand.

"Pleased to meet you," said Cochon. He had a slight droop to his lower lip. "And this is my colleague Herman Svaart. We represent Rumpelstiltskin, Inc. We need to speak with you regarding a consulting contract issued on Saturday, May 29, of this year."

"Uh-huh."

"The company wishes to cancel the contract. We'll be happy to pay a ten percent termination fee as soon as we take possession of the equipment that Rumpelstiltskin lent to your friend Paul Bridge."

"You should ask him about that."

"He's neither at his home nor at his office. And I see that he's not with you. Would you know where we can find Mr. Bridge?"

"No," I said. Over in the limo, dark Gyula's expression was studiously bland, and perhaps a bit mocking. Was there any chance that Veeter actually knew that I'd dropped Paul in Chinatown? But Cochon looked convincingly frustrated. As if I'd outmaneuvered them. Big Owen twisted his neck impatiently, like a bird eager to peck.

"Don't you want the cancellation fee?" said Cochon, pulling in the corners of his mouth. "Note that, in accordance with clause twenty-seven of our contract, if we deem your behavior to be obstructive or dilatory, the cancellation fee is voided, regardless of whether we receive our equipment."

I hadn't noticed that clause. "I'll see what I can do," I said finally. "Are we done here?"

"We're prepared to institute a lawsuit against you," said Svaart. "If you defy us, you can expect to be served papers quite soon." His beard wagged up and down as he talked.

"Let me talk sense to the guy," said Gyula, getting out of the limo. He took hold of my upper arm and none too gently dragged me off to one side. "You guys playing the market?" he asked in a low tone.

"This isn't really about money," I said.

Gyula snorted derisively. "Of course not, Professor. Look, I gave you a break. So now you help me pay off my mortgage, hear? Three hundred grand."

"I gotta go."

"Don't fuck with me, Bela." He jerked his head towards the big guy by the car. "You don't want me to put Owen on you."

"Give him me," called the thug, recognizing the import of Gyula's gesture. "I am respect." He had a loud, high-pitched voice.

I made it into my apartment. My band-mates weren't there yet. Maybe they were partying after school.

I was angry at Veeter for canceling my contract, and very glad I'd stashed Paul and the magic teapot at Tang Fat. I got out some fresh paper of my own and began rewriting Paul's notes. As I worked, I understood them better and better; I began tightening up the ideas, mixing words, pictures, and equations as was my wont. It would be great to find a simple open-source method for paracomputation, and to devalue Veeter's patents and techniques.

I was interrupted at seven by a knock on the door. Time flies when you're doing math.

Merry on my doorstep were Naz, K-Jen, Thuggee, and—Jutta Schreck. The four of them were smoking a conical yellow hash joint. Jutta had a pale face, high cheekbones, platform-soled black boots, strawberry blonde hair, and ripe curves. Her makeup gave her a stern, ultra-metal look—shiny silver lipstick and eye-covering chromed contacts. But she was laughing, a barking sound that came out *tjachz, tjachz*.

"Bela," she said, handing me the fat fuming roach. "We get down to it, hound. We rock it for Cammy Vendt."

Jutta lived up to her reputation, and then some. She played like nothing else mattered, as if music were a language that she'd been speaking for a thousand years. She was fast and sensitive, she read our unspoken vibes. She was the musician that Cammy might have grown into, with craft and cunning layered upon still-burning passion.

The rehearsal was emotional. At times it felt as if Cammy were right there, a ghostly wave-pattern in the overlaid moires of sound. K-Jen had written a long song about the murder, "Leaf-Blower Man," and it took four run-throughs till I could play that one without breaking down.

All the while, the music was thinking for me. Even while I was screaming the choruses and bending my staircases of notes, I was getting ideas about the Gobrane, about devolution, about paracomputation, and about Paul's mind model.

The rehearsal over, Jutta left me with a lit reefer in my hand. I sat down alone and worked for another couple of hours, and by two in the morning I had the impression that I knew both how to make pirate copies of the Gobrane, and how to carry out those knuckle-walking devolution techniques. I decided to post my results on the web so everyone could see them. The sooner I could devalue that prick Veeter's intellectual property, the better. I typed up my explanations and scanned in my figures and equations.

Made sly by the pot, rather than posting the info to my own home page—which was vulnerable to being taken offline by the Heritagists—I posted it via Pollinator, a nimble spambot maintained by an ex-Humelocke math student friend named Onar Anders, who'd moved to Tonga. Assuming Onar approved of you—and he liked me fairly well—his Pollinator would send out a hundred thousand anonymous helper-bots to post your information worldwide into guestbooks, comment threads, and the home pages of free trial accounts opened on the spot.

Pollinator signaled my successful post with an animation of an exploding dandelion head. I'd gotten over. I'd given away my information. And if I was right, then before long everyone would have an open-source paracomputer. That would teach Veeter to short me on my contract.

When I woke late the next morning, Tuesday, I immediately thought of some major holes in the midnight logic that I'd posted worldwide. Oh well, it was a start. I very much wanted to ask Paul about how to fix my ideas, but with Veeter on our case I didn't want to risk blowing Paul's cover by calling him. Come to think of it, if Paul was online, he'd probably notice my posts on his own. He'd love reading them, and he'd love finding the holes. Visualizing Paul's reactions made me smile.

I phoned Alma to see how she was doing. Her cell phone was turned off so I used the Ziff landline. Her father Gary answered.

"Hi," I said. "This is Bela Kis. Can I talk to Alma?"

"Rock and roll," said Gary. "I saw some of your concert. Washer Dump?"

"Washer Drop," I said. "I wrote a song," volunteered Gary. "Want to buy a song? It's called 'Tequila Memories.' I could sing it for you now."

"Maybe when I come see Alma," I said. "Can you put her on?"

"Hey Pete," called Alma's father. "Where's Alma?"

"Stinking up the shitter," said Pete's voice in the background. "Whoops, here she comes."

I heard a clatter and some hissed whispers, and then Alma was on.

"Bela?"

"Hi. I miss you."

"I can't wait to get out of here. Stop it, Pete!" More rattling and the slam of a door. "I wasn't in the bathroom like he said. I was feeding the fish and cleaning the filters in Mom's aquariums. She's hardly home at all these days. She started some new antidepressants and she's like a jumping bean now. What's up with you? Are you over your guilt trip?"

"Getting better. I'm going to Cammy's funeral today, and that benefit concert is gonna happen tomorrow night. It's good to be doing stuff. You still up for seeing me early Thursday morning?"

"With your surfboard," said Alma. "Sweet. I can't wait for Big Sur. I've got my board and suit here, you know. I've been practicing with Pete."

"One thing," I told her. "I just saw two of Veeter's lawyers. The contract is history. And they were threatening to serve papers on me. I'm wondering what that even means."

"God dammit. Veeter wants to cancel your consulting contract? It's as bad as you said."

"Easy come, easy go. Don't forget, I've got the rock-star thing happening too."

"But why does that pig want to sue you? You should be suing *him*! Did you and Paul do something skeevy?"

"Well I—I better not go into details on the phone. So do you know about serving papers?"

"I do. When you go corporate, I can be your CEO. Listen up. When someone wants to sue you, they run to the court in tears, and they hand in some papers saying, *waaah*, Bela did this and that to me, and I want the courts to do such and such to Bela to make it fair. Now, the court isn't going to consider the case until they're sure that Bela knows what the crybabies are saying about him. So some reliable individual has to, like, physically put a copy of the complaint papers into your hand and testify in court that you got them."

"So I can stall by avoiding the papers."

"Yeah, but that's not a long-term solution."

"If I stall long enough, maybe things will change," I said. More noise in the background at Alma's end: Gary Ziff yodeling "Tequila Memories."

"Don't stall about picking me up on Thursday morning," said Alma.

"Would six a.m. be okay? I might come straight there from the concert."

"I'm sleeping on a fold-out bed in the garage, actually. Pete's hogging my old room. So just creep into the garage and kiss me awake. I'll be glad to see my Prince Charming."

"I love you, Alma."

"I'm glad."

I spent another couple of hours working on my open-source paracomputation project, and got nowhere. The harder I looked, the more errors I found.

And then I went to Cammy's funeral at a graveyard in South San Francisco. Quite a few people turned up, many of them strangers to me. The dirt hole in the ground was a model of the Cammy-sized hole in the world. I was having trouble accepting her death as real. Near the end of the service, I noticed Cochon and Svaart edging toward me through the crowd. I did a slow-motion evasion, sidling through the mourners, but when I reached the edge of the party, I had to break into the open. Cochon and Svaart kept on coming; it ended with me running full tilt across the gently rolling green hills of the graveyard, tears in my eyes, the white stones like numbers.

I slept on Naz's couch Tuesday night to avoid the lawyers, and all day Wednesday I hung out at Naz's family's store.

I didn't think much about math that day, I was thinking about the coming concert instead. Thuggee used my Bel Paese to ferry equipment to Rubber Rick's Globo Club in the Mission district of San Francisco. And, last of all, I told him to load the squinty whale with my two surfboards and my two wetsuits and bathing suits and park the car behind the club. Two of everything just in case I needed spares. I myself took DART and the bus to the concert.

Rubber Rick's club was an old warehouse, big enough for several hundred people. An enormous bar ran all along the left-hand wall. The floor was shellacked concrete, with a scattering of green plastic garden-furniture tables and chairs. A low stage stood at the far end, with black-painted plywood partitioning off a backstage area.

As show time drew near, I was back there with Naz, K-Jen, and Thuggee, taking turns checking out the crowd through a black-gauze-covered porthole. Rubber Rick was at our side.

"Where's Jutta?" said Naz for maybe the seventh time.

"I talked to Siggy fifteen minutes ago, man," said Rubber Rick. He waggled his tongue. "Siggy's her himbo-slash-bodyguard." Rubber was an older guy, in his forties, with an odd, zigzag comb-over and a close-cropped devil beard. He claimed he got a lot of sex. "Siggy says, *opanować się*," continued Rubber. "Means 'be cool' in Polish. Jutta likes to get lifted before she comes on. You gotta know that." He was wearing a cell phone headset.

"In other words she's shooting up," said K-Jen in tart, California-girl tones. "How headbanger. I hope she remembers our songs. Do you have the playlist, Bela?"

"Here," I said showing it to her. "And somewhere in there we goose the energy with the AntiCrystal cover we practiced."

"Crying Chainsaw Clown," said Naz. "That song is god."

"What about the second set?" said Thuggee.

"There might not be a second set," I said. "If there is, we play everything again faster and louder."

"Are those Cammy's parents drinking at the bar?" said K-Jen, peering through the black gauze. "The mother looks trashed. Aren't they from, like, Iowa?"

"A kind word for everyone," I said. "Ohio. They buried their daughter yesterday. You should say hi to them. Are you nervous?"

"Poor things. Yeah, I'm half-thinking there's a second creep out there waiting to get me."

"Maximum force tonight," said Thuggee. "Look." He held up a black aluminum baseball bat. "I will be showing this to the crowd."

"Thuggee wanted to bring a machete," said Naz. "But I said he'd end up cutting off his foot or my hand when the music got good to him."

"We'll have Jutta's guy Siggy onstage too," I told K-Jen. "Don't worry. Everyone here tonight loves us."

"The human part of me is scared," mused K-Jen. "But the career part is bummed that I'm not the new vlogger on *Buzz*. Didn't Leni say I could go next after Cammy?"

"Maybe, but, you know, they're rethinking it all. They picked an engineer for now, I looked at him on the web today. He's an employee of Veeter's down in Watsonville. Henry Nunez? Chief technologist at a company called

Membrain Products. I guess Veeter figures the exposure could help the Membrain stock. They're thinking about an exponential growth rate, like distributing a million vlog rings in the next couple of months, if you can believe that. For the ultimate reality show."

"Why show a million people when they could have shown *me?*" said K-Jen, actually serious. She was absorbing the rock-diva thing really fast.

"At least Rubber Rick is webcasting our show," I said. "You'll get your fame soon. Washer Drop is riding a spike, too." On the inside, I was thinking my own thoughts about Henry Nunez. I'd watched Alma, Lulu, and Leni talking to Nunez in his vlog. Nunez seemed like a genuinely nice guy, friendly and intelligent. Alma had been flirting with him in her generalized cast-bread-upon-the-waters fashion, and Nunez had casually asked her out to dinner. To my relief she'd turned him down. But she'd left the door open for a follow-up invitation. Alma would know that Nunez could soon be a high-tech billionaire. And the guy definitely wanted a girlfriend. On the vlog, after Alma had turned Nunez down, Lulu had pushed in and *she'd* had dinner with Nunez—computer science lug Lulu with her plaid schoolgirl skirt, big red lips, and messy bangs—and Leni had gotten really mad about it. I hadn't gotten around to checking how Lulu's date with Nunez and fight with Leni had worked out. Things were happening too fast.

"Jutta's here," said Rubber Rick, breaking my reverie. He hurried to the front of the club.

Right after he left, two people pushed backstage. A straight-looking man and woman, dressed in nearly identical black outfits: jeans, turtlenecks, and leather jackets. I'd seen them yesterday; they'd been at Cammy's funeral. At the time, I'd thought they might be cops.

"Bela Kis?" said the woman in that certain tone. She was short and intense, with dark lips.

"Don't tell me you're going to arrest me," I said. "Is this about Veeter's paracomputer?"

"National Security Agency," said the guy, showing a badge. He had a wobbly halo of curly hair; he was a bit older. "I'm agent Kenny Jones and this is agent Mary Smith. We're from the government and we're here to help you." He chuckled at the old line, showing his teeth in a smile.

"Please don't bust him," said Naz. "We're about to play a gig."

"We know that," said Mary Smith. She had oval black-framed glasses and she wore her dark hair in a ragged shag. "You guys rock. Can you three clear out and let us talk secret stuff with Bela?"

"We can perform an equipment check," said Thuggee. "Unless you want them to be gone, Bela?" He hefted his bat, looking like he'd enjoy using it.

"Think of us as backup security," said Kenny Jones, flashing that winning grin again. His irregular teeth gave him an honest look. "No worries."

K-Jen was still peering through the porthole into the club. "Rubber Rick's leading Jutta into his office. He's drooling on her hoochie-mamma dominatrix-wear. God, he's cheesy. I don't even want to think about why he has that name."

"Do think about it," suggested Naz. "Write a song about him."

"Hipster Love Monkey," suggested K-Jen, breaking into song.

> *Peel my rubber banana,*
> *I'll groom your mangy tail.*

Laughing and joking, my band-mates made their way across the still-dark stage and, prompted by K-Jen, continued over to the bar to introduce themselves to the Vendts, K-Jen acting very sympathetic. She was kinder than she liked to let on.

"What do you guys really want?" I asked the agents, turning my attention back to them.

"Agent Jones and I handle the wack reports for the NSA," said Mary Smith, squinting up at me and adjusting her glasses. "Unexplained phenomena. No stone left unturned. Mostly it's bullshit, but you're a special case. You made our month." She opened her purse and took out a subcompact laptop.

"You talked about aliens a few times on your vlog," said Kenny Jones. "And that popped up in our media filters. No big deal, but then the murder and the Congressman Veeter connection jumped you up the priority scale. So yesterday we took a look at your files."

"Jackpot," said Mary Smith. "Remember when you said, 'I saw flying alien cone shells reflected in my guitar'? It's a go-flag when we hear something that unique. The nut jobs always imagine the same familiar things. I went into your vlog and adjusted the viewpoint so that we were staring into your chrome guitar from the same angle as you, zoomed it up a little, and *yeah*."

She clicked an icon on her laptop's screen to start a slow-motion view of my chrome guitar at the San Jose show. The image was dim, warped, grainy. At first it was hard to read, but then it popped into focus for me: the dark night sky, the oval faces of the crowd, and hovering above them were the two big cone shells covered with the down-pointing orange and white triangles in patterns like rivulets, their alien stalk eyes staring out the screen at me.

"So they're real," I said, letting out a long breath. I looked at the two agents, seeing them as people instead of as cops. "Any idea why the aliens are only visible in mirrors?"

"I imagine they're projecting virtual images of themselves," said Kenny. "And the images are maybe out of phase with our reality? But a mirror-reflection swings them into synch. I might as well confess that I'm a mathematician too." He patted my knee and gave me a damp smile, licking his upper lip. "We have more in common than you think." A federal agent was cruising me?

"We have another video," said Mary. "But we're not sure if—"

"Not sure if you can handle it," chimed in Kenny. "It's of Cammy Vendt."

"Show me," I said grimly. "I want to know."

"We went into the vlogs that Ms. Vendt's ring posted after her death," said Mary. "Watching for reflections." She glanced over at me. I nodded again.

The little screen popped up the very image that was most deeply engraved on my mind: inert Cammy with her blood trails woven across the road like the trunks of heavenly trees. The viewpoint zoomed in on her sunglasses lying beside her. I saw a tiny pale flicker in the one unshattered lens. The zoom increased; the pixels got blocky. I saw cone shells again, two of them, the same ones as before, I recognized the branching patterns of triangles on their shells. They were hovering over Cammy's nearly severed neck. Drinking the blood?

I felt a pain in my fingers; I was squeezing one hand with the other very hard. My breath was coming fast and shallow. Kenny patted my shoulder.

The cone shell snails were clearer than in the other video. Each of them had a striped breathing tube like a clam's siphon. Below the siphons were stalk eyes mounted on either side of a mouth snout. A slender red tentacle extended from each mouth like an unbelievably long tongue: thick at the base, thin at the tip. These tendrils were, horribly, reaching into Cammy's neck, pushing into her brain through her slashed-open spinal cord.

"That's enough," I said, my stomach heaving.

"I think they were carrying out some kind of anatomical investigation," said Kenny, closing the display.

"Or maybe they were stealing her soul," I said bleakly. "This is all my fault, you know. The alien cone shells came from Haut to me. And Cammy wouldn't have died if I hadn't left her at Paul's. I should have loved her while I had the chance."

I heard loud thumping from the stage. Naz adjusting his drums. I ran my hands over my face, trying to shake off the new images, trying to bring back my focus. The agents stood there watching me.

"Go away," I said.

"Here's a laser pointer," said Mary, handing me an object like a pen. "If you see aliens at any time tonight, beam this at them. Kenny and I would really really like to talk with them."

Kenny hefted his briefcase. "I've got an electric-net-gun in here. Rangers use them for mountain lions. We figure there's a chance that we might be able to trap the cone images and rotate them into solidity."

There was something very odd about these two. "You're not from the NSA at all, are you?"

"Trust us," said Kenny with that bogus toothy smile again. I heard Jutta's growly voice out on the stage, arguing with K-Jen about who should stand where.

"Thanks," I said, shoving the pointer into my pants pocket. "But I can't think about your problems now, guys. Whoever you are, whatever you want. I'm on."

"If—if the aliens help you off Earth," said Mary Smith, taking my sleeve and staring into my eyes. "Take us with you."

I pushed past her onto the stage, hungry for the music.

I'd like to say the show was a triumph, but there were problems. Thuggee had forgotten about setting up monitor speakers, so we couldn't hear ourselves very well. With no monitors, the sound seemed to disappear into the club like water in sand. I couldn't even tell if I was on-key. After limping through the first song, I stopped the show for a few minutes so we could set up extra speakers pointing back at the band.

And then we tried "Leaf Blower Man." What with having just revisited Cammy's murder vlog, I had trouble on this song too. My voice was cracking so much that I couldn't do the choruses. My fingers were shaky; I screwed up the chords.

All along, Jutta's beat had been leaden and a bit off, but it wasn't till the next number that I realized just how loaded she was. It was like she'd sent a radio-controlled robot to stand in for her, dressed in thigh-high boots and a leather bathing suit. I went over to her and pumped the neck of my guitar, urging her to pick up the pace. She ignored me, rocking to her own rhythm, frozen-faced, her chrome eyes reflecting the room. At least I wasn't seeing any cone shells in the reflections. The "agents" Kenny and Mary were stationed right in front of the stage.

To get some energy, I led the band into our AntiCrystal cover, and that finally woke Jutta. She bared her sharp teeth in a smile, left the smile in place, and growled the words of "Crying Chainsaw Clown," playing a funeral dirge that accelerated into a rocket launch. The song was very East European, very metal, deeply good. Jutta plowed on past the ending and we stretched out, getting into a groove for the first time tonight, the music meshing like the wheels and levers of a locomotive. We wrapped up the number with multiple repetitions of its psychotic chorus.

Crying chainsaw clown—her head is on the ground.
Crying chainsaw clown—my head is on the ground.
Crying chainsaw clown—your head is on the ground.
Crying chainsaw clown! Crying chainsaw clown! Crying chainsaw clown!

The cartoony, English-as-a-second-language lyrics seemed uncannily powerful to me tonight, and for the first time ever I was able to break my voice into the heavy-metal falsetto register, screaming my heart out like AntiCrystal's Wacław Smorynski.

Some kook started to climb on stage right around then, but when he saw the way Thuggee and Siggy came for him, he hopped back to the floor no doubt. Siggy was a smooth-muscled athlete, wonderfully tan. He looked like a leather shark with legs. And Thuggee was truly ready to bust a head.

We played a lighter number, and then I made an announcement.

"We're here tonight to honor the memory of Cammy Vendt. All the profits from this show will go into a special Cammy Fund at the Fugue Music Network, to help out other struggling musicians. And if you can donate a little extra money, Rubber Rick's got a bunch of buckets set up along the bar. I only knew Cammy for a little while, but she was—she was a bright spirit. She was smart and together and beautiful and she rocked. We're gonna close this set with one of the songs that Cammy loved to play. But first I'd like to tell you that Cammy's parents are in the house. Let's show them how we feel about their girl."

The clapping and cheering went on for quite a while, and segued into a chant of Cammy's name. Her parents were standing by the bar, smiling and crying, Klaus's arm around Dagmar's shoulders. As the chanting died down, Naz whacked his drum, I struck a chord, and we were into

"Oil Pig." It was good. Jutta was on it, channeling Cammy, fresh and bouncy instead of decadent and monumental.

And then the set was over and Rubber Rick brought up the lights. Thuggee was hugging K-Jen, holding up her hand, and Naz stepped forward, grabbing K-Jen's other hand. The crowd was clapping. I wanted to go talk with Cammy's parents, but right then I noticed Cochon and Svaart pushing towards the stage, Cochon holding the dreaded papers. On a sudden inspiration, I aimed my laser pointer at them so that the red dot played across Cochon's bald dome.

Whump! A sparking metal net settled over Cochon and Svaart, making them jump and shout. Kenny Jones was in a firing stance, his legs well separated and his arms cradling a heavy tube-gun. Apparently it held another round, for he was turning his head my way, wanting for me to signal another target . . .

But by then I was gone—out the back door, in my squinty whale, driving to Chinatown.

I left my surf wagon in the beat old Vallejo Street Parking Garage at the border between Chinatown and the mostly Italian North Beach. Just a block from the Tang Fat Hotel.

It was nearly one in the morning by now. You could have fired a cannon down Stockton Street, it looked that deserted. Up ahead was another pedestrian, a tall, ungainly woman bundled up in a cheap black cloth coat and carrying a couple of shopping bags. Her head was swathed in a dark kerchief with gold Chinese characters on it.

As it happened, she too was headed for the Tang Fat Hotel. This was a stroke of good luck: I could follow her in without having to try and rouse the super. I stepped up my pace so as to reach the tiled steps of the rooming house right on the woman's heels. Not turning to look at me, she bent over the doorknob, awkwardly scrabbling her key into the lock. Some of her hair showed under her kerchief: black and coarse.

"I have a friend staying here," I said in my halting Chinese. Although the tall woman didn't answer, she allowed me to push into the hallway after her. It was lit by the dimmest imaginable bulb in the ceiling fixture, maybe three watts. I headed up the stairs after the woman. I hadn't yet glimpsed her face. I noticed a nice smell of warm food trailing from her tattered shopping bags. I realized that I was quite hungry.

I must have been following the woman too closely, for halfway up the stairs she paused and swung her leg backwards as if trying to kick me in the face. "Excuse me," I said in Chinese. She cast a quick glance down at me, her face shrouded, a sparkle of light catching one of her eyes. And then she made a muffled sound that sounded like a giggle. God forbid that she was expecting me to make romantic advances! She turned away and continued stomping up the stairs.

We reached the third floor landing together. The kerchiefed women went to the far end of the hall, paused by a doorway, looked back at me, and crooked her finger. She was very definitely laughing.

"What's wrong with you?" I demanded in Mandarin.

"No speak Chinese," said the woman, pushing back her kerchief.

"Roland!" I exclaimed, recognizing my thesis adviser. He grinned. This was the first time I'd seen him since the Summit Psychiatric Center, and the stay seemed to have done him some good. He actually seemed to be in a good mood.

"You're just in time for supper," he told me, knocking on the door. Paul Bridge opened the heavy dead-bolt to let us in.

The room was a refitted broom closet with a quality lock—the lock being perhaps the main selling feature for a room in this kind of place. The room was so cramped that the door couldn't fully open without hitting the short, narrow bed set against the opposite wall. There was no window. The sole light was another of those three-watt bulbs in the ceiling. The floor was dirty brown and black linoleum. In addition to the flimsy bed the room held a rusty triangular metal stool and a second bed, folded in two and squashed behind the door against the left wall. Paul's few possessions were tidily arranged in his Stanford duffel bag on the right.

The three of us sat down side by side on Paul's thin foam mattress, Haut in the middle with the bags of food in his lap. The shiny teapot with the paracomputer rested upon Paul's stool, connected by a cable to the laptop on the floor beneath it.

"Glad you showed up," said Paul, handing me a plastic fork and a styrofoam box of warm ravioli. He and Haut each got the same. In addition, we had garlic bread, some tiramisu, braised greens, a bottle of red wine, and a couple of artichokes, everything shaded gray in the dim light.

"The midnight feast of the mad mathematicians," said Haut, starting to chuckle again. "An esoteric ritual of the arcane cult." Maybe he was a little *too* cheerful. You never knew with him.

"S'good," I said with my mouth full. "So what's up?"

"We've been trying to make money," said Paul. "Speculating. Roland's been staying here too."

"I'm the runner," said Haut, gesturing at his long blue dress. It had sailor-style white piping on the lapels. "Disguised to blend in." I could see now that he was wearing yellowish pancake makeup in addition to his blunt-cut black wig.

"Oh, nobody would give you a second look," I said.

"I fooled *you*, Kis. On the stairs you were trying to peek up my skirt."

"Imagine my disappointment," I said. "And all you've been doing is speculating? That's what my cousin Gyula would have done. How lowbrow. How middle-aged. I posted a rewrite of your axioms for the Gobrane, Paul. Plus a plan for a people's paracomputer. There's some errors I was hoping you'd help me fix."

"Didn't see the post," said Paul. "Roland and I've been doing other stuff too. Working on a paper about his paradox. Much further-out than anything I'd be doing at Stanford."

"That's more like it. And don't forget we want to change the past. Oh, speaking of Gyula, he thinks I should give him three hundred thousand dollars. Tell me how much you've made. One million? Twenty? A half-billion?"

The two were quiet for a minute, and then Haut spoke up. "We lost all our savings and we've run up about ten thousand dollars apiece in credit card debt," he said. "It's been a complete fiasco."

"But now you can help us set things right," Paul told me, hugely biting into his tiramisu. "I strongly suspect that we've been using the wrong morphonic model. Roland kept changing it."

"What market have you been speculating in?" I asked.

"Chip futures," said Paul. "Just like Veeter. That's the only market we have a good codec for. The codec that Veeter figured out. And we already had all his data on the laptop, and the model that you wrote, so what the hey. But it didn't work long enough for us to really get ahead of the game. The accuracy kept going down."

"And then I improved on your model," said Haut. "And our losses got worse."

"Were you updating the full terabyte of chip-industry data?" I asked.

The two mathematicians looked at each other.

"My understanding was that it would be enough to just update the current ticker prices," said Haut in a small voice.

"Pinheads. You've been playing the market for three days solid—and doing it wrong?"

"Two and a half days," said Paul. "You have to help us recoup." He picked up the laptop and began clicking windows, dribbling food on the keys. "So, okay, it costs two hundred dollars to download an up-to-the-minute version of the full chip-industry data set. But our bank and credit cards are maxxed out. Give me your bank card number, Bela, and we'll hit the chip futures one more time, okay?"

"I don't have a bank card," I quickly replied.

"Bullshit," said Paul, totally not going for it. "Give me the number and I'll tell you about Roland's paradox. And maybe I'll look at your crappy, broken axioms. When did you post them?"

"Monday night after I got stoned with my band."

"Oh, forgive us for not getting on that immediately, Kis," said Haut in his sarcastic professor tone. "Paul and I are planning a major paper on my paradox. I seem to be having an *annus mirabilis*. Perhaps in the fall I'll have time to see if anything can be made of your little fantasia."

Out in the hall a woman was screaming in Chinese. From what I could make out, she was a drunk hooker who'd been shorted of her pay. Now she began kicking the door across the way. The door crashed open, a man's voice roared, and a bottle shattered. A slap, sobbing, another door slam, silence.

"Your unsavory landsmen, Bela," said Paul. "You marooned me in a real dump."

"We didn't want Veeter to find you, remember?"

"I wonder about that," said Paul. "Maybe he knows exactly where we are. Maybe he's playing cat and mouse."

"I wonder too," I echoed uneasily. "For sure he'd be interested in what we're doing. He'd probably be glad we're still working with his paracomputer. I think he only cut us off so that we wouldn't taint his reputation any further. And I guess Doakes's staff doesn't want us Humelocke Common Grounders in on their new technology. If Van could quietly watch us, he would."

"Look, Paul, the fresh data's downloaded and ready to unlock," said Haut, watching the computer screen. "Cough up your bank card, Kis. All we'll charge on it is two hundred for the data-access fee, and two thousand for our new speculation nut."

"Oh, all right," I said. It would, after all, be nice to have some real money. "But let Paul do the clicking. Don't forget to roll back to my original model, Paul. The way it was before Roland spoiled it." I took out my wallet and told him my bank card number and my password. "I got some money from Leni, but after renewing my lease, I only have a few hundred dollars in my account," I said. "The good news is that I'm allowed up to three thousand on instant credit."

Paul clicked away for a few minutes, fiendishly buying and selling chip futures. The membrane in the teapot glowed and danced: scrolls and gliders, stripes and spots, jaggy blocks and washes of color—like a cartoon of an inside-out dream. Whenever I could tear my eyes away from the Gobrane, I checked Paul's progress on the laptop screen. So far so good. But our margins for error were getting smaller with each transaction. The reliability of our data set was beginning to fade. I could see this physically on the Gobrane. The patterns were less crisp than before.

"We've got a million," announced Paul. "Most optimal. Credited to Bela's account."

"Good," said Haut. "We'll share it three ways. But keep going. Go for more!"

"Don't," I said. "The data's too soft now."

"So get fresh data," said Haut. "Why stop?"

We were interrupted by another outburst of noise: A man pounding on our door and yelling, "Where my nice girl?" He was, I gathered, a Chinese pimp. His intense, high-pitched voice sounded vaguely familiar.

"Not here," I shouted. "Across the hall."

The man switched to the other door. We heard the door fly open. The same man as before began to yell. We heard the thud of a fist, the breaking of a chair, a woman's harangue, and then the new man's tenor voice quietly laying down the law.

"Never mind them," said Haut. "Go on, Paul."

I was beginning to feel uneasy. "Show me Roland's big paradox now," I said. "We can always make more money later. It's like you're using a beautiful scarf to shine shoes. Show me the paradox, and then let's get out of this place."

"Here's the paradox," said Paul, digging out another of his neatly written lined-paper pads.

"Oh, come on, dog, I want a demo, not a freaking math paper. I'm not an academic anymore. Can we make the paradox *run* is what I want to know. Can we really tear a hole in spacetime?"

"We've been, uh, hanging back on that," said Haut. "How far is your car from here?"

"Couple of blocks."

"I'd suggest that before we try any experiment, we be fully prepared to relocate," said Haut. "The demo might cause a disturbance. But, hell yes, I want to see it, too. Give me that laptop, Paul. I'll download our model onto the paracomputer. And the codec is trivial. It's a one-line program, Bela."

"Like a liar paradox?" I asked. "A sentence that says, 'This sentence is false'?" Across the hall things had quieted down.

"More or less," said Haut. "A program that tells the Gobrane to predict the opposite of what it predicts it'll predict. It's akin to calculating the sum of an alternating infinite series: one minus one plus one minus one plus one forever—does it sum to zero or to one? It's not so much the potential for self-contradiction that matters, you understand, it's the divergent regress of self-reference. You've heard of the Margolus-Levitin theorem?"

"Barely," I said. "I heard Veeter mention it when he talked about your paradox."

"You told him about my paradox, Paul?" Haut was instantly outraged.

"It was all under nondisclosure, Roland. It's not like he's gonna publish it."

"Easy for you to say with your fat grant," fumed Haut. "You're giving away my leverage! I should crush you like a—"

"Academic fame doesn't matter anymore, Roland," said Paul. "We've got money from the market, and as for power—we're close to altering reality! And to think I was so worried about getting back for a meeting with my department chair."

"Can one of you finish telling me what we're talking about?" I demanded.

"There's a maximum computational rate that any limited region of space can perform at any given energy level," said Haut, composing himself. "That's the Margolus-Levitin limit. It's high—maybe ten-to-the-fiftieth bit-flips per second on your teapot paracomputer—but I've proved that in the process of trying to, as it were, unpredict itself, a paracomputer running my paradoxical program will overshoot the limit. A *digital computer* has a built-in maximum capacity, but there's nothing other than the geometry of space to stop a naturally occurring *analog paracomputation* from growing without bound. And we know from Einstein that space is elastic. I predict that, in order to preserve the Margolus-Levitin condition while expanding without limit, my paradoxical paracomputation will deform the Gobrane's space. A spherical volume around the Gobrane will bulge out into hyperspace and—"

"And if the bulge touches another sheet of spacetime, we get a tunnel!" shouted Paul excitedly. He was kneeling on the floor, stashing his few possessions in his little red bag.

"All this from a one-line program?" I asked.

"It doesn't even have to be a program that comes in via a codec," said Haut. "We should be able to initiate the behavior on the Gobrane by electrically zapping it in a particular spot. The paradoxical point. Paul and I calculated its location this morning in terms of the fixed point of a matrix self-map. The eigenvector. The paradoxical point's coordinates involve our old friend the golden ratio. Delightful. That's part three of our paper."

"Sweet," I said, thrown back into my old admiration of Haut's mathematical technique.

With all his gear packed, Paul was compulsively arranging the trash, nesting the containers and fitting them into the empty shopping-bag. A spare steamed artichoke remained from our meal.

"This can be our test particle," he told Haut, fastening his wristwatch around the plump gray-green bud. "And I'll throw in my watch to check for temporal effects."

"Surreal," I marveled. "So *what's* going to happen to the artichoke?"

"Nothing," said a voice from the laptop computer. Veeter's face appeared in a window on the screen. "I'm not going to let you maniacs do this."

"Are you live?" I asked the window. "Not a tape, not a simulation?"

"It's the real me," said Veeter. "Didn't it ever occur to you so-called geniuses that I'd be watching you through the laptop I gave you? Hanging back and learning from you? Oh, and I enjoyed that broken little paracomputer recipe you posted Monday night, Bela. But don't do that again. Frank Ramirez's staff wanted to have you shot. I had to spend some of my political capital to save you."

"You're talking about the vice president?" I said uneasily. "Why would he care?"

"From now on, the paracomputer is top-secret classified, and talking about it is a treasonable offense warranting termination with extreme prejudice, as they say. I can't afford to protect you again. The fun's over. And as for this crazy experiment you're about to pull, if that were to cause any major damage, it would be terrible publicity for—"

As surely as if I had a prediction machine embedded

in my brain, I saw what was coming. Veeter was going to send a signal to the laptop, a signal that would pass through the connector cable and disable the Gobrane. With a seamless, smooth gesture that was utterly one with the inspiration to act, I snaked out my hand and disconnected the laptop from the little brass teapot.

"I don't know you guys anymore," said Veeter, and with a slight popping sound, the laptop screen blanked out.

"You screwed things up again, Kis," said Haut, blindly tapping at the laptop's keys. "Why'd you yank the connector? The laptop's gone dead. And did you hear what Veeter said? Now I'll never get a grant from him."

"Ramirez wants to kill Bela?" said Paul, more to the point. Across the hall a cell phone rang twice and stopped.

"Let's run the experiment right now," I said. "Duh, Roland, the reason I unplugged the teapot was so Veeter couldn't disable the Gobrane." I peeked into the pot. The colorful membrane was as lively as ever. "Hurry and zap it like you two said. At the paradoxical point. Maybe those flying alien cone shell snails can help us."

"They're real?" said Haut, growing pale. "The doctor said I'd only imagined them. I don't want this!" He got to his feet and made shooing gestures with his hands, backing towards the left side of the room. "You're a menace, Kis!"

The pounding on our door resumed.

"Bela Kis!" shouted the same high-pitched voice as before, and now I realized who was out there: Veeter's muscleman, Big Owen, also known as Yuan from Shanghai. He'd be in here quite soon—to kill me, or just to confiscate the Gobrane?

I feared the worst. I yanked the laptop's power cord from the wall, took out my pocket-knife, cut the cord in two, and stripped the insulation off the wires leading from the plug. My hands were shaking, and it took longer than I liked. "Stick the plug back in the outlet," I told Paul, handing it to him. "Then zap the Gobrane where Roland said."

"Don't," said Haut from behind me. "No cone shells."

I spread my arms, blocking Haut from reaching Paul and the magic teapot.

"Do it," I told Paul. "Otherwise Owen breaks my head."

"I'm down with this," said Paul leaning over the Gobrane. "Be cool, Roland."

The door was shaking under Owen's fists, but still it held. That dog across the hall was barking again, and the woman and man were out there too, discussing every move in rapid Chinese.

With a quick, precise gesture, Paul touched the bare-tipped wires to certain spot upon the elliptical Gobrane: near the teapot's spout and a bit to one side. The para-doxical point. A spark jumped; our little ceiling light died; there were exclamations from the hall.

Behind me, Haut moaned.

The Gobrane glowed. A nested pattern of red and blue raced from the zapped spot to the edges and back, the oval patterns moving at uneven speeds, overtaking each other to form fringes of green and yellow. The core of the pattern was alternately red and blue. Yes and no. Zero and one. The Gobrane was trying to predict the opposite of what it predicted.

Owen had begun ramming our door with his shoulder. Although our fine, strong dead bolt was holding up, I could hear the wood around it splintering. In the dark it was hard to be sure how soon the door would give way.

The flicker of the Gobrane doubled and redoubled its frequency. Soon my crude human eyes could distinguish only a steady mauve ellipse. Something odd was happening to the noises from the hall—the thudding, the barking, the Chinese commentary—the sounds were slowing down. As if the air were turning to honey, to cough syrup.

"I better back off now," said Paul, placing his wrist-watch-wearing artichoke upon the open lid of the teapot. "Only another couple of seconds till it passes the flat-space Margolus-Levitin limit. And then it'll bulge."

"They'll eat me!" cried Haut. Paul stepped back to my side of the room.

And then a lot of things happened. The mauve ellipse within the teapot rose up in a bulge, with the artichoke wobbling on top of it; the bulge ballooned into a ten foot puffball of light, resting like a genie upon the tea-pot. Where the puffball touched the ceiling, the building materials crumbled away. Scraps of lath and plaster dropped through the air, silhouetted like dark snow against the glowing lavender light. The closer the flakes were to the light, the faster they seemed to move.

Looking into the ball was like staring into a tunnel. At the far end were green islands and floating blue—lakes? Wiggling seas of water against a clear sky, with dozens of lush islands to explore. The ball was the door to another world. A cord like a vine or a kelp stalk stretched along one side of the tunnel from the other world to our own.

The far end of the stalk disappeared into one of the seas and the stalk's near end tapered to a point on the left side of the ball.

Peering deep into the tunnel, I saw that our test artichoke had fallen through; it was dwindling in size as it approached the other end; it was a tiny speck amidst the far floating archipelago. A distant triangular shape darted at the artichoke, then snapped to attention. It aligned itself towards us, pondered for a fraction of a second, then flew decisively our way, growing larger as it approached.

I could see the brown and white triangular markings upon the creature's shell, its wavy mollusk foot, its bunched eyes, snout, and siphon. Yes, the approaching alien was a flying cone shell snail.

With the strength of a madman Roland Haut clawed past me, literally climbing over my shoulders. He threw himself towards the magic teapot, perhaps hoping to break the link to unknown other world.

Just after Haut launched himself, the hall door gave way and flew open, thudding into the bed, covering my thesis advisor from view. I heard Haut's drawn-out, dwindling whoop, more ecstatic than desperate. Had he fallen into the tunnel? At the same time, the man who'd broken our door began a lurid kung-fu scream—and abruptly stopped.

The mauve light went out; at the same time the room echoed with a sound like a cannon shot or a clap of thunder. The floor rocked and vibrated as if from an earthquake. In the sudden dark, something clattered against the ceiling. I felt an updraft of wind. And then the room was still. I heard excited voices in the hallway. In the distance, sirens were approaching.

"Wow," said Paul, leaning against me.

"Come on!" I said. "We gotta bail!"

We got to our feet and half-closed the door. Most of our ceiling was gone, with pinkish light coming in from the low night clouds of San Francisco. Tang Fat tenants were milling in the hall, questioning and discussing. But there was no sign of Haut, and no sign of Owen.

Paul had a little flashlight stored in his tidy red duffel bag, and he knew exactly where to find it. He made me wait an endless fifteen seconds while he shone it around the bed and floor, looking for the magic teapot. But it, too, had vanished.

And then we were down the fire stairs and out the rear door into a stinking, offal-strewn alley that led back out to Stockton Street, now crowded with excited locals. Some gestured at the sky, some pointed at us. A cop car and a fire truck were blaring their horns and loudspeakers in front of the building, and still more sirens were on the way.

We trotted around the corner to the Vallejo Street Garage and hustled up to level three where I'd left the squinty whale. Parked next to it was, somehow unsurprisingly, Gyula in the white Hornswoggle limo. This time he was alone.

"Where's Owen?" he asked.

"I couldn't say." I noticed that he still had a laptop and the paracomputer on the seat next to him. They were both turned off.

"Veeter says you've been cut loose," Gyula told me. "On your own now. He's not gonna sue you. And there's no murder contract on you just yet. But if you talk about— what was the word?"

"Paracomputation."

"If you mouth off about that, or post anything about it on the web—" Gyula drew his finger across his throat.

"This is for real?" I said.

Gyula shrugged, his stubbled face dark in the dim light. He got out of his car and came close. The nearby sirens echoed in the parking structure's concrete walls.

"Talk to me," he murmured.

"You're still looking for a payoff?"

"Three hundred kay."

"Don't got," I lied. "I can get you a hundred. And you give me that little magic teapot. Tell Veeter somebody stole it from your car. You don't know who. Don't tell him till he notices. Later tomorrow."

"A hundred fifty, and I'll throw in my pistol. I lost that too, say. I got drunk in Chinatown. Wasted on O. Rolled by the lotus blossoms. Grieving for Owen. Plenty of places open this late, if you know where to look."

"Good deal, Gyula. I'll get the money to you later."

"Transfer it to this account by tomorrow," said Gyula, writing some digits on a card and handing it over. "Under the name of Sino-Ugric Services."

"You got it."

"Thanks, Cousin Bela." Gyula gave me a wolfish smile and headed out of the garage on foot.

It was almost four in the morning now. Paul and I tooled south on Route One, heading for Cruz, two surfboards in the back of my beater, a nine millimeter pistol in my pants pocket, and a magic lamp in the glove compartment.

FIVE

mathematicians from galaxy z

We made a pit stop just south of SF in the gritty beach town called Corona. I visited a cash machine by a Monogrub burger place. I really did have a million dollars in my bank account now. I withdrew my daily maximum, three hundred bucks. And then I tanked up my car while Paul got some supplies. "I'm taking Alma surfing in Big Sur today," I told him as the squinty whale lumbered back onto the highway. "I'll drop you off in Palo Alto."

"No way," said Paul. "I want to see Alma too. I want to go to Big Sur. We can run Haut's Paradox again. Make a new hypertunnel."

"What about your big meeting with the chairman this afternoon? Can't miss *that*, Paul."

He gave me a haughty look. "I'm beyond this Earth's academic games. The hypertunnel changes everything. I'll come to Sur with you and we'll make a tunnel we can travel through."

"But I'd like to see Alma on my own. It's been a few days. I want to work on—on our relationship." With any luck, I'd slip into her bed in the garage before daybreak and we'd make love.

"Oh, I won't interfere," said Paul, still taking that lofty tone. "We need to stick together for now." He turned his head and stared out the rear window. "Is something following us? In the air?"

I half-suspected he was trying to spook me. "You think the cone shell came through the tunnel and stayed?" I said, firmly keeping my eyes on the foggy road. Steep cliffs dropped to the Pacific on my right.

"I think she ate Owen and maybe Haut and then she flew out through that hole in the ceiling," said Paul. "With the tunnel closed, she's trapped here. She's probably hoping we'll open up another tunnel so she can fly back."

"She?"

"I picked up a vibe that this particular alien is female," said Paul. "From the little bit of her that I saw. Owen opened the door at just the wrong time."

"I bet he thought so, too," I said.

"The tunnel didn't stay open for very long," mused Paul, off on his own train of thought. "A hyperdimensional tunnel like that needs a lot of mass at our end to stabilize it. When we make the next one, we should set up the paracomputer in, like, a cave. Or under a heavy bridge. So we'll have plenty of time to go through and look around. You know any places like that?"

"Miller Beach," I said. "There's an amazing natural bridge in the water. A massive craggy stone haystack with a little square passage through it. I've always thought it's like a door to another world. You see postcards of it. We could set our paracomputer to running Haut's Paradox on a ledge inside that natural bridge, paddle out past it, turn around, and when the tunnel opens up we surf through!

Crunkabunka, dude." I paused, thinking of Alma again. "Hypothetically speaking, that is. But are you really sure about missing your big meeting with the chairman?"

"I'm telling you it doesn't *matter* if I miss the damned meeting," said Paul. "If we make it though the tunnel, we'll never see this sheet of reality again. We'll surf out to a higher level of existence, locate an alternate Earth, and surf back to that one. Instead of back to this one. Cammy can be alive there, Bela. We can undo the murder."

The ultimate adventure. And a release from my guilt. The cliffs had leveled out; a meadow sloped down to the sea on our right. The squinty whale's headlights were carving white cones into the fog. I checked the rearview mirrors. No sign of a flying cone shell alien. Was Paul spinning wild plans just to get another shot at my girl?

"Here's the turnoff for Palo Alto," I said. "I still think maybe I should drop you off. I don't want you near Alma."

"Don't be so uptight, Bela. I accept that Alma's decided on you. I'm not gonna try to snatch her away." He snickered ever so softly. "Of course if she *asks* me to—"

"You give us some privacy when we get there, you hear me, you gunjy freak? We're gonna sleep for awhile. I'll get in her bed and you—you can stretch out in the back of the station wagon."

"What am I, your dog?"

"Try to think about somebody besides yourself for once in your life, you autistic prick."

"I'm thinking about saving Cammy," said Paul.

It was still pitch dark outside. I couldn't drive very fast. Paul had his window open and I could hear the sound of the surf. "What makes you so sure that we can alter reality?" I asked after a time.

"Did you notice the vine thing that was growing through the tunnel? Off to the left?"

"Yeah."

"I figure it was a connector cable. Something at the other end is passing the code for our universe through that cord. Universal dynamics says that all of spacetime can be computed from a simple seed, you know. All the future and all the past are determined by a small pattern that's fed into something like a cellular automaton rule. Change the tiniest tip-ass bit of that seed, and everything's different over here."

"Jump to conclusions much?"

"I've been thinking about this for awhile, Bela. And the patterns of light on the Gobrane confirmed my theory. I was watching them closely. The fact that those elliptical bands remained in an eccentric configuration, and that their successive widths were in the golden ratio—I strongly suspect there's a morphon-theoretic proof that *therefore* the cable is indeed the carrier of our cosmic seed."

"No doubt," I said absently. I was too tired to let Paul frogmarch me off to Mathland. But one thing was nagging at me. "What about that million dollars we'd be leaving behind us here? Should we bring it with us?"

"It's hard to run with the weight of gold," said Paul. "The million was Roland's thing. I was just interested in figuring out how to *get* it. We can always get more, wherever we wind up. We're mathematicians."

"I'll pay off Gyula in any case," I said. "For the good karma. And maybe give the rest to someone worthy?"

"Whoever you like," said Paul. "Except my parents. They couldn't handle it." We were nearing the outskirts of Santa Cruz. It was about five a.m., with a faint grayness in the eastern sky.

Although I'd never been to Alma's house before, I'd checked the route on the web. I found the Ziff compound easily enough: a sandy lot with a single-story stucco house flanked by a little garage with a peaked roof and a concrete driveway holding a Bogoturf-topped panel truck and an oil-dripping motorcycle with a surfboard rack. The garage, where Alma was staying, had a row of tiny, curtained windows in its pull-down door.

I parked in the street, locking the Gobrane in the glove compartment. "Stay," I said to Paul as I got out.

"Whine," he said, dogging my steps.

I felt the weight of Gyula's pistol in my pants pocket. What the hell was I supposed to do with it? I'd never fired a gun in my life. I glanced up through the thick predawn fog, cocking my head to listen. All was calm.

The garage had a regular door on the side. I tapped lightly, and hearing no response, I eased it open and peeked in. The garage was fixed up with furniture and a square of carpeting. Alma was sleeping beneath a cotton blanket on a fold-away double bed across the room. A faintly glowing seashell night-light illuminated the pleasant landscape of her horizontal body.

"I'll crash right here," said Paul, wriggling past me like, yes, a dog and settling himself on an empty daybed just inside the door. A sleeping bag happened to be rolled up on the daybed; before I knew it, Paul had squirmed into the bag, tucked his head between two sofa cushions, and had fallen—or had begun pretending to have fallen—asleep.

I closed the door and undressed. I slid my stuff under an armchair and got in bed with Alma. I spooned up behind her; with a sleepy purr she molded herself against me. A peaceful minute passed and then her head popped up.

"Bela?"

"It's me. Here for our trip to the beach."

She rolled over and kissed me. "I missed you. Are you better now?"

"I guess. The funeral's over. And Paul and I have this plan to—" I thought better of immediately going into the details. "Oh, I'll tell you later. Basically everything's fine. The concert was great. Did you watch it on the web?"

"We don't have a decent link here," said Alma. "Nothing ever works in this house. I'll be glad to get back to Humelocke." She cuddled against me and we kissed again.

Paul let out a sudden sharp snore.

"What's that?" demanded Alma, sitting up and staring at the quilted figure on the day-bed.

"Paul."

"You brought him along? Isn't he supposed to be in Palo Alto? Did you go out of your way to pick him up?"

"Well—he and I were doing some stuff up in the city after the concert last night, and he was begging to come to Big Sur with us, so I thought—"

"He insisted because he misses me so much," said Alma, a little smile playing over her lips. "What am I going to do with you two mathematicians?"

"Stick with me," I said pulling her back down. "And forget Paul. Washer Drop is gonna be humongous. And Veeter's not suing me anymore." I ran my hands under her nightgown. Paul's breathing had switched to a light, steady snoring.

"Don't, Bela. Not with him here."

"If we're quiet he won't notice."

"Well—maybe. You do feel awfully good."

We were almost at the point of no return when Alma's head popped up off the pillow again. "I hear something! Right outside the door! It better not be Pete."

"I don't hear a thing."

I got in one more kiss, but then Alma heard another noise. "Go see what it is, Bela."

"Okay."

There was indeed a sound outside, a stealthy, rhythmic crunch, as of someone tip-toeing across sand. Maybe it was Pete circling the garage, hoping to do a peeping Tom number on his sister? I considered getting the gun out from under the armchair and busting a cap in Pete's face. A moment of pleasure, a lifetime of pain. Don't do it, Bela. I took a deep breath, slipped on my shoes, and went outside naked.

As soon as I opened the door, the crunching stopped. The fog was palely luminous with dawn; I could see all around the yard. Gary Ziff's pumpkin patch was well established, with thick vines, yellow blossoms, green leaves the size of dinner plates, and lovely beads of dew upon the leaves. But nobody was walking around, nobody was hiding behind the garage. Maybe the tilled soil had been shifting on its own. Whatever. I went back inside, pulling the door closed ever so gently so as not to wake Paul.

But Paul was gone from his spot. He was naked in bed with Alma.

"Oh, no *way*!" I said.

Alma giggled, sitting up with the sheet across her breasts, looking perky and jazzed. "Maybe we should—you know." she said. "The three of us. Just this once. I've always wondered how—"

"I am not going to do that," I heard myself say. "Not with my girlfriend. And come on, Paul, you're a good guy, but rolling around naked with you is—"

"If it's okay with Alma, why not?" said Paul. "Do I disgust you?" His expression was earnest and pleading. Vulnerable and yearning. Deeply human.

"Get out of our bed," I said.

"No," said Paul, grabbing the headboard with one hand and the mattress frame with the other.

"Jerk." Rather than fighting him, I simply squeezed into the bed between him and Alma.

"You're so *possessive*, Bela," said Alma with a disappointed little laugh. "I mean—I could tell you boys what to do."

"We're going to sleep," I said, feeling tired and square.

It took awhile for the three of us to drop off, crowded like sardines, Paul too stubborn to leave. I didn't get into my really deep sleep until the sun was up.

I awoke to the sound of arguing. Alma and her father. Oh shit. He was standing at the foot of our bed, glowering, sneering, leering. It was midmorning; a shaft of sun sliced through the room, highlighting the heavy gold chain around Gary Ziff's neck: a flat-linked chain with an X-eyed smiley face medallion hanging in the open collar of Gary's parrot-patterned shirt.

"—in here enjoying a three-way," Gary was saying. "And that's cool, but meanwhile there's a skeleton wrapped in snot right outside. Look at it from my standpoint, Alma. I gotta call the law."

"You're spun," said Alma wearily "As usual. You're not thinking straight. Call the cops and I show them your and Pete's stash. All of it."

"Let us get dressed, Mr. Ziff," said Paul. "Then we'll talk."

"I thought you two boys were on the up and up," said Gary, his teeth flashing through his walrus mustache. "Ph.D.s. Mathematicians. And now you're coming on like the goddamn Manson family." He took a half-step towards us, balling his fists. "If you harm one hair on my little girl's head I'll—"

"Dad, *please*," said Alma, bursting into tears. "Get *out* of here."

"I'll be in the yard," he said, and stepped out, slamming the flimsy door.

"I'm sorry about him," said Alma to me, drying her eyes. "Oh, this is so embarrassing. You have to get me out of here right away." She darted around the room, putting on clothes. For now she was ignoring Paul.

Paul looked over at me, the two of us together in bed. I met his eyes. For a moment it felt like looking in a mirror. We were wearing the same smile. Rueful, embarrassed, amused, eager for the coming day's adventures. You had to love the guy.

"Mr. Ziff's wearing Owen's chain," he said.

"I know," I answered. Over the weeks I'd learned a bit about the habits of cone shell mollusks. Not that the aliens would necessarily behave exactly like South Pacific cone shell snails. But I recalled that, after eating, say, a fish, one of our ordinary cone shells eventually regurgitates any indigestible remains, wrapped in a packet of mucus. "Did you hear the digging in the garden last night?"

"Yeah," said Paul. "I guess she's hiding there."

"Under the sand," I said. "That's how they like to rest. With a siphon sticking out."

"Get dressed," said Alma, at the mirror brushing her hair into two little pigtails. She wasn't really listening to us. "Be ready to defend me."

"For sure," I said. "I'll get you out of here really fast. Next stop Miller Beach. I've got my two surfboards in the squinty whale."

"Will you bring your own board?" Paul asked Alma as he pulled on his pants. "So we have three? I want to try this too."

Alma frowned at him. She was all tidy now, with her makeup in place. "I thought you had a big appointment with your chairman today," she said coldly. "You were talking about it all last week. We'll drop you at the bus station."

"You want to get rid of me?" said Paul.

"Paul, about last night—" Alma shook her head. "That wasn't the real me talking. That was sexual rhetoric. Actually I'm a prude. I'm trying to make a life with Bela. Get it through your head. Bela's the one I've chosen. The decision is final."

"But I have to come along today," insisted Paul. "Bela and I want to try this experiment with the Gobrane. We'll be surfing that square natural bridge at Miller."

"That's true, Alma," I put in. "Paul and I do have a plan."

"Please, Alma," begged Paul. "I'll be good."

"Oh, all right," said Alma, relishing the attention. "One more day with my two lovers. Do you think I'm horrible?"

"You're hot," I said.

"You're the best," said Paul. "I love you."

"Please don't ever say that to me again," responded Alma.

"And remember, after Big Sur we really and truly split. That's my board up on the rafters, Paul. You can carry it. And grab my wetsuit off the peg too. And the yellow bikini."

"Alma!" Gary Ziff's voice was right outside.

"He's so skeevy," whispered Alma. "He's been laid off for a week. Hitting his bug-powder-sinse bong twenty-four/seven. He won't really do anything to us. He's probably leading up to asking us for money. I wonder where he got that gold necklace. It almost looks real. What were you guys saying about it?"

"Your Dad might as well hear the explanation, too," I said, opening the door. "Let's get this over with."

"You go first," said Alma, hanging back.

Gary Ziff was out there alone, his long curly hair hanging down to his shoulders, his bald spot showing in the bright sun. I wondered where his wife and son were. I noticed that both the family vehicles were gone. The neighborhood was very quiet; it was a little past ten a.m. of a dead Thursday morning in June.

"Are you in a cult?" asked Gary, glaring at me. "Or queer? Is that it?"

"Of course," I said, feeling strong and heartless. "I only slept with Alma so I could get at Paul. You like that necklace? Consider it Satan's gift." I scanned the ground and, yes, there beneath one of the pumpkin leaves was a pile of bones with a skull on top. The little bundle was slick with mucus. The half-digested rags of Owen's pants and red tank top lay beneath the bones. The hair on my neck rose, but I kept playing it tough. "You could be next," I told Gary, pointing at the human remains. "Let's bury this crap, and that's the end of it. I'll give you a hundred bucks."

"No," said Alma's father, drawing together whatever dignity he'd once had. "This isn't right. And I don't want you seeing my daughter anymore. Murderer."

"Oh god," said Alma, stepping into the yard. "There really *is* a skeleton?"

"It's Owen," I sighed. "Veeter's muscleman bodyguard? An alien cone shell ate him and spit him out. And your Dad took the gold necklace off the bone stack. Bad karma, Gary."

Gary just looked at me, his eyes tired, bloodshot, sad. It suddenly struck me that he was, after all, a suffering fellow human. A worried father. Not a knock-em-down inflatable Bozo-the-Clown doll.

"You need help," he said quietly.

"You killed Owen?" echoed Alma. She'd never believed in the cone shell aliens. She took a step forward, a step back, put her hand to her mouth. "That's what you did to the *body?* Oh, Bela. Yes, Dad, call the police. Hurry."

"The cone shell is right there!" exclaimed Paul, pointing.

I saw the siphon now, protruding from a dense clump of sunlit pumpkin leaves. It was striped red and white, the size of a man's arm, gently waving, tasting the air. It knew we were here.

"I'll get 911," said Gary, hustling towards the house.

"Don't!" I hissed. "You'll ruin everything!"

Perhaps the alien cone shell heard us, for now with a great sliding of gravel, she lifted up from the pumpkin patch, here for real, no longer a mirror-image. Paul gave a low whoop; Alma moaned. The monster was fully ten feet long. Paul had claimed she was female, and somehow this felt right.

Her shell was a conical spindle, four feet across at one end, and tapering nearly to a point at the other end. The hovering shell was decorated with streamers of overlapping white and reddish-brown triangles, wrapped around it like complex cellular automaton patterns. Protruding from the shell was the alien's snail-like body, irregularly striped in red and white. In front she had an upcurved breathing tube, or siphon. Below the siphon was her mouth tube, with her dark, shiny, watchful stalk-eyes on either side.

As Gary reached the little concrete slab outside his house's back door, the cone shell's mouth opened a bit. A red proboscis emerged like a slender tongue, rapidly growing longer and thinning at its tip. In a flash, the red tendril had stretched a full twenty or thirty feet to find purchase on the back of Gary's neck. I saw a brief puff of whitish vapor, smelled something bitter. Gary dropped to the ground, twitching.

The cone shell sped towards Gary, her proboscis withdrawing into the recesses of her mouth-tube—which was opening up like a funnel, as if to swallow Gary whole. All of this was happening in silence, everything brightly lit by the June sun. Alma was too shocked to scream. She outran the cone shell and threw her body protectively across Gary's. I admired that. I had to help my Alma. I pulled out my pistol and ran at the shell, sick at the thought of killing such a remarkable being, but not knowing what else to do.

"I your friend, Bela," said the alien as I aimed my gun at a spot between her eyes. "No hurt me." The sibilant voice was coming from her mouth tube, as if from an elephant's trunk. She was only a foot or two away from me, floating at my chest level. She smelled of the sea, of decaying meat, and of her alkaloid venom. This was real. I was next to an extraterrestrial. My trigger finger unclenched. I just had to talk to her. Was anyone else watching? I glanced around and saw no neighbors. Everyone in this Cruz neighborhood was at work or surfing or stoned, the tiny lots and houses quietly baking in the mid-day sun.

"Kill it, Bela," said Alma, her arms covering her disabled father. Gary Ziff was on his side, curled into the fetal position with his eyes closed. He'd stopped twitching; he almost looked content.

The cone shell's mouth tube flexed and whistled. "I your friend, too, Alma. My name Rowena. I help you go La Hampa."

"La Hampa?" said Paul, right at my shoulder. "That's those islands we saw at the other end of the tunnel?"

"I live," said Rowena. "Osckar live. Nataraja live La Hampa. Nataraja jellyfish make your world. You meet jellyfish she make your way."

Rowena had saved us from Owen and Gary, and now she wanted to help us pass through the hypertunnel and fix the past! In other words, the cone shell snail was our ally—although there was still the question of whether she'd caused Cammy's death.

"Can you pick up Owen's bones?" I said to Rowena, not quite ready to talk about Cammy, nor to ask what she meant by a Nataraja jellyfish. I reset the gun's safety and shoved it in my pocket. "Otherwise we'll get blamed. Spit them in the ocean or something."

"No," said Rowena, refusing my request. "You come back new world anyhow."

"She means that after we go to, um, La Hampa, we'll return to a parallel world," Paul remarked to me. "Like I said. The new Earth can have a different past. Calm down, Alma." He reached down to pat her shoulder, but she ignored him.

"Bela!" she said accusingly. "That thing killed a man and it poisoned my father!"

"Father like," said Rowena. "Conotoxin."

Gary had indeed relaxed. He lay sprawled across the low stoop, eyes closed, his face turned to the sun. He was smiling. "Come on, Dad," said Alma tugging at him. "Sit up."

Gary shrugged her off, and settled onto his back. He raised his hands and began slowly moving them back and forth, savoring the play of shadows on his eyelids.

"Oh great," said Alma once again halfway between laughter and tears. Gary seemed to bring this out in her. "He's tripping. I hate my family. I hate my life. I hate men."

Gary giggled.

"Let's go surfing," said Paul.

"Yes, yes," said Alma a little desperately. "Anything to get out of here. Wait, I forgot my bag." She headed back to the garage.

I noticed a shovel leaning on the fence. I began digging a hole in the sandy soil of the pumpkin patch to bury the bones. Even if we were out of here, there was no point leaving the problem for poor old Gary. Paul and Rowena watched me dig.

"What about Cammy?" I asked the cone shell now. "What were you doing to her body?"

"Sorry you sad," said Rowena. "I make bet with Osckar. I bet you guys not predictable. He bet you are. So we test. My sister and I learn one human axiom system. We learn Cammy. Peek in her head. Then we look back your past and see if Cammy axiom system make fast predict what she do. I bet no, Osckar bet yes. Osckar right. This Earth is docile."

"Axiom system?" exclaimed Paul. "You know about axioms?"

"I am mathematician. Osckar mathematician. Like you. That why we friend."

"Did you make Sandoval kill Cammy?" I demanded. Nudging Owen's slimy bones into the fresh-dug pit was bringing back the full horror of Cammy's murder. I missed Cammy's husky voice, her wised-up face.

"Bad man kill her," said Rowena. "If we not there he do same. You come La Hampa, you meet Nataraja jellyfish, she make your way."

"What's taking Alma so long in the garage?" said Paul distractedly. "Maybe we should leave without her." He began scuffing sand into the hole, trying to make my job go faster. "Hey look," he exclaimed. "My watch was under the bones." He picked it up with his handkerchief and wiped it off. "It's still running. That's terrific." He slipped the watch onto his wrist, then glanced over at mine. "Seems like it lost two minutes. Hmm. I'd say two minutes is exactly how long it was over there on the other side. Rowena swallowed it with the artichoke and came charging right over to save us from Owen." A little cautiously he reached out and patted Rowena's shell. It echoed like a drum. "Thanks, Rowena. Our new math pal."

"You didn't see what she and her sister did to Cammy's body," I said, shoveling the last of the dirt into the hole. "Cammy's vlog showed them reflected in her sunglasses, Paul. I didn't tell you this yet. This creepy man and woman in black showed it to me in a video last night; they said they were from the NSA, but that was bullshit. Kenny Jones and Mary Smith? Come on. I don't know *who* they really were. But my point is that in the video, Rowena and her sister were poking tendrils up into Cammy's neck after she was dead."

"Get over it!" exclaimed Paul. "They were studying her brain's program like Rowena just said. Time to move on, okay? Now we go to La Hampa and undo the murder. I say we leave Alma here and hit the road."

Right on cue, Alma appeared at the garage door. She'd redone her makeup and packed her bag. "Can you carry this for me, Bela?" she called.

"Okay." I smoothed out the sand I'd shoveled, then laid some sticks and leaves over the disturbed spot of earth.

"Can you meet us at Miller Beach?" Paul asked Rowena.

"I follow," said the cone shell alien.

"You're going to fly right behind us?" I asked the cone shell. "People might—"

"I fly high," said Rowena. "Bye."

She drifted upwards like a helium balloon, her image dwindling to a normal seashell, to a triangle, and then to a dot that hovered above us in the sky.

I got Alma's bag and we headed across the yard. Gary Ziff sat up and blinked as we drew even with him. He was still wearing Owen's gold chain.

"I better buy that necklace off you, Gary," I said, hunkering down at his side. "Bad karma," he said, fumbling for it. He couldn't quite coordinate his fingers. I took the necklace off him myself.

If our trip to La Hampa worked, it could really be that I was leaving this universe for good. And I'd never see this particular Gary again. "Here you go," I said, taking two hundred dollars out of my wallet and tucking it into his jeans. "Take care of yourself, man. I'm sorry I was ragging on you."

"Peace," said Gary, gently waving his hand.

"Oh, stop jerking him around," Alma told me in a sharp tone. "And don't think I didn't hear what you said to him when you first came out of the garage, you heartless bastard." She planted a long, fierce kiss on her father's cheek, then strode out to my squinty-whale station wagon. Paul and I followed, carrying Alma's surfboard, her wetsuit, her bikini, and her suitcase. Alma got in the front seat with me; Paul sat in back. For the moment none of us talked.

While I was getting the whale turned around, Pete showed up on his motorcycle, his surfboard on the side-rack.

"Stop," commanded Alma.

Reluctantly I rolled down my window so Pete could peer in at us. He had his long wet hair in a ponytail, revealing the hard-weathered planes of his face. "Where the fuck you fuckheads goin'?" he asked companionably. "Surf's down."

"We're gonna try Big Sur," I said.

"Hyperspace surfari," said Paul, trying to be cool. Pete leaned down to get a look at him, then shook his head, as if unable to come up with a sufficiently profound insult.

"Keep an eye on Gary," Alma called across me. "He's tripping his balls off."

"No way. Where'd he score?"

"I thought you'd know," said Alma evasively.

"Laugh a minute, this family," said Pete. He held out his hand, showing off a loose-fitting vlog ring. "Check this out, I got it for free at the Pleasure Point Monogrub with my breakfast burrito! They're starting this contest, *One in a Million*, to find the person with the wildest life. Our Monogrub is the pilot project, they just began giving out the camera rings this morning. I'm gonna be a star! I was surfing tubes and vlogging it live, you feel me? I'm on the web."

"The cops are gonna be watching you through that thing, Pete," I said.

"And the Heritagist campaign committee," added Paul.

"Aw, I can take the ring off if I get into anything sketchy. You two guys want to be worrying about taking good care of my baby sister. Or I'll waste your ass." Pete's hog rumbled onto the concrete driveway as we drove off.

"We Ziffs may be dysfunctional," said Alma, settling into her seat with a sigh. "But we look out for each other." She adjusted her two pigtails. "Maybe everything's okay. I was waiting in the garage till you were done burying the bones. That was good, Bela. Gary never will sort out what really happened. Give me the gold chain."

What the hell, I handed it to her. She took a tissue from her purse and polished the necklace, examining it in the light. "I wake up in bed with two guys, and one of them gives me bling from a murdered thug," she said, putting the gold chain around her neck. "Evil glamour." She regarded herself in her compact mirror, looking somewhat mollified. "It's like a rap video. And I've always been such the good girl. Tell me the whole story now. Oh, and let's pick up some breakfast burritos too. At Monogrub, so we can see about the *One in a Million* pilot project."

The south side Santa Cruz Monogrub was indeed handing out vlog rings to all comers. Everyone who wore a Monogrub vlog ring could be accessed on the Monogrub-sponsored *One in a Million* website, and you could vote for whose life was the most interesting to watch, with weekly prizes for the winners. If the project went well, it might soon go all over the Bay Area, and then maybe statewide and even national.

"This is beyond selling out," said Paul, regarding the garish, echoing Monogrub dining area as if he were from Mars.

"Leni is getting some serious money from Monogrub," said Alma. "Not to mention a grant from the NSA. So do I ask for three rings?"

"No way," I said. "What with the weird science we've got planned for today, we don't want to be carrying around surveillance cameras! And, you know, Veeter's gonna be coming after us when he finds out about—"

"Save it for the car," said Paul.

On the way out of Cruz we passed a branch of my bank. I went inside and wired Gyula's money to his account. And, what the heck, I transferred the rest of the million to my mother.

As I drove down Route One towards Sur, Paul leaned forward to be part of the conversation, and we told Alma everything we knew, eating our road food as we went along. Paul was talking more than I liked, trying to show off for Alma. It was a drag having to compete with him every second. Finally, as we followed Route One through the strawberry and artichoke fields, he dropped off to sleep.

"I don't ever want to share you," I told Alma. "I hope it doesn't sound sexist, but I want you to myself. I don't want to have to worry all the time. Our relationship should be, you know, a safe haven. A port in the storm. A cozy room where we can relax."

Alma patted my leg. "I'd like that too, Bela. Maybe now you understand how I felt about you mooning over Cammy."

In my opinion the situations weren't at all comparable, but for once I had the sense to hold my tongue. "You and me, Alma," is all I said. "I want the relationship to be about you and me." I had to be extra nice, because I was about to ask her to do something hard.

"I think I love you, Bela," said Alma, looking very cute with her pigtails sticking out. "I would never ever go back to Paul again."

"I'm glad," I said.

The sun sparkled on the bay, with the Monterey peninsula showing on the southern side. We had about another hour's drive till Miller Beach.

"What did Paul and that—that Rowena thing mean about a parallel world?" Alma asked. "You're going to jump through a tunnel of some kind? And the idea is to try and undo Cammy's murder?"

"I feel like we've gotta try," I said. "Rowena's from some kind of higher universe that she calls La Hampa."

"Odd name," said Alma. "La Hampa in Spanish means the underworld. Did you know that? Underworld like gangland."

"Whatever. But it's not gonna be sinister at all. Paul and I glimpsed La Hampa; it has blue seas and green islands."

"And when you're done there do you come back here to me?"

"Well, that's the catch," I said. "That's what we have to talk about. If someone could change the past of their world, and still be in their same world, it wouldn't work.

The world wouldn't be able to settle down. For instance if I reached back in time to keep my parents from meeting, then I wouldn't have been born, so I wouldn't be around to reach back and keep them from meeting, so I'd be born the same as before and end up wanting to reach back in time to keep them from meeting—like that."

"You don't want to come back here from La Hampa?"

"I'm telling you I *can't*. It's a standard argument from the philosophy of science. Arbitrary reverse causation in a single, logically consistent world is *a priori* impossible. If Paul and I go through the tunnel and do something over there to change Earth's past, then when we come back it has to be that we're actually coming back to a different Earth. The new Earth will be in a parallel universe, or maybe it'll be a nearly identical planet that's somewhere else in this universe, but a long way away. The new Earth will be *like* this Earth without actually being the exact *same* Earth. That's what Rowena meant when she said, 'You come back new world.'"

"Why does she talk so weird?" said Alma, temporarily evading the issue. "I can't stand it."

"That's, you know, the Asian way," I said. "Don't forget I'm half Chinese. We string together ideograms and don't worry about grammar. Like a series of pictures. Rowena learn talk eat Owen brain."

"The rhetoric of glyphs," said Alma with a distracted giggle. But then her face turned serious. "You're telling me that if you and Paul go through the tunnel and I stay here, then I'll never see either of you again. It'll be like you both died on me today." She took my hand, holding onto me.

"That's it," I said. "And that's why I want you to come with us."

"I knew it. All this just for Cammy?"

"It's not only about Cammy, so please don't be jealous. I also want to do it because it's such an amazing adventure. And, listen, if you won't come along, then I won't go. I just decided that. But, hey, I really *do* want to see La Hampa."

"What about the alien cone shells?" protested Alma. "If we go over there, won't they kill us?"

"I think they really do mean to be our friends," I said. "Rowena only ate Owen to protect Paul and me. And she didn't actually hurt your father. And supposedly it wasn't her fault that Sandoval killed—killed Cammy."

"Oh I don't know," said Alma, suddenly angry. "I thought we were just going surfing. Why do you have to make everything so weird? Why do you have to pressure me?"

She fell into a sulk then, staring silently at the landscape as we powered past Monterey, and waving off my attempts to resume our conversation. I gave up and drove in silence. The Bel Paese's big engine purred, eating up the miles; Paul breathed softly in his sleep.

Alma finally spoke again when we began swinging along the high cliffs of Big Sur. "That car's been right behind us for the last few miles," she said, peering through the rear window.

"I know," I answered. It was a red Crevasse coupe with a couple of guys in the front seat, the passenger taller than the driver. They'd been following us ever since we'd crossed the road from Watsonville. "I figure those are Veeter's boys. From the Membrain plant that's down this way."

"What?" asked Paul, waking up and looking back. "What would they want?" He sounded cranky and querulous.

"By now Gyula will have told Veeter that he lost the paracomputer," I reasoned. "And Veeter will figure that you and I have it. And he'll want it back. Because he doesn't want us to make another hypertunnel. We might make his top-secret product look unsafe."

"And I guess they used my mind-simulation program to predict you'd drive to Big Sur," said Paul, wanting to brag for Alma again.

"That Mickey Mouse hack doesn't work for shit," I said shortly. "You know that. Veeter's in the government now. He tapped our phones. We talked about Sur on the phone, didn't we, Alma?"

"Yeah," she said, still turned around in her seat. "And, *duh*, Pete vlogged us." The red Crevasse was holding a steady two hundred feet distance behind us. "That's Henry Nunez driving. He's nice, and he's bound to get rich. I met him the other day when Leni gave him the vlog ring for *Buzz*. And he asked me out. Did you watch that? I said no, and he took out Lulu Cliff instead, and she gave him a blowjob in his car after dinner, right on the vlog, and now she thinks he might ask her to marry him, but of course he won't, the first-date blowjob strategy never bags the guy for more than two weeks. And meanwhile Leni got so jealous that she fired Lulu. Poor Lulu's lost her job with *Buzz*, just as vlogging is really starting to take off. The skinny tall guy riding beside Henry is a total thug gangbanger, by the way, I met him too. Tito Cruz. I think even Henry doesn't like him. I hate security guards." She touched her X-eyed smiley face medallion. "Peace, Owen."

"I wonder how rough they plan to get," I said. "Did you hear that Vice President Ramirez wants to kill me, Alma?"

"Like he'd care about you," said Alma, really doubting me.

Paul rolled down the side window and stared up at the sky. "I see Rowena," he said. "Way up high."

"She's going to attract attention," said Alma. "Once Bela, Rowena, and I go through that tunnel, nothing here matters," said Paul in a flat tone. "We're not coming back."

"Bela told me that," said Alma. "And you'd leave me without a qualm?"

"You bet," said Paul. "The Alma on the next Earth will like me better. And the quantum-mechanical no-cloning theorem implies we can't have more than one of each of us per Earth. So if you came, you'd only be in the way."

"*Hmmpf*," said Alma, annoyed.

There wasn't much traffic on the road just now, and the red Crevasse came at us. It sped up as if to pass us, then locked speeds. I looked over. Nunez was a short guy with a ponytail and a round, pleasant face. He was intently focused on his driving. I was in such a high-adrenaline state that I was noticing tiny things, like that Nunez wasn't wearing his vlog ring.

Meanwhile rangy Tito was brandishing a single-barrel, large-bore shotgun and gesturing with his free hand for us to pull over. His Adam's apple worked up and down as he waved the gun. Nunez glanced over with a concerned expression, perhaps telling Tito to be careful. Tito ignored him and leveled the shotgun at—

"Shit," I said, mashing the accelerator. The squinty whale's V-8 engine was ready for the attack. We sprang forward, leaving the Crevasse well behind. I drew the pistol out of my pocket and handed it to Alma. "Show them this if they pull up again."

"Maybe I should waste Paul for them instead," said Alma, tapping the gun against her medallion and aiming it at Paul's head. "*Viva la vida loca.*"

"Don't fuck around, Alma," snapped Paul.

"You wanted me to fuck around last night," she said, delicately licking the tip of the barrel. "Horn-dog. Do you understand now that you and I are over?"

For once Paul had no comeback. Watching Alma from the corner of my eye, I loved her more than ever.

The road was straight and I was going a hundred. The Crevasse was well behind us. But my suspension and alignment weren't the best, which meant that the view through my windshield was a blur. We came up on a pair of camper vans like they were standing still. I fishtailed around them in one smooth motion, getting back into our lane inches ahead of an oncoming line of cars.

"Sweet," said Alma, looking back. "I have an idea. There's this gravel road that loops inland just before the Kerouac Bridge. The bridge is only about a mile ahead. It's the Coast Road that you'll want; it branches off to the left; it cuts into a tall embankment. We've got such a big lead now that you can whip into the Coast Road and Veeter's guys won't even see. They'll drive past. And then we take the Coast Road down about ten miles to where it rejoins Route One, and while we're doing that, they give up and go home."

"They'll go wait for us at Miller Beach," objected Paul. "Slow down. We're gonna crash."

"We never said Miller Beach on the phone or to Pete," said Alma. "They'll check some other places first. Get ready to turn left, Bela." I was up to a hundred and ten.

I slowed down, but not all that much. The main road was a little sandy, and the Coast Road was gravel, so I figured I could do a controlled drift for my turn. I'd slide sideways into the pocket. The trick would be to start the turn early.

I think I would have made it if it hadn't been for the two bicyclists. They came wobbling out of the Coast Road about a quarter second after I entered my drift, some two hundred feet north of the intersection. If I kept going, the car's side would swat the cyclists like gnats. So I tried to pull out by giving the car more power and twisting the wheel to the right.

Error. The squinty whale squirmed like a live beast, wholly out of control. And then my massive, overpowered station wagon shot through the guard rail to the right of the bridge, out into achingly beautiful steep-walled gorge where Kerouac Creek meets the Pacific.

Time went very slow. I looked at Alma, at Paul, and at Alma again.

"Bela," she said. "Bela." I took her hand.

We were in free flight, right at the high point of our arc. Slowly my whale began tipping forward, following the weight of her big engine. The aquamarine and ink-blue water was so exquisitely shaded, the traceries of white foam so delicate. In silence I accepted this final gift from Gaia.

But then something thudded against the car's roof with a resonant splat. The squinty whale shuddered, swayed, and began to rise, slowly and then faster. I myself felt grow lighter—I was bobbling on the seat.

"Rowena!" shouted Paul. Alma and I began to cheer.

Yes. Rowena the flying alien cone shell snail had fastened her great foot onto us! Her eyestalks bent down to peer in through the windshield. We waved and cheered some more. Our arms flew about like crazy rags; Alma's medallion danced in the air. Rowena had an antigravity thing happening for us.

Her red-and-white-striped mouth tube curved around to poke into my window. "Which way Miller Beach?" she said.

We leveled out at maybe a thousand feet and followed the Big Sur coast south, cruising along as silently as if we were riding a balloon. The three of us were floating off our seats and giddy from our narrow escape with death. We had all the windows open to savor the delicious, thin, salty air.

"I don't want this anymore," said Alma, handing me my pistol like it was a turd or a dead rat. "We're in a new video now."

"Right on," I said, hurling the weapon out my window. "Shed the lead. Not our style."

"Good," said Paul. "You were freaking me out with that thing, Alma."

"Don't dis me again," said Alma lightly. "And I'll be your friend. I'm on this trip all the way."

"You are?" I asked, laughing elatedly. "We can go through the hypertunnel?"

"I almost died five minutes ago," said Alma. "So this is extra time. Like found money. Why *not* do something wild? It beats looking for a nonexistent job."

"You do understand that you won't be able to come back to this same world?" I asked.

"I guess. Not that I necessarily think you and Paul know what you're talking about. But—" She smiled softly, letting her eyes rove over my face. "I don't want to cage you, Bela. And I don't want to take the chance having you permanently disappear. And, Paul, I'd miss you too. I'm coming to La Hampa, boys."

"Isn't she great?" I said, turning to grin at Paul. The most he could muster was a shrug. "Hand me the para-computer from the glove compartment," he mumbled. "I'll get it ready."

In ten minutes Miller Beach was in sight, a long strip of white at the base of steep, rocky hills still slightly green from the winter's rains. Island-sized rocks hunkered in the surf offshore; a lagoon spread to the left.

"Right here," I called, pointing downward and rapping on the windshield. Rowena saw my signal; she'd kept one of her eyestalks bent down our way.

The beach rushed up at us like a zoom into a satellite map. The sand was dotted with people when we started down, what with it being noon in June. The sight of my mollusk-draped car falling from the sky sent them screaming and running away.

After that kind of entrance there wasn't much point in trying to be low-profile. I had Rowena plop us down right at the edge of the water: two mathematicians, a rhetorician, and three surfboards in a dirty white squinty whale with a primered fender and a yellow hood.

Fifty feet into the ocean was an enormous hump of rock with a square natural bridge in it. The Miller door. You could see right through it to the open sea beyond. The waves were breaking outside, with the surge periodically rushing through the square hole, sending low circular point-source wave fronts towards the shore. The surf was mild enough that even during the surges, some breathing room remained at the top of the hole.

We stepped onto the sand. "A magic gate to another world," said Alma, staring at the square natural bridge. "Are we really doing this?"

"I ready," said Rowena, peeling her snail-foot off the roof of my car.

"Me too," I said, getting the boards and wetsuits and bathing suits out of the back: red trunks for me, flowered ones for Paul. I gave Paul the full-body wetsuit and kept the shortie. "Here, Paul, see if you can get this on. Just leave your clothes on the beach. The zipper goes in back. Is the paracomputer set?"

"Yeah," said Paul, handing me a largish ziplock bag. The Gobrane teapot was in there, also a battery wrapped in black electrical tape with two wires sticking out. Paul had picked up the extra stuff at that Corona gas station on our way down to Cruz.

"We can get a spark by touching the wires," said Paul as he pulled on my flowered trunks and began puzzling over his wetsuit. "I figure the whole system is more or less waterproof, but we might as well keep it in the bag till the last minute. There's one problem, though."

"You're *not* ditching me!" said Alma, wriggling into her pink and green wetsuit.

"We've established that," said Paul impatiently. "Can I talk? My problem is that I have no idea how to surf."

"Just stay between us," said Alma, tucking her gold necklace inside her wetsuit. "I'll tell you what to do."

"You're good at that," sneered Paul.

"*Bitter* horn-dog."

"Come on, Paul," I put in. "Keep it together. Be a mathenaut." Even though I wasn't coming back to this world, out of long habit, I took my car key and tucked it into a zipper pocket of my wetsuit.

Some of the people who'd run away were edging closer now. Rowena hovered alertly above us, the tipmost end of her red proboscis protruding from her mouth.

"Are you shooting a movie?" called a teenage boy with zits and a blonde pompadour. "Gynormous surfin' scifi flick," responded Alma, playing with the rhetoric. "Please stay clear so we can get this next shot, sir."

"Awesome," said the kid. He craned upwards. "Where'd the helicopter go?"

"Wasn't any helicopter," said a darkly tanned woman behind him. "That cone thing was carryin' the car."

"There was too a helicopter just a minute ago, Mom," shrilled a little girl in a red bathing suit. She had a voice like a dentist's drill.

"Stand back!" I shouted. The three of us had our wet-suits on and our boards under our arms. I had the para-computer in my hand. No need to answer more questions. We trotted down to the water, Rowena floating through the air above us.

"So here's the plan," I told Paul and Alma. "We paddle out to that square hole in the rock; I set this gizmo on a ledge; Paul sparks it in the right spot for Haut's Para-dox; we paddle out further while the Gobrane bulges and makes a ball of light inside the arch. We turn around and surf into the light—which will be the mouth of the hyper-tunnel to La Hampa. Doesn't totally matter if we catch a wave, by the way. Paddling would be fine."

As usual, the frigid Big Sur waters gave me an ice cream headache all over my body. We were halfway to the rock when, damn, a helicopter did appear, a sleek black job with no markings, roaring out from behind a cliff to the left. I could make out a single pilot in the cockpit. Two additional figures were peering out through an open door in the helicopter's side.

The infernal machine hovered over us, flattening the waves around us, its loudspeaker broadcasting commands. A woman's voice. "Please return to the beach immedi-ately. Bela! Paul! Alma! Please let us join you. Bela! Paul! Alma!"

I glanced up and recognized the people in the heli-copter door: the supposed NSA agents Kenny Jones and

Mary Smith, he of the curly hair and she of the pointy glasses. Kenny was holding his electric-net-gun.

I called a warning to the cone shell, but my voice was lost in the copter's hideous clatter and roar. No matter; Rowena had more tricks up her snout. She darted out her red-tinged proboscis, sending it toward the black helicopter. The slender thread twined upward through the prop-wash, feeling its way. It found purchase upon the side of the helicopter and encircled it like a nightmarishly fast-growing vine.

The proboscis wove a field of dark light around the helicopter and some odd transformation began. The chopper dwindled as if moving further and further away, but yet it remained not very far overhead. It took a second to realize it was shrinking.

"That's Cal Kweskin and Maria Reyes!" called Paul, staring up at the dwindling helicopter. Those were the names of the Stanford mathematicians whom we'd been racing for the Morphic Classification Theorem. Like I said, I'd never met them—but Paul knew them well. They had a research contract from the NSA—so they hadn't been entirely lying when they'd claimed they were agents. And that black helicopter seemed like an NSA-type chopper for sure.

The tiny Cal Kweskin seemed elated by the bizarre change they were going through. Joyfully he tossed his tubular gun out the helicopter door—it dropped past my face, the size of a toothpick. Though it was hard to judge, the helicopter looked to be the size of a seagull now. Rowena withdrew her proboscis and, with an energetic roar, the tiny chopper sped out to sea, the minute figures on board waving in glee. Weirder and weirder.

Alma and I exchanged glances, mustering the courage to continue.

"Once again, Humelocke shows Stanford how it's done," said Paul, pleased by the encounter with his new colleagues. "Look out, guys, here comes a surge."

We paddled further out through the surf.

In another few minutes we were inside the square stone passage. Rowena took up too much room to stay in there with us; she flew on through and waited on the ocean side. The surf was bigger than it had looked from the shore.

A wave broke outside, filling the square hole with rushing foam. I kicked against the currents, banging my knees and elbows against the jagged wall. Up near the top I saw a suitable ledge, flat and nearly a foot wide.

Alma was at the ocean end of the passageway, working the ebb and flow as gracefully as an otter. She had hold of the plastic leash cord that dangled from Paul's board.

"Let's start Haut's Paradox," I said to Paul, leaning in towards him. I opened the ziplock bag and squeezed the battery and teapot together. "I'll hold it and you move the wires."

"Okay," said Paul, reaching forward. Another surge of surf came through just then and it took a minute to reposition ourselves. As I kicked and paddled, I happened to glance back at the beach. I saw a short man and a tall man, Henry Nunez and Tito Cruz, with Tito carrying his shotgun.

Alma saw them too. "Stay with it, boys," she urged us. "We can't turn back *now*."

Paul and I hunched together like two desperate mountaineers trying to start a fire. Tito was yelling. Out in the sea, another wave was breaking. But now the wires met; a tiny spark flickered against the wiggly surface of the computational membrane. Yes. The off-center oval bands of red and blue began to pulse.

"Go!" I said, shoving Paul forward and letting the surge lift me up to the shelf. I laid the teapot on its side and paddled on through the stone arch, my motions lit by strobing red/blue light.

The sea was wilder by far than it had been fifteen minutes ago, the waves rough and badly formed. A hill of water rushed at us, as if bent upon hammering us into the rock. Alma and I ducked under the crest, holding Paul's board from either side.

Paul caught a lungful of the icy water and emerged coughing. The sea tilted down and then up; a bigger wave was on its way. We turned our boards back towards the shore. Rowena steadied herself in the air above us, preparing to jet forward.

The square natural bridge housed a bulging egg of mauve light. The sea churned where the light touched it; bits of the rock walls were chipping away and swirling into the dimensional hypertunnel. I heard a boom—Tito's shotgun or a wave hitting a rock?

Chilled, bruised, and terrified, Alma and I knelt upon our boards, holding the gasping Paul steady. The big wave rose behind us. I felt scared; and I kept wishing I'd phoned to say goodbye to my Ma. I hadn't had the nerve. At least I'd transferred that money to her.

As I was thinking all this, we were sliding down the wave's face as if sledding a hill of glass, steering ourselves towards the glowing oval that filled the square hole. The roar of the surf faded; the waves off to the sides became sluggish mounds; the flying droplets of spray behind me hung pulsing in the air.

I felt a rush of wind as Rowena sped past us, plunging headlong into the light. We followed in her wake, Alma first, me second, Paul trailing a bit behind.

The hypertunnel was constricted, wrapped round upon itself, a region of radically warped space. A gnarled cord ran along one side of the hypertunnel. I saw no signs of the natural bridge's walls in here, only the sea, the air, the cable, our bodies and, in the distance, triangular Rowena and some spots of blue and green.

We three glided from beneath another natural bridge, this one high, lacy, and delicate, set in a calm aquamarine sea and surrounded by a faint blue glow. Where the waters of Big Sur had been icy and brutal, this sea was warm, nurturing, and fanned by a gentle breeze.

The mysterious gnarly cable through our hypertunnel had a bend in it here; it disappeared downwards into a small whirlpool. We kicked past it easily enough, our boards sliding across the glassy water, Alma still first, followed by me, and then Paul.

Ahead of us was Rowena the cone shell, flying towards a high-crowned green island nearby. Hearing a noise behind us, I looked back at the elegant natural bridge with its egg of hypertunnel light. A seagull-sized helicopter came powering through, passing overhead and shooting upwards, growing in size as it rose.

"The Stanford spies in their Pig machine," I said. "I wish they'd crash."

Quite abruptly, the chopper slammed into the sky. Some flaming pieces of wreckage dropped down to our ocean, while other bits melted into the sky itself.

"Whoah!" said Paul. "Take back that wish."

"I didn't mean I wanted them *dead*," I said hurriedly. "I hope they're okay." The sky was odd-looking. It was shiny and close, like a not-all-that-high ceiling. I could faintly see three human figures floating—behind it. "They're alive!" I exclaimed, feeling relieved. "A woman and two men. And they're swimming?" But now they grew hazy and faded away.

"It's like there's multiple levels to this world," said Paul. "Is that another ocean up there? I think they swam through it."

"I'm glad they're not dead, but I don't like them glomming onto our adventure," I griped. "When Cal and Maria came to see me last night, Maria asked me to take them with us. It was like she *knew* we were hypertunneling over to La Hampa."

"Well, yeah," said Paul. "I gave them some hints. I was making a lot of phone calls last week when I was high on speed. I couldn't shut up."

"You were horrible," put in Alma.

With the noise of the chopper gone, I could hear a

slight hissing from the hypertunnel and the natural bridge, a sound like the electrical buzz around a high-tension transformer. I paddled away from it, keeping pace with Alma.

The scene before us resembled the island-sprinkled seas of Micronesia, save that floating in the sky were enormous balls of water like time-slowed drops of spray. Nine of them. Each of these slowly drifting orbs was bespeckled with its own set of islands. And amidst the toy water planets hovered a small sun, not overly bright.

"Gorgeous," breathed Alma.

"La Hampa," I said. "The underworld."

"Overworld," said Paul. "Heaven. Nobody was able to stop us. And we can go back whenever we like. Unless—"

As if linked to a single axle, our heads turned to look back at the hypertunnel's mouth. And just then—*blip*—the glowing oval shrank to a point and winked out. The blue nimbus faded from the natural bridge and all was still. It was so very quiet here.

"Oops," I said. Surrounded by this calm, enchanted seascape, that was about as upset as I could get.

"Darn," said Paul, equally mild. "I figured the mass of all that rock would hold the hypertunnel open. I just hope the La Hampans will help us go home."

"Oh stop analyzing everything to death, you two," said Alma. "It's time for fun." She slid off her surfboard, wormed her way out of her wetsuit, and kicked down into the water, looking around, her gold medallion and bright bikini flashing through the blue water. After a bit she emerged laughing. "Wow."

"Fish?" I asked.

"*Yeah.*"

I slid in and peeled off my wetsuit. I tasted the water; it wasn't salty. Without really thinking it over, I swallowed a bit of it. It felt tingly in my gullet. And now I took a deep breath and dove down, eyes open. The water felt good on my eyes. Somewhat magically, I could see nearly as well as if I were wearing a face mask. The obliging, unearthly water was acting like a lens.

I was surrounded by a shoal of perhaps five thousand tiny tropical fish, similar to the zebras or tetras you'd see in someone's home aquarium. Their bodies moved like iron filings in a magnetic field, with ropes and scarves of density emerging from the parallel computations of the school. I swam below the school and looked up towards the surface. The quivering fishies were green or gray or blue, depending on the precise angle of light, each watery, gleaming shade lovelier than the next.

I surfaced, grabbed a breath, and swam down deeper. Some of the little fish followed me, changing their shapes as they swam. They morphed into yellow and white oval butterfly fish with Turing-style leopard spots and tiger stripes, and as I went still deeper, they became parrot fish the size of salmon, with their scales shaded in rust and acid green, their mouths beaky, and tiny chartreuse fins on their sides. It was very odd and even a little creepy to see the fish morphing as they whirled around me; it was as if they were taking on the shapes I wanted to see.

I was almost at the bottom now; it looked interestingly shiny and smooth. I kicked for it, arms outstretched.

To my surprise I shot through the shiny film and into the air of a twilight sky. I'd entered an enormous, dimly lit bubble of air that lay beneath the sea I'd been swimming in. The bubble contained its own little sun and its own floating water planets, ten of them. The sun was nearby, faint and blotchy, the size of a sports stadium. Fluttering along with me were some of the parrot fish, who'd now become parrot *birds* with chartreuse wings. I happened to think of a long-tailed white tropic bird just then, and one of the parrots took on that form as well.

All very magical and mysterious. But how was I to rejoin Paul and Alma? I had no way of moving back upwards; indeed I was dropping at an ever-faster rate through the dimly lit air towards a particular water ball that held a green-black island with a murky lake. Even so I was calm—I had the sense that I might be able to dive painlessly into the approaching water planet. On its island stood a little square cottage. Light flickered at me from beside the house, as if someone were aiming a mirror at my eyes to blind me. Faintly I glimpsed a figure in white. Roland Haut!

Over the beating sound of the air, I heard a whistling noise. A flying cone shell was swooping towards me from above, avid and intent, quite menacing in the gloom. The birds around me squawked and fluttered.

"Don't!" I screamed. "Don't eat me!"

The shell's dark red proboscis shot out, wrapped around my waist, and pulled me towards a snout with a familiar mouth. Rowena.

"He crazy," she said, suctioning her slimy foot to my

bare back. She began powering upwards towards the underside of the sea I'd come through. She seemed to be in a hurry.

I heard a faint crackling from the island far below; a bolt of energy sizzled past us, heating my skin and incinerating a couple of the parrots. A ray gun? I got no explanation from Rowena. She pushed through the thin skin of the high sea and reunited me with Alma and Paul.

"Luau now," said Rowena. "Talk math." She flew some distance towards the nearest island, pausing this time to make sure we followed.

"What the fuck happened to you?" asked Paul as we paddled. "We thought you'd drowned."

"There's—another sky down there," I said. "A giant air bubble with its own floating seas. Someone else lives down there. I think it's Haut. He was shooting at me, the asshole." I craned up at the sky *above* our sea. It glistened; it was concave. "And we're inside an even bigger air bubble right now. Look—" I pointed at the local sun. "That's a ball of fire only a few hundred yards across. It's not all that far. See how it reflects off the dome of our sky? The sky's a film of water, I tell you, and there's another ocean surface above that and—"

"Do you have to turn everything into a mind-breaking math trip, Bela?" interrupted Alma. "I want to go to the luau." She paddled out ahead of us, Paul and I following in her wake. Alma was graceful and alluring in her yellow bikini. She was my girlfriend and we were on our way to a luau with alien mathematicians. I relaxed. I drank some more of the delicious water. It was all good.

"*Investigations of Curved Surfaces*," said Paul, staring fixedly at Alma. This was a the title of Carl Friedrich Gauss's classic treatise about how to assign a numerical curvature value to each point of a surface. Hills and valleys are regions of positive curvature, with the size of the curvature measuring how sharply the local landscape differs from a plane. Saddle-shaped mountain passes are regions of negative curvature whose numerical size is, again, proportional to non-planarity.

"I'd say Alma's butt cheeks have a curvature of four at their local summits," continued my mathematician pal. "With the value dropping to negative two at the arch of her back. The numbers being based on a one-meter unit, you understand."

"Don't slobber over her," I said. "Alma is a person. Think of her as a friend. Like a sister-in-law."

"I want her back," said Paul.

"I'm not having this conversation. Let's talk about the big picture, dog. Did you even hear what I said about the bubbles before?"

"La Hampa is a fractal," said Paul simply. "Seas inside bubbles inside seas inside bubbles forever up and down. With islands on each sea and a sun in every bubble. And no doubt the space inside the bubbles has a negative Gaussian curvature proportional to the radius of the bubble, so that, in effect, you shrink to fit as you explore downward, and you grow to take up more room if you fly up through the sky to the next level."

"Yes!" I exclaimed. "That's it!" Good old Paul.

"I wonder why Roland shot at you," said Paul.

"Maybe it was Rowena he was aiming at," I said. "You know how paranoid he is about cone shells."

"He'd not gonna be a happy camper here," said Paul, shaking his head with a little laugh.

Rowena's verdant island domed up from the water, the very image of a tropical hideaway. Thickets of red-blooming shiny-leaved bushes lined the shores amid stands of succulent broad-leaved stalks dangling purple flowers and clusters of bananas; higher up the island's slope were gnarly lop-leaved trees bearing heavy oval breadfruits and ivory blossoms; the island's summit was crowned by tall, swaying palms. Springs trickled from the dark soil; ferns and fat-leaved epiphytes nestled in the tree crotches; vines twisted about the mossy trunks; bright birds fluttered from branch to branch.

The sea was so clear that it was as if our surfboards were gliding through empty space. Orange-pink, mauve, and pale-green corals encrusted the island's submerged rocky base with flat spiral dishes, brain-shaped lumps, and staghorn antlers bearing exquisite lavender tips.

Innumerable fish finned amidst the living stones. I saw, for instance, a school of twenty tiny black-and-white arrowhead-shaped damselfish just below the surface, each of them a slightly different size; they hovered over a chartreuse flat-topped tree of coral, nipping in and out of the nooks, disappearing like magicians hopping into each other's pockets.

We followed Rowena straight through an inlet into a calm lagoon with sand on the bottom and a smooth rock ledge at the shady far end. I saw a fire in a pit back there.

Waiting on some comfortably curved rocks by the fire were six aliens: Rowena's cone shell sister, the two big cockroaches I'd seen in my mirror, a pair of man-sized lizards, and a flat white mollusk with a crest of branching tendrils. This last creature resembled a six-foot-long sea slug of the type called a nudibranch.

Let me interject that these alien creatures weren't *exactly* like over-sized cone shell snails, cockroaches, lizards, or nudibranchs. I speak of them that way only as a convenience. The so-called roaches had humanoid hands; the lizard aliens had pinkish skin, little blue bat wings, and colorful triangles ridging their long tails; the by-now-familiar cone shell snail aliens had unearthly jets in their rears; and the nudibranch-like creature's tree of soft palps was, as I'd soon learn, a specialized electromagnetic sense organ rather than a mere gill.

"Happy greeting," said Rowena, flying out to meet us. "Introduce Jewelle."

"Hello Alma hello Bela hello Paul," said the second cone shell in a breathy singsong. She rose into the air and extended her red proboscis-tendril to help Alma step on shore.

The smooth stone edge of the lagoon had regularly curved steps rising out of the sea. Glancing down into the water, I noticed a fancifully arched door with colorful borders set into the submerged wall.

"That our house," remarked Jewelle, noticing my glance. "Unger sleep there too."

"Come on, don't be shy, I'm Tanya," said one of the cockroach aliens, stretching out her pale purple hand.

"Welcome to the Nanonesia level of La Hampa." Her faceted deep-green eyes were familiar from my Ratvale mirror. Her narrow lips bent upwards in a welcoming U, revealing yellow, unthreatening teeth.

Tanya helped me up the steps onto a kind of patio, smooth as marble and patterned with intricate pastel scrolls. Her hands were soft and sticky, vaguely unpleasant to the touch. She had a pungent smell like ammonia. I took a step back from her, feeling vulnerable.

"One ground rule," said Tanya. "If any of you humans plays rough with us, you're all outta here. You want to pass that word on to Roland Haut. We like it peaceful in Nanonesia, and any species wants to fight, they're eighty-sixed."

"Two to the eighty-sixth is the largest power of two that doesn't have any zeros when you write it out in decimal," said the other cockroach, who'd flopped down on his belly to goggle at Paul, still lying on his board. "Lemme ask you this. What's the biggest Mersenne prime you got? I'm only asking for the lizards' sake, mind you. My name's Osckar, and I'm a hierophantic logician from—whaddaya, whaddaya, call it Galaxy Z." Galaxy Z or not, Osckar and Tanya talked like New Yorkers.

"The biggest Mersenne prime that I heard of lately is two to the 25,964,951 minus one," said Paul, math robot that he was. I would have liked to ask Tanya what she knew about Haut—how had he ended up with a ray gun on an island in the world below? But it was hard to get a word in edgewise with all the alien mathematicians here.

"My condolences," the female member of the lizard

couple was saying to Paul, ironically drawing out the word. She fixed him with one of her large, golden eyes. "Your puny Mersenne prime is only enough to make a fourteen-million-digit perfect number. In our world, googol-digit perfect numbers are a commonplace. And we've proved there are infinitely many bigger ones, as well." She gestured delicately towards herself and the other lizard. "I'm Vulma and this is Mulvane. We're number theorists." She tossed her head and twitched her colorfully ridged tail. She had meaty rear limbs like those of a *T. rex*.

"Charmed," chimed in Mulvane, baring his long rows of teeth in a smile. A whiff of carrion rode upon his lukewarm breath. Even so, he seemed no more menacing than the average European math professor.

"Number theory's a baby pool," said Osckar the cockroach dismissively. "Logic's the open sea. Hey, speaking of logic, whaddaya got for provably unsolvable systems of Diophantine equations back on Earth? I'm talking clean and simple here. None of those furshlugginer Gödel numbers." His wing covers twitched as if he were shrugging.

Paul answered something I won't bore you with, and Vulma one-upped him again, and Osckar said something nasty about number theory again, and Mulvane got mad.

"Logic is for unstable, disorganized individuals who don't know their own minds," said the lizard number theorist, angrily fluttering his little wings.

"Space shape more important," put in Jewelle. "Number and logic just game."

"And don't, ah, forget infinity," came another voice. "Listen to Unger." At first I couldn't tell where the voice came from, and then I realized the nudibranch was making sounds by vibrating his upper surface. An orange band around his edge rippled as he talked. Although he had no eyes, those soft ivory branches upon his back were sensitive to the motions of our bodies.

"Hi there, Unger," said Alma, waving at him. "Don't tell me you're a mathematician, too?"

"Unger is a point-set topologist turned transfinite set theorist," said Unger. "He can't tell a raven from a writing desk." Pause. "That's a joke. The raven's, ah, digestive tract and two beak-nostrils being homotopic to the three holes formed by the desk's, ah, four legs and three cross-bars? Stay awhile and Unger can educate you about Cantor's Continuum Problem. The true power of the, ah, continuum is alef-two. And the next cardinal in the beth power-hierarchy is alef-seven. Big, ah, surprise. To enjoy the proof, amathematical Alma, you might get Rowena to load you up with a conotoxin sting for mind expansion. Like your Dad. Or the Nataraja can make you some, ah, pot. I'll pace you by eating grork."

"Don't make fun of my father," said Alma, confused. "How do you weirdos know so much about us? For that matter, how do you know English?"

"Siddown already," chirped Tanya. "Then we'll talk. Don't listen to Unger. Mollusks are—let's face facts—slimy. Why get high when you got hierophantics?"

We folded our wetsuits for cushions and settled onto the rocks. "What do you mean by hierophantics?" I asked, intrigued by the word.

"The Hierophant is a Tarot card," volunteered my knowledgeable Alma. "A trump of the Major Arcana. It shows a wise woman who explains mysteries. At least I think she's a woman. Hiero + phant is mystery + show; it's like hiero + glyph is mystery + symbol."

"Just so," said Mulvane, turning his scaly, clawed hands upward. "And hierophantics is an advanced style of thought that one absorbs in La Hampa. The human race's adoption of language and of writing were first steps towards hierophantics."

"Osckar and me have taken a zillion steps more," bragged Tanya.

"Maybe our Morphic Classification Theorem is hierophantic," put in Paul.

"I think so," said Rowena. "Hierophantic mean speed-up. Long story short."

"Oh stop it with the math," said Alma, toying with her X-eyed smiley face necklace. "I thought this was supposed to be a luau. Back home that means a party?"

"Eat, eat, eat! Drink, drink, drink!" said Tanya. "That's the way you learn hierophantics." She tugged over a clear crystal basin that was filled with—really big worms. Or snakes. Or, no, they were sea cucumbers, white with dark brown leopard spots; they had stubby leg bumps and little fans of feelers at their front ends; each of them was roughly the size of a salami.

"Ice cream? Nxgan? Pizza? Grork?" said Osckar, picking up a pair of the heavy, drooping invertebrates and offering them around. "Whaddaya, whaddaya, the Nataraja sea cukes give it to ya just the way you want it, red-cold or ice-hot."

"You inverted the thermal intensifiers," said Mulvane in a supercilious tone.

Alma shied away from the sea cucumbers. "Ick! Won't any of you tell me how you learned English? How about it Tanya? You're all different kinds of aliens, right?"

"We're as diverse as it gets," said the lively female cockroach. "Our races emigrated to La Hampa forever ago. We came from planets scattered all over the infinite multiverse."

"It's *not* infinite," said scaly Mulvane, his wings standing out for emphasis. "And it's *not a* multiverse. It's one exceedingly large but finite global universe with a complicated indexing system to pick out the local universes and the hyperverse stacks. Like a Library of Babel that has all the possible books. And there's no quantum mechanics required, I might append. Don't be sneaking in those spurious assumptions, Tanya."

"The Library of Babel *is* infinite if there's no upper bound to, ah, the size of a book," put in Unger, gently waving the ivory tree of sensors upon his back. "The fear of infinity is a kind of blindness. A disability. The fear of infinity destroys the possibility of, ah, seeing the real. It's quite obvious that infinity in its highest form has created and sustains us. Infinity is in every cell of your body and in each of your, ah, thoughts."

"You're an expert at being *blind*," sneered Vulma with a dismissive flick of her tail. "Light-blind, blind to logic, and blind drunk every night."

"Number theory is as cowardly as studying fish names instead of swimming in the sea!" exclaimed Unger. His body surface was heaving violently, making his voice quite loud. "Number theory is like looking at sex pictures instead of finding a mate! I pity you, lizard-thing."

"I'm not the one who's a self-fertilizing hermaphrodite," said Vulma, her long mouth wide-open in a grin. The aliens seemed to enjoy arguing with each other.

"Enough buffoonery," said Unger to change the subject. "I will, ah, answer Alma's question. The way we learned your language and your cultural history, Alma, was by looking at or by electrically sensing the, ah, patterns within the flesh of a Nataraja jellyfish that intersects a lake on the other side of that hill. We know your world in the limited fashion of peeping, timid number theorists. But now you're here in person. We exult to share our, ah, corporeal vibrations in depth. Thus this welcoming luau."

"You did more than watch us," I said to the aliens. "You reached into our world. We saw you in mirrors."

"Your jellyfish's body is like, whaddaya, an interactive vlog," said Osckar. "And, yeah, when we reach in, we come as mirror images to reduce the disruption. It's like our wave functions are ninety degrees out of phase."

"What is this jellyfish you keep talking about?" interjected Paul.

"One particular jellyfish make your world," said Rowena.

"Your jellyfish's cable generates one after another of your parallel universes," added Tanya. "And the series of universes is what we call a hyperverse. It's like successive drafts of a novel."

"Or like the output of a sculptor who finds successively lovelier images within a quarry's stones," said Unger. "Forms that approach the beauty of, ah, Alma."

"Why thank you," said Alma.

I was beginning to understand the meaning of the

gnarled connector cord I'd seen running through the hypertunnel from Earth to La Hampa. Some godlike jellyfish was in physical contact with our universe. According to Tanya, the jellyfish was feeding in a series of information seeds that specified successive versions of our world, thereby constructing or connecting to an ever-changing series of Earths, each of them somewhat similar to ours, and each of them supposedly a bit better than the ones before. My mind felt very clear as I formed these ideas.

"Look at Bela thinking!" said Osckar the cockroach mathematician from Galaxy Z. "I can see the mysto steam coming outta his ears. That's the hierophantics taking hold. You've been drinking the water, right?" He flopped two of those leopard-spotted invertebrates down in front of me. "Eat these and get even smarter," he added. The sea cucumbers pointed their palps at me, as if waiting for me to speak to them. But I wasn't ready for that yet.

"Maybe you want to poison us," said Alma as Osckar laid a pair of the fat, spotted sea cukes in front of her. "I still don't like the way that Rowena ate Owen and spat his bones in my backyard."

"Eating the first member of a race that we physically contact is typical of Rowena and her sister," sneered Vulma, filliping her tail towards the cone shells. "They're so literal-minded."

"Maybe Rowena was hoping to taste a human soul when she chowed down on that bodyguard schnook," said Osckar with a sarcastic laugh. "She's a real romantic, you bet."

"No taste soul," said Rowena. "*Those* humans predictable."

"How can a complex computation like thought be predictable?" said Paul. "Even if there is an axiom system for a human mind, deriving future mental states should take a really long time."

"Your world docile; your people docile," said Rowena. "Other world, other humans maybe not. Computation landscape always different. Like geology. Not docile everywhere."

Mulvane glared over at the cone shells. "Those two would be a bit more bearable if they'd speak properly."

"Unger would like to point out that Rowena and Jewelle use their, ah, special rhetoric by deliberate choice," put in Unger.

"Deep talk big block," said Jewelle. "Like hierophantic." Which was sort of what I'd been telling Alma about Asian versus Western styles of speech. Not that I could figure out what the hell Rowena had been talking about just now. What did she mean by docile?

By now Osckar and Tanya had set a couple of those nasty-looking sea cucumbers down beside each of us. The cockroaches were gesturing with their spindly arms to encourage us to eat.

"Notice that our sun's getting darker?" said Tanya. "Its brightness cycles up and down once a day." The dimmed sun looked a bit splotchy. "Dark means suppertime," added Tanya. "Eat!"

"Let's see *you* bite into one of those gross things, Tanya," said Paul, gazing down at his sea cucumbers.

The cockroach woman picked up a sea cucumber and sang to it. "I got a yen for nxgan! As if you didn't know, cukiepie." The creature morphed into a crisp brown packet like a giant deep-fried egg roll, glistening with fat and nicely folded. Tanya crunched down on it, spilling out lumpy orange liquid from its interior. "Scrumptious nxgan," she said, her voice sweet with saliva. She used one of her spare legs to push a gobbet of the orange stuff into her mouth.

My two sea cucumbers stretched comfortably, like a pair of starlets by a swimming-pool, turning their fans of sensors towards my face as if worshipping the sun. They really and truly wanted to be eaten. I was almost hungry enough to try.

"Maybe some baked tofu in a pita bread with pickled bok choy?" murmured Alma to her sea cucumbers. "And a big bottle of Beck's." Instantly the creatures morphed into a pita pouch and a damp green bottle of beer. Alma raised her eyebrows, but didn't touch the food. Meanwhile Paul asked his sea cukes to be a pork chop with French-fried yams next to a tall glass of orange soda. And I told mine to form roast rabbit, black rice with carrot puree, and a glass of red wine.

"I don't know," said Alma. "What if the food's full of sick eggs that'll hatch larvae inside us that eat our flesh and burst out—*yuuugh?*" She made a rapid gesture to mime something erupting through the wall of her abdomen.

"I figure if they wanted to kill us here, we'd already be dead," said Paul, prodding his crisp pork-chop with his finger. "Show us how, Bela. You the man."

"Oh, all right," I said. I took a sip of my wine and a nibble of my rabbit. Flavors bloomed in my mouth. It was as if I'd never properly tasted anything before. "Yeah, dogs,"

I said, digging in. "We're in heaven." The sun had turned silvery and spotty, like a moon.

As we ate and drank, the luau grew convivial. Hearing the laughter, the aliens' children came out from hiding, with several dozen small cone shells emerging from the water, and scores of miniature roaches scuttling down from the ruby-crystal pillbox roach house upon the hill. Mulvane went halfway up the hill and bellowed into a gold-framed mine shaft entrance to call his kids too: a trio of knee-high lizards. Tiny nudibranchs oozed forth from slits in Unger's skin to scavenge up the spilled scraps of the anemones and sponges that he was eating.

"You never really explained what the Nataraja sea cucumbers are," said Paul, finishing off a dish of ice cream he was sharing with two of the lizard children. "That word Nataraja, it means—what?"

"La Hampa is a place," said Mulvane. "This place. The Nataraja is the thing that lives in La Hampa. As it happens, the two are very nearly coextensive. The Nataraja fills every cranny of La Hampa, just as the superorganism Gaia fills every part of your planet Earth. All the levels of La Hampa are filled with the Nataraja: our Nanonesian level, the Subgum level below us, the Paradisio level above us, and so on up and down. Everything you see here is a some part of the Nataraja's interwoven life cycles. Everything other than us." He gestured at the seven alien mathematicians and their children. "We, like you, are visitors. Although perhaps our races have been here for so long that we've turned a bit Nataraja ourselves."

"We use the word '*Nataraja*' with you because in Earth's

Sanskrit language, *nata* + *raja* is *dancer* + *king*," said Unger.
"Nataraja is another name for dancing Shiva, the creator
and destroyer of worlds."

The island's trees were swaying in complex rhythms;
the patterns in the marble underfoot were slowly changing shape. Everything here—even the rocks, the water, the
air—was a living part of the Nataraja superorganism that
filled La Hampa. The La Hampan animals were as corpus-
cles in the Nataraja's blood stream. And my world's God
was a jellyfish that was part of the great Nataraja as well.
The ultimate reality was odder than I'd ever imagined.

Turning in on myself, I sensed the richness of my body.
I was an ecosystem, a colony. Perhaps, relative to a sin-
gle-celled bacterium in my gut, I too was a Nataraja of
incalculable significance and size.

The children had begun playing a game that Mulvane
called centrifugal bumble-puppy, drawing the name
from the human database. Responding to the children's
request, the Nataraja had set a little tornado to spinning
at the edge of the patio. The little cone shells, lizards,
cockroaches, and nudibranchs repeatedly hurled themselves into the tornado and were spewed out—the game
of the thing was to try to stay in longer than the others and, if possible, to climb up higher in the tornado's
column. Often as not the children landed in the water,
chirping, growling, and fluting with glee.

Mellowed by food and drink, we adults lolled around
the dancing fire, talking about math. In a sense mathematics is quite objective: the same deductions can become
known to everyone who starts with the same axioms and

definitions; the same abstract forms can be universally perceived. So it's perfectly possible to talk math with a cockroach from Galaxy Z.

This said, there's also a sense in which mathematics is subjective. If your language is unknown to me, I find your books unreadable; if you paint in colors invisible to me, I avoid your museums; if you travel by carriers I can't board, your journeys don't engage me; if your mathematical definitions and axioms seem arbitrary to me, I have little appreciation for your theorems.

Our math conversation with the aliens meandered back and forth across the fuzzy boundary separating information from noise. Generally speaking, the lizards were interested in numbers, the cone shells in space, Unger in infinity, and the cockroaches in logic.

In their home world, the lizard forbearers of Mulvane and Vulma lived underground. Their main concerns were tunnel branchings and family trees. They had very little appreciation for open space, for infinity, or abstract logic. But they were hellacious with the integers. They'd long since resolved the Riemann hypothesis and Goldbach's conjecture concerning prime numbers, which was big news for Paul and me. We would have liked to know the proof of the Riemann hypothesis, and they spent a few minutes trying tell it to us, but every concept they mentioned was unknown, requiring explanations that led to yet more arcane background material, with no solid ground in sight. We gave up. Next?

Given that Rowena and Jewelle's ancestors were from a water planet, they were experts on flow. Prompted by a question from Paul, Jewelle explained how a detour into seven-dimensional vortices led to an elegant proof of the Birch and Swinnerton-Dyer conjecture concerning cubic curves. And Rowena allowed that, thanks to hierophantics, she could solve the intractable Navier-Stokes equations for fluid flow—at least in what she called the "docile" worlds.

Unger told us that, being blind, he had little interest in space or number. For him the world was a system of electromagnetic fields, so he was perforce prone to viewing reality as an endless undivided whole. Unger believed in his mind's direct perceptions of impalpable form. According to Unger, infinite sets were as real as the objects that we non-nudibranchs saw with our crass eyes. And words, for Unger, were potentially infinite sets of etymological links and conversational associations, which made rhetoric a kind of linguistic theory of infinity.

Alma was vehemently bored by the math talk, and she started a side conversation about rhetoric with Unger. As they talked, Unger began turning some of the Nataraja sea cucumbers into a kind of stinging shrimp that he called grork. Eating grork seemed to get him drunk or high. And then, at Unger's urging, Alma told a little Nataraja sea cuke to turn itself into a fat, blazing marijuana joint.

While the children chattered around their tornado and Alma grew raucous, Paul and I kept our heads. We didn't want to miss a word. I, for one, felt like Aladdin in the treasure cave.

Osckar and Tanya explained that their ancestors were from a world near the core of their beloved Galaxy Z, a spot where solar systems were continually being torn apart by catastrophic close encounters. The all-but-inde-structible roaches were forced to emigrate to new worlds every generation or so, which meant that, for them, most concepts were utterly relative, and they preferred to focus upon the relations between axiom systems and the theorems that might be logically deduced.

In La Hampa, Osckar and Tanya had added the mysterious hierophantic technique to their arsenal of logical inference methods. In the grandiose style of mathematicians everywhere, they were overweeningly proud of their new technique. They said they were the best mathematicians in both La Hampa and in the entire multiverse—with the possible exceptions of Jewelle and Rowena.

The roaches claimed that, at least in the docile realities, hierophantics could collapse the natives' long, groping proofs and computations into a few ultraefficient steps apiece. As it happened, some of the alternate Earths were docile, and some were not—according to Osckar and Rowena, our Earth of origin was in fact docile, and that's why we were predictable.

"But I still don't get what hierophantics is," I complained. Weary of centrifugal bumble-puppy, the children had gathered around the fire; they were roasting snack foods on sticks. Osckar threw a few more branches into the flames. "You don't feel smarter yet?" he asked me.

"Talking to a filthy cockroach should make anyone smart?" said Alma, heavily lurching past us from where she'd been camped out with Unger. She looked zonked and irritable.

"You learn hierophantics from eating Nataraja sea cucumbers," said Tanya. "I'm tellin' ya, it's the food of the

gods!" Alma didn't do well with drugs or alcohol. I was
glad she only rarely overindulged.

"Sick cucumber eggs," she muttered as she disappeared
into the shadows. One of the little lizards staggered around
the fire, imitating Alma's gait. The little cone shells piped
appreciatively, their little black eyes dancing in the firelight.

I took another sip of my red wine, pondering the flavors. Was I thinking better than before? I glanced at my
watch. It said nine o'clock.

"You feel anything?" I asked Paul.

"I'm grouping my ideas better, yeah," he said. "I've got
this fresh concept about how to solve the paracomputational codec problem."

"Tell us about the codec problem again," said Mulvane,
picking his teeth with the tip of his tail. "I like that one."

So we talked about codec for a little while, but then
Alma came back and started heckling us. Unger had fallen
asleep, flattened out on the patio with his babies bouncing
on his back as if he were a trampoline. Hop on Pop!

"Rowena said you had a bet with her about predicting
the things Cammy did?" Alma said to Osckar.

"Yeah," said the cockroach. "And I won. I'm the brains
around here, can't you tell? I knew the score just by lookin'
at the Earth you came from. The shapes of your clouds
give it away. Docile. You're from a low-complexity zone
of the computational multiverse. A place where it just so
happens that all the big searches collapse. And that means
you rubes are a snap to predict. Of course now you're in
La Hampa, and eating Nataraja, and you're wising up."

Alma wasn't really listening. She had prepared a special
punch line she was waiting to deliver. "Cammy wasn't a

good choice for your test," she said heavily. "She was easy to predict. She was always a slut." The firelight glittered off her gold necklace.

I drew in a deep breath and exhaled. It occurred to me that there was no reason I absolutely had to stay with Alma once we got back home. Life with Cammy might actually be better. But for now I needed to stay calm and patient. I owed Alma that much. I was the one who'd talked her into this trip.

"It's about time for us to get some sleep," I remarked to Tanya. "Is there a place for us?"

"Make hut," said Rowena to the Nataraja at large.

A square of the patio rose up, rapidly forming a pleasant wood cabin with a thatched roof, big screened windows and a little porch. The room held a single giant bed lit by a small glowing orb on a table at the bedside.

"I want my own bed," said Alma, peering into the room. "A single. I don't want Paul horn-dogging me and Bela *protecting* me. I want space." Obligingly the super-king bed divided into three singles with night tables between them. The baby cockroaches ran up onto our house walls and began racing each other around it, their bodies never touching the ground. The baby cone shells paced them, flying in an endless circular caucus race.

This world was starting to give me the creeps. The trees writhed slowly against the dimly glowing sky. Luminous shapes moved about in the warm sea waters. The nine other water planets coasted their zodiacal routes. The gentlest of breezes toyed with my hair, as if taking my measure. Everything here besides us and the aliens was the living body of the Nataraja. I felt a little rush of claustrophobia. And my

stomach didn't feel so good either. I'd ended up eating yet
another Nataraja sea cuke for dessert—I'd had it turn into
fresh pineapple chunks on coconut ice cream. I could feel
the weight of the three alien sea cucumbers within me.

Alma delivered a parting shot from the hut's threshold.
"Math sucks. You're all losers." She shuffled into the room
and collapsed on the leftmost bed. One of the young lizards punctuated the moment with a belch.

"Why did you contact us in the first place?" Paul asked
the aliens, studiously ignoring Alma's remarks.

"To schmooze with you," said Osckar. "To have some
fun with math. And mainly to get ourselves a new sun.
They burn out, you know, they turn into water vapor and
dust. Ours is almost dead. Like an old lightbulb."

"The jellyfish for your world is big and ripe," said Tanya.
"She's just about ready to turn into a sun. That's what they
do. But she can't make the transition until the people of
your world begin finding their way over to La Hampa. The
hypertunnel produces a special energy. A feedback loop. It
probably would have happened on its own, but we're pushy.
We figured we'd try and help things along by talking to you.
That's why Rowena got in touch with that crazy professor
of yours; that's why Rowena nudged that bum into setting
the fire; and that's why Osckar and me reached out to Bela."

"I was so scared when I saw you two in the mirror in
my room," I said.

"Whaddaya, whaddaya. You and Roland Haut looked
like the hot prospects for getting the hypertunnel in
gear," said Osckar. "Of course Roland was a bust."

"What *about* Roland Haut?" asked Paul. "You mentioned him right when we got here. He fell through the

first hypertunnel we made, right? Bela said he saw him on the level below here and he shot at Rowena?"

"He scared," said Rowena. "He living alone on island in Subgum level." It occurred to me that the house I'd seen on the island on the inner sea was just like the house Nataraja had grown for us here.

"Haut completely freaked out when we tried to talk to him," said Osckar. "Fuhgeddaboutit. He popped out of the natural bridge half a day before you guys, and Jewelle nabbed him and brought him up here and we tried to give him a luau, but the guy is, whaddaya, xenophobic. Especially when it comes to giant cone shells. We couldn't talk to him at all. He darted into Vulma and Mulvane's tunnel and dropped through the bottom of the island to the level under ours. Subgum. Pretty dark down there. It's up to you to calm him down or, like Tanya told you first thing, humans are banned."

"Rowena says Haut got the Nataraja to make him a ray gun," said Tanya. "Makes it hard to pay a social call. If he's gonna act like a cornered rat, maybe just leave him to squeak alone in the dark. The Subgum level's sun is almost burned out, you know, and there's no jellyfish down there that's even close to turning ripe."

I felt a twinge of pity for Roland, frightened in the gathering gloom.

"I just hope he doesn't think of asking the Nataraja to rig him so he can fly up here," Osckar was saying. "If he shows, you boys talk sense to him. He's supposed to be this hot mathematician; so of course we'd be glad to chat with him. But if the guy can't deal, you wanna send him the hell home. I don't want him squatting here soaking up hierophantics and plotting against us. If Haut hurts one of us, it's the bum's rush for all of you."

"Drone, drone, drone," said Mulvane, yawning hugely, toothily. "Bedtime." He and Vulma made their way up towards the tunnel in the hillside, herding two of the young lizards and carrying the littlest, who'd already fallen asleep. And the cone shells slid down into the water, dragging the comatose Unger with them.

"Tomorrow you can meet your special Nataraja jellyfish," said Tanya the cockroach. She and Osckar were crouched down, letting the baby roaches fasten themselves to their backs. "Jellyfish Lake is right past where our house is. You go up the hill and then down into a crater."

"Show it to them now, Tanya," suggested Osckar. "I'm sorry I was sounding so bossy, boys. You can walk up with us and take a look before bed. It's quite a sight."

I glanced into our cabin; Alma was fast asleep. "I'll come if Paul will," I said, not wanting to leave him alone with my girl.

"I feel pukeful," said Paul.

I, too, felt very conscious of the mass and volume of the alien sea cucumbers in my stomach. But I was intrigued by Tanya's earlier remark that I'd learn hierophantics by eating the sea cucumbers. I was determined to digest them if I could.

"Come on, the walk will do us good," I told Paul. "It's not far."

It was a lovely tropical night. The sun was like a pale moon, casting gentle, dancing highlights upon the floating water planets of our small, domed sky. For the first time I could really sense the fact that this sky curved all the way around under us. We were inside an enormous bubble inside a water-planet inside a higher sky—the Paradisio sky.

Although the rocks underfoot were a bit rough and jagged, there was a clean path to the ridge. The baby roaches chirped to each other from their parents' backs. We followed Osckar and Tanya up to their low red-glowing house with the slit windows. Osckar and the little ones went inside, and Tanya walked us to the top.

Standing at the summit with six-limbed Tanya at our side, Paul and I gazed down into our island's center. The jungle plants were rustling, as if feeling the air. A few bats could be seen flapping raggedly above the tree line. And in the valley glowed a pale green lake, really just a pond. The glow was from thousands, no millions, of small moving forms within the water.

"Jellyfish Lake," said Tanya. "I'll tell them you're here."

"I'm not sure that—" I began, but before I could finish my sentence, the big roach alien had puffed up her body and sent out a chirp so shrill that Paul and I had to clap our hands over our ears.

A glowing circle of activity traveled through Jellyfish Lake; a brighter light flared in its depths. Slowly a great bell-shaped organism wallowed up from the water to hover a few feet above the lake's surface. Its luminous tendrils were as a waterfall of light. It pointed a tendril towards us. It knew we were here.

"*Come to me, Bela.*" I heard the words in my mind, not my ears. A quick glance at Paul showed that he heard nothing. The big jellyfish was talking to me, only to me. "*I am a gate for but one pilgrim*," said the sweet, liquid voice in my head. A woman's voice. "*Thou art my seeker.*"

I felt an immediate and very deep conviction that the jellyfish was indeed God. I had to fight an urge to gallop down the hill and leap into the luminous, teeming water. Whoah there, Bela, she's getting to you. A part of me was very afraid.

"Let's go to bed," I said, stiffly turning myself around. "That's one big-mama jellyfish," said Paul, still staring at the lake. "She wants Bela," said Tanya, acutely studying us with her dark-adapted compound eyes. "She'll have to wait till morning," I said, fending off the touch of the jellyfish's powerful mind. "When Alma's awake."

"Never *mind* about Alma," put in Paul. "Talk to the jellyfish now. You don't have to worry about Alma's wishes. Not after she calls us losers."

"Show us the way back down," I told Tanya.

We followed the big cockroach, her domed back silvered by the moony, mottled sun. Out towards the mouth of the lagoon, the sea's gentle waves were breaking in phosphorescent ripples. But all this beauty was as nothing beside my mind's images of the shining jellyfish, the Lady in the Lake, the one true Gate.

Tanya chirped farewell, waved her antennae, and crawled into her home. As Paul and I neared our cabin, we heard a heavy noise in the jungle; something or someone was blundering around. "I hope just that's one of the lizard people," said Paul. He raised his voice to call out a hello. But he got no answer.

"Could be a wild pig," I suggested. "A Nataraja pig."

We walked faster, stumbling over roots and skidding on the leaves and rocks. In between thoughts of the jellyfish, I wondered if Ma back home had noticed yet that I was gone for good. Poor old Ma. I was glad when we reached our hut, flimsy though it was. Alma was still asleep. I took the bed between her and Paul.

"The way I feel, I'm wondering if I should stick my fingers down my throat and throw up," said Paul. "Get it over with. Do you feel gnarly?"

"A little," I said distractedly.

"Did you actually see Haut when you fell through the ocean?" asked Paul.

"Um, no. He flashed a mirror in my eyes, and he shot at Rowena and me. Never mind that now. I keep seeing the afterimage of that jellyfish above the lake. She was talking to me in my head. Her voice—it was beautiful."

"She didn't talk to me," said Paul. "You must be the one who gets to make the wishes about our new world. That Ritalin I took in Palo Alto is where I went wrong. Tell the jellyfish no stimulants for Paul. Do you think she can change that?"

"She can do anything," I said. "She's God."

Paul grimaced. "Just because she controls the seed for our universe? A programmer *is* God for the creatures in a videogame, Bela, but in real life, a programmer's a geek. If you want to talk about God, maybe you should be talking about the Nataraja."

"I don't want to talk at all," I said, the jellyfish light pulsing behind my eyes, and the sea cucumbers heavy in my gut. "I want to sleep. Give me a glass of water, Nataraja." A glass of water appeared on the table by my bed and I drank it down.

My head cleared a bit. I gazed at Alma in the next bed over. She was vehemently slumbering. Alma never did anything by halves. The unpleasant things she'd said tonight didn't matter. I reached out and touched her smooth cheek with one finger.

Paul drank some water too, then shook his head.

"I'm too wired to sleep," he announced. "I want to figure out how our time relates to hampatime and to the many universes. I think it's significant that yesterday's hypertunnel from the Tang Fat Hotel came out here at the Nanonesia level too. And that my watch lost two minutes. Also I noticed something about the angle of the jellyfish's cable that—" He groped around in the air. "Can I have paper and something to write with, Nataraja?"

A lined pad and a number two pencil appeared on our table. Paul propped himself up with his pillows and began inscribing precise lines of symbols—for all the world as if we were back in our apartment in Humelocke. It was a comforting sight.

"Just don't bother Alma," I said, and pulled a pillow over my head.

SIX

the gobubbles

I had terrible, mathematically warped dreams, filled with loops, regresses, and higher-dimensional flips. Near dawn I dreamed I was awake and sitting up, and that our hut turned into its own mirror image, with Paul's and Alma's beds changing place. In my dream the room flipped again and again, spinning as if upon a hyperdimensional lathe. My rectangular bed was at the still core, and the Nataraja jellyfish hovered at the foot of the bed, gazing at me through limp eye slits, her mouth a ragged rent. I paddled at the air to escape her; my bed was a surfboard tracing a downward gyre upon the funneled wall of a giant maelstrom. The jellyfish bobbed at the base like a bright bubble of foam. I descended ever faster. When I hit the jellyfish, she'd turned to glass; I crashed through the skylight of a 1940s factory. Urgent, oily machines picked me off the floor and transformed me into a thousand pasteboard Tarot cards. I was the Hierophant in every deck; the decks were in the rear jeans pockets of school-girls and Ferris wheel attendants across all the hill towns of Ohio and Kentucky, the great wheels skeletal against orange sunset skies, their hubs lit with pulsing glows. My stomach cramped and an alien worm shot through the thin paper wall of my body. My blood covered the Tarot cards, the wheels, the jellyfish. And when I reached for Alma, I found Paul's stiff tool rising from her dark furrow—

Yuuugh!

I sat up groaning, this time truly awake. Alma was still asleep to the right of me. Paul's bed was empty, scattered with closely written papers. I could hear his voice outside, some way uphill from our cabin. I couldn't make out what he was saying, nor could I be sure if anyone was answering him.

The sky was getting brighter. According to my watch it was five in the morning. My stomach was okay now, and my mind felt preternaturally clear. I was thinking faster, and in a higher-level way than ever before.

Paul was talking to Roland Haut. I made this deduction all at once, with no additional evidence and no intervening steps.

For the moment, the *feel* of my rapid thought process interested me more than the conclusion. Was this what the aliens had meant by hierophantics? Perhaps, as Tanya had promised, I'd been learning hierophantics all night by digesting the flesh of the Nataraja sea cucumbers. And hierophantics was what? Think of it this way. Hierophantics was to me as math would be to a nonmathematician: an arcane way to supercharge one's mode of thought.

Where my mind had once been a thicket, it was now an orderly bed of flowers. My perceptions and emotions were automatically constellating themselves into crystalline patterns. I felt sure that Paul was talking to Haut, and that they were scheming about how to keep my Alma from accompanying us to the new Earth.

I reasoned that Paul wanted my Alma out of the way so he'd have a good shot at the new Alma on the new Earth. And why couldn't we just have *both* Almas on the new Earth, one for each of us? Because of an esoteric quantum-information-theoretic result Paul had mentioned earlier: the no-cloning principle. I'd never fully understood quantum information theory before, but this morning the discipline was hierophantically clear to me, as was the chain of reasoning that led from the no-cloning principle to the ironclad conclusion that only one version of a given person can be on a given Earth.

Moving silently, stealthily, I left the hut and crept uphill through the jungle, rapidly calculating the forces and the angular sweeps of my leg and arm motions—so as to minimize any crackling of the underbrush. Moments later I was lying on a mossy rock, peering at Paul and Haut through a scrim of ferns.

Haut was dressed in a silky white robe that the Nataraja must have made him, an angel's outfit. On his back were a pair of insect-style wings, transparent and irregularly veined like those of a giant housefly. His robe had a large lump in one pocket.

Haut and Paul were sitting on a fallen log by the side of a little stream, orchids and butterflies all around them. Despite my expectations, they weren't talking about Alma at all. They were talking about math; to be more precise, they were talking about Haut's new solution to a problem in higher analysis involving the axiom of hyperdetermi-nacy and projective sets of Hilbert-space vectors.

"It's a really major result," said Haut. "I can hardly believe how easily I'm making these discoveries. The lon-ger I stay here, the smarter I get."

"You should move to this level and be friends with the aliens who've colonized Nanonesia," said Paul. "They're mathematicians, Roland. Our crowd. Last night they were telling me—"

"I don't want to be near them," said Roland, frowning and shaking his head. "Giant cone shells, roaches, lizards—ugh." He patted the bulge in his robe. "I'm just glad I have this wonderful ray gun. I came across five of those lizards in the cave I crawled through to get here, and I cleaned them right out." He glanced around. "I do like the bright sun-light on this level. Maybe I should clean out all of Nanone-sia so I can live here with Alma. She'll come to me after you and Bela go back. I dazzle her, you know. I could tell when she visited my office with Bela." He gave a fatuous chuckle.

Paul's face had clouded over. "You're—you're saying you killed Mulvane and Vulma? And their kids? Damn you, Roland, they were the same as *people*. Number the-orists. I was eating *ice cream* with those kids last night." Paul rose to his feet. "That was an evil, evil thing to do. I can't believe you murdered them in cold blood." Paul pressed his hands to his temples, thinking. "And now the aliens are gonna give us the boot. Look, that plan we were talking about? You're gonna have to be ready to carry it out in an hour or two. And you're not coming back with us, right? I'd almost rather you didn't."

"I'll stay on," said Roland calmly. "I'm sensing profound new consequences of the ideas you were just telling me about the mathematical physics of La Hampa and the Earths. A nice start, that, Paul. And now the master can finish the apprentice's work. When I'm done, I'll be like a god. I'll set up the perfect world for myself and return in clouds of glory. Don't worry, Paul, after you see me at that lacy natural bridge this morning, you won't see me again. So you're foolish to be angry with me."

"Whatever," said Paul curtly. "I gotta go."

I barely beat Paul back to the room. I positioned myself on the edge of my bed as if just waking up. Paul looked abashed to see me. And no doubt my face wore an odd expression as well.

"Almost dawn," said Paul, forcing a hearty tone. "I've been barfing all night, that and doing mathematical physics." He waved his hand at the papers on the bed. "I figured out a result. La Hampa's time dimension is the same as the stacking direction of the alternate Earths. It's a virtual dimension that you might call 'otherness.' Hampatime is otherness."

"I heard your voice outside," I said, testing him. "That's what woke me. Who were you talking to? Roland Haut?"

"No, no," said Paul, squeezing his eyes shut to mime sincerity. He always did this when he lied. "I was retching and mumbling to myself. Making noise to scare off the pigs, bats, and jellyfish."

Fine. For my part, I wasn't going tell Paul I knew he was lying. In order to shepherd Alma back to an altered California, I'd need to stay a few steps ahead of Paul's little games. Meanwhile, disturbed though I was about Haut's murder of the lizards and about Paul's plans for Alma, I was genuinely curious about what Paul said he'd proved.

"Hampatime is otherness?"

"There's a whole lot of Earths," said Paul. "You can think of the Earths as drawings on a stack of papers, one Earth per sheet. And each drawing is a little different. Our Nataraja jellyfish keeps making our drawing better. Revising it. My calculations indicate that she makes precisely one new version of Earth for each week of hampatime that elapses here. Every Friday. She'll make a new one today. Note that since the time here is totally different from Earth time, that means we're likely to tunnel back to the same Earth-time that we left from. A little after noon on Thursday, June 3."

Alma shifted in her bed, making a grumbling waking-up noise. Dear Alma. "Our world's been revised all those times, and things are still so screwed up?" I said, trying to absorb Paul's strange notion.

"A certain amount of unhappiness is inevitable," said Paul. "It's the natural order of things. Also keep in mind that a Nataraja jellyfish's idea of a better and more interesting world might not be the same as ours. We should remember to be amazed that Earth hangs together as well as she does. Sunlight, gravity, clouds, oceans, life—things are very together. Complaining about, say, President Doakes's reelection is like bitching about one crooked bump of paint in van Gogh's *Starry Night*."

"Oh, you're *dazzling* me, Paul," I said. My anger over his intended betrayal of Alma was heating up. "You're not talking about the really important thing, are you?"

"How do you mean?" he said evasively. He busied himself gathering his wetsuit and his papers. "I think we should get going on the trip home right away. It's getting light now. I'll talk to those roaches and cone shells about opening another hypertunnel. It'll lead to the jellyfish-god's latest version of Earth. You see how that works? We can't tunnel back to a version that corresponds to an earlier hampatime. We can't go back to our old Earth."

"Yeah, I get it," I said impatiently. "But the important—"

"You go see that freaky jellyfish and make your wishes," interrupted Paul. "I don't need to be there for that. Just be sure and tell her there's no meth or Ritalin for Paul on the new—"

"The *important* thing is that you're going to try and ditch Alma," I exclaimed. "Because she loves me. You're gonna want to be with that *other* Alma on the new Earth. You think that if the other Paul didn't take speed, then the other Alma would still be living with him. Call them Paul-2 and Alma-2. You'll boot out Paul-2 and settle down with Alma-2 yourself. Our real Alma would get in the way. You already said so before."

"And what about you and Cammy-2?" challenged Paul. "Isn't that what this is all about?"

"Stop *arguing*," muttered Alma, waking up. She was tan and lovely. "God, you two are uptight." She yawned and stretched an arm, holding her sheet over her breasts. "Were you talking about me? Was I bad last night?"

"You were being yourself, Alma," said Paul. "I gotta run." And then he was out the door. "That cuke-weed was wack," said Alma. "I was acting like my father. Ugh. But today I'm good. I feel—smarter." She laughed. "As if that were even possible."

"I'm smarter too," I said, sitting down on the edge of her bed. "It's the hierophantics kicking in. Paul puked, so he didn't absorb as much as us. We can think rings around him now."

"I always could," said Alma. "When it comes to things that really matter." She was silent for a second. "Okay, I just pieced together what I heard while I was waking up. Paul is planning to leave me here."

"And Roland Haut is gonna help him," I said. "The issue is that there's gonna be copies of you, me, and Paul in the world we go back to."

"*And* a Cammy for you," said Alma in an aggrieved tone. "I wonder what *I* should ask for?"

"I'm sure you have a plan," I said. "Last night you said that all the rest of us were losers."

Alma guffawed. "I said that? It's that jealousy thing. And feeling less-than because I don't dig math. What I want is a career in politics, Bela. I want to be a speechwriter, or maybe run for office myself. Senator Alma Ziff. And you can be my little house-husband. With his cute equations."

"Last night you said—"

"Let go of it, Bela. Do you still love me?"

"I do." I lay down next to her and kissed her. "You're fun," I said. "I'm starting to realize it's okay that you're so high maintenance."

"What do we do about Alma-2, Bela-2, and Paul-2 when we go back?" asked Alma, molding herself against me.

"Supposedly the new Earth's reality would get unstable

if there were two copies of anyone," I said. "So I figure we'll bump those guys back through the hypertunnel into La Hampa. And then they're on their own."

"That's kind of pushy isn't it?" said Alma. "Kicking them off their home world? Not that I mind being pushy. Do you actually think they'll be at Miller Beach right near the natural bridge? Conveniently positioned to be forced into the hypertunnel?"

"I think the jellyfish will fix it that way. Or maybe it'll happen automatically. There's higher-order patterns that I don't understand. I think no matter when we leave here, we'll end up back at Big Sur on June 3, with our counterparts in the water near the bridge."

"So then what's the rush?" said Alma cozily. "I'd like to hang around and explore La Hampa for awhile. Don't you want to? What's so great about another Earth? Same old, same old."

"You have a point." Lying here with Alma, saving Cammy didn't seem quite so urgent anymore. The laws of logic ensured that I could never change the past of Earth-1. Cammy-1 was dead for good and she wasn't ever coming back. For the first time I fully accepted this. But there was still the problem of Roland Haut.

"Let's stay here for a month," suggested Alma.

"Well, the aliens are gonna want to evict us," I said after a pause. "Haut killed Mulvane and Vulma and their kids."

"No!"

"And Haut's promised Paul to keep you from going back through the hypertunnel," I added.

"Haut's going to kill me?" said Alma, hierophantically getting the picture. "Maybe not. He wants you to be his mate."

"Yuck," said Alma. "Death before dishonor." Despite all the problems this morning, her mood remained sunny. It was like she wasn't taking anything that seriously. "So if you're about to leave, you're gonna visit that jellyfish to make magic wishes, right? I'm going with you. I'm not gonna be the submissive girlfriend cheerleading on the sidelines." She gave me a kiss. "You should be the one to cheer for *me*."

"Yay, Alma!" Swept into her giddiness, I hopped up and executed a convincing Herkie cheerleader jump, with my legs stretched like a hurdler's, one fist on my hip and one hand high in the air.

"You're on my squad," said Alma. And then we made love.

Afterwards we found Paul by the lagoon with the cone shells and the cockroaches on the marbled patio. The baby cone shells and roaches were romping around playing centrifugal bumble-puppy again.

"Paul says you three are tunneling back today?" said Osckar. "Busy, busy."

"I hear there were three others who came through with you," said Tanya. "They're up at the next level, the one we call Paradisio? If you bump copies of yourselves back here, maybe we'll send the copies up there too. Nothing personal, but, mathematically speaking, you people aren't all that interesting."

"What *about* those people above the sky?" said Alma, gazing up. She was dressed in her bikini and necklace. "From the helicopter. The woman and the two men. Why can't we go hang with them, Bela? Instead of with Paul the traitor and Haut the killer. Come on."

"Go for it, Alma," said Paul. "But Bela and I are going back today. Right, Bela?"

"Maybe not," I said. If we moved to Paradisio, the Nanonesian aliens might leave us alone, even after they found out about Mulvane. "I'm sticking with Alma, whatever she does. We can talk to the jellyfish, sure, but we're thinking we might stay here for a few weeks."

"Yay, Bela!" said Alma.

"Jellyfish almost ripe," said Rowena, her voice a windy gust from her striped mouth tube. "Soon she make sun. Then no more Earth tunnels."

"Miss Glyphic English is trying to say that if you want to talk to the jellyfish, you have to do it soon," said Tanya. "Each of the jellyfish is a god for a series of versions of a particular world. And once the beings from a jellyfish's worlds begin finding their way to La Hampa, the jellyfish is almost done with that stage of her life. She gets so much energy from the tunneling that she becomes a La Hampan sun. It's all part of the Nataraja life cycle."

"I do want to make sure that Cammy gets to live in another Earth," I said.

"And that I don't have my problem with speed," put in Paul with an earnest smile. "Don't forget to ask for that."

"You actually think that staying clean is all it would take for you to keep me?" put in Alma, reading him like a book. "I wonder. I do have that security-seeking side to my personality, but, Paul, you're such an insufferable—"

"God dammit, Alma," snapped Paul, "If you don't watch yourself—"

"Why even futz around with wishes?" interrupted Osckar. "You newcomers always want to do that. Breathing down God's neck. Like she doesn't know what to do on her own? You're so much wiser? Dear God, don't forget to make the plants grow. Dear God, make sure that cows give milk. Dear God, let me crawl up my butt and shovel out my own crap because I'm worried my colon doesn't know what to do."

"It just seems best to stick to our original plan," I said, feeling foolish.

"Is there a very last Earth that our jellyfish-god is gonna make?" asked Alma. "A best of all possible worlds? The final draft of the Big Bestseller?"

"Unger and Mulvane argue about that all the time," said Osckar. "Unger thinks that a world's jellyfish flares up in a, whaddaya, infinite Zeno series without a limit point. Like always covering ninety percent of the remaining distance without ever reaching the goal; I'm talking 9, 9.9, 9.99, 9.999, and so on, forever falling short of the perfect 10.0. But number-skulled Mulvane says that *obviously* there's a very last one, the final best version of whatever world that jellyfish was working on. We should find those two characters and get them to argue for us. I know Unger's sleeping off those grork toxins, but where *is* Mulvane? And Vulma? Usually they're up bright and early with the kids."

"Roland Haut murdered them and their children in their sleep," said Alma. "Roland flew up from his island, crawled up through the lizards' tunnel, and incinerated them with his ray gun. You might as well know."

"Alma!" exclaimed Paul in a scolding tone. "Don't listen to her," he told the others.

Tanya twisted her head from side to side, the light glinting off the facets of her eyes. She looked at us one by one, and then at the vacant black mouth of the lizard's tunnel on the hill above.

"Oh hell," she said sorrowfully. "It's come to that? Poor Mulvane and Vulma. And those sweet children. Haut's gonna pay. And it's back through the tunnel with you three."

"Eat Haut," said Jewelle, her red stinger lolling in her mouth.

"It's not our fault that Haut's crazy," put in Alma. "I'm scared he wants to kill *me*. That's why I told you. And Paul here wants Haut to stop me from going back. If I try and go through that tunnel, Haut's going to pop up from the water and shoot me!"

"Good," said Tanya. "That way we'll catch him. You're bait. Get them moving, Osckar."

"Whaddaya, whaddaya, the bum's rush," said Osckar, pointing his antennae towards our surfboards at the edge of the lagoon. "Hop on the boards and start paddling. Right now. Goom-bye."

"At least let Alma and me talk to our jellyfish before we go," I begged. "Please, Tanya."

Tanya and Osckar touched antennae in a quick private consultation.

"Oh, all right," said Tanya after a bit. "The more the jellyfish deals with you, the sooner she's likely to become a new sun. And we need that. We'll give you half an hour. Meanwhile Paul here gets on his board and swims out to the natural bridge to wait. Jewelle, you guard him. And Rowena, you escort these two to Jellyfish Lake and then bring them out to the natural bridge too. And no funny business, Bela. You know what those cone shells can do."

"Thank you, Tanya," I said. "See you later, Paul." Alma and I hurried up the hill. As we passed the lizards' tunnel mouth, I noticed a smell of charred flesh. "Haut never did like number theorists," I remarked to Alma. "He's an analyst."

"There's rival schools of math?"

"*Oh* yeah. You could learn math if you wanted to, Alma. Now that you know hierophantics."

"Why bother."

Seen from the ridge in the daylight, Jellyfish Lake looked small and turbid. As we scrambled down the rocky path to it, I began seeing jellyfish near the surface, myriads of them softly beating.

"Hello," I called when we reached the water's edge. "We're here."

There was no visible response.

"Maybe we should swim out," said Alma. "Do they sting?"

I waded in to knee level and touched a few of the jellyfish. They slid across my fingers as harmlessly as wet Jell-O. "No sting," I said. "They feel good, actually."

"Let's do it naked," said Alma, slipping out of her bikini and laying her necklace on top of it. I left my trunks on the shore, and the two of us swam out into the lake. Trees shaded the edges; the gentlest of Nanonesian breezes riffled the surface. The little sun's rays were angling down the ridge into the greenish-yellow, algae-rich water, warming it to nearly the temperature of a bath. And all around us pulsed the jellyfish, millions of them.

Each jellyfish was a little dome, with four short, dangling arms beneath it like the legs of a table. The domed bells were pulsing in waves that moved out from the center, bounced off the rim and returned to the center, there to begin a new cycle. This meant that the smaller jellyfish were pulsing faster: less distance from center to rim. I pointed this out to Alma; she'd already noticed, hierophantically enhanced as she was.

We dove down to about twenty feet, looking for the big one from last night. My visual field held only sunlit yellow-green water and jellyfish, everywhere and at every angle. It was hard to tell which way was up. There might have been about sixty jellyfish touching my body at any one time, four big guys, eight mediums, sixteen smalls, thirty-two tiny ones, like that. A power law.

"It's incredible to imagine that each of them keeps creating new versions of some particular world," I said to Alma when we got back to the surface. Rowena was floating in the air, twenty feet above us, watching.

"It's incredible that we haven't found the big jellyfish yet," said Alma. "I'm starting to feel itchy all over. I'm about ready to get out. They do sting a little bit, you know."

Just then we felt a cold flow of water against our feet, an upwelling as something huge moved towards the surface.

"Here she comes," I said.

Without even slowing down, the giant jellyfish moved into our location, engulfing us. And now Alma and I were inside a damp, echoing body cavity. Somehow the little space loomed as large as a cathedral. The floor was as a glassy sea, and in the center stood an alabaster throne ringed by an emerald rainbow. A figure stepped from the throne and walked slowly towards us, a form like a four-armed Shiva with a woman's face. Each of her gestures was ideally formed and laden with meaning; each gesture was a novel, a theorem, a cosmic work of art.

"Welcome Bela and Alma," came the voice in my head. "You are as one flesh, one seeker. I bid you bow before me. I am your God."

Gladly I knelt. Peace filled my heart. I thought to glance over at Alma; her face was suffused with joy. The jellyfish telepathy was hitting us both. For half an instant I flipped back to a not-so-pleasant image of us squeezed into a sac in the body of an alien coelenterate, but then a tingle ran through my brain and I was again seeing the sacred figure, the holy dancer, the end of every quest.

She danced on, her limbs tracing slow, exquisite paths. Alma and I sat cross-legged, holding hands. Veils streamed from the goddess's arms, the motion-trails weaving into a glowing cable that led away from the throne, across the sea, dwindling into the distance where a tiny planet Earth floated at the long cord's end. I could see the ice-caps, the continents, the clouds.

"What do you seek, Bela?" asked the goddess. "Utter your heartfelt wish."

I found myself unable to speak anything but the truth. "I wish I'd made love with Cammy at my mother's house after the Washer Drop concert in San Jose," I said. Abruptly Alma dropped my hand. "And that I hadn't left Cammy alone in Palo Alto," I added.

"And the wish of your friend Paul?" said the goddess, gazing at me with endlessly deep eyes.

"Oh, Paul wishes he'd never been on meth or Ritalin," I said grudgingly. "Let all this be so," said the goddess, with a smooth gesture of an arm. "What do you seek, dear Alma?"

"I—it doesn't matter," said Alma in a small voice. "I don't want to go back to Earth with him."

"Yet you and this man are as one," said the goddess.

"Let me stay!" cried Alma.

"You will part," said the goddess. "And join again. Remember the last things."

She made a final fluid hand gesture and released us. The water rushed in upon us and we were on our own, far below the surface of Jellyfish Lake. It was a long swim up; we emerged coughing and gasping for air.

"Look, Alma," I said, as soon as I could talk. "The guy who slept with Cammy-2 is gonna be Bela-2, not me. I'm still faithful to you."

"For how long?" she demanded. "Screwing Cammy was your *first wish* to God! And there I was feeling like you and I were practically married. I'm such a sucker. You're on your own now, Bela, I mean it. If I can find a way, I'm not going back to Earth at all. I'll go find those Stanford people who came through in the helicopter."

Rowena was above us, still standing guard. "Come lagoon now," she said.

In silence we two walked back over the ridge, got our bathing-suits and wetsuits together, and paddled out toward the natural bridge. It was tougher than it had been paddling in. A tide was running, and the wind had risen enough to make some waves. Alma was sulky and balky, but Rowena kept urging her on, even to the point of threatening to sting her.

We found Paul floating out there with Jewelle watching him. There was no sign of a hypertunnel. "About time," said Paul as we pulled up next to him. "Are you going to make a hypertunnel for us, Rowena?"

"You do," said Rowena. "Pray jellyfish."

"Not me," said Paul. "I already put in a lifetime's worth of that prayer shit, growing up as a preacher's son."

There'd been no religion at all in my family, other than some perfunctory Confucian ancestor ceremonies. But the divine dancer had converted me.

"The jellyfish is God," I said.

"And Bela couldn't wait to tell her that his biggest wish in life is to fuck Cammy," said Alma. "Can you believe that?"

"Did you tell her about getting me off speed?" asked Paul. "Yeah, yeah," I said. "She said okay."

"Thanks, dog. Now pray for the hypertunnel," said Paul. Certainly I could imagine praying to the divine jellyfish. But with Alma angry, Paul dubious, the wind rising, and the cone shells no longer so friendly—I found it hard to focus.

"Please make a tunnel back to Earth for us," I said into the air.

"Let me stay here," added Alma in a more fervent tone. "I don't want to go. Help me, jellyfish. Help me, Nataraja."

"Pray better, Bela," said Jewelle. "Like magic spell."

"Tunnel, tunnel, tunnel," I chanted. "Earth, earth, earth. Please send us back, dear God of Jellyfish Lake." No tunnel appeared. The breeze freshened; low clouds scudded by. I heard a rumble of thunder.

"Oh, hell, I better show you how to use the unknown tongue," said Paul. "Like my Dad. *Wah, wah, ooth wun graar umb-umb-umb ka-wheeee!*"

And still we got no tunnel. But now the hierophantic part of my brain showed me the special incantation, the precise sequence of sounds that I needed to make.

"*Inch'allah tekelili eloi uborka Gaia*," I said. As I intoned the formula, I visualized the glowing dancer within the jellyfish. Something wriggled beneath the surface of the sea; swirls eddied the water beneath the arch.

"Look out!" yelled Alma, eager to get away. "There's a whirlpool! It'll suck us down!" She paddled off to the side.

Rowena flipped out her long red tongue to pull Alma and her surfboard back into our midst. The cloudy sky began spitting rain. The sluggish eddy beneath the arch wasn't anything like a hypertunnel yet.

I said the magic spell once more. "*Inch'allah tekelili eloi uborka Gaia.*" With a sharp crack of thunder, a giant streamer of light pulsed up from the alien mathematicians' island behind us. I saw the face of the goddess within the fiery pillar. And now the column of light split into branches. Most of the branches went up through the sky—but one arched like a rainbow, alighting upon the natural bridge and bedecking it with a crown of purple flames.

Thunder rolled again and a squall pelted me, stinging my skin. The tongues of flame licked into the space beneath the bridge; the maelstrom in the sea rose up to became a waterspout within the bridge's arch. The twisting vortices of fire, air, and water wove themselves into a glowing egg: the mouth of a hypertunnel.

"You go," said Rowena, propelling my surfboard forward with the lip of her shell. The alien mathematician showed no emotion, and she offered no fond good-byes—just a shove. Geek. It was Haut's fault that the La Hampans didn't like us anymore. I'd kind of hoped to see him appear by the bridge and get eaten by Jewelle, but that no longer seemed to be in the cards.

I was sliding steadily towards the hypertunnel now; it felt as if I were on rails. As before, the flow of time was distorted near the tunnel's mouth. The raindrops ahead of me were rapid streaks; the ones behind me hung vibrating in the air. I craned back over my shoulder to see what was happening to my two companions.

"I'm not going back with them!" Alma yelled, trying again to paddle away. From my vantage point, her voice sounded deep and slow. "If you don't want me at this level, bump me up to Paradisio!" By way of answer, Rowena propelled her towards the arch in my wake. Alma's gestures sped up as she came, the mauve glow of the hypertunnel's mouth glinting off her X-eyed smiley face medallion.

Paul was taking up the rear. "Don't kill Haut," he told Jewelle, his voice thick and syrupy. "He's nuts, but he's my friend. If you catch him, just send him through the tunnel after us."

"You go," said Jewelle, as cold as Rowena. She shoved Paul after Alma and me.

I looked up ahead, making sure I was heading directly into the hypertunnel. In just a moment I'd be in. Down near the core of the egg, I could see a tiny image of the Pacific surf lit by the good old California sun.

Glancing back again, I saw Paul trying to push Alma off to one side so she'd miss the tunnel. For once these two were in agreement. Rowena and Jewelle flew towards them and—

Haut shot up out of the water like a breaching whale. He was still in his white robe, with those furiously beating gossamer wings strapped to his back, the wings etching frantic figure eights into the air. In his right hand he clutched his red and yellow ray gun, an anachronistic wonder-weapon with Art Deco fins. The apparition was comical, but Haut was aiming at Alma and preparing to—

Jewelle descended upon Haut from behind, her mouth distended into a hideous floppy funnel, her stinger darting for the math professor's neck. Haut managed only one shot before he disappeared into Jewelle's crop. Although he'd aimed well, the hierophantic time-warped Alma managed to roll off her board before the beam hit; the gun's rays bounced off the water and into the mouth of our hypertunnel, lighting it up like a neon tube.

And then I was well into the tunnel, its hyperspace corridor tight and weird. It was all I could do to stay on my board. I saw Paul, myself, the still-lingering energies of Haut's blast, the vine-like control cord of the jellyfish—but no Alma.

I heard a low rumble as Paul and I popped out from the Miller Beach natural bridge into the oncoming icy surf. Just ahead of us were three surfers: identical copies of Alma, me, and Paul. The Paul-2 was riding midway between Bela-2 and Alma-2; he was kneeling on his board rather than standing. The three had caught a wave and were heading to my right, on course to avoid the big rock behind me that held the natural bridge. But I just happened to be positioned so as to block their path.

Bela-2 shouted a warning to the others, then veered to my left to keep from hitting me. Paul-2 and Alma-2 followed his lead. As they passed, Alma-2 yelled "Goober!" at me for cutting in on them—and in that split second our eyes met. She was wearing the same yellow bikini, but no gold necklace. She recognized me; her jaw dropped. The wave carried her past me. Again I heard a rumble.

Turning my board around to stare at the natural bridge, I saw no sign of Alma-1 coming out. But the glow from within it meant that the hypertunnel remained open. I was still expecting her to appear.

Paul-1 was closer to the rock, ideally situated to block the Earth-2 surfers from any route save into the glowing square hole. He was paddling hard now, as if trying to leave an escape route for Alma-2. But fate was such that the three whooped and went for it, just as we three would have done. They disappeared into the square hole.

All this time the rumbling had been growing; now it rose to a sharp peak. Dust sprang from the natural bridge; the stones tottered; foam and ripples surged from within the square arch.

I paddled towards it, my stomach hollow with fear. The glow in the door was gone. Though the stones were still shifting, Paul had gone all the way in; a moment later his voice echoed off the stones, shaking with grief.

"Alma! Alma! Alma!"

Paul and I fished her out from the water, pathetically limp, her skin cold, her ankle still leashed to her surfboard. One of the falling rocks had crushed the back of her head.

"Which Alma is it?" I said, feeling unworthy for asking.

"She's not wearing that necklace," said Paul slowly. "I guess it's Alma-2. This was supposed to be my Alma now. All those grandiose maneuvers of ours, Bela, and all we did was kill her."

"If you hadn't gotten Haut to come and shoot that ray gun into the tunnel—" I began.

"Don't," said Paul, his voice low and sad.

Another rock dropped from the arch above us, nearly hitting us. We barely noticed.

"My Alma's still alive in La Hampa," I said, feeling desperate. "She stalled Jewelle and Rowena from pushing her through the hypertunnel. I bet they had to settle for carrying her up to Paradisio."

"Or maybe they *did* push her through the tunnel and her necklace fell into the ocean," said Paul. "Maybe this is Alma-1, and Alma-2 is in La Hampa. Either way—we suck." He wept as he kissed Alma's pale, cold cheek. "I loved her as much as you did, Bela."

My shield of denial gave way. This was Alma, and the 1 and 2 business didn't matter. This beloved woman was dead. I threw back my head and howled.

Paul and I floated Alma to shore on her board, her blood running freely into the sea.

Some of the same people as before were on the beach: the boy with the blonde pompadour, the leathery woman, the shrill little girl. And there, sitting on some towels, was Cammy Vendt, wearing her black jeans and sleeveless T-shirt.

"Is Alma hurt bad?" she cried. "She's dead," said Paul

flatly. He turned to me, his face working. "Look who's waiting, Bela. Lucky you."

"Don't," I said. "We have to stay friends. And maybe—" But now Cammy and the tanned woman had come running out to us.

"Get the ranger, Tyler!" shouted the brown-skinned woman, and the blonde teenage boy sprinted away. As if creepily fascinated, the little girl in the red bathing-suit inched towards Alma's limp body.

Cammy hugged me. She smelled good; she was lithe and warm in my arms. "Oh, Bela, this is grim. That was an earthquake, you know. And you're okay? Poor Alma. I'm sorry, Paul. You were a great couple."

"We could have been," said Paul distractedly. He walked over to Cammy's towels and lay down on his side, curling himself into the fetal position.

"Stop that, Ashley," said the tan woman to the serious-faced little girl, who was holding out her hand towards Alma. I now noticed that the girl was wearing a vlog ring.

"It's gonna help my ratings, Ma," said Ashley. "I'll be one in a million!"

"You want me to take that thing away?" said her mother. "Go sit down."

Ashley stomped across the beach, scowling and delivering an angry commentary to her hand.

"How—how would a kid get a vlog ring?" I asked Cammy. It was hard to believe Cammy was here, back from the dead, with me talking to her.

She gave me a worried look. "We just finished writing a song about it with K-Jen, Bela. Evil Eye?" I still looked blank, so she continued. "Veeter and Leni Pex are giving vlog rings away with the meals at all the Monogrubs for their *One in a Million* show, and it's really a Heritagist data-mining scam? Come on!"

"Oh, that's right," I said. Apparently that show had been around longer on Earth-2.

Cammy stared searchingly at my face. I found it very strange to see her in motion, to hear her low, urgent voice. "Are you tripping?" she asked. "Or did you hit your head? Lie down for a minute, Bela. You're shaking."

I stretched out beside Paul, who was curled up with his eyes closed. Up the beach, the ranger arrived, a wild-haired, bearded Big Sur type wearing official green work clothes and a hat with an insignia. When the dark-skinned woman ran towards him, little Ashley darted over to us, camera hand extended again.

"Was she your girlfriend?" she asked, holding her vlog ring towards Paul.

"What the fuck?" said Paul, opening his eyes.

"Ooooh," squealed Ashley.

"Sir!" called the ranger, walking over with Cammy at his side and the tan woman and the blonde boy close behind. "Is either of you injured? I've called the sheriff and an emergency vehicle. One of you can ride to the hospital with your friend. They'll be taking her to Monterey."

"I'll go with her," said Paul quietly. "You and Cammy pick me up there, Bela."

Paul and I found some of our clothes on the towels; we got dressed.

"Paul's crying," said Ashley to her hand.

"I warned you, Ashley," said the tan woman, but the avid little girl stayed well out of her mother's reach, reporting the events and building up her ratings: circling us like a seagull as Paul and the EMTs carried Alma away; recording my minimal statement to the sheriff; filming Cammy and me leaving that unhappy beach.

My car was in the lot, much the same squinty whale as before, although the script chrome insignia on the tailgate now said "Golden Mullet" instead of "Bel Paese." I set down the surfboards and gazed at Cammy standing there tough and relaxed, Cammy watching me with alert eyes.

"You zipped the key into your wetsuit," she said, as if reading my mind. "Give it to me and I'll drive. You're in no condition."

I found the key and—wonder of wonders—in this world it still worked. I unlocked the car and slid in with Cammy, letting her take the driver's seat. It was kind of great to be alone with her. Yes, she was weak-chinned, slightly bucktoothed, and her lips were rather thin. But she had such poise, such grace, such womanliness. Cammy was vibrant and approachable and matter-of-fact.

Maybe things would settle down and be okay. I could do worse than have Cammy for my girlfriend. With all the alternate worlds to choose from, perhaps the death of one Alma on one Earth wasn't such a huge deal. Yes, I know that sounds callous, but that's where I was at just then. Maybe I was in shock.

I leaned over and slowly kissed Cammy. She wasn't surprised; she didn't pull back. I concluded that in this world we were lovers. Probably we'd fucked at Ma's.

Cammy drove up the winding beach road to Route One, then headed north towards Monterey. "You're still down with opening for AntiCrystal on Saturday?" said Cammy.

"Huh?"

"AntiCrystal. Wacław Smorynski? Chainsaw Crying Clown? Jutta Schreck? It was Jutta's idea, remember, she heard our San Jose concert on the web. And when the singer for their opening act OD'ed this week, Jutta thought of us. Jutta's my hero as a bass player. And Wacław is the greatest singer on Earth." Cammy pronounced his name with relish, using what must have been the correct Polish pronunciation: *Vahkwahv*. "There's gonna be a huge crowd. We'll have to step way up. We'll rehearse tonight—hopefully you're not too wrecked—and tomorrow. Don't even dream of holing up with Paul and Henry Nunez to work on the Gobrane. Our sound check at Heritagist Park is four o'clock Saturday afternoon."

I was relieved to hear her mention Gobranes. That meant that, if all else failed, I could eventually return to La Hampa and rejoin Alma. But—

"Heritagist Park?"

"The San Francisco baseball stadium, Bela? The Heritagists bought the naming rights a couple of months ago when they kicked off the hundred-percent campaign. You're tripping, right?"

"Um, I have memory loss. Now that we're alone, I guess I can tell you about it. You're not vlogging us or anything, are you?"

"Vlogging's for goobs anymore, with that Monogrub *One in a Million* show," said Cammy. "No way would I vlog now. I've never seen a new medium turn to shit so fast. You were hip to ride that edgy first vlog burst and get Washer Drop's music out there in time, Bela." She looked over at me, a half-smile on her lips. "You three huffed those conotoxins, huh? That's why you did such a—I'm sorry—such a fucked-up dumb-ass maneuver like trying to surf through that little square hole. It must suck to be tripping in the middle of a tragedy. I bet things seem horrible to you right now." She gave me a reassuring pat on the hand. "When I'm in a really bad place mentally, I always try turning it into music. Or I talk it out."

I took a deep breath and plunged in. "I'm a different Bela from the one you drove down here with, Cammy. I'm Bela from an alternate Earth. You died on that alternate world; a stalker stabbed you to death. I couldn't stand it, so I went up to a higher world and found my way to an Earth where you're still alive."

"Those are some twisted hallucinations all right," said Cammy shaking her head. "Are you so high that you don't even know it? Alma was showing us the squeeze-bulbs on the way down, remember? She got them from her brother Pete. Three doses."

"I'm not the same Bela that you knew. But I still want to be your lover."

"It's the old Bela that *I* want," said Cammy, kind of joking around. "Where's the *old* Bela?"

"Paul and I bumped him and the other two. We forced them into that natural bridge so they'd go to the higher world."

There was a silence. The car slowed down. "I hope

you're not saying you murdered Alma. Or that you imagine you did. Because if—"

"I wasn't even under the bridge when the earthquake hit," I said. "The *old* Bela was in there, but I was outside, waiting."

"Stop it!" said Cammy, giving me a hard poke. "You're creeping me *out*!"

I decided to back off. "Sorry," I said. "Maybe I'm hysterical. The shock of Alma's death. And, yeah, the conotoxins. Talk about a bad trip." Apparently conotoxins were a street drug on this world—put here as a cosmic joke on me by the jellyfish god.

"Just rest," said Cammy. "Forget what I said about 'talking it out.' If you're still tweaking this hard when we get to Klownetown, I'll score you some Quaak. Spun ravers always use Quaak to come down."

"What's Klownetown?"

"The place where you live, Bela? A university town across the bay from San Francisco? Named after the early Golden State settler, Willem Klowne. I learned all about him at dear old Akron High School."

"That town was called Humelocke in the world I came from," I said.

"Enough with the bootsy nightmares, bud. Bottle them up and make a song. We need two more by Saturday." Cammy fiddled with the radio. "There's hardly any stations—oh, here we go."

". . . week the hundred-percent campaign has been gaining a surprising amount of traction," said a journalist's voice. "When President Doakes proposed his hundred-percent campaign in his State of the Union message last January, the notion was derided and then ignored. But somehow a series of news developments over the last few days have brought the hundred-percent campaign to the front burner, and to full boil."

"I hate those freakin' anti-humanity pigs so much," said Cammy, reaching for the radio.

"Leave it on," I said, touching her hand. "I need this information so I can orient myself."

"Oh, this news is gonna be perfect for you, where your head's at right now," said Cammy. "It's gonna seem like you've ended up in a sick, weird, evil alternate reality. Feel it, bud, that's the world we're livin' in."

The show had switched to a tape of Joe Doakes at a recent rally. "In these perilous times, our nation deserves a hundred percent Heritagist government. We can afford no less. Now, I don't mean to question the patriotism and honesty of each and every member of the Common Ground party. But—if you buy a dozen eggs and one or two or three of them is rotten—common sense says you get your money back and a fresh dozen from the store." His voice was dry and humorless as a locust's chirp.

"What I'm saying is simple common sense," continued Doakes. "Over and over, the elected and appointed officials of the Common Ground Party have let our people down—in our Congress, in our courts, in our state legislatures, and in our governors' mansions. I'm proposing a hundred-percent Heritagist victory this fall. We won't settle for a mere majority. We've endured the sorry parades of Common Ground filibusters, we've seen our dreams die in the power-brokered special-interest Common Ground committees, we've tasted the lash of the willful, revisionist Common Ground courts." Doakes was a madman. But each time he stopped, his audience burst into wild applause.

"With complete control of the Congress and the state legislatures, we can use the constitutional power of impeachment to remove the activist Common Ground judges," rasped the mean little voice. "This is what the balance of powers stands for. With complete control of the Congress and the state legislatures, we will propose and, with the people's help, *pass* a constitutional amendment to remove the outdated notions of Presidential and Congressional term limits. This is what a stable democracy deserves. The success of the hundred-percent campaign will bring lasting homeland security, a wave of transformative legislation, and an end to the prideful tyranny of the courts. Our great nation deserves no less than the hundred-percent freedom that a hundred-percent Heritagist victory will bring." The applause crested like a thunderous wave, with the audience members cheering themselves hoarse.

"That was President Joe Doakes addressing a national congress of trade unions," said the journalist's voice. "Only a few months ago, the hundred-percent campaign seemed dead on arrival, yet this week President Doakes received a warm welcome from what had once been a Common Ground constituency. How is it that the hundred-percent campaign has made such inroads in the mainstream this week? Part of the explanation seems to lie with the new Heritagist publicity campaign being orchestrated by Congress's latest addition, the former high-tech executive and new Speaker of the House, Van Veeter."

"Your pal," said Cammy. "You should be ashamed."

I took in a little more news, and then I must have dozed off. When I awoke Cammy was parking the car on a hill overlooking the bay in front of the low, modern Steinbeck Memorial Hospital. "Here we are," she said brightly. "Got meds? Doesn't look like the earthquake had any effects up here. Oh-oh, there's Henry Nunez talking to Paul. Don't let him pull you into another big science powwow, Bela. We need to get back to Klownetown and rehearse."

Paul and Nunez were right inside the hospital main door in the waiting area, with Nunez's red car parked by the curb. From their body language, it looked as if Paul and Nunez were on very good terms. I saw no sign of that skinny mean security guy who'd been with Nunez before—Tito Cruz.

My mind was kicking back into gear; I still had some of that hierophantic thing working for me. In this world Cammy hadn't been murdered; therefore Veeter had kept Paul and me as consultants; therefore we were Van's and Nunez's trusted coworkers. Thanks to the four-way collaboration, the Gobranes were working really well; therefore the Heritagists were using the Gobranes to predict the effects of their news releases and ads; therefore the Heritagists had gotten the upper hand in manipulating public opinion. Veeter must have been doing some manipulating on his own hook as well, if he'd already become Speaker of the House.

"Hi Bela," said Nunez in an easy voice as I entered the hospital. "What a tragedy. Alma was a wonderful woman. So lovely, so interesting to talk to." He had a warm smile and pleasant eyes.

"We're about done here," said Paul. "They've notified Alma's family. I think I'd rather not wait for them."

He gave me a significant look, and I remembered Pete Ziff's last words to us: "You two guys want to be worrying about taking good care of my baby sister. Or I'll waste your ass." Of course that had been back on Earth-1, but the Pete of Earth-2 was likely to have the same attitude.

"It's a shame nobody could predict that little earthquake," said Nunez in his gentle tone. "Another few weeks and we might get tectonics modeled, too. You two should think about morphon structures for geology. After you're done grieving, of course."

"Oh, Paul!" It was Lulu Cliff, coming across the lobby from the ladies' room with her arms outstretched. She hugged Paul hard, for quite a long time, with tears running down her face and leaving trails of mascara. "You two were perfect together," said Lulu. "If there's anything at all I can do . . ." She stepped back and dabbed at her eyes, looking quite fetching in her sleeveless lacy lavender blouse, red miniskirt, and low, fleece-lined gold boots, with her all-purpose cell phone device clipped to one boot top. She leaned against Henry Nunez, keeping her eyes fixed on Paul.

"Soooo," said Cammy. "Do we go home?"

"I guess so," I said.

"I brought Bela and Paul some new toys," said Nunez, glancing around the lobby to see if anyone was filming us.

"Come on out to my car. And, Cammy and Lulu, this is one of those paranoid non-disclosure things, so—"

"Circle jerk time," said Lulu. "The boys and their toys. I love how you play bass, Cammy. I was thinking of writing a song for you about lugs and bis. I'm looking for a new career."

"That could almost be a title," said Cammy, evenly regarding Lulu from beneath her long, level eyebrows. "I like it. We need more numbers for the stadium concert Saturday night."

"It's so awesome that you're opening for AntiCrystal," gushed Lulu. "Henry got us really good seats. You should come see Washer Drop with us, Paul. You don't want to mope at home."

"You *should* go with her, Paul," put in Henry. "I didn't get a chance to tell you yet, Lulu, but I can't make it to that concert. We're putting in a new production line at the Watsonville plant this weekend."

"You're handing me off?" said Lulu, an edge in her voice. "After getting me fired from *Buzz?* Well, I think you're too short for me, how about that? And your company's core business sucks. Take me to the Washer Drop concert, Paulie?"

"I don't know," said Paul. "Maybe moping at home is precisely what I need to do. Alma's lying dead in a cooler about a hundred feet from here."

"Sorry!" said Lulu. "Let's go outside so we can smoke, Cammy."

"I have the title for your song," said Cammy as they made their way to the door. "'Lug Bi War Bride.' Patriarchy and the battle of the sexes. And it's like the singer is from another country."

"Yes!"

Cammy and Lulu stood in the shade of a eucalyptus tree, smoking and talking while Paul and I sat in the back of Henry Nunez's car with him between us. Henry reached up to the passenger seat and got two small, cubical, black leatherette cases for us.

"Look inside," he said with a low chuckle. "Gobrane, phase two. We've already trademarked it as the Gobubble. Van's written a new operating system for it. He's holed up on his ranch in the Santa Cruz Mountains."

I tipped back the hinged lid of my velvet-lined box, letting the sun shine in to reveal an object very much like a leathery soap bubble: a shiny, hollow, semi-transparent sphere with iridescent colors playing over its surface. When I pushed down on it, the skin dimpled. It felt tough and unlikely to pop.

"Do you have to mount a Gobubble in something else?" asked Paul, staring down at his magic ball. He'd taken it out of the case and was rolling it from hand to hand. "Like the way we put the Gobrane into a teapot?"

"Teapot?" said Henry. "Oh, right, you're talking about Van's prototype models, not about those clunky jobbies we've been shipping to D.C. inside the buzzing beige computer boxes—which makes them look like what the Government Purchasing Office expects to see. This week feels like it's lasted ten years, doesn't it? Forget about Internet time, guys, we're in the paracomputational Singularity." He prodded my Gobubble with his finger. "Does it *look* like it needs a support system?"

"No," I guessed. "It's stand-alone. It runs on solar power and it uses wireless web surfing to get data."

"Exactly," said Henry. "And of course it has global positioning, so it always knows where it is. We've reached a fully mature technology in two steps. We couldn't have designed the Gobubble without using our Gobrane paracomputers, by the way. We've been bootstrapping like crazy. Van ported an improved version of Paul's human-predictor app to the Gobubbles this morning." Henry's face was wreathed in smiles.

"Can you predict—Pete Ziff?" said Paul, glancing out the car window towards the street.

"You're talking about Alma Ziff's brother?" said Henry. "Maybe—especially if he's picked up one of those Monogrub vlog rings." He gave Paul's Gobubble a little pat. "It's all coming together so fast. Go ahead and ask, Paul. Ask it if it can do Pete Ziff. You're scared of Pete, huh?"

"I just talk to the Gobubble?" said Paul.

"Sure," said Henry. "That's the interface."

"Can you model Pete Ziff of Santa Cruz, California?" Paul asked his Gobubble.

"Yes," said the apple-sized ball, and its shimmering surface formed an image of Pete riding on his motorcycle down Route One, the wind blowing back his hair. Pete looked grim. He was wearing a vlog ring. The image was as perfect as if Pete were inside a toy snow-dome.

"Is Pete mad at Bela and me?" asked Paul.

"Pete is planning to inflict felonious assault upon you two," said the Gobrane. The image zoomed in on a detail. "Note the pool-cue club affixed to the frame of his motorcycle. The club is drilled out and weighted with lead." The picture did a fast forward to show Pete pulling into the hospital parking lot, yanking me out of Henry's car, smashing my head open with his pool cue, sprinting around the car to catch up with fleeing Paul, clubbing him as well, and then moving back and forth, beating our limp bodies at will.

"I knew I should have brought Tito," said Henry. "But I get sick of the way he spits out the window and it gets on my car."

"We're outta here, Henry," I said. "We can keep the Gobubbles?"

"Of course," said Henry. "Under nondisclosure, of course. You're going to Paul's in Palo Alto first?"

"Don't tell Pete," I said, already out of the car. "Hey, Cammy! We gotta run!"

"I'll come too," sang Lulu. "I'd like to see your house, Paul. And maybe you can get me into the grad program at Stanford. I call shotgun!" She giggled. "That takes on new meaning if you've ridden with Tito."

"Hurry!" I said. "Pete Ziff is about to show up and beat Paul and me to death with a pool cue."

The women sat in front, with Paul and me in back.

"Go towards the beach instead of towards the highway," I told Cammy. "So we don't pass Pete."

"I think you're right about him," said Cammy. "I remember what he said when we three picked up Alma."

Paul and I glanced at each other. Our new pasts were partly unknown. Just as we turned onto the Monterey beach road, I glimpsed Pete's motorcycle far uphill, pulling off the highway into the Steinbeck Memorial Hospital lot. We were safe, at least for now.

"Show us what's in the boxes," said Lulu as Cammy worked her way through Monterey and back to Route One.

"I'd like to," said Paul. "I'd like to use mine to keep an eye on Pete. But Henry said I shouldn't let you see the new devices. You're not spying on us for Van and Henry, are you, Lulu? Or for the Heritagists?"

"Leni's the one hooked into the Heritagists," said Lulu. "I was just hanging with Henry because I thought I might move in with him, or at least get a good programming job, now that my *Buzz* career's gone up in a catfight. You're the guy helping the Heritagists, aren't you, Paul? Like those scientists who built the hydrogen bomb. Myopic, in denial, sexually impotent."

"Soooo, let's assume you already know about these Gobubbles," said Paul, opening his box. "And to hell with nondisclosure. Gobubbles are prediction oracles."

"Yeah, I saw Henry's." said Lulu. "I even peeked at Van's source code for the operating system, not that any mere mortal can read it. Bottom line: a Gobubble is like a fortune-teller's crystal ball. And your group is giving them to the Heritagists for their hundred-percent campaign. You're *worse* than the bomb builders, Paul, you're like Hitler's death-camp architects. Suicidal, life-hating, and quite possibly incapable of love." Lulu had a take-no-prisoners style of flirting.

"Is Pete gonna chase us up the coast?" Paul asked his Gobubble, ignoring Lulu's taunts.

The bubble showed a scene of Pete sobbing over Alma's body in the hospital morgue, and then fast-forwarded to Pete drinking heavily in a Monterey bar. It made me queasy to be spying on the guy's life this way.

"Put it back in the box," I told Paul. "And let's put the boxes under our wetsuits in back. I'm thinking the Gobubbles can spy on us, now that they're wireless. Like Veeter's laptop before."

"Right," said Paul as we stashed the boxes in the rear. He gave Lulu a thoughtful look. "I wasn't impotent last time I got a chance to check. But I guess it wasn't webcast around here. What's all this about a Heritagist hundred-percent campaign?"

"Like you haven't heard of it?" said Lulu. "You're playing the innocent robot geek?" Cammy glanced sharply at us in the rearview mirror. "You have memory loss, too, Paul? Just like Bela?"

"I don't know what Bela told you," said Paul, cautiously. "I wouldn't want to contradict him."

"We got high on conotoxins with Alma," I said quickly. "And we forgot a lot of stuff."

"We even forgot about taking the conotoxins," said Paul with a rueful smile. "That's how bad off we are. Can someone inform my damaged brain about the hundred-percent campaign?"

So I told Paul about what I'd heard on the radio. Lulu and Cammy chimed in with more details. Veeter had been using the Gobranes to simulate people's reactions to possible Heritagist ads and news releases—with the result that the Heritagist candidates were hitting nothing but home runs.

Like, for instance, the probable Common Ground presidential candidate Winston Merritt was a clean-living, highly decorated war hero, while Doakes himself had been a party-animal draft dodger. But the Heritagists had come up with the angle of finding a few of Merritt's fellow soldiers to say that Merritt hadn't deserved his medals, and that Merritt had thrown his medals away, and that Merritt wasn't a real patriot. And the public went for it. Merritt wasn't even nominated yet, and his campaign was dead in the water. And it wasn't like there were any viable alternates. Every Common Ground candidate for every single office across the country was on the ropes. Thanks to the oracular Gobranes the hundred-percent campaign was all but assured of success.

Paul groaned and rubbed his face. "We helped do that? Is Roland Haut involved?"

"Your old thesis adviser?" said Lulu. "He's not in the loop, so far as I know."

"Good," I said. "Let's keep it that way."

"Maybe on this Earth, I never got high enough to phone him," muttered Paul.

"You're hallucinating that you're from another Earth too?" asked Cammy. "Like Bela? Is that a common side-effect of conotoxins?"

"Whatever," said Paul. "We're here now. We'll work with what we have. That story about the hundred-percent campaign—have you guys ever heard of the logician Kurt Gödel?"

"There's a classic mathematician pickup line for you," said Lulu. "Of course I've heard of him; I'm a computer scientist!"

"I'm thinking the hundred-percent campaign fulfills a prophecy of Kurt Gödel's," said Paul. "This goes back to the 1940s. Our Kurt, the king of logicians, was at the Institute for Advanced Study in Princeton, and he applies for his citizenship, and he hears that the judge might ask him some questions about the constitution. So Gödel studies the U S. constitution as only Kurt fucking Gödel can study a logical system. He's gonna pass that test. And supposedly he discovers some weird loophole via which our constitution allows a sufficiently ruthless president to install himself as dictator for life. Gödel runs to tell his pal Albert Einstein about this—Einstein's at the Institute too, he's like an uncle figure for young Kurt. They love taking walks and talking together; nobody else is as smart as these two. On the constitution thing, Einstein tells Gödel to calm down, and he even comes along with Gödel to his naturalization hearing, and when Gödel starts in on the judge about the impending Amerikan dictatorship, Einstein defuses the situation by cracking a joke and signing some autographs, and Gödel gets his papers and that's the end of it. But mathematicians have always wondered exactly what was that constitutional loophole that Gödel found. And now in this brave new world, I'm finding out that Gödel's loophole is for real; it's the hundred-percent campaign. Good work on picking such a wonderful Earth for us to live on, Bela."

Veeter's limo showed up at Paul's house in Palo Alto at the same time we did. Cousin Gyula was driving as usual. And sitting next to Gyula was big Owen, still alive on Earth-2.

Van said he needed to talk to us in private, so Paul and I went into the house with him while Cammy and Lulu waited by the car, working on the words and moves for "Lug Bi War Bride," using Gyula and Owen as their test audience—Gyula was enjoying it, but Owen seemed to have no idea what was going on.

Veeter was carrying a metallic umbrella. He popped it open as soon as we were inside Paul's house. The thing had a foil skirt hanging down around it and some electronic boxes taped to its ribs; one of them was an audio jammer emitting a jagged hiss. Veeter beckoned us to get under the umbrella with him. The three us were so closely crowded together that I could smell the other two men's breath.

"This is my state-of-the-art privacy chamber," said Veeter. "I call it a hushbrella. The reason it looks so funky is that I made it myself—otherwise it would have an NSA microphone in it, right? I'm staying at my ranch up on the ridge just now, so I ran down to see you in person. The good news is that I'm the Speaker of the House now. And we've got those new Gobubbles to program, which is fun. The joy of tech. Everyone already knows that you showed a Gobubble to Cammy and Lulu, and that's not a big deal, but please, boys, for your own safety, be careful of what you say about the Heritagists. I've got enemies."

"Ramirez?" I guessed.

"Quick as ever, Bela," said Van. "Yes, Ramirez is deep into the NSA. He's got access to all the Monogrub vlog data-mining results. And Cal Kweskin and Maria Reyes are reporting directly to him. And there's other agents as well.

I wouldn't be too sure about Leni, for instance. *Buzz* was a prototype for the Monogrub *One in a Million* show, which is totally NSA." Veeter shook his head. "Can you imagine? People are volunteering for intimate surveillance!"

"I thought that show was my idea," said Paul.

"That's what Leni wanted you to think," said Veeter. "If you review the tapes, it's quite clear it was her idea."

"Paranoia, *the* destroyer," I intoned, harking back to the day when I'd fantasized that Haut might shoot me from his office window.

"It's not paranoia when it's true," said Veeter. "The reason we need to worry about Ramirez is that I just got Joe Doakes to promise me the vice-presidential slot on the ticket this fall. I used a carrot and a stick. For the carrot, I showed him some Gobrane predictions that make it clear the switch is a slam dunk for the hundred-percent campaign. For the stick, I told him that I'd stop supplying and programming the Gobubbles if he didn't put me on the ticket."

"Pull the plug, Van," implored Paul. "Don't help the Heritagists anymore. Disable the Gobranes and Gobubbles that they already have."

"Actually, I thought of that," said Veeter. "I'm pretty uneasy about what's in the cards. But it's too late to freeze out Doakes and his handlers. Kweskin and Reyes have all our data, all our notes. They can replicate anything that we've done. Even if I pulled out completely, at most they'd lose a month of time. And the elections are still five months away. Doakes knows my stick is weak, but he likes the smell of the carrot. Ramirez is unpopular in all the mainstream demographics. Even the Latinos don't like him; they know the guy's an amoral thug. And Gobrane simulations show that Ramirez is the one factor that could drag down the hundred-percent campaign. I'm the best man to replace him."

"But why not pull out anyway?" I asked. "Like Paul said. Why help Doakes at all? You're not a fascist, Van. You're a regular guy. Practically a mathematician."

"Face it, if things go as the Heritagists plan, there won't be another free election for many years to come," said Van. "It'll take an armed revolution to get them out. I want to stay on board to try and keep things from getting too far out of hand. You don't know how it is in the inner party circles. They're talking about brainwashing and assassination squads, about torture and secret prison camps."

"What if I gave the Gobubbles to the Common Ground party?" I asked. "You'd be dead," said Veeter. "And it's not even clear that the Common Grounders would have the balls to use Gobubbles the right way. Winston Merritt, for crying in the sink? He's letting a draft dodger wipe the floor with his Medal of Honor."

"I'd be dead?"

"Believe it. All three of us might be hit pretty soon, as a matter of fact. Yesterday I heard that Ramirez is so steamed about getting bumped off the ticket that he wants to do something drastic. That's why I'm holed up on my ranch with my guards and some robot defenses I've put together. I've been running Gobrane simulations of Ramirez around the clock, but of course his boys are doing the same on me. It's like chess. I came here to warn you two that some of the scenarios get ugly."

"Why not give Gobubbles to everyone in the world?" suggested Paul. "If the Heritagists were discredited, they wouldn't have the power to come after us."

"That's a thought," said Veeter after a pause. "The open-source path to liberation. Maybe I should tell you the Gobubble recipe."

Cammy and Lulu interrupted us then, saying that Gyula wanted Veeter out in the limo to take a secure call from Washington. Van was out there a long time, leaving his hushbrella in the kitchen with us. Lulu, Paul, Cammy, and I ate some food from Paul's fridge. Lulu was still flirting hard with Paul and he was starting to go for it. Although the women thought we were being pompous, Paul and I got under Van's hushbrella for a side conversation.

The topic: Should we jump back to La Hampa? Neither of us was up for repeating the whole rigmarole right away. After all, we weren't particularly welcome in La Hampa anymore, and if we traveled to yet another Earth, that one might be even worse than Earth-2. The divine jellyfish's notions of "better world" were, to say the least, inscrutable. Nevertheless, we agreed that if things got desperate we'd bail, assuming we could make a hypertunnel again.

"Super secret spy stuff," said Lulu as we emerged. "Are you boys bi?"

Paul found this amusing. "Stay here with me tonight, Lulu," he said. "You can straighten me out. Or kink me up. Either way. You're fun to have around."

And then Veeter came back in, looking very grim. "Let it come down," he said. "I need to talk to Paul alone under the hushbrella."

I was curious of course, but by now Cammy was seriously impatient with all the male secrecy. She and I said goodbye and headed out for Klownetown alone.

My alternate life as a rocker pulled me back in. We had a great rehearsal with Naz, K-Jen, and Thuggee. They were very stoked about playing with AntiCrystal on Saturday; the promoters had given Thuggee three dozen tickets to the zone by the stage, and he shared those out.

Fueled by a mound of take-out Tanzanian rice and fried bugs that Naz brought, we ran through our whole repertoire, including two new songs: "Lug Bi War Bride," and a political call to arms by K-Jen attacking the Heritagists' hundred-percent campaign. She called her song "Hundred-Percent Asshole."

At first I thought that maybe we'd have a chance of reaching more people if we called it "Hundred-Percent Tyrant." But K-Jen said I was being as wimpy as Winston Merritt, the impotent stuffed-shirt-mandarin Common Grounder candidate, and that these desperate times called for radical confrontation. So, okay, we did it K-Jen's way, using the title for a chorus and hammering out fresh verses as we went along. Pretty soon the song got good to us. It gave me goose bumps to imagine playing our inflammatory anthem to tens of thousands of people at no less a venue than Heritagist Park.

We caught our breath for a few minutes, and then somehow I got into a gentle ballad inspired by Alma's death, and by Cammy's death before that. I was calling it "Where Are You?" and I drew some of the imagery from the visions I'd shared with Alma inside the Nataraja jellyfish.

It was odd, odd, odd to see people die. The world rolled on the same as before, as heedlessly as if a person were an ant or a wildflower or a puff of wind. Nature kept on making more and more of everything, and never mind that birth is a death sentence. And now that I'd been to La Hampa, I knew that creation was even more prodigal than I'd ever imagined. There were worlds upon worlds filled with people struggling and swarming like fretful gnats, all of them doomed to vanish into dust while the cosmic dance spun on.

After the deaths, I was very grateful to see a Cammy standing there calm and solid and alive, drawing beautiful music from her bass guitar.

Thuggee, K-Jen, and Naz left, and Cammy stayed over—this was no big deal for her, as she'd already slept with a Bela. I had a moment of hesitation as we got into bed together; I missed Alma-1, and I felt sad and guilty about Alma-2. But the Almas were nowhere on this Earth, and Cammy was right here in my bed: her shape, smell, voice, and touch crowding my senses. I wasn't going to flub my chance again.

The sex was great. Cammy tasted good: her mouth, her skin, her body, her pheromones like keys fitting into rusty locks. We talked awhile after we were done; I told her a little more about how I'd gotten here; she still didn't really believe it. She especially didn't like the notion of me raising her from the dead by tunneling to a parallel reality—nobody wants to hear someone talk about their murder. So I dropped the topic, and we chatted lazily about our music and our plans for the band, and then we made love again. The second time around, I realized that sex with Cammy wasn't all that different from sex with Alma—which had always been great, too. Like most men, I'm ridiculously easy to satisfy.

I awoke near noon, still tired. My hierophantically supercharged brain had been spinning all night long. Cammy was gone; she'd left a note; she was in San Francisco to meet with Wacław Smorynski to work out a deal where we could use some of AntiCrystal's equipment—they had, like, sixty thousand watts worth of amplification on tap. She'd be back for rehearsal around six o'clock. XXX, Cammy.

I got out my Gobubble and had a good look at it while I ate some leftover rice and fried grasshoppers. The paracomputer was rubbery, the size of a nectarine, and with a faint organic smell—a whiff of the sea, a sniff of decayed meat.

It would have been an exaggeration to call the Gobubble a perfect sphere. Its shape was continually undergoing minor adjustments: flattening out like a tangerine, bulging out one end like a pear, forming a faintly indented hourglass waist, or all of these at once, leading to wandering patterns of bumps. Nor was the ball totally smooth at the small scale; its surface was alive with goose bumps and shivering ripples. As I nestled it in my hand, I could feel it pulsing and wrinkling like the skin on a bald gnome's head.

"Can you predict me?" I asked the Gobubble. The pastel shades of its shimmering surface flowed and interlocked to form an image of me sitting at my kitchen table.

I set the bubble down and stared into it. "I'm going to raise one of my hands in a second," I said. "Show me which one."

The little figure inside the bubble raised his left hand. So I decided to raise my right hand, just to prove the Gobubble wrong. But even before my right hand started to move, the Gobubble caught up with my intentions and changed its image to match. I altered my plan and raised my left hand instead, but by the time my left hand was in the air, the Gobubble had gone back to showing my left hand in the air as well—just like it had predicted in the first place.

I felt within myself, wondering if I still had access to the hierophantic mode of thought. Perhaps I'd be harder to predict when I remembered to think in the advanced La Hampan way. After a moment's introspection, I felt my new techniques kick into gear. I gerrymandered my thought maps into new districts, zoomed out to see higher-order patterns, and began short-circuiting long deductions with lightning-fast jumps.

"Predict what I'm going to write," I told the Gobubble, then put a piece of paper down in my lap and scribbled a hierophantic conclusion that popped unexpectedly into to my head, to wit: "Cammy is fucking Wacław." Geez. Could that be true?

But before dealing with this unexpected content, I wanted to finish my Gobubble test. Holding the paper pressed flat between my two hands, I regarded the iridescent ball. The Bela figure inside had his hands in the same position as mine.

"Show me your paper," I said. "Predict what I've written."

Obligingly the Gobubble Bela opened his hands and, oh wow, his paper said, "Cammy is fucking Wacław," in the exact same handwriting I'd used.

Which meant that the Gobubbles really could predict me, even when I got all hierophantic on their ass. But being unpredictable wasn't my front-burner issue anymore.

"Show me what Cammy's doing right now," I told the Gobubble.

The gleaming ball shuddered, cleared, and there was Cammy, nude and sensual on a king-sized bed with a stunning view of the Golden Gate Bridge through pink silk curtains. A slender, pale-skinned guy with weird crystal-patterned tattoos and lank, greasy blonde hair was on top of her, his butt dancing, his softstubbled face rubbing her smooth-skinned cheek. Cammy's eyes were slitted with pleasure, with lust, and she was whispering his name, pronouncing it that special way: "Vahkwahv, Vahkwahv, Vahkwahv."

"Enough," I told the Gobrane. "And that's only a prediction, right? Not a videotape or a real-time vlog ring image?"

"Just a prediction," said the Gobrane, its surface taking on the mottled, live-paisley look that it had when it wasn't computing much of anything in particular. "But I'm always right. I know from the Grand Hotel hall cameras that she's in his room."

I remembered something that Cammy had said to me on the way to our San Jose concert. "Sex isn't that big a deal to me. It's like brushing your teeth. I don't see why everyone gets so bent out of shape." But, dammit, how could she be up for another lover so soon after sleeping with me? I'd thought only men were like that.

I heard a motorcycle in the street.

"Oh shit, Pete Ziff!" I exclaimed, running to check the lock on my door. "Is he coming here to get me?" I asked the Gobubble over my shoulder.

"In less than two minutes," said the Gobubble, "He'll kick in your door. Might as well leave it open so you don't have to repair it."

"Simulate him for me," I said, undoing the lock. "Quick. Help me figure out what to say." An angry Pete appeared in the Gobubble, facing a cringing Bela.

"I'm really sorry," I said tentatively into the sphere. "It was an accident. An earthquake." Pete's pool cue swung down; the little Bela crumpled.

"Reset," I said, and the scene returned to the same spot as before. "It was Paul's fault," I essayed. "He steered her into the rocks." Once again, Pete's club slammed into the virtual Bela's head.

I could hear Pete's real world feet on the Ratvale stairs. I tested a third line on the Gobubble simulation: "You have to help me stop the Heritagists!" The Pete image paused.

And now, in the real world my door flew open, and the real Pete came stalking in like a movie monster, carrying the heavy sawed-off pool cue in his hand. Quickly I tried my line again.

"You have to help me stop the Heritagists!"

Pete paused and—lowered his club. "*Those* mother-fuckers? Are you sayin' it's their fault Alma's dead?"

"No, dog," I said, winging it. "But why kill me and go to jail? Listen, I've got plans. But first take that off that vlog ring. I told you before, you're wack to be wearing a cop spy camera all the time. Especially if you're planning murder one."

I had Pete off-balance now. Almost sheepishly he pulled off the vlog ring and then—being the kind of guy he was—threw it on the ground and stomped it to bits.

"*Right* on," I said. "You and me can help save the country, Pete. And talking about fault—if you hadn't given us those conotoxins—"

Abruptly his face tightened, he flopped down on my couch and burst into tears. "I been thinkin' that myself. I'm not dealin' that shit no more. Last night I took all those nasty little snails out of Sarah's aquariums and—"

"You were milking the venom yourself? No wonder it was so strong. The natural bridge looked enormous to us, Pete, it was like a train tunnel to another world. Even so, we would have slid through fine if it hadn't been for the earthquake." Pete's expression was hardening again. I was talking too much. But I couldn't stop myself. "Listen, dog," I blithered, "I'm thinking about ways to bring Alma back. I'm into some weird science like you wouldn't believe." As I said this, it struck me that, if Alma returned, it wouldn't be to this world. The jellyfish god was all done with this world. Any further changes in it were up to the folks living in it now. Up to people like Pete.

He smoothed the planes of his face with his grimy hands, wiping away all traces of the tears. His hand strayed back to his pool cue. "You slushed geek. I oughtta—"

"Look at this ball," I said, frantic to win him over. "It predicts the future."

"Huh?"

"It's a new kind of computer called a Gobubble. The Heritagists are using them to rig the election. They can see what's coming, so they know what to put in their ads." The Gobubble was of course reporting on my saying this, but I didn't care. I was gearing up for all-out war. I picked up the ball and handed it to Pete. "Try it out. Ask it something."

"About what?"

"I don't know. About whatever you're planning to do today."

"Planning to kick your ass."

"Not that. Come on, Pete, we can be on the same side. Ask the Gobubble something useful. Then you'll begin to understand."

Pete hefted the ball dubiously. "Is Navaho Jack gonna have a good sprocket for my bike at his Oaktown junkyard?" he finally asked.

The ball responded, thank God, showing a scene of Pete talking to a rough character in a sleeveless work shirt. The guy was telling Pete to try Jeremiah's junkyard over in Bayview.

"*Hmmpf*," grunted Pete, just like Alma would have. "Is Jeremiah gonna have the sprocket?" he asked the Gobubble.

The ball displayed Pete sitting outdoors on a broken-down cloth couch with a rawboned, wild-eyed guy in a straw cowboy hat. Mounds of junk towered all round, with a few beat old camping trailers scattered among them. Resting on Pete's lap was a large, toothed metal gear: a motorcycle sprocket. The demented-looking virtual hick with the virtual Pete was drinking a long-neck bottle of beer from a cardboard case sitting on the ground beside the couch.

"Good old Jeremiah!" said Pete, hefting the Gobubble with a pleased air. "Of course. Hey, do I have a chance of spending the night with Lizard Girl?"

The scene shifted to show Pete, still in the same junkyard, talking to an alert, pleasant-faced woman with a hard-core beehive hairdo and lizards tattooed on her arms. She was standing by a rounded aluminum trailer with a *T. rex* painted on its side.

"You can test out different lines that you say to her," I told Pete. "So you can see how she'll respond."

"Fuck me!" he said into the ball, and the Lizard Girl image turned her back and walked away. "You're beautiful!" he tried; Lizard Girl laughed and wandered off to drink beer with Jeremiah. "I'm so unhappy," said Pete; the virtual Lizard Girl took his hand and led him into her trailer. "All right," said Pete, handing back the Gobubble. "Now I've planned my day."

"Hold on," I said, A full-blown scheme of action for unseating the Heritagists had hierophantically formed in my mind, and this was a plan I didn't want the Gobubble to overhear. I put the Gobubble back in its case and stashed the case under the pillow in my bedroom.

"I'm serious about fighting the Heritagists," I told Pete, coming back into the kitchen. "My idea is to pirate thousands of copies of these Gobubbles and give them away at our stadium concert with AntiCrystal tomorrow." I had a strong suspicion that Veeter had told Paul the recipe right after we'd left yesterday. "The Heritagists will lose their power over us once everyone else has Gobubbles, too. People will be able to look ahead and see what Doakes really plans: the poverty, the pollution, the prison camps, the endless war."

"What use would I be to you?" said Pete. He looked very open just now. Seeing the sad lines on his troubled face, I realized that he had an innate tendency towards depression and—what had Alma said?—low self-esteem. Poor guy, the sister who loved him had died. I took a chance and hugged him.

"Alma loved you," I said.

"Her funeral's on Tuesday," said Pete, stepping back and regarding me. "We're gonna scatter her ashes at Pleasure Point. She'd want you there. And that Stanford guy." He meant Paul.

"I'll be there," I said, feeling a sense of deja vu. Another funeral for a girlfriend. I was a jinx. I had a sudden image of the depression morphon—a teapot whose spout runs out of the pot's bottom, spilling all the tea on the ground. I took a deep breath and pushed past it.

"You *can* do something, Pete. Come to the Washer Drop concert at the stadium tomorrow and help spread the Gobubbles around," I handed him six of the tickets Thuggee had left with me. "Bring some friends." A Crew badge lay by the tickets, and I gave that to Pete too. "This'll get you in without having to be searched. It might be that we'll need some extra security. It'd feel good to know we have a guy like you on our side. Bring weapons."

"Sweet!" said Pete, actually smiling as he regarded the tickets. "I'll bring Lizard Girl and Jeremiah and Prescription John and Wrong Wave Jose and—" His face fell again, thinking of his sister.

"We'll be doing it for Alma," I said.

After Pete left, my thoughts turned back to Cammy. It didn't seem likely that our romantic relationship would get all that far. I shouldn't ask much from her along these lines, lest love-problems break up our band. And then I thought of Roberto Sandoval, Cammy's murderer on Earth-1. Should I be worrying about him on Earth-2?

I went and fetched the Gobubble again.

"Show me Roberto Sandoval of San Jose, California," I said.

"No data," answered the Gobubble in a sulky tone. Its surface was a pattern of blots and loops. "His sister's name is Eva," I said, remembering this from the last time around. "He lives with her on, um, 11th Street."

"Okay," said the Gobubble, displaying a visa photo of a dark woman with a crooked face. "I have Eva Sandoval's cell phone number. Should I call that for you?"

"Yeah," I said. I had no idea what I was going to say. I was letting my hierophantics do the thinking.

A voice came on, speaking Spanish, then switching to English. Yes, this was Eva Sandoval. I heard noise in the background; it sounded like a restaurant. Just to get something going, I introduced myself as Curt Girdle, a publicist for the band Washer Drop, and said I was interested in talking to her brother Roberto.

"I don't know where he is."

"You and Roberto won a pair of free tickets to the Washer Drop show tomorrow night," I said. "They're opening for AntiCrystal. It's at Heritagist Park, the base-ball stadium in San Francisco."

"Washer Drop again?" said Eva in an impatient tone. "You haven't pay Roberto enough last time. Not his fault that girl left too soon." Aha. Someone in the background was yelling at Eva in Spanish. "Just a minute, Julio, I'm on the phone, I got business."

"Can Roberto take the train to the stadium?" I asked. "One of us could meet him at the Willie Mays statue outside it. The train stops right across the street." I was winging it, waiting to see what developed.

"He don't never take the train," said Eva. "Send a driver like last week."

Oho. "You mean—last Saturday morning?" I said.

"Saturday morning your car came taking Roberto to Palo Alto, no?" said Eva. "And you haven't pay him his second half. You bring that when you picking him up tomorrow."

"Where's Roberto right now?" I asked.

Eva's voice turned suspicious. "You the same guy, no? Friend of Frank Ramirez?"

"Yeah, yeah," I said. "I'll call again later." I stared absently out my window at Haste Street as the scrolls and gliders of my thoughts processed my inputs. Last week Vice Presi-dent Frank Ramirez had arranged a ride for Roberto San-doval to Palo Alto so that Sandoval could murder Cammy Vendt. Why? To smear Veeter and the paracomputation technology that was scoring so many points for Veeter in the Heritagist party's higher circles. Did that mean

Ramirez would strike at Cammy again? Not necessarily; his primary target was, after all, Van Veeter. Ramirez's next hit might come from a different angle.

As for Sandoval—assuming Earth-1 matched Earth-2 in this respect, Sandoval had been a hit man, not a stalker, and all the statements he'd made had been false. But then why the multiple stab wounds on Earth-1? Because making the slaughter splashily sensational had been an essential part of his PR-directed mission. And perhaps he'd been enjoying himself as he stabbed Cammy-1 sixteen times. With the Vice President Ramirez in his corner, Sandoval would have expected early release from prison, regardless of the savagery of the crime—so he'd made the most of his opportunity.

I felt very uneasy now. Again I asked the Gobubble to show me Roberto Sandoval; again I drew a blank. I figured the NSA was masking his data, at least from me. Again I checked on Cammy; she was still in bed with Wacław. I phoned her cell.

"Yeah?" said Cammy.

"Having fun?"

"What's on your mind, Bela?"

"I wanted to warn you about Roberto Sandoval. The guy Thuggee threw off the stage at the San Jose concert? I didn't stress this enough last night. Sandoval was, you know, the bad guy in the other world that I was talking about. He's here, too."

"Bela—"

"I have some information that makes me think Sandoval might come after you. So please be careful. Don't be alone."

"I'm not alone."

"I know," I said. "And ask Wacław to have one of his road-ies give you a ride when you come back. A guy with a gun."

"Just chill, Bela." She rang off.

Okay, I'd warned her. But I still couldn't let go of the Sandoval thing. The fact that his sister Eva had seemed a little surprised by my call meant that Ramirez hadn't yet asked Sandoval to do a follow-up attempt at a hit. So now I started worrying that my call itself would in fact trigger such a hit. So I called Eva up and told her not to do anything, never mind, forget it, and Roberto should stay home. She hung up on me, too.

Maybe I really was going crazy. Maybe I was one rigor-ously logical step from fingerpainting the walls with my own shit. Maybe I'd taken conotoxins yesterday, and I'd hallucinated the whole deal about La Hampa and the two Earths. I needed reassurance.

"Show me Paul Bridge," I told my Gobubble.

"I have weak, fluctuating data for him," said the Gobub-ble. "And intermittent interference. The image will have very low reliability." It showed me a picture of Paul sit-ting in his back yard sunning himself with his shirt off. That was unreliable all right. Paul hated sunbathing. And then, suddenly the image of Paul switched to showing him bowling, which was also out of the question. I fig-ured he'd found a way to thwart the Gobubbles' ability to predict him. Good old Paul.

I called him on his phone.

"How's it going, dog?" he said. "You and Cammy?"

"Okay," I said, not wanting to feed still more info into the phone tap. "You and Lulu?"

"Gettin' gooder by the minute. She's my kind of woman: brilliant and perverse."

"I'm wobbly, Paul. Was our trip real?"

"Hyper real." His voice was calm and comfortable.

"I need to see you," I said. "I'm thinking of the Humclocke math picnic." At the first departmental math picnic Paul and I attended together, we'd spent a memorable hour blowing soap bubbles.

"Me too," said Paul, on the beam as usual. "Come by tomorrow morning."

"See ya."

That night Washer Drop had another good rehearsal, with the band in an ebullient mood. Cammy was a little distant with me, though, treating everything I said like a joke. When we finished playing, she asked Thuggee for a ride back to San Francisco. As they prepared to go, I loaded Thuggee down with warnings about Roberto Sandoval and the nefarious NSA minions of Frank Ramirez's Heritagist henchmen.

"Lighten up, Bela," said Cammy. "What are you, my Dad?"

"Klaus Vendt," I said. "That's me."

"How the hell do you know his name? I never told you that."

"I met Klaus and Dagmar at your funeral in the world where Sandoval stabbed you sixteen times. That's why I keep telling you to be careful."

"Washer Drop singer-guitarist Bela Kis suffers delusional psychotic break," announced K-Jen into the Monogrub vlog ring she insisted on wearing. "Band members are increasingly concerned."

"Our man's in training for his big match with Wacław is all," said Naz, sending a shower of beats from his drum-vest and singing a couplet.

Gobubble goblin wonder-wall,
Who's the hundred-percentest dreg of all?

"Bela's a *way* better fuck than Wacław," said Cammy. "Except when he starts ranting about resurrecting me. Nail me to the cross, Bela, nail me to the cross." She danced down the Ratvale stairs with her arms stretched out and gracefully swaying.

"I am on the very highest alert for conotoxic hyperspace hit men," Thuggee told me, feigning a salute.

Goofing and pranking, my band made their way to the street. I watched them out my window—waving to them, laughing with them, loving them. Maybe everything was okay. I went to bed alone and I got my first good night's sleep in several days.

I woke fresh and rested on Saturday morning. The La Hampan hierophantic brain-boost had finally worn off. I didn't miss it. I'm smart enough just being a mathematician.

I jumped in the squinty whale and drove to Paul's, bringing my Gobubble in its case in the back of the car. I would have liked once again to ask it what Paul was up to, but I didn't. Whenever I was using my Gobubble, the Heritagists were spying on me.

Paul greeted me with a smile. An odd smell wafted from his house, accompanied by a staticky hiss. Resting on the hall table was a Gobubble showing Paul mowing the grass around his house while lustily singing the "Star Spangled Banner."

"That's Special Paul," said Paul. "He lives in my Gobubble to blind the Pig's eyes. Come on in my kitchen." He led me through a foil-covered plastic curtain he'd rigged up across his kitchen door. "It's like a big hushbrella in here. A temporary autonomous zone."

He'd papered the ceiling, walls, window, and floor of his kitchen/work-room with aluminum foil. The long sheets were tidily aligned, and he'd taped a plastic tarp over the foil on the floor so that we didn't tear it when we walked around. An audio jammer sat on the counter pulsing out its pseudorandom hiss. And the microwave oven was humming with its door open, filling the aether with electromagnetic interference.

It smelled like the ocean in Paul's silver kitchen—and like a Chinatown butcher's shop with offal piled in the alley. I breathed through my mouth, not my nose. Pots of turbid, glistening fluids sat upon his stove. A laptop computer and a homemade bubble wand rested on Paul's kitchen table beside a steel mixing bowl filled with foamy, iridescent liquid. The counters and the floor were strewn with—Gobubbles.

"Way to go, Paul! Did Veeter—"

"He gave me the recipe right after you left the other day. How to make the bubble fluid, and how to put his morphonic operating system onto it. And he gave me a download link for the operating system, source, and executable. Remember that phone call he took in his car, and then he said 'Let it come down'? He'd just found out that Ramirez outmaneuvered him. Van's not gonna be on the ticket after all—Ramirez told Doakes that if he was dropped, he'd tell the press the details about how Doakes has been gaming Tariq Qaadri's terrorism to help the Heritagists in the polls. Skyscraper-bomber Qaadri pops up to scare our voters whenever there's an election, and Doakes makes sure that nobody catches Qaadri. Van actually gave me an access code for this secret video that shows Doakes's personal chopper air-lifting Qaadri outta the siege in Lilliputistan to his safe haven in Blefescustan. The Presidential seal on the helicopter is, like, covered with black paint, but you can see its outline anyway."

"Whoah. Van gave you all that?"

"He says he's had a change of heart. Says he hadn't realized just how rotten his grand old party had become. But I think mainly he's mad that he's out of the power loop. The guy's a politician. He wants us to bring down the administration so he can step in. Dig it, he's Speaker of the House, and according to the Constitution, that puts him third in line after the Prez and the Veep. So, like I said, he gave me the recipe. And when Lulu left on Friday morning I got busy. I was able to get some supplies from the Stanford labs."

"Good deal," I said. "And Lulu? You really like her?"

"She reminds me of myself," said Paul, which was his highest form of praise. "She's off at the admissions office trying to become a Stanford CS grad student. I could get serious about her. But just now my heart is still a little—

you know. Off-line. How about Cammy? Are you living the dream?"

"She spent the night with me on Thursday, and it was great. But then Friday she hooked up with Wacław Smorynski. I don't know. I miss Alma."

"Me too," said Paul quietly. "And what about Pete Ziff? I've been expecting him to kill me even before I'm martyred by the Heritagists." He said this in such a flat, offhand way that I couldn't tell if he was kidding—or if he cared.

"I used Gobubble simulations to defuse Pete; I tested out his reactions to possible approaches, and I found a line that worked. He's not such a bad guy. He'll be scattering Alma's ashes at Pleasure Point on Tuesday. You should be there, too. You were her boyfriend in this world."

"Yeah," said Paul sadly. "And I screwed it up. I'm really something. First I killed Cammy by not taking her to the train station, and then I killed Alma by encouraging Haut to show up with his ray gun." He held up his hand. "Don't interrupt me, Bela, I have to speak the truth. I've been thinking about it. It was Haut's energy ray that triggered the earthquake."

"Who knows, Paul," I said, patting his shoulder. "Maybe the jellyfish god made Earth-2 this way on purpose. Or maybe she couldn't help having it turn out like this. Everything in the world is inextricably interlinked. Maybe something good depends on our pain right now."

Paul sighed and rubbed his face. "Funeral on Tuesday? Yeah, pick me up on your way to Cruz. Assuming we're still here in three days. Assuming people are still having funerals by then. Henry Nunez was right, we've entered a technological singularity. And just wait till we hand out ten thousand Gobubbles at your stadium concert tonight. That's the plan, right?"

"You can make *ten thousand?*" I said. "You're my hero, dog. Tell me about your process." Looking more closely at the Gobubbles scattered around the room, I noticed that they were all showing images of Paul doing wildly improbable things, with no two of the images the same. "Why is every one of these Gobubbles simulating you?"

"They're testing the draft versions of Special Paul," said Paul, his gloom lifting.

"What is this with Special Paul?"

"He's gifted," said Paul. "He's so bright it's frightening. But he's intermittently chaotic. I keep Special Paul running on my personal Gobubble out in the hall; he's like my screen saver. He screws up the web's Paul Bridge data-set updates on a realtime basis. And that makes me Gobubble-unpredictable. But before we get into that, I'll show you how to make Gobubbles."

"Yeah."

Paul stepped over to the kitchen table, clearing his throat like a professor. "To make a Gobubble, you blow a bubble from this goo," he said, jiggling the steel bowl of glistening liquid. "Bovine pancreatic juices mixed with kelp-stem pulp and a bit of hog melanin in a gelatin, glycerin, and detergent base. The base produces extremely long-lived bubbles, and the organics catalyze a colorful activator-inhibitor paracomputation. Oh, and the recipe includes traces of magnesium and gallium for the wireless access."

"No way is a soap bubble going to be pulling in the wireless web unless it has some kind of ground-level program to begin with," I said, thinking out loud. "So you must be loading Van's operating system onto the membrane while you blow the bubble, right?"

"Behold the magic wand," said Paul. His bubble wand had a comb of copper teeth around the bubble hole. A wire led from the teeth down the handle to a laptop computer. "The laptop feeds an electromagnetic signal into the bubble wand," continued Paul, dipping it into the shiny fluid. "It sets up certain eddy currents and long-term resonant vibrations in the spherical membrane, yes. These currents and vibrations constitute Van Veeter's Morphonic Operating System for the Membrane Paracomputer, Release 2.0, Spherical Version. MOSMP 2-SV. Here we *go*."

He pursed his lips and puffed a gentle stream of air. The Gobubble swelled, wobbled, and came free. I caught it in my hand. Its surface was slightly rippled; it was patterned with azure spirals and ecru polka dots.

"Show me what Cammy's doing," I said on a whim.

"No data," answered the newborn Gobubble.

"This bubble doesn't work!" I exclaimed.

"Duh? The kitchen's a temporary autonomous zone, remember? No wireless, no web. Take the Gobubble out in the living-room, and it'd work just fine, although the Heritagist data-mining bots might squawk about an extra bubble coming on-line."

"Okay, so now tell me why all the other bubbles in here *are* working—and showing *you*."

"These are special bubbles; they have the Special Paul screensaver. Special Paul doesn't need web access to run. How'd I make him? I studied Veeter's operating system and figured out a hack. The Special Paul screensaver is based on the NSA's Paul Bridge simulation that I snarfed off the web. Except I added a chaotic cubic wave equation into its update step." He gestured around the room. "It's computational pseudorandomness that makes these Pauls special. It took me quite a few tries till I got my algorithm just right. The big win is that now I can carry a Gobubble around and use it to predict things—and with Special Paul as my Gobubble's screensaver, the Heritagists can't be using the bubble to track me."

"Could you do that for me?" I said. "I have my Gobubble in my car. I didn't bring it in because I'm so worried about the spying problem."

"Suffer the little Gobubbles to come unto me," said Paul, patting his laptop. "I can make a Special Bela screensaver for you, dog."

So I fetched my Gobubble from the car. When I took it out of its box, my Gobubble was off-line due to the wireless shielding in Paul's kitchen; it was showing wavy vermilion grids with lemony horseshoes. Paul used his landline to get the NSA's data set on Bela Kis; built a Special Bela simulation using his batshit cubic wave equation; and waved his magic bubble wand to put Special Bela onto my Gobubble.

My Gobubble displayed an image of me driving my car across the Bay Bridge towards Klownetown. In the middle of the bridge I slammed on my brakes, causing a chain reaction pile-up behind me. Ignoring that, my image began walking back towards San Francisco. And that was only scene one. Over and over the image wavered and displayed fresh notions of what the absurd Special Bela might do. He was, successively, smearing brown shoe-polish on his car; masturbating over an anatomy book in the Stanford Library; eating a Monogrub triple burger; building a campfire out of dynamite sticks; shopping for an SUV; and doing pushups on a floor covered with shattered bottles.

"Special Bela," said Paul. "Keep him near you always, my son. But right now, park him in the living room. From now on, you can use your Gobubble without the Heritagists tracking you. Whenever it has a spare moment, your Gobubble will be running Special Bela to ruin everyone's predictions about you."

"That's so great," I said. "Yesterday I was trying to falsify my Gobubble's predictions about me and I couldn't do it. Even when I was using hierophantics."

"That doesn't surprise me," said Paul. "Hierophantics is software. You're still working with the same brain, with the same physics. We're in what Rowena calls a docile zone of reality. In principle you'd expect most naturally occurring processes to be computationally unpredictable—but that doesn't absolutely have to be the case. In the docile worlds, the underlying cosmic computation happens to be a simple, predictable one, and predictability cascades out of that. In docile worlds there actually *are* computational short-cuts for predicting natural phenomena. The physics on Earth-2 is predictable."

"How do you know?"

"Yesterday I was testing my Gobubble on falling leaves, on candle flames, on the clouds, on the weather, on a dripping faucet—it was predicting them all. Nature isn't nearly as gnarly as we always thought. At least not on Earth-2 and not, for that matter, on Earth-1."

"Our home Earth never felt docile to me."

"*Yeah*, it was docile; that's why Osckar won the bet against Rowena. We're predictable. Why? Humans are physical systems; the physics of Earth-1 is docile; therefore the humans of Earth-1 are predictable. But, at least while we were there, Earth-1 science never reached the point of being able to make the predictions. However, on Earth-2, paracomputation has taken off. Earth-2 science has reached the point of being able to make the not-so-difficult-after-all predictions about our docile reality. The Gobubble can predict human behavior."

"I'm finding this hard to believe," I said. "Okay, maybe we don't have ectoplasmic souls, maybe we're just physics, but physics is supposed to be computationally irreducible. Unpredictable. Intrinsically random. Nondocile. Fierce!"

"Not when you're in a docile zone like Earth-2," said Paul with a shrug. "But that doesn't have to stop a couple of crazy mathematicians from making things weird enough to be fun. Check *this* out."

He produced a gas-powered leaf blower from beneath the kitchen table. Wired copper bubble wands were taped to the nozzle, fed by plastic tubes snaking back around the engine to a plastic gas can filled of bubble goo. Three more full cans were under the table.

"The craziest mathematician of them all," I said admiringly. "You're a monster."

"My motorized multiwand bubble blower can pump out ten thousand bubbles in under five minutes. I'm bringing it to your concert tonight. Lulu's coming with me."

"Power to the people," I said, handing him two tickets and Crew passes. "Which reminds me: I gotta head up to Heritagist Park for our sound check with AntiCrystal."

We made some plans for what to do after the concert, and then I was back in the squinty whale, with Special Bela busy in the Gobubble next to me on the passenger seat. Special Bela was canvassing door-to-door for the Heritagist party.

I had it in my mind that we should be playing "Hundred-Percent Asshole" when we released the bubbles at the concert's end, so at the sound check I talked up the song to AntiCrystal, that is, to Wacław Smorynski, Jutta Schreck, guitarist Stanislaw Mostowski, and drummer Abdul Mohammed.

Being near the AntiCrystal members felt like mingling with gods: each of them had the indestructible aura of a Platonic archetype. I hardly knew which of them to stare at. Seeing Wacław in the flesh, glowing and twinkling, any thought of my being jealous about Cammy and him evaporated. This guy was way out of my league. AntiCrystal was an astronomically bigger name than Washer Drop. Even so, I kept pitching the notion of them playing our new song until, what the hey and *opanować się*, Wacław, Jutta, Stanislaw, and Abdul said yes.

They were loose enough to think it would be would be a fun goof to surprise their fans by a two-band encore jam with the Washer Drop newbies. It helped that Jutta had become obsessed with Cammy and with our song "Oil Pig"—which was why we'd been asked to open for them. And that, by now, Wacław had a thing for Cammy. Jutta was flirting with me too, I think, but I kept my distance. She was pretty formidable with her mask-like expression, mirror-reflecting full-eye contact lenses, and thigh-high silver leather boots—even though she was laughing and smoking pot and goosing people with the tip of her bass guitar.

I could hardly wait for dark, and finally it came. The concert was everything we'd hoped.

Washer Drop played the first set. It was amazing to perform at such a big venue. According to the roadies, we had a gate of thirty thousand souls in those towering stands. In the audience near the stage lurked Paul and Lulu with the tanks of bubble goo and the bubble machine, temporarily idle. I was glad to see them securely stationed in the midst of Pete and his dreggy posse: sociopathic Prescription John, manic Jeremiah, hypervigilant Lizard Girl, and the nihilistic Wrong Wave Jose with his pompadour and his grommeted earlobes. I was a little concerned that Sandoval might show up to execute a hit on us—although so far he was nowhere to be seen.

Thanks to the massive AntiCrystal sound system, our music overflowed the huge outdoor space. It was mind-boggling how one little flick of my guitar pick could stir so vast a volume—literally hundreds of tons of

air were undulating with the motions of my fingers. And
to sing a phrase and have thirty-thousand voices call it
back at you—talk about positive feedback! This beat the
hell out of publishing a math paper. I felt merged into the
public hive-mind like never before.

And when the giant, fueled spaceship that was AntiC-
rystal came onstage, we saw what it really meant to work
a crowd. Wacław was an amazing frontman: wildly charismatic and lithe as a flickering flame, his voice smoothly
rocketing up past the heavy-metal falsetto register into
the operatic zone, his face a Punch-and-Judy show of
conflicting emotions. Jutta Schreck was a cartoon super-
heroine come to life, a jolly powerful robot, and not too
high at all tonight. Their guitarist Stanislaw Mostowski
was a hyperactive maniac, splitting his notes in two, and
then splitting them again, his mouth wide open, stomping around the stage in a spraddle-legged crouch. Abdul
Mohammed was shamanic and magical; even amidst his
most explosive fireworks of sound, his arms remained
somehow languid, floating above his drum kit like kelp
stems in surf, his drumsticks always where they needed to
be, calm at the heart of the maelstrom.

As AntiCrystal ended their set with "Crying Chainsaw
Clown," Paul started up his bubble machine, its leaf-
blower roar barely audible over the rhythmic chanting of
the crowd. The bay breeze began sweeping great drifts of
the Gobubbles across the crowd. Paul had programmed
his electric wand to load this batch with screensavers
showing realtime predictions of things that would happen
if the Heritagists met with success in November.

Wacław beckoned to Washer Drop; we were waiting at the rear of the stage. We stepped into the light and plugged in. A melee had broken out in the audience near the stage. Security guards were trying to force their way into the crowd to get at Paul and his motorized bubble blower. But a bunch of dregs were holding back the guards, and Wrong Wave Jose was leaning across to smack the guards' heads with Pete's pool cue.

"We've got a hundred-percent problem in this country," I yelled into the mike, my voice booming back at me. "See your future in the bubbles! See what the Heritagists want with their hundred-percent campaign! And, thank you, thank you, thank you, AntiCrystal for letting us play this song! Joe Doakes is—A Hundred-Percent Asshole!" I swung my arms down like a conductor and the bands dug in, K-Jen and Wacław screaming the lyrics with a classic dreg/metal mix of joy and defiance.

It was a wild ride. Naz and Abdul were pounding the drums in a goose-stepper's march, Cammy and Jutta were bubbling up fat sarcastic bass notes, Stanislaw was playing a wallpaper of paisley-shapes and I was stabbing rusty triangular knives of ostinato guitar feedback into K-Jen's stark text.

He's a hundred-percent jerk—Never had to work.
He's a hundred-percent war—Our friends are dying for.
He's a hundred-percent Pig—Why let him be so big?
He's a hundred-percent hate—Stop him now, it's late!

We all had mikes, and we came in together on the chorus, with the crowd pumping their fists and roaring the words along with us, over and over again, Wacław's hugely amplified voice soaring above it all, barking out the refrain with a quirky passion that made each repetition new.

> *Hundred-percent* asshole!
> *Hundred-percent* asshole!
> *Hundred-percent* asshole!

The promoters cut the power to our amps after perhaps the thirtieth repetition of our chorus, but they were way too late. We'd gotten over.

And yes, I know the lyrics look crude on the printed page, but forget not the transformative power of rock and roll. Imagine, if you will, thirty thousand people screaming these words at once, and imagine ten thousand Gobubbles floating among them, with each bubble showing a simulated moment of the projected hundred-percent Heritagist administration: truculent Joe Doakes announcing another war in the service of big business, police attacking poor people with clubs, industrial pipelines pouring poisons into rivers, American tanks razing mosques and minarets, hard guy Frank Ramirez telling FBI agents to shut up, another skyscraper collapsing from a terrorist bomb, peevish Doakes and his marshmallow family hobnobbing with glittering billionaires, a fresh-faced American soldier dying, a cancer-stricken old woman staring into an empty cupboard, a child in a nightgown begging outside a factory, heavy rain washing away the soil of a clear-cut forest, Doakes testily signing another tax cut for the rich—hundred-percent asshole!

Backstage we were filled with a sense of imminent rev-olution. Cammy was hanging tight with Wacław. K-Jen was flirting with Stanislaw, and Abdul was playing with Naz's drum vest. A dauntingly merry Jutta Schreck gave me a big kiss and rubbed my face against her pumped-up tits. But I was worried about the Heritagists. Even if we'd struck a decisive blow against their empire, they still had time to gun me down. Paul and I were planning to lie low in San Ho.

Quickly I disguised myself as an AntiCrystal fan. I rubbed some of Jutta's pale make-up on my face, squirted my hair with Abdul's green hair gel, and painted on K-Jen's black lipstick and dark eye shadow. To complete the look, I pulled on an black XXL AntiCrystal concert T-shirt showing a busty devil-girl playing a crystalline guitar in front of three empty crosses and an atomic mushroom cloud.

And then I melted into the night, with Special Bela in my pants pocket jamming all predictions of my next move.

SEVEN

the best of all possible worlds

Most people in the audience lucky enough to snag a Gobubble had taken it home with them. Yet a fair number of the bubbles had blown loose in the wind. Outside the stadium, the iridescent spheres were bouncing past on the sidewalk, each of them holding an image of some different person's future. Homeless people were busy collecting the bubbles, stuffing the futures into ragged sacks.

I'd thought maybe the Heritagists would be out in force trying to confiscate the Gobubbles. But it seemed like for now they were off-balance, perhaps even stunned into silence. Surely that wouldn't last long.

I'd arranged to meet Paul at the commuter-train station across the street, and there he was, dressed up like a Washer Drop fan in a red T-shirt showing a grinning washing-machine embedded in the roof of an SUV with an X-eyed pig hanging out the door. Paul had gel-dyed his hair black and moussed it into a Mohawk, had attached a temporary ring to his nose, and had decorated his arms with press-on tattoos. We high-fived each other, looking for all the world like a pair of seasoned headbangers on their way home to San Jose.

"What a concert," said Paul. "You outdid yourself, Bela."

"We shouldn't use our real names," I cautioned.

"We'll be Joes," said Paul. "Okay, Joe?"

"Sure thing, Joe. A hundred-percent!"

"Hundred-percent asshole!" echoed Paul, and his cry was repeated by half a dozen people around us.

"Hundred percent!" I yelled again, and got the same enthusiastic response, this time with twenty voices chiming in. The phrase had a stickiness to it; people liked to say it. With any luck, in a few days the response would be universal.

A lot of the people in the train car had Gobubbles from the concert; Paul and I switched seats after each stop to get an idea of what people were doing with the bubbles.

A smooth-talking backwards-baseball-hat-wearing guy was wooing a full-lipped beauty. She had a Gobubble, and he didn't. "Let me stay over tonight," he said. "I don't want to be apart from you. We'll go to the beach in the morning." The woman looked in her Gobubble, and saw him sneaking out of her house the next morning before she woke up. "I don't think so," she said. "But you can drive me home from the station."

A ruminative, slow-moving boy in an SJSU cap was playing on-line poker on his pocket computer while watching himself in his Gobubble. His actions were fully in synch with the Gobubble's predictions; he bet big and won when the bubble predicted he'd bet big and win; he bet small and folded when the bubble predicted he'd bet small and fold. I visualized the positive feedback loop as a teapot morphon with its spout pouring into its top. "What would happen if you did the opposite of what the Gobubble predicts?" Paul asked him. "Why would I do that?" said the boy, brushing Paul off.

A rough-skinned guy with burr-cut hair was watching predictions of lottery drawings in his Gobubble: tomorrow's Pick 3 and Fantasy Five. He jotted down the numbers to bet. "Tomorrow's gonna be the last day ever for lotteries," Paul murmured to me. "With thousands of people picking the correct winning numbers, the pay-off will be less than the ticket price."

A lean, hungry, business-obsessed guy was leaning over his Gobubble talking to it, honing his Monday morning pitch, attentive to the simulation's reactions. I remembered how I'd used my Gobubble to get on the right side of Pete Ziff.

Two giggling Goth girls were playing Scissors-Paper-Rock while watching their Gobubbles. The Gobubbles kept changing their predictions of course, each bubble reacting to the new data put out by the opponent's Gobubble. An ongoing negative feedback loop; two morphonic fish chasing each other with rakes. Even so, whenever the girls finally did stick out their fingers to show their final picks, the Gobubbles always had them right.

An academic type with wire-rimmed glasses was watching us watching the girls. "Check this out," he said to me. He wagged his finger at his Gobubble. "In one minute you'll be white or red," he instructed his Gobubble. "I'm going to ask you to do two things: Predict what color you'll be in one minute, and set your color to the opposite of what you predict."

"I can't do that," piped the Gobubble, "It would be a contradiction."

Paul and I played dumb, but after the guy got off the train, Paul said, "It looks as if Van Veeter's current operating system tries to block Haut-style paradoxes in the software. That could make it hard to build another a hypertunnel."

"We didn't use software at Miller Beach," I pointed out. My Gobubble was displaying Special Bela watching golf on television. "We just zapped a spot on the Gobrane."

"Yeah," said Paul. "We used a point whose distances from the two edges were in the golden ratio to each other. But on a sphere there's no edges to measure from."

"Maybe zap a Gobubble in three spots," I suggested. "One zap sets the north pole, the second zap sets the prime meridian, and the third zap can do the golden-ratio thing in longitude-latitude coordinates."

"Let's try that tomorrow," said Paul. Our half-empty train was rattling into San Jose. "Where are we gonna stay tonight?"

"How about my mother's place," I said. "I miss Ma."

"Her house is gonna be totally staked out, Joe."

"I have to see her now," I said stubbornly. "I was wrong to leave Earth-1 without saying good-bye."

"It's not the same Ma here, Joe."

"I don't care. And she'll know someplace we can stay. Don't worry about the surveillance, I know a back way. We can walk to Ma's from here."

We followed the edge of the tracks for awhile, then climbed down into a gully and worked our way up a dry creek bed. Walking the secret byways of my boyhood filled me with nostalgia. With Earth-1 forever behind me, I could never truly go home. But here I was anyway.

We came up from the creek bed and through a bamboo thicket to the rarely used back door of Ma's garage. Paul and I slipped in there beside Ma's little white car. Fortunately the garage's big front door was closed. Standing well back from the slit windows, we could see a black car parked across from our driveway with two figures in it.

The garage had a side door that led right into the kitchen. I stood there listening, wondering if Ma was alone. I could hear her TV; she was watching the late news. She would have known I was giving a concert tonight.

Just then the announcer began talking about our show, with our music faintly in the background. The Heritagists had regrouped; the attack machine was in gear. The Gobubbles were "interactive occult amulets based on illegally obtained top-secret government intelligence technology." People were required to turn in their Gobubbles to the police—or face the possibility of criminal prosecution. The foreign AntiCrystal band members were being expelled from the country. Dreg rocker Bela Kis and Stanford mathematician Paul Bridge were being sought in connection with felony charges of violating the Homeland Security Act.

"A hundred percent," murmured Paul.

I tapped very faintly on the door to the kitchen. Ma had sharp ears. Right away the door swung open and there she was, no taller than my chest, her eyes like inquisitive quotation marks, her face lighting up. She gave us a good once-over, smiling at my green hair and black lipstick, and at Paul's Mohawk and nose ring.

"Ma," I whispered, touching my finger to my lips.

"Bela," she breathed. We hugged. Ma put her hands on my waist as if hefting me, the way she liked to do. Weighing her baby.

Paul made a sleeping gesture, putting his hands by the side of his head. Ma nodded knowingly, pursing her lips to exaggerate the gesture, stretching her neck forward and nodding for a very long time. She went back into the kitchen, exclaiming, "Where *is* that cat?" for the benefit of any audio bugs, and returned with a note written in Chinese.

It was an introduction to Mabel Wang, the plump old widow of Wing Wang. Mabel was the sister of Wah Woo, who was the husband of my mother's father's first cousin Shirley Woo, who was also the grandmother of Ling-Ling Woo—the high school girl whose interest in the vlog footage of me in the shower had inspired my song "Bela's Weenie." Aunt Mabel, as I called her, was a remote enough relative that her house was surely unwatched—indeed, it was doubtful if any official databases even registered the fact that I had any connection to Mabel. My relatives were all kind of sneaky.

I hugged Ma again and she patted my head. It was painful to part, knowing that I might soon leave this world as well. As Ma said good-bye to me, she looked just the slightest bit uncertain—and she was never uncertain.

It broke my heart. Could Ma at some level sense that I wasn't her natural-born Bela-2?

With a heavy heart I led Paul back through the bamboo, down into the streambed, across the soccer field at the elementary school, through a culvert under the Guadalupe Freeway, around a lumberyard, and up a gravel alley to Mabel Woo's tiny cottage. I hadn't been there in years.

It was two a.m. and we had to knock for quite awhile. For the longest time old Mabel pretended she didn't hear us, but when we wouldn't let up, she finally shuffled from the bedroom and peered through the little glass window in the door. Given that we were still dressed as dreg/metal concertgoers, Mabel's expression was suspicious and sour. Fortunately I had Ma's note to press against the glass, which made all the difference.

"Little dragon!" she said letting me in. "You dressed for stage! Famous musician. Your mamma Xiao-Xiao tell me." She touched my cheek and my lipsticked mouth and looked at her finger to see if the colors came off. "You need wash," she said, and flicked her finger against Paul's nose ring. "In China we lead cow that way. I Bela's Aunt Mabel. You like Chinese food?"

"I'm Paul," he said, unclipping his nose-ring and smoothing out his hair. "Yes, thank you, Mabel, I'm quite hungry. And would you happen to have some beer?"

"Tsingtao," said Mabel. "Four big bottle. We make after-hours party. Very nice waking up to see you two boys. I was dreaming about husband Wing's funeral. Every night I dream it again. Too lonely being old. All my friends dead. My son Jackie only visit once in a while. He very busy San Francisco." Jackie was the bookkeeper for a Chinese tong that owned several of the residential hotels in Chinatown, including the Tang Fat. Mabel bustled across the room and lit a candle inside a red lantern above her miniature dining table. I'd been fascinated by Mabel's place as a boy; it was like a doll's house.

"Do you have a computer?" Paul had to ask.

"Of course," said Aunt Mabel, "I modern woman. Jackie give me. You play with computer tomorrow. Big after-hours party now."

I was still totally wired from the concert, and Paul, he now confessed, had taken a little taste of Pete Ziff's meth. We ended up eating, drinking, and talking with Mabel for several hours; after the beer was gone, Mabel brought out some clear Chinese liquor that tasted like paint remover. Mabel was up for hearing us talk for as long as we were able.

When I explained to her that it had to be a secret that we were here, she reminisced about how, back in China, her mother had hid a cousin for a whole year from the Red Guards, keeping him in the hayloft above the cow with the nose ring like Paul's. She never asked why the law was looking for us; she only said she'd be glad to shelter me and my friend for as long as we liked.

Dawn was breaking when we finally crashed. Aunt Mabel's house had only two rooms; Paul and I slept on a quilt she laid on the little living room/dining room/kitchenette floor. I woke in the late morning, head throbbing, tongue salty and dry.

Paul was busy on Mabel's laptop, a clunker with a faint, fuzzy screen and a slow landline link. He informed me that, over the last two hours, he'd pollinated the world with:

- The Gobubble recipe, which he knew by heart.
- Practical tips about how to make a serial-bus bubble wand for programming your Gobubble.
- An archival copy of the source and executable code for Veeter's Gobubble operating system MSOMP 2-SV.
- A digitally signed and authenticated copy of the NSA video of Doakes's helicopter rescuing Qaadri from the American troops in Lilliputistan.

Good old Paul. I drank a quart of water from Mabel's wee sink. I could see her through the window, in her backyard watering her many roses, wearing a white bonnet with an enormous bill. It was another ruthlessly sunny California day. I peered over Paul's shoulder at the computer. "Nobody can trace this back to Aunt Mabel's machine?"

"You gotta trust Onar Anders," said Paul. Like me, Paul had known Onar before Onar left our math grad program to become the chief web honcho for the Kingdom of Tonga in the South Pacific, there to provide such sorely needed computer liberation tools as his Pollinator ware. The laptop gave a beep and displayed the fluffy white ball of a dandelion head. Paul had gotten over. Onar's bots had posted our subversive info on hundreds of thousands of sites worldwide. "The small axes are chopping," said Paul. "Cutting the big tree down."

I was glad, but I felt uneasy. "What if, um, Doakes's agents get to us before he's out of power? I'd feel more comfortable if I knew we could tunnel back to La Hampa."

"So let's do some experiments," said Paul. He dug down into his baggy pants pockets and produced his Special Paul Gobubble. The bubble showed Special Paul standing in a long, long line outside a breakfast spot in Los Perros. "Let's try zapping this bubble in three spots like you said. We don't necessarily have to go through if it works. We can always get another bubble. Battery?"

After some poking around, I found a flashlight, electrical tape, and wire in a drawer near Mabel's sink. I remembered that drawer from when I'd been a little boy. Mabel's place was like a sailboat, with each object stashed away in its one particular place.

"Better take our experiment outside," I said. "If we make a tunnel in here, Mabel's whole house could get sucked in." If I'd been holding a walking stick in my hand I would have been able to touch every wall in this room, the place was that small.

In the yard Mabel cheerfully sprayed water at us, then asked what we were up to.

"We have these fortune-telling balls," I said, showing her my Gobubble. "You can ask them questions and see the future. And now Paul and I want to zap one with the battery from your flashlight and see if it gets big."

"Like firework?" said Aunt Mabel. "I stand ready with hose."

"Good idea," I said agreeably. "But keep a good distance back." Paul was bent over his Gobubble, battery and wires in hand. So far not much was happening. "How you mean fortune-telling?" asked Mabel after a bit. "Can I ask about stock market?"

"Um, you can try," I said. "But aren't the markets closed today? It's Sunday, right?"

"Shenzhen Exchange in China is trading seven days," said Mabel, starting towards Paul. "I following Asian blue-chip stocks. I want to ask which will be biggest gainer today."

"Hold on, Aunt Mabel, let Paul do his thing. You can use my magic ball instead." Special Bela was using a noisy, gasoline-powered, high-pressure water pump to hose off his SUV. A man's hose for a man's car. I handed the Gobubble to Mabel. "Just ask it whatever you're interested in." I turned my attention to Paul, who didn't seem to be getting anywhere. "You did understand what I said about the three points?" I said.

"Duh!" he said sharply. "It doesn't work. A simpler way to express your notion is to pinprick a right triangle that has two of its sides in the golden ratio to each other, by the way. And that doesn't work either." He fumbled around some more, teasing his Gobubble with tiny sparks—but to no avail. "We need a better idea," said Paul, flopping back on the grass and tossing aside the battery and wires in disgust.

"Let me keep these to try later," I said, picking them up and shoving them in my pocket.

"Fine," said Paul, staring up at the sky.

"Look here, Bela," said Mabel, still busy with my Gobubble. "ZTE do very well today. Spike ten percent."

"ZTE?" I walked over to her to see.

"Zhongxing Telecommunication Equipment," said Mabel. "High-ranking. Chinese wireless company. You think I should buy a hundred share?"

"Don't gamble unless you can afford to lose," I cautioned. "The economy's gonna be thrashing for the next few days. That prediction could be wrong. The Gobubble predictions feed back into the system and alter what they're trying to predict."

"I call Jackie now. Buy two hundred share."

"Please don't," I said.

"Not worry," said Aunt Mabel. "I no tell about you. I tell him I have dream."

She phoned Jackie and placed her order, but a few minutes later Jackie called back with the news that the Shenzhen exchange had closed down. He hadn't been able to place Mabel's trade.

"Your ball no good," said Mabel. We were back in the house now, Mabel busy at her little stove, fixing rice-flour pancakes for our breakfast. Paul and I were slouched on her couch.

"It's like that Scissors-Paper-Rock game on the train," said Paul.

"I put on TV, we watch real news while we eat," said Mabel, setting down the pancakes on the table. "Maybe hell break loose from what you bad boys do." She nodded towards the shelf with the bottle of clear, oily Chinese liquor. "Hair of dog?"

"God no," I said.

The TV news was wonderful. All the networks were airing special reports on a nation in crisis. At long last the news media had turned on their puppet masters. The journalists, too, had been peering into Gobubbles to see the real future that the Heritagists had in store.

Over and over the TV showed the video of our president's helicopter rescuing the terrorist Qaadri from our troops. Violent street demonstrations against the Heritagists were in progress all across the nation. The White House was under siege, surrounded by a crowd of demonstrators estimated at a hundred thousand, and growing by the minute. Police cars were being overturned and set on fire. The president had scheduled a special address—and here he came.

It was a classic performance. Doakes was like a wounded shark snapping at his own dangling guts. The Gobubbles were Satanist; the Common Grounders were traitors; Van Veeter was a criminal; the demonstrators were terrorists; war was peace; slavery was freedom; ignorance was strength; and more than ever we needed a hundred-percent Heritagist victory in November. To my delight, the megacorporate news station had the nerve to post a hip, mocking caption across the bottom of the screen while Doakes was still ranting: *100% A-Hole?*

Paul and I stood up and cheered, with Mabel smiling at us, not quite sure what was going on. And that's when we heard the knock on the door.

Framed in the door's little glass window was the face of Ling-Ling Woo, her mouth open in an excited smile, her ponytail sticking straight out from the back of her head.

"I tell her keep the secret," said Mabel, even as Ling-Ling came bursting in.

"Aunt Mabel!" she shrilled. "You've got Bela visiting? Oh. My. God. Your concert last night was *so* awesome, Bela! I was *there*!" Her voice shot up on the final word, twisting it into a squeal. "I had no! Idea! You'd be here! I've been out all afternoon trying to sell these, like, raffle tickets for my band so we can go to Hawaii for the band contest at Christmas? But everyone's like, let us watch television, and I'm like, *why?* Is something happening?" Not waiting for an answer, Ling-Ling jabbered on. "Please buy some tickets, Aunt Mabel? Five dollars each. And my friends won't even *believe* that I saw you, Cousin Bela. Look, guys!" She stretched out her hand towards me—and that's when I noticed she was wearing a vlog ring.

"Take her outside for a minute," I told Paul. "And then bring her back in."

"What are you *doing*, you weird man," cried Ling-Ling as Paul bundled her out the front door. "Are you a total freak?"

"Do you know cousin Gyula's cell phone number?" I asked Mabel.

She did. I got Gyula on the phone and talked Chinese with him, asking him to meet us at the lumberyard. He was in a good mood. He said he could be there soon. Paul brought Ling-Ling back in. I loosely tied Mabel's quilt over the angry Ling-Ling, covering her and her camera so she couldn't report which way we went. Sirens were approaching.

"Bye, Mabel. Tell them you don't know anything."

"I don't speak English," she said in Chinese, her wiry

arms wrapped around the enquilted Ling-Ling. "Good
luck, little dragon. And you be quiet, niece!"

Paul and I crouched at the back of the lumberyard for
what felt like forever, squeezed under the shelter of a
crooked pile of plywood. We could hear sirens and cop
loudspeakers all around the neighborhood. A chopper
was beating the sky. We distracted ourselves by talking
some more about how we might get Haut's Paradox to
work on the Gobubble. But just now we were fresh out
of ideas. We were stuck on Earth-2, in the midst of the
anthill we'd stirred up.

Whoosh, Gyula pulled up in Veeter's white Hornswoggle stretch limo with the dark glass and the official plates.
Gyula had a Gobubble mounted right on his dash. The
bubble was set to show an aerial view of the neighborhood streets one minute from now; Gyula was playing
the cop patterns as handily as an old-school videogamer
leading Pac-Man away from his ghostly enemies.

Quite soon we were doing a hundred and twenty miles
an hour on Route 280 heading north out of San Jose. Paul
and I were in front with Gyula; the passenger compartment was mounded with guns and ammo.

"Glad you called," Gyula told me. "Van wants to see
you guys. He's getting ready to make his move." He was
cheerful, pumped up. "Van figures Doakes and Ramirez
will have to step down now," he continued. "And thanks
to his Gobubbles, he's next in line. Speaker of the House."

"Van's at his ranch on Skyline Boulevard?"

"With his personal guards and automated defense

system. He doesn't trust the Secret Service. We've got me, big Owen-slash-Yuan, Tito Cruz, a new guy Tito brought in, I forget his name, and now you two. Plus the robots and the Tomahawk missiles. We're armed and dangerous, bud. Van's Liberation Army. Reach back there and pick weapons, in case some fool might want to fight." Gyula's excited grin reminded me of the old days when he and I would amass fireworks for the Fourth of July.

Paul and I peered into the back seat, with Gyula watching in his mirror and swerving a bit as he gloated over his stash: four Colt .45 automatic pistols like L-shaped candy bars, two MAC M10 submachine guns resembling green quarts of milk with nozzles, an M16 assault rifle, an all-metal Barrett 50 caliber semiautomatic rifle like a farm implement with two hand-grips, and a pair of insectile RPG-7 rocket-propelled grenade-launchers with a dozen rockets piled into a wooden box.

"Maybe one of you should fire off a rocket," said Bela. "There's a chopper on our tail. And they're using a Gobubble to predict us as fast as I can use my dashboard Gobubble to predict them. We've got to shoot them."

Paul and I looked at each other. "We're mathematicians," I said presently. "Not terrorists."

"I'm not into murdering strangers," added Paul. "Let's see how we do using *my* Gobubble." He threw the one on the dash out the window and replaced it with his. "Mine jams the Pig's predictions." He turned to stare out the rearview window. "And what if that's only a traffic helicopter, anyway?"

"It's NSA," said Gyula. "Look at the freakin' cannon on it." As he drove, Gyula was continually speeding up and slowing down, one eye always on Paul's Gobubble.

But even Paul's special Gobubble could keep us safe for only so long. Soon the chopper's savage roar was directly overhead. Three rounds pounded the car roof and dust popped from the upholstery overhead.

"There was no way to dodge that one," said Gyula. "At least we're armored. Up to a point. But I'm seeing all the paths from here as dead ends unless we fire that rocket. Come on, Bela. Don't be a wimp. It's them or us."

"You shoot, Gyula," I said. "I'll drive."

"Okay, professor," said Gyula, glad to get his hands on the guns. "Get ready."

"You monitor the Gobubble for me, Paul," I said. "I'm gonna have to focus on the road."

Gyula opened the sunroof and slammed on the brakes so that the chopper was way out ahead of us. The gun-ship's turret rotated, swinging our way "Go, go, go!" yelled Gyula, worming over the seat-back into the rear of the car as I slid into the driver's seat.

"Speed up right now, Bela," said Paul, staring in the Gobubble. I mashed on the gas; the acceleration flattened me against the back of the seat. And as we went under the chopper, Gyula fired the rocket.

The whoosh was deafening; the car filled with smoke. Glancing in the mirror, I saw an orange ball of flame with the helicopter wobbling brokenly to the side of the road. Gyula had taken off its tail; possibly the passengers were alive.

Meanwhile, coming up fast behind us was a cop car with his flashers on.

"Right lane," said Paul. "Slow down. Twitch left!" A bullet ripped through the car's right fender. "Real fast again," said Paul. I heard more bullets whizzing past. "Can't you go faster than that, Bela? Left lane! He's coming. He's blocking off our strategies. He's gonna get us. Shoot him, Gyula!"

Baring his teeth in a stark grin, Gyula leaned out the side window, holding the 50-caliber rifle's two implement grips, wedging its butt against the window frame. He blasted off a few shots, but then the gun clattered onto the 130-mile-per-hour pavement. The rifle's powerful recoil had twisted it from even Gyula's strong hands.

"It's okay, you got him!" cried Paul. "You hit his engine block! Look at that smoke and steam! He's pulling over!"

And then I was off 280, slithering uphill on Alpine Road, shaded by oak trees, with the sun-yellowed fields flashing past. Thanks to Paul's anonymizing Gobubble I dodged the cops all the way uphill—now and then ducking into someone's driveway to avoid an encounter. I offered to let Gyula take the wheel again, but he said I was doing fine. He got a kick out of seeing his brainiac cousin play the gangster.

Up on the ridge, three unmarked black cars had road-blocked Skyline Boulevard, just a half-mile short of the turnoff to Van's house. Gyula reached past me to hit a custom switch on the dashboard; it raised the Hornswoggle three feet off the ground. Without slowing down, I swerved onto the rugged yellow-grass shoulder, closely following Paul's Gobubble instructions, swooping and swerving like a salmon swimming upstream. We had a clear path past the roadblock. The agents were shooting at us, but thanks to Paul's instructions they kept missing us. We were the good guys in this movie.

"Our futures dead-end when we pass those cars," said Paul in a worried tone. "They'll be firing at point-blank range."

"Hell they will," said Gyula. He launched an airborne rocket low over the agents' heads and toggled yet another switch on the dash. This one unleashed a blanket of fire from beneath our car. Our would-be captors scattered like termites off a campfire log.

"Flamethrower system in the trunk," said Gyula happily. "Nozzles on both sides of the car. You can turn it off now."

As we sped down Van's long driveway, I noticed metallic figures loping through the dry weeds like double-jointed aluminum deer. They were carrying rifles mounted on their backs. "Armed robots!" exclaimed Paul.

A high, green steel fence surrounded the core of Veeter's property, with a watchtower every twenty yards. Robot machine guns tracked us from the two nearest towers. A roboticized cannon was waiting at the main gate; it recognized us and moved to one side. Three honest-to-god Tomahawk missiles were set up on portable launch-pads just inside the gate, with spider robots perched on their controls. Silicon-Valley Van was even ready to fend off an air strike.

His house was out of sight from the gate, fifty yards down the ocean side of the ridge and set right into the hillside, much of it underground, with oak trees all around it and a patio made of smoothed-off giant boulders with a view across the rolling Santa Cruz mountains to the low afternoon sun gilding the fog-blanketed Monterey Bay. Van stood at the near edge of the patio beckoning us, big Owen at his side.

I asked Paul's Gobubble on the dash what awaited us in Van's house. But Van had a jamming system as good as Paul's. The Gobubble wasn't showing anything meaningful.

"You talk to him, Paul," I said, getting myself a submachine gun from the back. "I'm staying out here in case something's screwed up. I'm paranoid."

"Tito said I should bring you and Paul in together," said Gyula, climbing out of the bullet-pocked rear door. "He's coordinating security."

"Tito sucks," I said, thumbing the safety off the MAC M10 and checking that it was fully loaded. "I'm staying the fuck out here." I was a little deafened from all the gunfire. It was hard to tell how loud I was talking. I rolled down the driver's-side window. "Don't try anything on me," I told Gyula.

Gyula stared in the open car window at me clutching my submachine gun. "Little Bela," he said softly. "You think I couldn't take you down right now?" He reached in and patted my cheek. "Don't hurt yourself." I was way out of my depth here.

"I'll check things out and come right back," said Paul.

Still sitting in the driver's seat, I watched Paul and Gyula walk around the side of the house to the patio. They talked to Van for awhile, and then they went inside. Right before they went in, Paul looked over and gave me a last wave. And then they were gone, leaving fat-necked Owen alone on the patio, watching me with eyes as unreadable as Rowena's. I noticed that in this world Owen had his gold chain again.

Nothing happened for a little while. I got out my Gobubble with the battery and wires and began exploring the problem of setting up an Haut's Paradox on a sphere. I had the placement of the sparks right; after watching Paul, I knew the golden ratio by heart. But nothing was happening. It occurred to me that the *timing* of the sparks could be important. In the case of the Gobrane that hadn't been an issue, as we'd only needed the one spark. But with three sparks—maybe you had to wait till the effects of each previous spark had wrapped all the way around the little ball. Yes. The correct model here was, I now realized, the cake morphon instead of the rake morphon.

I zapped the ball a few times, getting a sense of the cycle time and how to spot it. So, okay, if I did one spark, waited a cycle, did the second spark, waited a cycle, and—

Two shotgun blasts boomed from Van's house. Owen disappeared from the patio, running heavily into the house. Pistol shots and a scream. I stared at the house through the open car window, clutching the MAC M10 on my lap. Should I quick try and open a hypertunnel? Or start the car and go for the gate? Or run in to save Paul and Gyula? But were they even alive? And what chance would I have against professional killers? I hesitated, torn, feeling like a coward.

A figure burst out of Van's house, running towards me with a shotgun in his hand. With a shock I recognized the bestial features. It was Roberto Sandoval.

Sandoval raised his shotgun, aiming at me and displaying some kind of badge. He had blood on his hands. "Freeze!" he yelled. "You killed them! You were jealous that they loved each other! Get out with your hands up!"

Reacting faster than thought, I hit Sandoval in the chest with a burst of submachine-gun fire. *Hell*, yeah. He fell onto his back; his legs beat a tattoo on the ground; he lay still. I got out of the car. I'd killed him, just like I'd wanted to. So why did I feel so bad?

"Good, Bela," said Gyula, limping into the yard, blood all over his shirt-front. "You're learning." And then he pitched forward, dead, the closest thing to a brother I'd ever had. I started crying.

I was pretty sure that Van and Paul were dead, too. Owen and Tito's voices were coming from the house, Tito's voice high-pitched and speedy, Owen's low and halting.

Time for me to leave? No, man. I had to see this to the end. I dried my eyes on my shirtsleeves and reloaded my MAC M10. Holding my gun at the ready, I stepped into the house—and faced Owen holding a shotgun aimed at my chest. Fortunately I had my submachine gun aimed directly at him.

"Brother Yuan," I said in Chinese. "Be my friend."

"Ugly guy shit crazy," answered Owen in the mother tongue. His flat moon face was slick with sweat. "Shoot the boss and your friend. Write blood on wall. Shoot Gyula. Run outside. He say blame you or he kill me too."

"Sandoval's dead," I said. "It's safe now. I no shoot, you no shoot. Agree?"

Owen studied me for the longest time and finally, in

unison, we lowered our guns. I reached out my left hand and shook with Owen.

"Shanghai," I said.

"California," said Owen, with a tentative smile.

"Yo, yo, yo!" came Tito's voice from the next room. "Help me out. I need a doctor."

He was stretched out on the floor, wearing a mournful expression and bleeding lightly from a superficial gunshot to his thigh. He said he wanted an ambulance, but he didn't really look that bad. I took his weapons away, then tore some bath towels into strips and tied them around his wound to fully stop the blood.

In the course of getting the towels, I got a stomach-turning glimpse into the ghastly charnel house of Van's bedroom. Paul and Van lay dead and naked on the blood-drenched bed, each of them shot in the chest and the head. Oh, Paul. Our long journey together was over. Ramirez had set up the crime to look like an occult sex murder. He'd scrawled my name and a five-pointed star in blood on the wall. Wipe it off? Better idea: get the truth out.

With Tito's bleeding stanched, I circled around the house looking for a sample vlog ring—and soon I found a whole box of the Monogrub models that Rumpelstiltskin was producing. I opened one of the bubble packs, slipped on a ring, and it went live. Before continuing, I used some voice commands to reroute the ring's wireless output to Pollinator—lest Monogrub quash the news.

"I'm Bela Kis," I told the vlog ring then. "I'm at the house of former congressman Van Veeter, who's just been murdered by Roberto Sandoval." As I talked, I made my way back into the dining room where Tito lay on the floor. "Sandoval was brought into Veeter's home as an extra bodyguard by Tito Cruz. Tell us about it, Tito."

"I can't," said Tito, tightening his long lips. "Get me to a doctor, okay?"

"Sit him up and make him talk," I told Owen.

Owen cracked his knuckles as if preparing for exercise, then hunkered down and propped up Tito, moving him as easily as a rag doll. Owen's hand was gripping the back of Tito's neck, the other was poised on Tito's wound.

"Hurt him now?" said Owen.

"I'm scared to talk," said Tito, his eyes darting around. "They'll get me."

"It was Ramirez, right?" I said. "Tell us your story and he'll go to in jail instead of you. This is going out national, Tito. Ramirez won't have a place to hide. If you stay quiet, you'll be the one in prison—and Ramirez will have you killed in the yard."

"Okay," said Tito with a long sigh. "Here's how it came down."

In a few minutes he'd laid out the whole deal. He had some bad debts; his old gang was gonna ice him; he got a call from Ramirez himself that he could clear things if he'd bring a special guy into Van's staff, a San Jose hit man named Roberto Sandoval. Sandoval's job was to kill Van and Paul—and to frame Bela for the killing. Tito didn't like the setup, but what could he do? Nobody could go up against Ramirez. Owen was supposed to play dumb, and Tito was planning to play the unsuccessful hero. He'd shot himself in the leg.

"Just to be perfectly clear," I said, "You're talking about Vice President Frank Ramirez?"

"That's it," said Tito. "He phoned me or Roberto every day. You could check the phone records."

"Thanks," I said. "You still want an ambulance?"

"I don't want nobody coming in here till the shit storm's over," said Tito, awkwardly getting to his feet. "First car to reach our gate's gonna be Heritagist hit-men, and the second and third ones too. Don't worry about this scratch on my leg. It ain't shit. I made it myself, I can fix it myself. Van always kept a bitchin' medicine cabinet." He hobbled towards the bathroom, leaning on Owen's shoulder.

I heard sirens beyond the front gate, stalled for now by the crackling gunfire of the robot guards. I discarded the vlog ring and went out to the patio. The sky was red; I was about done here.

I'd found a world where Cammy still lived, and I'd taken a shot at making her my lover. That hadn't worked out, but oh well. In a way, I'd avenged her murder, which was good. And on the wider scale, I'd saved the U.S. from a Heritagist dictatorship. And that was even better.

But in this world, Paul and Alma were both dead.

I didn't want to be here. I wanted to get back to Alma.

I drew my Gobubble, battery, and wires from my pocket.

Timing the sparks did the trick. A moment later my Gobubble began pulsing ruby and sapphire colors that merged into vibrant amethyst. It grew to several meters in size, a jewel beyond price. Within its clear center I could see the water worlds of La Hampa. I backed off, took a running start and leapt into the hypertunnel.

This time around, I emerged in midair, amidst water planets bobbing beneath a shiny sky that curved around to make a vast hollow sphere. A bright little sun glared over my shoulder. I didn't see any planet resembling the one with the alien mathematicians; none of the jiggling orbs seemed to hold an island with a Jellyfish Lake. Up above me, the hypertunnel was already gone.

I was falling towards the nearest of the planets; it boasted a large, curved island with a long beach and a waterfall-bedecked central mountain. I noticed five thatched houses along the beach and some figures sitting in the shade. They showed no sign of noticing me. I strained my eyes against the beating air, trying to see if my Alma might be on the island. But I couldn't even be sure the figures on the beach were human.

"Give me an easy landing, dear Nataraja," I said aloud to the distributed Nataraja-being that filled La Hampa. My prayer was answered; I cut into the water as cleanly as a high diver.

Fish schooled around me. I spread my arms to slow my descent towards the dimly gleaming sea floor—which I knew to be the sky of a lower level. I passed a long twisted piece of metal: the blade of the NSA helicopter that had delivered those Stanford mathematicians. This meant I was in Paradisio, the level above the Nanonesia of the cone shells and the cockroaches. I kicked my way back to the sea's upper surface.

As I emerged, something bright and fast flew low over my

head—a butterfly, a hummingbird? No, it was bigger than that, a meter long. It circled back towards me, a cartoony humanoid form with two bell-bottom legs, a lumpy ovoid bottom, a tapering torso chest with tear-drop arms, and a translucent bulb-head with a pair of antennae. Another alien.

The figure hovered above me, glowing in rich neon colors: seaweed-green legs, carroty-red bottom and arms, cobalt torso, robins-egg-blue head-bulb, and lilac antennae. The more I looked at it, the brighter it shone. I smelled ozone, as if from an electrical generator. I hoped the alien wasn't about to sting me.

"So say something," I said, treading water in the warm, clear sea. "I'm a human named Bela. What are you?"

The alien tweeted a word so fast that I couldn't make it out.

"Come again?" I said.

"Jimbo," chirped the little figure. "Jimbo, Jimbo, Jimbo." It pooted four short-lived cannonballs of light from the funnel-bottoms of its legs, each with an image inside. The result was a crystal-ball comic strip explaining the origin of the Jimbos. Glowing magnetic tornados lifted free from a speckled Sun to float across space. The space eddies touched down on a nearby planet's atmosphere—was that a future version of Earth? The magnetohydrodynamic swirls came alive with neon colors and took on playful forms: Jimbos. The Jimbos tagged after people like pet balloons, one per person.

"Jimbo, Jimbo, Jimbo!" said the alien again.

"Bela, Bela, Bela," I said. "You can be my Jimbo, if you like."

Vibrating with enthusiasm, the Jimbo flew right through my head; I grunted in fear, but all I felt was a brief tingle. Perhaps it had harvested some of my thought patterns? Fine. I stopped worrying about the Jimbo for now.

Instead I began worrying about drowning. My clothes were seriously dragging me down—I was wearing jeans, an AntiCrystal T-shirt, and leather boots. I got my clothes off, bundled everything inside my jeans, rolled them up, and tied the legs around my waist. With that done, I swam towards the island, with my Jimbo cheerfully buzzing around my head.

The first person I saw as I waded ashore was Paul Bridge. For a crazy instant I thought I was dead in heaven. But then I realized it was the Paul-2 whom we'd bumped to La Hampa when we'd invaded Earth-2.

"Bela?" he said, looking surprised to see me. He was sitting in the shade of a palmy tree, playing chess with a buxom blonde woman, a stranger to me. She and Paul-2 were naked. Two Jimbos hovered above them, shapes painted upon the air with colored light. The music of a sitar and tabla was drifting down the beach. The unseen sitar player was an amateur, repeatedly stopping and starting over.

The blonde woman's hair was short, dense, and close-cropped like velvet flocking, with the sharply delineated hairdo extending down the back of her neck and onto her spine. She had the face and figure of a movie star. She wore huge diamonds set into the lobes of her ears, a diamond in her navel, and a snake tattooed around her bare waist. A live tattoo: the snake was slowly circling

around, moving higher up her torso like the stripe on a
barber-pole.

"Pips, Bela," said the woman, glancing at me. "I thought
you were playing with Chockra?"

"I'm a different Bela," I said, stepping into the shade of
their tree. My Jimbo buzzed a loop-the-loop around the
other two Jimbos.

Paul-2 cocked his head, examining me, figuring things
out. His Jimbo was a winged lime-green barrel with a
cubical maroon robot head. "You're the one who forced
us into the tunnel?" asked Paul-2.

"That's me. And now I came back to La Hampa. I'm
glad to see you, Paul. The other Paul is dead now. Paul-1.
Ramirez's hit man got you. Him."

"That political crap seems so far away," said Paul-2. "It's
better here. I just wish I could go down to Nanonesia and
meet those alien mathematicians I've been hearing about.
But Duxie says we can find more of them at higher levels.
So what happened to Alma?"

"That's what I was gonna ask you," I said evading his
question. "Isn't Alma here?"

"*Your* Alma's here," said Paul-2. "But not my Alma. She
didn't make it through the tunnel. We found your Alma
here with those Stanford mathematicians—Cal Kweskin
and Maria Reyes. We're working on a generalized theory of the La Hampan cosmology and cosmogony, by the
way. Your Alma's taken up with a man from the future.
Nordal. But I was asking you about my Alma back on
Earth. Is she okay?"

"Um—" I didn't want to tell him.

Sensing my discomfort, the blonde woman interrupted. "I'm Duxie," she said, holding out her hand. She was so beautiful that it was hard for me to look directly at her. Especially naked. "Pips, other-Bela," she continued. "I'm from a future Earth, year 2204. Three friends and I hypertunneled to La Hampa using Haut's Paradox on our Jimbos. We just got here. The Jimbos have replaced what you called—was it a Gobubble?" She extended a graceful hand and her Jimbo perched on it unsteadily: a two-legged figure with a pleated skirt, a taffy-twisted torso, and a ball head with a short, cylindrical nose.

"The Jimbos are symbiotic sentient magnetohydro-dynamic paracomputers," put in Paul-2. "The real deal. From the Sun. They feed on our thought patterns, and the odd scrap of excrement now and then. In return they act as computers and cell phones. They love gossip. But tell me what—"

"We came out ten thousand four hundred La Hampan levels higher than Paradisio," resumed Duxie. She had a vibrant, well-modulated voice, and she liked to talk. "It's so crowded up there right now? Lots of people like to emigrate here, particularly from our decade. But no matter when someone comes from along our timeline, they show up on the same La Hampa day. Oh, there are some other humans who've been in La Hampa a week longer than our crowd; but they're from what they call the Earth-1 timeline. They think they're just so prixy. Turns out they've been pushing into our timeline and bumping people into La Hampa for two centuries. I hate them so much. They call us Earth-2, like we're copies or something. Just to bust free, we four—me and Erman, Chockra and Nordal—we thought it would be flippy to dig down to the La Hampa level with the earliest hampajumpers of all. You guys. The *real* aristocrats!"

"They're two couples," put in Paul-2. "Open marriages." The halting sitar music had stopped.

Duxie's Jimbo gave Paul-2's Jimbo a little kiss—for all the world as if the Jimbos were autonomous thought balloons. "We *discovered* you!" said Duxie. "I'm proud. It was tricky, because when you swim down through a waterworld's ocean and find ten new planets, well, you have to pick one planet to dive into for the next level down, and so on and on, which makes a lot, a lot, a lot of paths. Erman says that to even write that number, you'd need a one with ten thousand zeroes after it?" She swept her hand over her lovely blonde head, to indicate the complexity of this concept.

"I think La Hampa's an endless fractal," said Paul-2. "That reminds me, Bela, your Alma claims that, of all the places to be, we're exactly one level above some so-called Jellyfish Lake where a giant jellyfish is supposed to be spinning out all the alternate Earths. That sounds a little too pat for me. A coincidence like that is so—"

"She's right," I said. "Nanonesia level. It's where we landed on our first hampajump. It's no a coincidence at all. It stands to reason the very first hypertunnel from any of Earth's timelines would lead to Earth's God."

"God?" said Paul-2 with a derisive laugh. "Maybe I'm missing something. Anyway, come on, you still haven't told me about my Alma."

"I wasn't done telling the other Bela how we found you," said Duxie. "So hush, Paul. It was my husband, Erman, he had the idea of using Jimbos to help us find the path, Bela. Before we hampajumped, we already knew a little bit about what to expect, thanks to all those pushy Earth-1 pigs who've popped up in our timeline over the years. So Erman had the idea of digging out gobs of info about the famous Bela from the Monogrub archives—everyone knows that he hampajumped after the second American revolution, and since he was such the vlogger there was a lot of info to go on. So we muxed together a special Jimbo personally tailored for Bela. And once we're in La Hampa, our tailored Jimbo sniffs Bela out like a dog finding his master. And thanks to our rocket-pod fields, it only took us an hour to dive down the ten thousand levels. *Whoosh*, what a blur. Ta da! Not only did we find Bela, there's a Paul here, and an Alma, and those three others, and now a second Bela. It's like discovering the Garden of Eden!" She pointed up at my dancing manikin of light. "See Paul, the other Bela has a Jimbo too. Our Jimbos spawned off helpers for everyone."

"Hi, other Bela!" exclaimed a familiar voice behind me. Could it possibly be—yes. I turned to see: Bela-2. He walked up to me with a coppery-skinned Indian-looking woman at his side, the woman was as movie-star-beautiful as Duxie. They were naked too. Bela-2's expression was a mirror of mine: recognition, surprise, pleasure, fear. Our Jimbos looked the same. Duplicate people were okay in La Hampa.

"This here is the surf-kook Bela who bumped us over here," Paul-2 told Bela-2. "He showed up alone just now."

"What happened to our Alma?" asked Bela-2, glancing past me as if expecting to see her there. I knew that strained, wistful look very well. And now I could see him starting to get angry. So predictable.

"She's dead, okay?" I said, brusque in my rush to finally get this over with. "There was an earthquake and a rock fell on her head. I'm sorry. I miss her. Boo hoo hoo, like that. I came back here to find Alma again, as a matter of fact. She's here, isn't she? My Alma?"

"You killed our Alma?" cried Paul-2.

"*You* killed her," I said. "You were there steering her into the tunnel as much as I was. The first version of you, that is."

"Bastard," said Paul-2.

"Let's be calm," said the beautiful dark-haired woman with Bela-2. She smiled at me and took my hand. "Pips, other-Bela. I'm Chockra from 2204."

"Duxie was telling me," I said, looking her over. If Chockra liked Bela-2, for sure she'd like me. "Is *everyone* beautiful in the future?"

"Just about," said Chockra. "Biotech, you know." Her Jimbo was elephant-like: a pale violet ellipsoid with four short blue legs, a pair of yellow disk-ears, and a long, curved tube-trunk.

"There's some retroheads who keep themselves old-bio on purpose," said Duxie. "That can be groasty or prixy. It all depends." She patted Paul-2 on the cheek. "But the real old-bio is definitely erot, eh Chockra?"

"That's what we were hoping when we sent our special Jimbo after Bela!" said Chockra, twining her arm around

Bela-2's waist. "And that's why your Erman's with that ugly little Maria and my Nordal's with Alma-the-bitch. Wait till they see me with *two* Belas!" Chockra smirked and crooked a finger at me, wriggling the finger like a worm on a hook. Her elephant-shaped Jimbo flew over to touch Duxie's peg-nosed one, exchanging some naughty thoughts. The two women laughed for what seemed an unnecessarily long time. I felt awkward, out-of-the-loop.

"The futurians are airheads," Bela-2 told me. "Predatory sexual tourists. I figure they've had it soft and easy all their lives."

"Cosseted imperialists exploiting salt-of-the-earth types like you," I said. "Destroying your moral fiber by teaching you Kama Sutra positions and the sitar."

"It's good to have an intelligent conversation for once in my life," said Bela-2 with a smile that mirrored mine. "With you here, I finally I have some hope of being understood." We gave each other a smooth high-five, our hands moving in unison.

"How long has it been for you since Miller Beach?" I asked him.

"Paul and I just got here today," he said. "Alma and the Stanford people have been here a week. Cal, Maria, and Rick. They say it's Thursday in La Hampa. According to the futurians, no matter where on the Earth-2 timeline you hampajump from, you show up in La Hampa on this same Thursday."

"Sounds right," I said. "When I left Earth-2 just now, it was Sunday afternoon. Three Earth days after I bounced you. La Hampan time is really independent from the Earth timelines."

"Paul and I have been working out the theory of it," said Bela-2. "Along with Cal and Maria. You'd think the futurians could tell us this stuff, but they're not that big on science, any of them. Stop scowling at him, Paul. It's not like he knew what he was doing."

"He killed Alma."

"One Alma," I said. "On one Earth. And *I* didn't kill her. Mainly it was the fault of Paul-1. Your twin. And he's dead too." I sighed and rubbed my face. "This could be heaven, if we don't make it hell."

"How many Earths are there?" said Paul-2 after a long pause.

"Billions," I said. "Trillions. Maybe more. Paul-1 claimed he'd proved that every week the divine jellyfish makes a new Earth. She's revising it, shooting for a perfect world. *Hampatime is otherness.* Like Duxie says, we called our starting world Earth-1 and your world Earth-2. According to the alien mathematicians I met here, Earth-1 was the first timeline where any humans ever discovered hampajumping. So that means all the human hampajumpers are from Earth-1 or Earth-2."

"Hampatime is otherness, eh?" mused Paul-2. "I like that. Me, I've been focusing on a different slogan. *Hampascale is time.* The further along one of Earth's timelines you lie, the higher is the hampascale you jump across to. One level equals about a week. Interesting to see the one-week interval popping up in both contexts. Like how pi turns up in all kinds of math. But I wish you wouldn't keep saying God is a jellyfish."

"I tell you, she makes a new Earth every Friday." It felt good to be arguing with Paul again. So much better than having him dead. "And those are the only times when anyone can hampajump back. You can't jump back into your own timeline because of time-travel paradoxes, you have to jump into the timelines of new Earths. Like I did with Paul-1. And from what Duxie says, it sounds like a bunch of future Earth-1 people managed to hampajump back to Earth-2 at the same time I did, only further into Earth-2's future."

"Can I, myself, go back to Earth or not?" asked Paul-2, beginning to look confused. I was happy to be dazzling him, although I knew that before long he'd understand La Hampa better than me. "Not that I want to leave," he added. "I like it here. Duxie might rocket-pod me to the higher levels where all the futurians live. But could I go back to Earth if I wanted to?"

"The divine jellyfish decides who gets to hampajump into the new versions of Earth," I said. "When I jumped from La Hampa to Earth-2, I had to pray to the jellyfish for her to open the gate." I recalled the extra streamers of light that had gone up through the sky. "I think she made gates for future Earth-1 people at the higher levels too."

"And we'd be jumping to Earth-3," said Bela-2, right on my wavelength. "Tomorrow. The jellyfish god makes Earth-3 tomorrow, which is Friday in La Hampa time."

"Exactly," I said. "I have a feeling that Earth-3 is gonna be her final draft. She might not want to mess it up with any extra people from Earth-1 or Earth-2. Which means we could all be stuck here for good."

"This all makes perfect sense to me," said Bela-2. He was only one who understood me at all. "I'm seeing a morphonic heptagon made of seven fish."

"Dude," I said. "What I was thinking." We beamed at each other.

"It's like listening to Isaac Newton and two Thomas Jeffersons, isn't it?" said Duxie with a rich giggle. "We studied about you in school, Paul and Bela. About your inventions, and about Bela bringing down the—was it Whig?—dictatorship."

"Heritagist," I corrected her.

"Whatever. Erman should be here." She glanced up at her Jimbo. "Call Erman for me," she said.

Her Jimbo extruded a glowing bubble from its nose. The bubble hovered before us, displaying a man's dark, ideally handsome face.

"Come on down the beach, Erman," said Duxie. "Bring the others, too. Paul and Bela are being profound. And we've got a new visitor. No, I'm not going to tell you. Get off that girl and come see."

"Pips," said the man. Squeezed in next to his face in the bubble was the face of the Stanford grad student Maria Reyes, aka Mary Smith.

"Everyone paired up instantly," Bela-2 told me. "Like a freakin' Club Med. Paul and Duxie. Chockra and me. Erman and Maria. Alma and Nordal. Alma's mad at Paul and me about some stuff that you other guys did, so all Pauls and Belas are out of the question for her. Oh, and Cal Kweskin hooked up with his helicopter pilot, Rick. How's my Cammy, anyway? I hope that's not bad news, too."

"She's fine," I said. "But now she's with Wacław Smorynski. We played a reality-altering concert at Heritagist Park Saturday night. We had some killer new Washer Drop songs."

"God, I wish I'd been there for that," said Bela-2. "You'll have to tell me every detail. I don't know when I'll get that kind of gig again. Well, maybe after Chockra takes me way up the hampascale to where all the people from the future are moving in. They're gonna have cities up there. I'm looking forward to it."

"Is it hard to play the sitar?"

"Yeah," said Bela-2. "But I love how gnarly it sounds. The Nataraja made me a really good one. Now that you're here we can jam together. I'd be happy to go electric. And we'll need drums and a bass."

"A bass player like Cammy or Jutta Schreck," I said. "Jutta stood in for Cammy with Washer Drop at Rubber Rick's back on Earth-1, you know. I've still got to tell you about all that. And about the encore jam at the stadium show. We did a song called Hundred Percent Asshole."

"I can almost hear it," said Bela-2.

But now I saw the other couples coming down the beach toward us. Cal and Rick. Erman and Maria. Nordal and—Alma. I dropped everything and ran toward her.

"Alma! I came back!"

I guess I'd figured she'd hug me and we'd be right back where we used to be. But my Alma could hold a grudge.

"Hello, Bela," she said coldly. Her Jimbo was a squat, armless, three-legged figure with a blank onion-head and two pig-tails. "Rowena carried me up here last week," said Alma. "How was Cammy?" She took a step back lest I try and embrace her.

"Look, Alma, I came all the way back here because it's you that I—"

"Meet Nordal, Bela," she said. "My new lover. I met him this morning. Nordal, this is the original Bela."

"I bet you wish you had one of your horses here to ride," Nordal said to me, grinning and shaking my hand. His teeth were flawless and white. "Marvelous beach." With his perfect face and muscular torso we could have been in Malibu.

"I never rode a horse," I said. "I had a station wagon."

"Oh, with a team of four horses?" said Nordal.

"With an internal combustion engine," I said. "It burnt gasoline."

"Ping!" said Nordal, laughing. His Jimbo was a bowlegged figure with spaghetti fingers and a potato head. It poked Alma's Jimbo with one of its long fingers and Alma smiled.

"Are you getting telepathy through your Jimbo?" I asked Alma. "I don't pick up a thing."

"That's because nobody's sending to you," said Alma. Her Jimbo whacked mine with one of its pigtails, and suddenly I heard Alma's voice in my head. *"Nordal's an idiot,"* she said.

I wasn't sure how to send a message back to her, so I just smiled. There was hope. Or there would have been—but then of course Paul-2 told Alma about us having killed Alma-2 on Earth-2, and that got her angry with me all over again.

As the sun dimmed, we picnicked on a batch of transformed Nataraja sea cucumbers that Erman and Nordal fished out of the water. This time I was careful not to overeat, and my stomach felt okay. The hierophantic clarity kicked in. But it wasn't much of an evening.

Although talking to Paul and Bela-2 was nice, I pretty much knew what they were going to say. The futurians were bone dull, and didn't really take anything we said seriously—they acted like we were pets. As for the Stanford mathematicians and their pilot, they were friendly with Paul, but snotty to the rest of us. And Alma was still mind-gaming me.

I ended up sleeping in the cabin with Chockra and Bela-2. When they started making love, Chockra lustily encouraged me to join in, and maybe we two Belas could have gone for it, but I knew Chockra would tell Alma. I didn't want to tangle things up even more.

What it was, the bloody killings at Veeter's estate had taken the wind out of my sails. Seeing Gyula die, and then blowing away Sandoval with a machine gun, and then finding Paul and Van butchered—it had done something to my head. I didn't want any more craziness. I wanted to settle down.

The next morning we all went for a swim in the ocean, me and the five couples: Paul and Duxie, Bela-2 and Chockra, Erman and Maria, Cal and Rick, Nordal and Alma. We were in a cool spot with deep water, paddling around with the eleven Jimbos hovering over us. By now, I'd figured out how to send mental messages to Alma with my Jimbo: it was simply a matter of silently talking to her. My Jimbo would somehow pick up what I said, pass it to Alma's Jimbo, and she'd hear me in her head. I could tell from watching her face.

"*I love you,*" I told her. "*I want to marry you and have a family.*"

She knit her brow and shook her head, smiling just a little bit. I swam closer to her. Nordal was talking about horses again.

When something brushed my leg, I thought it was Alma, playfully kicking me, but it was a sharp, abrupt swirl in the water. All at once, Alma and I were spinning in rapid circles about each other, in the grip of a narrow, intense whirlpool.

The thread-like vortex sucked Alma and me through the shiny bottom of the Paradisio sea and popped us into the Nanonesian sky. The Nanonesian sun was nearly dead, but in its faint light I saw the island of the alien mathematicians directly below us. Our Jimbos were gone, either left behind or crushed out of existence by the forces drawing us downward.

Ever-vigilant, Rowena and Jewelle flew up towards Alma and me. But we spun past them, riding the vortex that had pulled us down from Paradisio. Twisting and twirling, haloed by an uncanny cerulean light, we plummeted towards Jellyfish Lake.

The jellyfish god rose from the lake's dim waters to meet us in midair, level with the island's ridge. Once again we were inside the jellyfish's body; once again we saw the divine six-limbed dancer, her face beautiful and terrible to behold.

"My creation is nearly done," she said, weaving patterns with her arms. "I've fashioned a final, perfect, unpredictable world—and now I'll become a sun." In the virtual distance I saw a fetal Earth cradled in nets of light.

"What about us?" said Alma. She was holding my hand.

"You must return," said the goddess. "You were the first couple to tunnel here from any of my worlds and survive—for the sake of symmetry you must close the circuit."

"I'd feel bad bumping people from Earth again," I said tentatively. "If we do go, can we make some special requests about the new Earth?" asked Alma.

"Trust in God," said the dancer. "I bless you."

Everything around us melted into white light.

It was Thursday, June 3. Ma was off at her restaurant prepping for lunch. Alma and I were alone in Ma's kitchen, eating cereal and looking at apartment ads. I was due to start as an assistant math professor at San Jose State at the end of the summer, and Alma was going to move in with me. Alma was studying the employment ads as well; she was hoping to find a job in public relations.

Suddenly she looked up from the paper and gave me an odd look. "Bela! It's like I'm waking up. We had other lives before this. The white light—the jellyfish sent over our memories instead of our bodies!"

An image of dead Alma-2 flashed past. I heard a snatch of Washer Drop music against a crowd's roar. I smelled the sweet breeze of Nanonesia. My two sets of memories were bubbling through each other, oil and water. The goddess had embedded the Bela-1 memories in the brain of Bela-3. I remembered something wonderful.

"Show me your hand, Alma!"

Alma held her left hand out towards me and smiled. Yes, she was wearing a diamond ring. I'd given it to her last week.

"A perfect world," I said. "You're going to marry me?"

"Yes, Bela."

I could end my story there, but I owe you a few what-became-ofs.

In this final Earth, Paul and I had shared an apartment at Berkeley, and he had a crush on Alma, but Alma didn't leave with Paul on graduation day. And I never hooked up with those kids to start the Washer Drop band. I'm a little bummed about that part. But I can still play the guitar pretty well, and I remember all our songs.

I checked for Cammy Vendt on the web; she's in a Redwood City band called Aternal. Alma and I went to see them play at a club one night. They weren't that great. I hung around afterwards, half-heartedly trying to get invited to jam with them, but they thought I was just a slumming professor.

I remember the Gobubble recipe quite well, and a few weeks ago I managed to make a sick-smelling, long-lived, iridescent bubble. But I don't have any kind of paracomputational operating system for it—and on this Earth, there's no Van Veeter, Henry Nunez, or Roland Haut; no Membrain Products and no Rumpelstiltskin, Inc.

Not that a paracomputing Gobubble would necessarily be such a powerful tool here. The thing is, this is a nondocile world. I can see it in the clouds, in the water running from a tap, in the motions of the leaves. The natural computations of this world are truly unpredictable.

And what about Paul? He has a job at Stanford and is living in faculty housing—the same as before. But in this world, Paul and I didn't write theses on universal dynamics; we didn't even have the same advisor. Paul's Berkeley thesis was "Noncommutative Spaces of Chaotic Quivers," and mine was "A Hypergeometric Theory of Ampleness."

Before paying my first visit to Paul, I spent a week writing up the Morphic Classification Theorem from memory—reproducing precisely the same paper as the one we'd written with Roland Haut. I figured that if Paul were to become interested, I might take him on as a coauthor; if nothing else, this would help my chances of publication. And in any case, I wanted to see what Paul-3 made of our Earth-1 work.

I found Paul friendly, but a bit distant—he was still peeved that Alma had picked me over him back at Berkeley, even though he's got Lulu Cliff living with him. She's taking grad courses and working as a sysop in the Stanford CS department.

I hinted around about the other worlds, but Paul showed no knowledge of them. Only Alma and I have those memories; I think we're the only extra people whom the jellyfish moved to Earth-3.

When Paul sat down to read my outre paper, he quickly found a large, unfixable hole in the proof. I was very deeply shocked. I'd always imagined mathematical truth to be absolute, the same in every world.

Now, I'm quite positive that I wrote up the paper just the same as before. And there's really no chance that Haut and the rest of our thesis committee could have overlooked so big a hole back in Humelocke. The only possible conclusion is that mathematics really can be different in different worlds.

The mathematics of Earth-3 is fierce, nondocile, and gnarlier than the math of Earth-1. The subtle insight that makes our old proof wrong was somehow unthinkable in those other worlds. More things are possible here.

As this sank in upon me during the days to come, I felt a sense of liberation. Did I really want to live in San Jose? No. I realized I want to live in the South Pacific, in a place like the La Hampan Nanonesia.

Fortunately Alma is up for the adventure. We'll have a Santa Cruz beach wedding in August, and then we'll leave for the Earthly paradise of Micronesia. I've found a teaching position at Palau Community College, and Alma's landed a job selling ads for the *Palau Horizon*, a weekly newspaper. She's thinking of becoming a dive-guide as well. Our future's unpredictable.

As my last project before leaving California, I've been writing up these adventures. I always wanted to write. The other day, I met a retired math prof from San Jose State who might help me get the book published. He says I should call it a science-fiction novel, of course—not a memoir.

I'm liking it on Earth-3. In a nondocile world like this one, it's as if every single object can have free will. I love the way that feels. And I believe what the jellyfish god said: this is the best of all possible worlds.

There's still bad news in the paper, of course, and sometimes I quarrel with Alma. But that's in the nature of things. A rapidly flowing stream has ripples; chaotic motions have sharp turns; societies have pockets of pain; your moods change unpredictably; the old die to make room for the young; whaddaya, whaddaya.

We've got it good.

afterword

I majored in math in college, and I earned a Ph.D. in set
theory and mathematical logic in 1972. Subsequently
I worked as a mathematics professor for a number of
years—eventually switching to being a professor of computer science at San Jose State University in Silicon Valley.

In 2003 I briefly entertained the idea of writing an auto-
biography called *Memoirs of a Crazy Mathematician*. But I
had second thoughts about publically labeling myself as
crazy. I liked that title, though, and I liked the idea of
writing about mathematicians. So I shifted to the notion
of writing an SF novel entitled *Crazy Mathematicians*.

Before tackling the novel, I spent over a year writing
a hefty nonfiction tome with a long title: *The Lifebox, the
Seashell, and the Soul, or, What Gnarly Computation Taught
Me About Ultimate Reality, the Meaning of Life, and How to
Be Happy*. I finished the first draft of the *Lifebox* book in
the fall of 2004.

While writing my tome, I'd been making plans for my
novel—which I ended up calling *Mathematicians in Love*.
I habitually keep a booklength set of notes about the
writing of each of my books. Early in November 2004,
I wrote this in my *Notes*: "I'm happy and excited that it's

going so well. Running and running and finally jumping into the air, flapping, and yes, once again I'm aloft."

By July 2005, I'd finished the first draft of *Mathematicians in Love*. My Tor Books editor, David Hartwell, made some useful suggestions for revisions, as did my science-savvy friends Scott Aaronson and John Walker. Tor published the novel in 2006. You can learn more about my process in the full *Notes for Mathematicians in Love*, which are online at the book's home page, along with reviews, and with some paintings that I made while writing the book:

www.rudyrucker.com/mathematiciansinlove

I had two primary goals in writing *Mathematicians in Love*.

First of all, I wanted to give a realistic picture of what mathematicians are actually like. And, in doing this, I wanted to give my readers a sense of what it's like to do research on higher-level mathematics and to convert the results into applications. I used a writing method that I call transrealism—that is, I transmuted some of my personal experiences into SF scenes.

I first described transrealism in my 1983 essay, "A Transrealist Manifesto." Philip K. Dick was definitely a precursor of transrealism, but for a number of years, I was the only self-avowed transrealist writer around. The style finally seems to be catching on. In an October, 2014, article in the British newspaper, *The Guardian*, critic Damien Walter says that my notion of transrealism has grown into "the first major literary movement of the 21st century."

As well as drawing on my experiences with mathematics and computer science, *Mathematicians in Love* incorporates material that I garnered in March, 2005, on a scuba-diving trip to the islands of Micronesia and Palau. While I was there, I went swimming with a zillion jellyfish in Jellyfish Lake. A perfect fit for *Mathematicians in Love*—a gift from the muse. One more connection: in 1983 I was, for a brief time, the singer for a punk band called The Dead Pigs.

My second goal in writing *Mathematicians in Love* was to dramatize some contemporary scientific ideas about the nature of our physical world. The idea is that, if you think of physical processes as being like computations, some interesting facts emerge. In particular, it seems that a wide variety of natural processes are complex or gnarly in similar ways. Examples would be the weather, an ocean wave, the growth of an organism, and the working of a human mind.

In his 2002 book, *A New Kind of Science*, Stephen Wolfram proposed two principles regarding these gnarly physical computations.

- All gnarly computations are equivalent. Any one of them can simulate any of the others.
- It's impossible to make useful predictions about gnarly computations.

Putting the second principle a bit differently, most natural processes are computationally irreducible—that is, we can't find quick-and-dirty shortcut methods for predicting their outputs well in advance. So, yes, you can *simulate* a natural process—but, as far as we know, in our

Rudy Rucker is a writer and a mathematician who worked for twenty years as a Silicon Valley computer science professor. He is regarded as a contemporary master of science fiction, and received the Philip K. Dick award twice. His forty published books include both novels and non-fiction books on the fourth dimension, infinity, and the meaning of computation. A founder of the cyberpunk school of science-fiction, Rucker also writes SF in a realistic style known as transrealism, often including himself as a character. He lives in the San Francisco Bay Area.

also from rudy rucker
and night shade books

Night Shade Books' ten-volume Rudy Rucker series reissues nine brilliantly off-beat novels from the mathematician-turned-author, as well as the brand-new *Million Mile Road Trip*. Conceived as a uniformly-designed collection, each release features new artwork from award-winning illustrator Bill Carman and an introduction from some of Rudy's most renowned science fiction contemporaries. We're proud to make trade editions available again (or for the first time!) of so much work from this influential writer, and to share Rucker's fascinating and unique ideas with a new generation of readers.

Turing & Burroughs
$14.99 pb
978-1-59780-964-1

Saucer Wisdom
$14.99 pb
978-1-59780-965-8

White Light
$14.99 pb
978-1-59780-984-9

Million Mile Road Trip
$24.99 hc
978-1-59780-992-4
$14.99 pb
978-1-59780-991-7

The Big Aha
$14.99 pb
978-1-59780-993-1

Spacetime Donuts
$14.99 pb
978-1-59780-997-9

Jim and the Flims
$14.99 pb
978-1-59780-998-6

The Sex Sphere
$14.99 pb
978-1-94910-201-7

The Secret of Life
$14.99 pb
978-1-94910-202-4

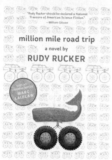  
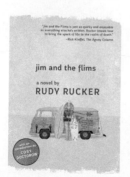  

world, running any simulation is going to take about as much time as it would take to watch the process unfold at its own pace.

Okay—but what if this second principle were wrong? What if we lived in a world where rapid predictions were in fact possible? What would that be like?

You'd be living in a novel called *Mathematicians in Love*.

Rudy Rucker
Los Gatos, California
December 1, 2014.